I0690037

VICTIM IMPACT

FRAN McDONNELL

POOLBEG

Published 2023
by Poolbeg Press Ltd.
123 Grange Hill, Baldoyle,
Dublin 13, Ireland
Email: poolbeg@poolbeg.com

A catalogue record for this book is available from the British Library.

ISBN 978178199-455-9

www.poolbeg.com

About the author

Fran McDonnell was born and raised in Newry, County Down. She has a degree in Nursing and worked as a nurse in England. She also has a Master's in Women's Studies. After travelling, Fran did a Diploma in Kinesiology and set up her kinesiology clinic in Limerick city. She lives in County Tipperary where she grows vegetables and enjoys watching beautiful sunsets.

Fran has also written the gripping thrillers *What Lies Hidden* and *Broken Silence*.

Acknowledgements

Thank you to Paula Campbell of Poolbeg Press for giving me this life-changing opportunity. I am so grateful.

Thank you to Gaye Shortland, my editor, for knowing and caring about my characters and for keeping me true to who they are. It is a pleasure to work with you.

Thank you to photographers Fran Veale and Niall Carson for their technical advice about cameras and sending pictures. They did their best to explain it to me. Any inaccuracies are mine. Thank you also to James and Michael from the Newry Computer Centre. When I lost the whole book you managed to retrieve it. Panic averted.

Thank you to my beta-readers Mum, Dad, Nuala, Aileen, Anne Marie, Joan Lonergan and Mary McInerney. Your feedback and continuing encouragement is heartening.

Thank you to Liam McDonnell, my nephew and alpha-beta reader. Once again, in this book your insights were one hundred per cent. Without you, I would never have been published. Thank you for your faith, support and commitment.

Thank you, Mum, for all the time and energy you have put into reading all the drafts and checking and rechecking for consistency.

Thank you to my readers for their kind words and enthusiasm for my stories.

Thank you to my friend, Denise, for all the adventures and for your support and wise counsel. You have helped me in countless ways that have made my life better.

To Mum, Dad and Nuala, thank you for . . . everything.

DEDICATED TO
NIALL McDONNELL

Chapter 1

A bell was ringing. Isobel registered it and slowly her mind came up through the layers of dreaming. A phone. Disorientated, she lay still. It was dark. Rain pattered onto the skylight above her head. The ringing stopped. Isobel moved. It was cold in her room. Reluctantly she reached out from under the warmth of the duvet for her bedside clock. She focused blearily. It was seven o'clock. She groaned. The ringing started again. She must have left the phone downstairs last night.

Isobel sighed, climbed out of bed, pushed her feet into her slippers and made her way carefully down the stairs. Her mobile was on the kitchen counter. Still ringing.

"Hello?" Even to herself her voice sounded hoarse with sleep.

"Auntie Isobel?"

"Jack, is that you?"

"Yes."

"Aren't you in Belfast?"

"Yes."

"Why are you ringing me so early? Is something wrong?"

Isobel could hear some sharp intakes of breath. She was awake now. She forced herself to be calm. Her mind quickly flicked through possible scenarios. Someone from the family sick or in an accident? It was unlikely that Jack would be delegated to phone her – therefore, he was probably in trouble himself. His family was closer to him, she was in Limerick – much farther away. She could feel her mind start to spiral with worry. She shut down those imaginings and took a deep breath.

She spoke softly. "What is it, Jack? What's happened?"

She could hear sobs. She injected some more power into her voice. "Jack, I know you're upset but try to tell me what's happened."

She could feel a knot of anxiety in her stomach. She closed her eyes and called on all her reserves. Taking a deep breath, she opened her eyes and said calmly, "Whatever it is, we'll sort it out." She hoped this was true. "What happened?"

"Two . . . two of my friends were . . . were attacked last night and one of them is . . . is . . ." The sobs deepened.

"What happened to one of them?"

"He's dead . . . Michael's dead."

Isobel murmured words of comfort, her mind reeling.

"Where are you? Who's with you?"

"I'm at the Royal."

"The hospital? Are you alright?"

"Yes, I'm OK. Dad is here with me."

Isobel felt her shoulders relax. Her brother, Dave, was there. Thank goodness. Dave was a few years older than her and had always been very protective. She heard some nose-blowing.

"But I want you to come up too. Can you? Please? You know about crimes and you know about dealing with the police."

Isobel felt herself tensing again. "Are you in trouble with the police, Jack?"

"No, no, that's not it. I would just feel better if you were here."

"Can you put your dad on?"

"Right."

She could hear noises and voices in the background.

"Hi, Isobel. I'm out in the corridor. This is awful."

"Dave, what the hell happened? Is Jack in trouble with the police?"

"No, no, nothing like that. In fact, he tried to help his friends last night when this happened. Sorry about ringing you so early. It puts your heart crossways, doesn't it?"

"It certainly does."

"Jack rang me at three o'clock this morning. My heart is still hammering. It seems that two men attacked Michael and Charlene, Jack's friends. It happened outside a pub. They both sustained head injuries. Michael died and Charlene is in intensive care. They may have to operate. Her parents are here. Jack helped at the scene. He's very upset. It would be great if you could come, Isobel."

Isobel mentally scanned through her plans. She hadn't yet gone back to work and so there was nothing major that needed to be cancelled. She could manage a trip up north to Belfast.

"OK. I have some things to sort out before I can leave and it's a four-hour drive. Where will I meet you?"

"Charlene is at the Royal Victoria Major Trauma Centre. She's . . . she's critical. Can you meet us here?"

Isobel did some hasty mental arithmetic. "I'll be with you between twelve and one o'clock. Tell Jack I'm on my way."

"Thanks, Isobel. He'll be relieved."

Isobel ended the call and sat down. She looked at her watch. It was ten minutes past seven. Ten minutes in which she had experienced dread at what had happened to Jack, relief at his safety and then been cast to the depths again on hearing of another family's tragedy. Life could change in such a short space of time, a moment really. She shivered. She heard the wind whistling at the patio doors but that wasn't it – it was as if someone had walked over her grave. Her mind flitted through the two police cases she had been involved in. In both instances an initial contact had led to her investigating a murder. There was truth in what Jack had said about her – undoubtedly that was experience.

She gave herself a shake. She needed to pack, put out the rubbish, sort out the perishable food, not to mention shower and dress and have some breakfast. A lot to do before she was ready to get on the road.

Isobel walked along the corridor leading to the Major Trauma Centre. The Royal Victoria Hospital, or "The Royal" as it was commonly known, had gained its Royal Charter in 1899. Isobel had done a placement there as a psychology undergraduate. That had been in the older

4

building which dated back to 1903 and comprised long Nightingale wards. However, the MTC was in a modern building, state of the art, with access to specialists of every discipline. She knew that was an advantage for Jack's friend, improving her chances of survival. Once again her thoughts went to Charlene's family. What an ordeal for them!

As she came through the outer door she passed a room and heard her name being called. Dave came out into the corridor after her.

"You made good time."

Isobel hugged him. He was a foot taller than her. He had the same dark hair – while his had a smattering of grey at the temples, she had an ash front.

"Yes, I reached Dublin after all the commuters had gone to work, so traffic wasn't too bad. Where's Jack?"

"He and Charlene's mum are with her at the moment. He'll be back out in a few minutes." He gestured to the room. "We can wait in here."

"How is Charlene doing?"

"She's critical, unconscious." He rubbed his hand across his mouth. "The doctors are worried about the pressure on her brain. She may need surgery. It's a waiting game. It could go either way."

Isobel nodded and followed him. The room was bright and furnished like a sitting room to give the illusion of comfort to distressed relatives.

She sat on a sofa. Almost immediately she heard some doors banging and Jack appeared. She barely had time to take in his dishevelled blond hair and worried blue eyes before she was enveloped in a hug.

"I can't believe this is happening," he said. "I keep hoping that I'll wake up."

Dave reached out and rubbed his son's shoulder. "I know, son, I know."

"It seems as if I'm in a nightmare."

Isobel gave Jack an extra squeeze and then held him at arm's length. His pallor showed the deep shock and trauma he had suffered.

"Why don't we go to the canteen for a cup of tea and we can talk?"

She saw him frown.

"I don't want to leave in case anything happens to Ch-Charlene." His voice caught on her name.

"I understand, but I've been driving for four hours and I definitely need something."

"Charlene's mother is with her," Dave said. "I'll stay here. I can ring you if . . ."

Jack thought for a moment, then nodded. "OK."

Isobel put her arm around him and steered him towards the exit from the unit.

Chapter 2

Jack refused to take anything at the canteen counter except a coffee. Isobel, knowing how easy it was to end up dehydrated and faint with hunger in times of trauma, tried to no avail to get him to take a sandwich. She took tea and a sandwich for herself.

All around, a mixture of nurses, doctors, other hospital personnel and relatives sat at tables consuming a variety of meals, snacks and beverages, and chatting. The atmosphere was cheerful and vibrant, a contrast to the shocked and anxious state Jack was in. Isobel led the way to a table by the window. The tables nearby were empty, creating a sense of isolation and privacy.

They sat and she said, "Tell me everything from the beginning."

Jack rubbed his hands over his face and heaved a deep sigh.

"This year one of my modules is cinematography. For the assignment we have to work in groups of five and make a short film."

"That seems ambitious."

"We have to write a short story, have people play the roles, find a location, film and edit it. Charlene and Michael were in my group along with Noah and Rachel. Rachel and I developed the story. Everyone approved it so we moved on. It's like making a real movie – we even have to audition people to play the roles." Jack gave a little grin. "And, believe me, some people really want to be in the movies."

Isobel smiled.

"Charlene and Michael were delegated to organise the camera and also to find locations for the different scenes."

Isobel nodded.

"Most of the story is fine and will be relatively easy to shoot but some of our story takes place at night on the street. Charlene and Michael had a number of possible locations in mind. They were supposed to go to each place and record a small amount of footage, at night, so we could be sure that the lighting would work and the film wasn't going to be too dark."

Isobel suspected that Jack was focusing on these details because he was reluctant to recount the next part of the story. She nodded in encouragement but said nothing, deciding not to break his thread. Better to let him exhaust the avoiding strategies.

Jack took a deep breath. "We had a meeting yesterday evening at five o'clock. It turned out that Charlene and . . ." his voice faltered, "and Michael . . . had taken no shoots in the different locations for the street scene at night." He swallowed. "The rest of us were really annoyed. We had done the major part of the work so far, and they hadn't done their part. It meant that we still couldn't decide on a location where the lighting would be right at night and that put everything back." He shrugged. "We have a deadline." He fell silent for a while, staring at the table. "It seems so unimportant now . . . a deadline when . . ." he looked at Isobel, "when Michael is dead and Charlene is fighting for her life." He snatched a paper napkin from the table and wiped roughly at his eyes.

Isobel murmured, "I know."

She had heard this so many times, had been there herself. When life re-orders your priorities, it's so easy to judge what you've done, things that in the usual run of life were normal reactions but, against the backdrop of a crisis, seem cruel or needless or suddenly unimportant. That guilt, that regret, the last things said, they could crucify. She knew words were inadequate, they always were, and yet she also knew she had to start Jack on the road to making peace with himself about what had passed between him and his film colleagues.

"Jack, you weren't to know what would happen."

"We were cross with them." He shook his head. "I was angry. I said they weren't taking the project seriously. I told them that they had better go out and get those recordings that evening." He rubbed his hand across his eyes. "They said they would. If it wasn't for me they wouldn't have been there then. They wouldn't be . . ." Tears rolled down his face. "It's my fault. If I hadn't pushed them, they wouldn't be . . ."

Isobel could feel her heart contracting in sympathy. She let Jack cry for a few moments and, when he had wiped his face and composed himself again, she said, "No, Jack. It wasn't your fault. You just asked them to do their part in the project. The person, the only person, responsible for what happened to Michael and Charlene is the person who attacked them, no one else. There was nothing you could have done to stop that person. You're not responsible for what happened."

Jack studied Isobel for a few seconds then nodded very slightly. "Charlene said that they did plan to go that evening but it's hard not to feel guilty."

"I know."

Isobel could feel that he was less agitated, more at ease, but also very tired. She realised that he'd probably had no sleep. He had talked enough for now.

"Let's go back," she said, "and see how Charlene is doing."

Chapter 3

As Jack and Isobel approached the family room in the MTC, a figure loomed in the doorway.

"Mr. Griffiths, you're back," Jack said. "What did the police say?"

Mr. Griffiths stepped back into the room. Isobel and Jack followed him, taking seats on the sofa as he settled himself in an armchair. He was a tall man with a balding head. His skin had a flush of red that suggested high blood pressure or a fond relationship with alcohol, or both.

He scowled. "Nothing."

"They have no leads?" Isobel asked.

"None, or nothing that they were prepared to share with me. They gave me the old party line of pursuing enquiries. *Bullshit*." His face became redder as he talked and his scowl deepened. "Do they think I came up the Lagan in a bubble? They have nothing. I can tell." After a few moments' silence he looked at Isobel. "Who are you?"

"Isobel McKenzie, Jack's aunt."

"Where's Dad?" Jack said.

"Someone from his work rang. He had to find somewhere private to have a phone meeting." Mr. Griffiths pursed his lips. "Charlene is still unconscious. Do you want to go in to her again for a while, Jack?"

"If that's OK, yes."

"You go ahead. Maybe they think you're the boyfriend, I don't know, but you helped my daughter when she needed it so you go right ahead. I'll stay here and keep your aunt company."

Jack left.

Mr. Griffiths frowned. His eyes turned towards the window, his thoughts miles away.

Isobel waited. She understood how his mind might wander as it tried to come to terms with his daughter's life-threatening condition.

After a few minutes, she said, "I'm very sorry about Charlene. How is she doing?"

His face trembled under the weight of his shock and sadness. Quickly he regained control. "At the moment the doctors are monitoring things. They may have to operate to relieve pressure on her brain but for now she is stable." He looked down at his hands. "They don't know if she'll recover. We have to wait and see. The staff want us to talk to her. They say she maybe can hear us. Jack's good at it." He looked up, his face tortured. "I find it hard. I don't know what to say other than I love you, please get better." He shook his head. "It's a waiting game."

Isobel nodded. She suspected that he was more a man of action and that of all things to wait passively was the hardest for him.

"I heard Jack talking about you to his dad earlier," he said, "when he wanted to phone you. You're a psychotherapist."

"Yes, I am."

He paused and then said, "Dave was glad you were coming. He hoped you could help Jack. Jack told me and my wife everything, even about the disagreement they had with Charlene. He's blaming himself but we know it's nothing to do with him. I've told him that."

"Thank you. I really appreciate that."

"Charlene always found it hard to buckle down and do the work. She's bright enough but likes the good times." He was silent for a few moments. Eventually he roused himself. "Sorry, I should have introduced myself. My name is Tony." He stood and moved towards her, his hand extended.

Isobel stood too. At five-foot two and curvaceous she felt small beside this bear of a man. She guessed he had less than ten years on her forty but, weighed down with worry and stress as he was now, he seemed much older.

The hand that engulfed hers was surprisingly soft and belonged to someone who worked at a desk rather than did physical labour.

Seated again, he gestured with his phone. "I looked you up when I heard Dave and Jack talking about you. You had your own private practice in psychotherapy."

She could feel one of her eyebrows rising but she said nothing.

"You also got yourself in the paper when you were involved in a rape case in Limerick a few months ago.

From what I read – and what Dave later told me – you were of great help to the Garda. And also were involved in a case in London." He met her eyes, watching.

She looked at him but said nothing. She couldn't help thinking that this man would be good in business meetings.

"I have to say, what I read interested me greatly."

She inclined her head.

"As you've heard, I've been to the police. Charlene and Michael were attacked near one of the student bars. Their mobile phones were taken and their money and bank cards. The police think it was a robbery that got out of hand, maybe someone on drugs who, in the heat of the moment, hit them too hard. The PSNI have looked at some CCTV in the area and so far it has revealed nothing in terms of progressing the investigation." He paused. "Basically, while they will continue to look into it, they have made noises suggesting that in opportunistic crimes like this it can be difficult to find the perpetrator." He looked at Isobel. "And, frankly, that's not good enough for me. I watch enough TV to know that the first few days of an investigation are crucial. I know that time is of the essence and that the longer things go the less chance there is of finding who did this."

Isobel felt her heart contract in empathy. Not finding a perpetrator, not feeling any justice, could lead to a deepening rage inside which poisoned life and relationships.

Tony met her eyes. "And so, I've been thinking. I have a proposition for you, a job offer really."

She raised an eyebrow.

"I want you to look into my daughter's attack and see what you can find out."

Isobel frowned.

Tony sat forward. "I'll pay you a consultancy fee. I want you to find out who did this to my little girl."

"Mr. Griffiths –"

"Tony."

"Tony, I'm sure the PSNI will do everything they can."

"Maybe. But to the officers, Char – Charlene is just some victim. But to you, well, to you, she's a friend of Jack's and while Jack is unharmed I'm sure you've had a shock too." He paused, looking at her intently. "Maybe it felt like a taste of how easily something bad can happen and completely upscuttle your life."

Isobel shivered.

"I think that with your training and being Jack's aunt you will be able to get the students, the people in the bar, to trust you, to talk to you. Maybe you can uncover something that the PSNI can't. I want you to find out what you can."

"Tony, I don't think –"

"This isn't a vigilante thing. I don't want to take the law into my own hands. I just want the perpetrator found and punished and you could help in doing that." He frowned. "Do you think that I would still be in business if I went with something that I believed was half-assed? This is my daughter, for Christ's sake! Do you think I'm going to entrust finding her attacker to people that I have doubts about? I'm prepared to pay you. Find out what you can. Anything you find, you turn over to the police."

Isobel stayed silent.

"Think about it," he said. "I'm sure, having driven up from Limerick, you are going to be around for a few days. No doubt Dave and Jack would like that." He pulled a business card from his pocket.

She glanced at it: **Tony Griffiths, CEO of Techsol**. A computer company.

"I mean it. Think about it. You can phone me with your answer. What have you got to lose?"

"I'll think about it."

Tony suddenly seemed to shrink back into himself. "I just want everything done to find who did this to my little girl, everything – that's all I can do for her now – that, and be here, and pray."

And suddenly he was no longer the business executive trying to get what he wanted but a father consumed with pain, who was trying the best way he knew to feel like he was doing something, anything, to help.

Isobel found this version of the man more compelling and she slipped his card into her shoulder-bag.

"I will definitely think about it."

"Thank you."

Tony stood up. "I'm going to go in to spend time with my daughter. To – to talk to her. I'll send Jack out to you."

Chapter 4

Jack led Isobel out of the MTC to his father's car. They could see Dave talking animatedly into his phone. When he saw them, he finished his call.

"Work problems," he said, nodding at his phone, as they climbed in.

"You're busy," Isobel said.

"Unfortunately, yes. Our production company is expanding at the moment so there are lots of meetings and, as the CEO, I need to be at most of them. Right – what do you want to do now?"

Isobel looked at her watch. It was already half past four.

"I have to contact the police," said Jack. "They wanted to talk to all of Charlene's friends. Mr. Griffiths gave me a number to ring."

"You'd better sort that out," Dave said.

Jack made the call. He gave his name and then waited.

"Yes," he said at length. "I was told you wanted to talk to me." He listened and then said, "Yes, I can meet you now. Where?" He listened again. "I'm not at my accommodation. I'm still at the hospital . . ."

Isobel whispered, "Tell them the Park Hotel. I'm staying there."

Jack nodded. "You can meet me at the Park Hotel where my aunt is staying. I'll wait for you in the foyer. Yes, half an hour."

When the call was over, Dave started the car.

"If you have stuff to do, Dave, I'll stay with Jack while he talks to the police and you can meet us again later."

Jack smiled. "That's fine with me. Isobel is probably more used to dealing with them anyway."

Isobel grinned. "You cheeky monkey!"

"That would be great," Dave said. "I had to cut short that call. I can finish up and when you've talked to the police we can all go for something to eat. I'm starving. I haven't eaten much today. Do you fancy an Indian?"

"Definitely," Isobel said and even Jack appeared slightly enthusiastic.

The Park Hotel was on the Malone Road and only a five-minute walk from Queen's University. Isobel got her keycard from reception and Dave went up to her room to continue his phone meeting.

Isobel and Jack took seats in the extensive first-floor foyer area. They chose a place in the corner with a degree of privacy and a window looking out on the front of the hotel. Isobel faced the door so she could watch for the arrival of the police.

She ordered tea and a jug of water. As she poured

water for herself and Jack, she saw a car pull into the hotel carpark. There were three rows of parked cars. As she watched, the car turned into each of the through ways and drove past all the cars, passing empty spaces, then pulled up in a no-stop zone at the front door of the hotel.

The police, no doubt.

A man dressed in plain clothes got out. He approached the steps of the hotel.

"The police are here, Jack."

Jack turned towards the door.

A minute later the man strode in. His gaze swept the room, settling on Jack, then he drew out his phone and tapped it. Jack's phone rang. Already he was on his way over.

"Jack McKenzie?"

"Yes."

"Detective Damien Doran."

Jack gestured towards Isobel. "This is my aunt, Isobel McKenzie."

The policeman nodded to her.

Damien Doran was, Isobel estimated, twenty-five – only five years older than Jack, but he seemed much more mature and world-weary. He was probably five foot ten to Jack's six feet. He had brown hair, which had probably been red as a child, and kind blue eyes.

He seated himself. A waiter appeared but he impatiently shook his head and the waiter withdrew.

Doran waited until Jack met his eye and then he said, "I'm sorry about your friend's death."

Isobel saw Jack pale.

"How is Charlene Griffiths doing?"

19

Jack inhaled deeply. "Still the same, critical, unconscious."

"I'm sorry." Doran paused while he pulled out a notebook and pen. "So what can you tell me about what happened last night?"

"Right. I was having a drink with some friends in the Lion. It was nearly closing time. Pat, one of my friends, texted me. He had gone out for a –" Jack hesitated, "a cigarette and discovered two people lying in the alley beside the Muse pub. They'd been attacked. We ran over to the Muse. Pat and some others were in the alley. There were two people lying on the ground, being given CPR. I know how to do it so I went to help." He stopped, overcome.

"Go on," Isobel said gently.

"It was only when I went closer that I saw it was Charlene and Michael. Pat hadn't said. He hadn't realised who it was."

Isobel reached out and squeezed his hand.

He took a deep breath. "It wasn't long before the police and some ambulances arrived. The paramedics took over. They whisked Charlene and Michael away to hospital. One of the policemen was trying to establish the identities of the vic– of Charlene and Michael. I gave them their names. He was trying to locate next of kin. I didn't know where Michael was from but I knew Charlene was from Craigavon." He swallowed noisily. "Charlene was so ill. I knew it would take her parents some time to get to Belfast so I went to the hospital." He looked at Isobel. "Then she wouldn't be on her own. There would be someone near her, until her parents arrived."

In that one statement Isobel could see and hear the

child she had watched grow up. She blinked rapidly to diffuse the tears that were pricking in her eyes.

"When I got to the hospital I thought I'd better let Mum and Dad know what was happening. I didn't want them to be worried and . . ." He hesitated.

"Maybe you wanted to talk to them," Isobel added.

Jack nodded. "Dad got a bit of a shock when I called. He decided to come down. He knew I was alright but he . . . "

There were a few moments of silence while Doran added a few words to his brief notes.

"Were you surprised that your friends were attacked?" he asked then.

"Very. A lot of students go to the Muse and there's never any trouble there. It's nearly all students and university people who use it. The owner has bouncers who make sure that no one gets out of hand. Usually the most exciting thing that happens there is that someone has too much to drink or goes off with someone that they shouldn't." Jack winced at what he had said and curled his shoulders. "Usually, anyway."

Doran nodded. "Yes. There tends not to be trouble there so we generally have very little to do with it."

"Mr. Griffiths told us that the CCTV from the area hadn't revealed anything," Isobel said.

"No, nothing really."

Isobel decided to apply a little pressure and see if she could learn anything. "He's very disappointed and finding that hard to accept."

Doran looked at her. "There's CCTV outside the Muse,

at the door, and in the smoking area. You can see Charlene and Michael coming out of the pub at ten to eleven. They walk in the direction of the alley. No one appears to be waiting for them. No one seems to follow them. No one is acting suspiciously before or after they leave the pub."

"What about the alley? Is there no CCTV there?"

"No. It's just an old alley, a laneway. It doesn't go anywhere. There's a staff door from the pub onto it, that's all. At the end of the alley is a gate to a derelict paper factory. It's padlocked."

For a moment no one said anything.

Doran turned to Jack. "Were Charlene and Michael a couple? Would they have gone into the alley for a –" he shrugged, "a romantic interlude?"

"No. They were just classmates." Jack kept his head down and fidgeted with his glass. He looked up at Isobel and she nodded at him encouragingly. He heaved a sigh and continued. "They were checking out the alley as a possible location for a short film that we were doing for one of our assignments."

"I see." Doran nodded. "And, to your knowledge, were either of them into drugs?"

Jack frowned. "I wouldn't have thought so. No, I'm sure they weren't."

"How well did you know them?"

"They're in my film class but I don't usually socialise with them."

"So more classmates than friends?"

Jack hunched his shoulders. "I suppose. The groups

were chosen by the lecturer. It's part of challenging us to work with people we don't know so well. I'm not even sure how well they knew each other before this assignment."

"So, to the best of your knowledge then, Michael and Charlene were in the alley checking it out as the location for a short film."

"Yes. That was what we had all agreed on at the group meeting."

"Do you know of anyone who had a grudge against either of them?"

"No! Of course I don't." Jack's voice shook.

"I'm sorry," said Doran. "I know this is upsetting but I have to ask. This is a murder enquiry."

Jack gave a small nod and swallowed noisily.

"Do you think, detective, that it's possible they were deliberately targeted?" Isobel asked.

Doran made a face. "At the moment, since their phones, bank cards and money were taken the thinking is that this was a random, opportunistic attack." He shifted uncomfortably. "I'm just covering all the bases."

"Do you suspect that drugs were involved?" Isobel asked.

Doran shrugged. "We know that there are more drugs around in the last few weeks. We think that the supply has changed."

"And do you think that these students were implicated in drugs?"

Doran shook his head. "Not especially. But this attack seems particularly vicious. I think it's excessive for petty theft."

Isobel had been paying close attention. He had said "the thinking" was that it was a random attack. The new information about drugs warranted a "we" but this last part was "I". Detective Doran had some theories of his own, it seemed, that were not subscribed to by his fellow officers.

"Of course," Doran continued, "much depends now on whether Charlene remembers anything when she regains consciousness."

"*If* she regains consciousness." Jack took a deep breath and exhaled.

And provided she hasn't suffered any permanent brain damage, thought Isobel. A sickening possibility.

"I think that's everything. If you think of anything else that might be helpful, ring me." Doran stood up. "Thank you for your help. I hope that Charlene . . ." he hesitated, "well, I hope that everything goes OK for her."

Jack nodded.

The detective left the hotel.

Jack shook his head. "They don't know anything."

"No."

"Poor Mr. and Mrs. Griffiths."

"Yes."

They sat in silence. Isobel mused over all that she had heard. Was the attack random, drug-related or personal? Obviously Doran was considering a number of possibilities. She wondered again if he was alone in that.

Jack's tummy rumbled.

Isobel laughed. "I hear you. Come on. Let's call your dad. He said he was hungry earlier and you are obviously starving too. It's time for that Indian."

Chapter 5

They took a taxi. It was seven-thirty and the evening was cold and dry. Isobel stared out the window at the unfamiliar streets. They were busy as workers hurried home or met friends for after-work drinks. The spirit of Halloween was evident in shop windows, and pumpkins and orange lanterns were strung over doorways. Belfast was buzzing. They travelled in silence. Isobel was glad of the respite after the long and intense day.

The entrance to the Indian was unobtrusive. Inside it was subtly lit with Indian lamps and between each table hung a voile curtain, creating the illusion of privacy and also a dreamy, tent-like atmosphere. Isobel could feel her shoulders descending from a place up under her ears. As she slid into her soft seat and received her menu, she relaxed for the first time since her phone call that morning.

She ordered her usual: chana masala with pilau rice and a glass of Sauvignon Blanc.

After they had all ordered, Dave asked, "How did the interview go?"

Jack shrugged. "Alright. There wasn't really anything new that I could add. I think Detective Doran just wanted to check out some theories of his own."

"Like what?"

"He mentioned some new drug wave in the city."

"Oh?" Dave looked disturbed. "He thinks Michael and Charlene were involved in drugs? Is that possible, Jack?"

"No, Dad, as far as I know there was nothing like that going on. And Doran said that the dominant thinking is that it was a robbery."

Dave shook his head. "But how much money could a student have on them? It seems such a waste, to kill one person and seriously injure another for their phones and whatever cash and cards they were carrying."

Jack winced.

"Jack, you did all you could," Dave said.

"I know." Jack's voice caught. "I just hope that Charlene recovers."

"Unfortunately, only time will tell. It must be very hard for Tony and Joan." He turned to Isobel. "Tony was very interested in your work, Isobel."

"Was he?"

"Well, he heard me and Jack talking about you and mentioning that you were a psychotherapist. Later on he told me that he had looked you up and found that piece from the rape case in Limerick and how you had been attacked. I told him that you had been helping the gardaí with the inquiry. Anyway we got talking and I told him all about how in Limerick you helped catch the rapist and also about London when you found those bodies and

26

helped catch a murderer. I think it really distracted him from the stress of what was happening."

Isobel frowned. "It didn't distract him. It gave him ideas."

"Oh?"

"He wants me to investigate Charlene's attack, to see what I can find out."

"Really?" Jack's head snapped up. "I think that's a great idea. Maybe you can find out who did this?"

"I hardly think that your dad would approve." She looked at Dave. "He isn't a fan of my investigating."

Dave put down his bottle of beer and looked at her. "Maybe in this case you could?"

Isobel sat back in her chair and folded her arms. "This, from the man who has constantly nagged me about my safety and discouraged me, no, fought with me, about getting involved in my previous cases."

"I know. I know. I've been less than supportive of your private-investigator skills. But, Isobel, I have to say, it's different this time. I think you should investigate this."

"I don't believe it. What brought about this complete change of direction in your attitude?"

Dave shrugged. "I suppose this time I'm involved."

Isobel waited.

"I think last night, when I received the phone call in the middle of the night, I got an awful fright. For a dreadful minute I – . . ." He swallowed. "When I found out that Jack was OK, I just felt relief. It took a minute for it to sink in that someone else was living my nightmare."

"I can understand that."

"I've met Tony and Joan. I see how distraught they are. Tony said the police talked to him about it being robbery and they warned him that they might never find who did it. He can't contemplate that. Neither could I. I would want everything that could be done, done. I would want no stone unturned. I would clutch at any straw. And the fact that you've been helpful in two cases, well, it's more than a straw, it's a lifeline. I'm asking you to see if you can help Tony."

Isobel shook her head. "Dave, I don't want to distract him from thinking about Charlene when she is so ill. Of course finding who did this is important but not more important than taking care of his sick child. And, as the PSNI pointed out, it won't be easy to find out who did this. I don't want to give him false hope."

Dave frowned. "I don't want you to give him false hope either. He just needs to feel that he is doing something, anything, everything, to find out who did this to his little girl." His voice caught. "Please help him. Even if you don't find who did this, he will know that he has done everything that he can."

Isobel rubbed her face with her hands. "I hear what you're saying but, because of the outcome from the last two cases I was involved in, he is going to be very hopeful and I can tell you that it seems already as if the PSNI have very little to go on."

Dave rolled his beer bottle between his hands. "And what is wrong with hope? Sometimes you need something to cling to, to get you through the days. If knowing that you're investigating helps Tony, what's so bad about that?"

Isobel took a mouthful of wine. She had to confess to

herself that following her meeting with Detective Doran her interest had been piqued and she had been making a mental list of the people she could talk to in order to try to get more information. She realised that maybe she had changed and investigating had become a way of processing information for her.

"Aunt Isobel, I want you to do it and I want to help. This has been horrendous. It still is. I want to help you find out who did this to Charlene and Michael." Jack sat up straight. "And I have a lot to contribute. I can find out easily about friends of Charlene and Michael that we can talk to." He pointed at his chest. "And they will talk to me, a fellow student."

Isobel couldn't help being impressed. It seemed that Jack was thinking along similar lines to her. And he had a point about being an asset.

Dave frowned. "Don't forget that you were attacked in Limerick, Isobel. You will both have to be careful." He leant forward. "I know I asked you to get involved but please don't take any risks. Talk to people, find out things, but be careful."

Jack smiled. "Does that mean I'm your assistant, Isobel?"

Isobel laughed. "I guess it does."

"Here's the food," Dave said. "At last. I'm starving."

As they ate conversation was casual and Isobel could see Jack relaxing.

When they had finished eating, Jack said, "You don't need to stay in Belfast, Dad. You can go back to Portstewart. If work is busy you probably need to be at home."

"How long are you going to be here, Isobel?" Dave asked.

Isobel shrugged. "I had thought that I would stay until the weekend."

"Great," Jack said.

Dave nodded. "If you're staying then I could go home, if that's OK with you?"

Isobel nodded. "Yes."

"If you need anything I can come back again."

"No, we'll be fine," Jack said. "We have investigating to do."

"And you have your studies," Isobel pointed out. "We'll keep in touch and update you, Dave."

Dave nodded.

"Excuse me." Jack got up to go to the bathroom.

When he left, Dave said, "How do you think he's coping with all of this?"

Isobel pursed her lips. "Considering everything, he's doing really well."

"I'm glad you're going to be here. It seems a lot to cope with and it's so upsetting. I can hardly believe it." He paused. "I remember when you were little Santa brought you that Sherlock Holmes storybook. Do you remember?"

"Yes." Isobel smiled.

"And you had to get a deerstalker hat. You were obsessed with Sherlock Holmes and so badly wanted to be a detective."

"I remember!"

"It's so strange that you have ended up being involved in cases as an adult."

Isobel shook her head sadly. "It's not like it is in a book. It's so much harder. The trauma that real people go through is terrible."

Dave nodded. "I'm getting a small idea of that this time. Does solving the crime help? Does it make things a bit easier?"

Isobel swallowed a lump in her throat. "It helps to know that the person responsible can't do it again. That helps me and I think sometimes it helps the people involved, but it doesn't change what happened, or the loss, or the trauma."

"No."

Jack came back and Dave settled the bill.

It was nine o'clock when the taxi dropped them at Isobel's hotel. Isobel and Jack walked Dave to his car.

Dave hugged Isobel. "Thanks for coming. I really appreciate it."

Isobel hugged him back. Somehow she felt closer to him tonight, as if he might now understand her better, and that felt good. She moved away as Dave hugged his son.

Finally Dave was in the car, the window open. He reminded them to stay safe and they waved him off.

Inside the hotel, Isobel said, "Can you arrange for us to meet and talk to the guy who found Michael and Charlene? Pat, was it?"

Jack nodded enthusiastically.

"I'm going to call Tony," she said.

Jack moved away, taking out his phone.

Isobel pulled up Tony's number. There was no answer. A few minutes later her phone rang.

"Hi, Isobel. I was in with Charlene. I had to step out to talk to you."

Isobel could hear a new tension in his voice. "How are things?"

"Not good. The consultant says the pressure is increasing in Charlene's brain. They're going to operate as soon as possible. I mean, tonight."

"Oh, I'm sorry."

"Are you ringing to tell me that you're taking the job I offered you?"

"Yes, I was actually, but this is not the time for discussing that."

"No. No. But I'm delighted. Where are you staying?"

"The Park Hotel but, Tony, I –"

"I'll take care of your expenses and pay you a fee."

"Tony, don't worry about that now. You need to concentrate on Charlene. We'll be thinking of her and praying."

"Thanks, Isobel. She needs all the help she can get."

"Let us know how things go."

"I will. Talk tomorrow."

Isobel hadn't noticed Jack coming to stand beside her.

"What?" he said. "Tell me."

"The doctors are going to operate tonight on Charlene."

"Oh, no!" Jack looked stricken.

Isobel hugged him. "Tony will let us know."

"Please God she'll be alright."

"Yes, let's hope for the best. Did you speak to Pat?"

32

"Yes, he said that we could come around now but maybe given . . ." He looked at her questioningly.

"Look, there's nothing we can do except wait." She thought that maybe having something to focus on rather than waiting for time to pass, for news to come, would help Jack. "Charlene is in the doctors' hands now. Talking to Pat is a small step in beginning to find out who did this. What do you think?"

Jack took a deep breath. "Let's do it."

Chapter 6

Jack led Isobel towards Queen's University then turned into the warren of streets known as the Holy Land. This was the main student area, houses that students rented interspersed with some family residences. Isobel didn't envy those people. She imagined that the streets could be noisy at night as the young people had fun and made their way to and from the pubs and parties that were a natural part of student life. Isobel couldn't say much in that regard – she had done her fair share of partying as an undergraduate.

The walk to Pat's house took twenty minutes. He lived in Bethlehem Street. Jack led the way to the blue door and rang the bell. It was opened quickly by a dark-haired youth, tall and thin, who was very pale.

"Hi, Pat. This is Isobel."

Pat nodded and led them through the hall to a sitting room. The ceiling was much higher than those in modern houses, speaking of the older era when the house was built. The walls were painted magnolia to which some posters of bands and films had been fixed. The carpet, a dark colour that was probably hiding stains, was heavy duty and slightly sticky. The curtains on the windows were closed and there was a small fire.

Pat took a seat near the fire.

Jack and Isobel sat on the couch which, despite its worn look, was comfortable.

"I can't warm up," Pat said, rubbing his hands together.

"It's probably shock," Isobel said. "Pat, why don't you go and get another sweatshirt and I'll get this fire built up. And, if you don't mind, Jack can get us all a cup of tea."

The boys left the sitting room, and Isobel heard Pat's footsteps on the stairs.

She found a firelighter and some sticks and strengthened the heart of the fire, then added more coal and logs.

Jack returned with mugs of tea and on the second trip a bag of sugar and a carton of milk.

Pat huddled into the fire which now was beginning to blaze and wrapped his hands around his mug.

"Jack was telling me that you found Charlene and Michael," Isobel said. "That must have been a terrible shock."

Pat nodded. "I didn't recognise them initially."

"Why don't you tell us what happened? You found them lying in the laneway beside the Muse?"

Pat nodded. "Yes, I was outside in the smoking area. I needed to go to the loo but at that time of night the pub was very crowded – both inside and out – and I couldn't be bothered battling through the crowd . . . so . . ." He looked uncomfortably at Isobel.

"So, you decided to nip down the alley and take care of business," she supplied.

Pat exhaled. "Exactly. The alley is normally kind of deserted and not really used for much. There are two small street lamps and also a couple of big rubbish bins. I went down to pee behind them where no one could see me and that's when I found . . . Charlene and Michael."

"Behind the bins?" Isobel asked.

"Kind of, yes. I only saw them because . . ."

"Because you were peeing."

Pat gave a wan smile. "Yes. They were behind the second bin." He put his mug down on the hearth and rubbed his hands together, looking down at them. "It took me a minute to realise . . . to figure out that I was really seeing people." He looked up uncomfortably. "I'd had a bit to drink."

"What did you do then?"

"I think I sort of stood there for a moment. I've never sobered up so quickly. I shook one of them gently and there was no response. I knew it was bad so I rang the police and an ambulance and then messaged Jack. He was in the Lion, which isn't far away. Then, well, I thought I'd better try and do something. He looked up at Isobel. "Michael, well, it never seemed good . . . but with Charlene I could feel a weak pulse. I must have shouted for help. I don't remember but I must have. Some people came and we tried to do something. It wasn't long before Jack arrived with some friends. We all tried to do what we could." He turned to Jack. "I didn't recognise them. Thank God you had your wits about you." He lapsed into a miserable silence.

"They were lucky that you found them when you did, Pat," said Isobel. "If you hadn't gone for a pee, well, God knows when they would have been found. Charlene is probably alive because of you."

Pat studied Isobel for a moment. She returned his gaze. What she had said was the truth. After a few moments he nodded.

"Did you see anyone when you went into the alley, Pat?" Isobel asked.

"No one. The PSNI asked me that too but I didn't see anyone. I've gone over it all day in my mind but, genuinely, I can't think of anything."

"Do you think you'll be able to sleep tonight?"

Pat nodded. "I'm exhausted. I was up all last night. I want to sleep. Just for a few hours, I want to forget."

She reached out and touched his arm. "You did really well, Pat. I mean it."

"Thanks."

Not long after, Jack and Isobel left.

As they walked back through the streets, Isobel said, "You must be tired too, Jack. Do you want to go home and get some sleep?"

"Not yet. Charlene could be in theatre as we speak. Is there anything else you want to do tonight?"

Isobel looked at her watch. It was ten o'clock. "I would like to see the alley where it happened."

Jack nodded. "OK."

"Are you sure?"

He linked his arm in hers. "Yes."

Chapter 7

The Muse was situated on the corner of Botanic Avenue and University Square. It was a large property. The front of the building faced onto University Square and had windows either side of a doorway. Lights streamed from the windows and from a light over the doorway.

As they drew closer, Isobel could see a notice on the wall beside the entrance. They stood side by side and read it. It said the Muse would be closed on Thursday night, as a mark of respect to Michael.

Isobel expected that an autopsy would be done very quickly. The results were probably not in question. It seemed from all she had heard that the cause of death would be blunt-force trauma. Perhaps there would be toxicology screens and forensic results but they took time.

"I must check social media later," said Jack. "There may be a vigil and there might be a Mass at the university. Maybe that's why they're closing on Thursday. I've been so busy thinking about Charlene that I never thought about that."

"It's alright, Jack. You've been at the hospital. Are you

sure you want to do this? Maybe it's a bit much tonight?"

"I have to face it sometime. Maybe getting it over with is the best thing to do. Maybe waiting only makes it harder."

Isobel knew there was never an easy time to do something that brought up trauma – but it was probably true that the longer you put it off, the larger it became in your mind. Maybe biting the bullet was the best approach, like getting back on the horse immediately.

"Are you sure?"

Jack took a deep breath and nodded. "Yes, I'm sure."

On entering, it was clear that the Muse was an atmospheric and popular pub. The bar was straight ahead. It was wooden and ran nearly the whole length of the wall. Behind the bar, wooden shelves held a variety of bottles of spirits, some looking quite ancient and definitely interesting. These were backlit. Serving customers was an attractive dark-haired man of about thirty and a red-haired woman about twenty. They were efficiently pulling pints and dispensing shots.

The customer area was large, with wooden tables and assorted stools and chairs. Each table had a candle. There were plenty of young people gathered in groups and there was the buzz of earnest conversation. Isobel guessed that the tragic attack was the subject of many of the discussions. A number of tables had older men and women, maybe lecturers or postgraduates.

An attractive woman, dressed elegantly in black, was circulating between the tables, collecting glasses and speaking to some of the customers. She looked to be about forty years old.

Jack waved at a young man seated near the bar. Behind him Isobel could see a sign for toilets.

"Can you show me the smoking area, Jack?"

He moved to the left and threaded his way through the narrow space between tables until he reached a door halfway along the left side of the room. They exited through the door into an area covered with a clear Perspex roof. There were posts marking the perimeter of the area. Between these was a rigid black material creating a half-height pseudo wall. The section was the length of the pub with another entrance to the outdoor tables and chairs from the street. There were some heaters that dispensed a weak heat and the roof was festooned with fairy lights in primary colours.

"So Pat was here," Isobel said.

Jack pivoted on his feet. "Yeah – and, as he said, it was probably too crowded to get easily to the toilets."

Isobel nodded. "So he decided to walk around the front of the pub and use the alley. He probably left through this exit." She pointed to the street access.

"Yeah. Trust me, walking through the bar can take ages because you know people and have to stop to say hello. If you need to go, sometimes, you need to go."

Isobel grimaced. "Too much information."

"I'm just filling in the detail. Are we doing a reconstruction?"

Isobel shook her head. "Just following in his footsteps."

She led the way out through the half-walls onto the street. She looked up at the walls of the pub. There was a camera on the corner of the building pointed back along the side where the smoking area was.

They went around the corner towards the front of the pub. The corner they passed had a camera facing the front door. As they passed the front door they noted another camera also pointed towards the door.

They arrived at the alley. There was no camera pointing at its entrance or down the alleyway.

There was no police tape across the entrance and Isobel wondered if some of the students had removed it. There was also no officer on guard so she assumed that any forensic assessment was finished.

There was no doubt that the alley was atmospheric. Isobel could see why Jack's film group had wanted it in their film. The tarmacadam at the entrance quickly gave way to a cobbled street. It was wider than she had imagined. There was room for a car with a small space on either side. The side wall of the pub had no windows overlooking it. The other side of the alley was walled, with barbed wire on the top. It was along this side that two lampposts were situated, their sulphurous light illuminating circles of subdued light and leaving most of the alley in semi-darkness.

Isobel turned in a full circle. The high walls on either side created an oppressive feeling, making the alley feel smaller, and the cobblestones added a historical sense of narrow spaces and dark deeds. She shivered.

"Come on," she said, moving further into the alley.

"Do you think it's OK to go in?"

Isobel paused. Was Jack asking because he wondered about the police and forensics or was he reluctant to go back to where his friends had been attacked?

"You can wait here. I just want to see where Pat found them and see if there's anything else . . ."

"No. I'll come with you." He stepped forward.

Isobel slipped her arm through his and squeezed gently. They walked forward slowly.

The alley stretched the length of the Muse building. She noticed three fans on the wall and wondered if they were for toilets or if the pub had a kitchen.

The bins were positioned halfway down, the lamps casting very little light on them. She wasn't sure if they were called hoppers but they were green plastic bins with lids on top. She released Jack's arm and walked over to them. Pulling down the sleeve of her top and using it as a glove, she lifted the lid of the first bin.

"Do you have you a torch, Jack?"

Jack brought up the torch function on his phone and shone the light into the bin. It was for bottles. Isobel moved to the second bin. It contained rubbish for landfill. On the ground beside the bin, Isobel saw a number of bouquets of flowers.

"I guess people have been remembering Michael," Jack said.

Isobel nodded. She examined the ground but there was nothing else to see.

She walked further down the alley and Jack hurried to catch up with her. "What are you looking for?"

"Nothing. I'm just looking."

The end of the alley featured pillars with old iron double gates looking the worse for wear, rusted and needing a new coat of paint. Above the gate was an old-fashioned stone arch. Isobel directed Jack's torch at the old lettering. Despite the weathering it was still possible to read: **McNichol Printers and Stationery**.

"I suppose the university has always attracted stationery shops," Jack said.

Isobel flashed the torch around the gateway. There was a relatively new and very sturdy lock on the gates. The pillars were weathered with the cap on one slightly misaligned.

"That capstone has got a bad knock," she said as she shone the torch on it. She saw some scrapes on the stone and also a green line of paint.

"I don't suppose it matters, there's never anyone down here," said Jack.

"That's just as well." Isobel turned to face the alley and the bins. "Where would you set your scene for the movie?"

Jack shook his head. "Oh, that all seems so unimportant now."

"Here? Or near where those lights are?"

Jack flinched slightly but answered nonetheless. "I don't know. We were waiting on the footage from Charlene and Michael." He looked around. "Nearer the lights. They would give a very atmospheric feel to the shot."

Isobel nodded. "Step back a bit and take a recording."

Jack hunched his shoulders.

"Please," she said. "I want to see what Charlene and Michael were meant to be doing."

"OK."

They walked back along the alley. Jack readied his

phone and moved forward from Isobel then turned with his phone raised. "Walk towards me, about three steps."

Isobel moved forward.

"*Stop!*" Jack said. There was a pause. "Take two more steps forward."

Isobel looked. She was now in front of the bins.

"I think that's a good place for lighting. We could probably have taken the shots with the action focused around where you're standing."

Isobel pivoted on her feet. The end of the alley was in almost total darkness. "OK. That's it, I think."

They walked back out of the alley and onto the street.

"So nothing that would help us find out who did this," Jack said.

Isobel smiled. "It's not like it is on TV. Most of the investigating I've done means talking to a lot of people, listening carefully to what they're saying and, if you're lucky, and I mean really lucky, finding something. There are no guarantees. You just have to see what you can discover. At this stage who knows what's important? But tomorrow I want to talk to some friends of Charlene and Michael. And, Jack," Isobel paused until he looked at her, "you don't have to do it if it's too hard."

"No, I want to. It was hard coming here tonight but I've done it now."

"You did well. I think that's it for today."

"I might go back into the pub and meet the friend I saw earlier."

Isobel smiled. "You do that. But, Jack, don't walk home alone, not with everything that has happened."

"I won't, I promise."

Isobel smiled. "Good. I'm going to get a cab. And, Jack . . ."

"Yes?"

"I'm having a bit of a rest tomorrow, so I don't want to see you until half-nine or ten o'clock."

"See you then."

It was nearly eleven o'clock when Isobel got back to her room on the fourth floor of the hotel. It afforded her a good view over the lights of Queen's university quarter. When she checked into the hotel all she had done was deliver her bags to the room before racing over to the hospital. Now she unpacked and laid out her toiletries in the bathroom, which was surprisingly spacious and had a bath. That decided it. Isobel made her way down to the bar and collected a glass of Sauvignon Blanc.

Returning to her room, she ran a bath and emptied in some of her pomegranate noir bath milk. Turning off the light in the bathroom and leaving the door open so that the light from the bedroom provided some illumination, Isobel relaxed. The four-hour drive had left its mark on her shoulders.

Images from the day floated through her mind. Most of the things were just flotsam and jetsam but she felt there were some pieces of information that were interesting.

Of course there were other possibilities but it made sense to Isobel that Charlene and Michael were in the alley just to assess it for the film. Pat had seen no one in the alley, or leaving it.

She sipped her wine. She thought that Detective Doran had made an interesting comment about the attack being very vicious. She felt there was something else but she couldn't think what it might be. The water was cooling so she stepped out of the bath, dried off and put on her pyjamas.

She wanted to do one last thing before she tried to sleep. She called Tony Griffiths.

This time he answered immediately.

"Hi, Tony. Is there any news on Charlene?"

"Yes, she's in theatre now. The operation is going to take a few more hours. We're waiting at the hospital to hear any news."

"We're thinking of her. Please let us know."

"I will."

"Night."

There was nothing more to do. She left her curtains open so that she could look out on the lights of the city. Somewhere out there was the person who had done this to Charlene and Michael.

Isobel slept.

In her dreams she was out in the country. Around the fields and along the road were dry stone walls.

Sitting on one of the walls was an egg. The egg had a young woman's face.

Suddenly a man dressed in black popped up behind the egg. He had a large spoon in his hand. He lifted the spoon and held it threateningly over the egg.

Isobel called out a warning but the egg appeared not to

hear her. Isobel started to run towards her but she was too late.

The man brought the spoon down on the egg's head. There was a cracking sound and the egg with the young woman's face broke into pieces that fell on the ground.

The man nodded and walked away up the field with his spoon over his shoulder. He was whistling a tune.

Isobel rushed forward. She picked up some of the pieces from the ground and tried to put them back together. A man and a woman came to help her.

Isobel woke with the lines of the nursery rhyme running through her mind. "*All the king's horses and all the king's men couldn't put Humpty together again.*"

Her eyes were wet with tears.

She prayed that the doctors and nurses in the Royal could put Charlene together again.

Chapter 8

It was nine o'clock before Isobel woke. Her dream lingered with her and she checked her phone. Tony had sent a message at seven that morning.

Surgery went well. Next 48 hrs critical. Talk later.

Isobel breathed a sigh of relief. At least the medical team had more success than she had in her dream.

She had a quick shower and went down to breakfast. As she exited the lift in the foyer, Jack stood up and came towards her. Isobel hugged him. He had heard about Charlene and was relieved. "I've something to tell you," he said, smiling, "but let's sit down first."

They found a table and ordered breakfast.

"Did you sleep last night?" Isobel said.

"Yes, though I didn't think I would."

"It was probably good to meet up with your friends."

"Yes, but everyone was talking about the attack. You couldn't get away from it." He made a face. "Lorraine, she's the owner of the Muse, gave me and some of the others who helped Charlene and Michael a free pint to say thank you."

48

"That was nice."

"Yeah. She's really good. She thought I might have trouble sleeping so she offered me some tablets that she found good when her mum was sick."

"Oh. And did you take some?"

Jack shook his head. "I accepted them but I didn't take any. She was trying to be helpful but I didn't need them. The couple of pints worked. I was exhausted."

Isobel smiled. " Do you have the tablets?"

"Sure."

Isobel reached out her hand. "Can I see them?"

Jack laughed. "Do you think that you might need them?"

"No, Jack. But I don't want you to take them either."

Jack handed her a blister pack with ten tablets in it.

She looked. It was Xanax, an anti-anxiety tablet which could sometimes become addictive. She really didn't want him to get into taking them unless absolutely necessary.

"Can I keep these?"

Jack shrugged. "Sure – I don't want them."

Breakfast arrived and Jack tucked in as if he were starving but, after a few mouthfuls, he put down his knife and fork.

"Isobel," he said, "I have found something new." He looked terribly pleased with himself.

"You have? About what happened?" Isobel put down her teacup and leant forward eagerly.

"Yeah. Yesterday, as you know, I was up in a heap, with being at the hospital, Mr. and Mrs. Griffiths, and you and Dad."

Isobel nodded.

49

"And loads of people were sending me messages asking about what happened."

"I can imagine."

"I didn't really look at them. There was too much going on. Anyway, it was only this morning that I started going through all my social media."

"Come on, Jack! You look like the cat that got the cream."

"When our film group got together Charlene set up a cloud account that all of us could access and upload things to."

Isobel could feel her eyes glazing over.

Jack picked up on her baffled look. "Basically, because we were going to be making the film together she set up a place where we could all access and save information about the project. I looked at it today and found that Charlene had uploaded some footage from the night she was attacked."

"*What!*"

"I know. Amazing."

"Let me see!"

Jack pulled out his phone and tapped and swiped. "Here we go!"

Isobel watched the video which showed a young man.

"That's Michael," Jack said.

Michael was dark-haired and pale-skinned with blue eyes. He looked serious in the picture, thoughtful. Isobel felt her heart contract for his parents and family and the loss they had experienced.

Michael was standing in the alley between the two lights. Then, he moved back and walked forward towards the camera and stopped.

Jack pointed at the screen. "Charlene must have moved further away."

On the screen Isobel could see the distance to Michael increasing.

"Now, Charlene must be getting him to walk towards her again."

Isobel saw Michael moving closer until he was in front of the lights. The camera swung wildly and then Isobel could see the face of Michael and beside him a pretty blonde girl with wideset eyes. Charlene. She smiled into the camera. Isobel felt tears in her eyes. Charlene now had probably had some of her hair shaved off for the surgery and was battling to recover.

Once again there was some wild movement on the screen and then the camera focused on Michael. He moved backwards, deeper into the alley, closer to the gate of the old stationery business.

"Actually, this is really good," Jack said. "The light in Charlene's shots is very much better than I thought it would be when we were there last night. The location was ideal for the movie. Sorry. Not relevant."

"Anything and everything can be relevant, Jack, in an investigation," Isobel said, seeing the guilt in his eyes.

He focused again on the screen.

"*Oh my God!*"

"What is it?" she asked.

"*Look!*" He pointed to the top left-hand corner of the screen. "You see here – right at the end of the filming. Look at what it shows!"

Isobel sat forward, frowning. "It's hard to see but it

looks like two people standing together."

"It does and if I play it again and you watch carefully you'll see, just before the recording ends, they turn towards Charlene and Michael!"

They watched the recording again.

"It's hard to see but I think you're right," she said.

"Those could be the people who attacked them!"

Isobel took a deep breath. "Either they are the attackers or they may have seen something. " She frowned. "Where are they standing?"

"Pretty far down the alley, I'd say."

"Didn't Detective Doran mention that they hadn't found any witnesses among the people in the pub?"

"Yes. I'm sure the police spoke to everyone they could but, you know yourself, some people may have left before the police arrived, especially if they had something to hide."

"True."

Isobel tapped her finger on her lip. "Those two people are either the attackers or the last people to see Charlene and Michael before they were attacked, so possible witnesses."

"What do we do now?"

Isobel sat back. "I'm thinking."

"What do we do?" Jack asked again, his voice higher this time.

There was only one thing that they could do. "We ring Detective Doran and let him know what you've found."

Chapter 9

Isobel was sipping her second coffee when Detective Doran arrived and joined them at their table.

"You have something to show me, Jack."

Jack nodded. "Yes, I have footage from the alley. Charlene must have taken it before the attack."

"*What?*"

"She sent it to a cloud account that the film group share."

Doran leant forward. "How come you're only telling us about this now, over twenty-four hours after the attack?"

Jack went white.

Suddenly Doran seemed much older than his twenty-something years.

"It's alright, Jack," Isobel said. "Just explain why you only found the recording this morning. You haven't done anything wrong."

Doran folded his arms.

Jack nodded. "I was busy. I was at the hospital, meeting Charlene's parents. Loads of people were sending me messages on social media, asking me about what had happened and how Charlene was. I didn't know what to tell them and I was upset, then Dad and Isobel were here and it was all too much so I stopped checking any of my media accounts. Last night, when I left Isobel, I met some friends and had a few drinks and then I slept. It was only this morning that I felt able to have a look at everything. That's when I thought of the cloud account."

Doran said. "Play the recording for me."

Jack played the short footage.

Doran watched it in silence.

"Again," he said.

Jack replayed it. He paused it towards the end and pointed. "There are two people standing there."

"Yes, there are. OK. I'm going to need a copy of the recording."

"I can email it to you."

Doran called out his email address.

Jack worked at his phone. "It's sent."

"This could be an important find," said Doran. "I need to get back to the station. I want a statement from you but I'll contact you about where and when. My boss, Inspector Williams, may want to speak to you himself as well."

Jack looked pale. "I'm not in trouble, am I?"

Doran shook his head. "No. It's just a shame that we didn't have this immediately."

"Well, there's nothing we can do about that," Isobel said. "You have it now. Do you think you'll be able to identify the people in the video?"

"I don't know. I guess the lab will have to see what they can do." He stood up. "I'll probably want that statement today so be available. And this is evidence now so do *not* show it to anyone else."

Jack nodded. "I won't."

Doran hurried out.

Jack shook his head. "How come I feel like a criminal?"

"You shouldn't. You've helped enormously."

"I'd better talk to Rachel and Noah and make sure that if they realise the film is on the cloud they keep it confidential."

He stood up and moved away as he talked on his phone. Then he searched his phone and talked again.

"All done," he said eventually, sitting down again.

"I don't know what it's possible to do in the lab. Do you think they'll be able to get clear images of the faces? The people were some distance away."

"It will depend on how good the original device that took the pictures was."

"I suppose we'll have to wait and see what the lab comes up with. In the meantime let's do what we intended and talk to some of Charlene's friends."

"We could visit the girls she lives with?"

"Excellent idea."

Charlene's accommodation was on Jerusalem Street. She shared a four-bedroom house with three other girls who were all sitting side by side on the couch.

Isobel and Jack sat in the armchairs opposite.

Fiona was a slim redhead with pale freckled skin. Her eyes were red from crying and had deep shadows underneath.

"You were there when they found Charlene, weren't you?" she asked Jack.

"Yes, shortly afterwards."

"I heard that she had surgery last night."

"That's right."

"I can hardly believe that this is happening. Charlene and I were at secondary school together. This was our dream, to be in college and sharing a place."

Isobel could see that Jack was unsure of what to say. "It must be hard for you," she said. "Are you doing the same course as Charlene?"

Fiona shook her head. "No. I'm doing history and English."

"Me too," said Anne, a beautiful blonde who was sitting beside Fiona. "We're all so shocked. Charlene was so . . ." she hesitated, "full of life."

"We were hoping for parts in that film you were making, weren't we, Anne?" said the third girl on the couch, a brunette.

Anne frowned. "Yes."

"I'm Bernadette," the brunette volunteered. "I don't know Charlene as well as the others. What happened is shocking. It would make you afraid to go out."

"How did you meet Charlene?"

"I only met her when I moved in. I knew Anne from the drama club. We were in a play together in first year. When Charlene and Fiona were looking for someone for the last bedroom, Anne suggested me."

Anne nodded. "Yes, *The Importance of Being Earnest*. I had a lead role."

"And were you hoping for a lead role in the film that Charlene was making?" Isobel asked.

Anne blushed. "As I said, there were going to be auditions but I did hope I would have a good chance. Perhaps Charlene mentioned me to you, Jack?"

Jack shook his head. "No, no, she didn't."

Anne nodded. "I suppose you weren't at that stage yet."

"No."

"Charlene was so excited about this film," Fiona said.

Isobel frowned. From what Jack had told her Charlene was dragging her heels on the lighting check. "Oh, was she?"

"Oh yes. She was going to no end of trouble."

Isobel looked at Jack who shrugged slightly.

"Really, what kind of trouble?" Isobel asked.

Fiona leant forward. "Well, don't tell her dad but she had spoken to his business partner in Techsol, Nathan Knight. She wanted advice about the best camera to use. Nathan is the technical expert in the company and Charlene's dad is the business head. She had sent Nathan some preliminary footage that she had taken and it wasn't good at all."

"Charlene had already taken some footage?" Jack asked.

Fiona nodded. "Maybe Michael had taken it but she wasn't happy with it, which is why she asked Nathan for advice. He was going to get her a really good camera, one like journalists use. Really expensive."

Jack raised his eyebrows at Isobel.

"Nathan said it would be better for night footage. It arrived on Monday," Fiona's eyes welled up, "in the afternoon. She was going to do some shooting that night.

She was so excited. She knew you were annoyed at her for delaying things but she knew that this special camera would ultimately help the quality of the film."

Jack looked bewildered. "We had a meeting and she never said anything about the camera."

"She wanted to surprise you. She knew you would be thrilled. She had a big reveal planned but instead . . ." Fiona burst into noisy tears.

Anne patted Fiona's hand. "She'll be alright. Charlene's strong."

Fiona wiped her eyes and looked again at Jack. "She said that the last project you had done was really good and this one would be even better."

Isobel glanced at Jack. He looked miserable.

"It's true," Anne said. "Really, she talked about nothing else. She got us all so excited about it. She was hoping to enter it in competitions."

Bernadette smiled. "Honestly, she had us convinced that the film was going to be amazing."

"Was Charlene having any problems with anyone?" Isobel said. "Was anything bothering her?"

"Why are you asking us that? I thought this was a robbery," Anne said.

Isobel winced. "That's something that the police are exploring. I'm just asking if there was anything upsetting Charlene at the moment."

"No, there wasn't. She was a normal student who was doing her best to get through her course. There was nothing bothering her. What is this? I think we've answered enough questions."

Anne stood up abruptly and moved towards the door.

Isobel was quite taken aback. Then she shrugged. "Come on, Jack. Let's go."

Anne ushered them to the front door and closed it behind them without a word.

They walked off down the street.

Isobel glanced at Jack. He looked stricken.

"Jack, don't take it to heart. You –"

"No, Aunt Isobel, don't! Charlene wanted to do a really good job. She was waiting for her new camera to do that." He swallowed with some difficulty. "I wish she'd told me that. I just thought that she wasn't taking the project seriously when in fact the opposite is true."

Isobel touched his arm. "Jack . . ."

He shrugged off her touch. "I know. It's just that I was thinking about her so negatively. We gave her and Michael a hard time and now I find out that she got a new camera, especially. *Shit. Shit.*"

There was a noise behind them. Isobel and Jack swung round. Fiona was running after them.

"I just wanted to answer your question," she said breathlessly. "I don't know what's wrong with Anne. She got so upset and annoyed that I didn't like to say anything."

"Go ahead," Isobel said.

"Charlene was worried about a number of things. I know that her dad is doing something with the company, going for a big deal. He's been working really hard and Charlene was a bit concerned that he was overdoing it."

Isobel nodded. "Thanks, Fiona."

"And . . ."

"There's something else?" Isobel asked.

Fiona made a face. "Yes. I'm sure it can't be relevant but . . ."

"If there is something else, please tell us, Fiona," said Isobel.

Fiona nodded. "Charlene had been getting some negative comments on social media. It was really bothering her."

"What sort of comments?"

"Oh, slagging her off. Saying she wasn't as good-looking or as important as she thought she was."

"Someone was trolling her?" Jack said.

Fiona nodded. "Yes. She tried to laugh it off and not let it affect her but it was really upsetting her and affecting her confidence. She didn't tell the others about it. She had asked Nathan Knight to see if he could find out who was doing it."

"How would he be able to help?" Isobel asked.

"He's a whizz on computers. Apparently there's very little that he can't find out if he really wants to. I didn't get to speak to her after she saw Nathan so I don't know what he told her, if anything. That's it. That's everything I know."

"Thanks, Fiona," said Isobel. "You've done the right thing in telling us."

"I've got to go." Fiona turned and ran back into the house.

"Poor Charlene!" Jack said. "Someone was trolling her and then we gave her a hard time . . ."

"If only she had told you that she was waiting on the new camera."

"I know. No surprise is worth the way I reacted."

"Charlene obviously thought it was. I wonder if

Nathan Knight had discovered who the troll was?"

"You can't really think that someone who was posting negative comments on social media went out and bashed Charlene on the head and killed the guy who was with her. That's a bit extreme. Surely it makes more sense that it was a robbery? That Charlene and Michael were in the wrong place at the wrong time?"

Isobel turned to Jack and spread her hands. "Maybe. But one of my favourite detectives, Inspector Gamache, says that the crime is related to the victim and that you need to look at the victim's life, at the people around them and the emotions that they engendered, to find who might have killed them."

"Does that apply if the attack was opportunistic?"

"No. But what I've learned from my last two cases is that you have to talk to lots of people and then sift through what they tell you to get to the truth."

Jack frowned.

Isobel continued. "Maybe what we're finding out has no relevance to the case but you can't know that until you check it out."

"I guess."

"And unfortunately you don't necessarily know what's important until late in the day. Looking into a crime is like walking in a fog – you don't really know where you are and you're not sure if you're going in the right direction."

Jack shook his head. "Sounds hopeless. Come on. I told Michael's girlfriend that we would meet her at eleven-thirty. We'd better hurry."

Chapter 10

Jack had arranged to meet Michael's girlfriend in the coffee bar of the Students Union. Jack set a fast pace of walking and Isobel felt a little short of breath and rather red-faced as she tried to keep up with him.

The Students Union was across the road from the main Queen's building. The Lanyon Building, named after its architect, was built in 1849 and was modelled on Magdalen College in Oxford. The imposing redbrick and windowed façade was iconic, even appearing on banknotes. It was one of Belfast's great architectural pieces and Isobel couldn't help but slow to admire it.

Jack quickly crossed the road and Isobel followed. In the Students Union café they joined the queue and collected coffees before Jack led the way to a table at the back of the room.

Two women sat at the table. Isobel was struck by their silence compared to the buzz coming from the other tables.

Jack said hi and went to bring over two more chairs to the table.

He and Isobel sat down.

"This is Isobel, my aunt."

"Hello," said Isobel. "I'm so sorry about Michael."

She looked at the faces in front of her, one fair, one dark. Where Charlene's friends had still some hope, here the grief was crushing. Most upset was the slight woman with blonde hair.

The dark-haired girl said, "I'm Brenda and this is Nicky, Michael's girlfriend."

Nicky dabbed at her eyes with a tissue, brushing away the fresh tears that those few sentences had generated.

"You were there on Monday night, Jack," she said.

"Yes. I'm sorry, Nicky. There was nothing more we could do."

"I know. Pat called the ambulance and they came quickly and you helped before they arrived."

"We tried."

"I know. I can't believe that I won't see him again. We had been going out together for a year and now . . ."

"Where were you, Nicky, when you heard about what had happened?" Isobel asked.

"I was in bed. Someone texted me that Michael and Charlene had been attacked. I didn't know then that he was dead. I only found that out later at the hospital. When I arrived they . . ." She dissolved into tears again.

Brenda hugged her and provided fresh tissues.

A few moments passed.

"How is Charlene doing, Jack?" Nicky asked.

Jack cleared his throat. "She had surgery overnight. The doctors have said that the next 48 hours are critical."

Nicky nodded. "The police have talked to me. They said that both Charlene's and Michael's phones and cards and money were taken. It's so hard to believe that someone would kill Michael for a phone and a few pounds. One minute he was talking to me about his project and a few hours later he was dead."

"He was talking about the film project?" Isobel asked.

"A bit. Michael and Charlene had to get the recordings from the different locations. You were in his group, weren't you, Jack?"

Jack curled his shoulders in as if he was trying to disappear. "Yes, yes, I was."

"Yeah, he told me about the meeting and how mad you all were about him and Charlene not having the recordings." She smiled. "He was laughing because, he said, Charlene had received a new camera that day, a really good one, and it was going to make the recordings so much better. He couldn't wait to show you all."

Jack shifted uncomfortably.

"So you were talking to him after the five o'clock meeting?" Isobel asked.

"Yes, we met for something to eat. I had a presentation to prepare so after eating I went to the library. Michael was meeting Charlene in the Muse at ten o'clock. They intended to visit all of the locations that night. I suppose they started with the alley because the Muse was an easy place to meet and they wanted to have a good look at the camera before they used it. He texted me later to tell me that they were going to the alley soon to make the first recording."

Jack cleared his throat and clasped his hands together.

Nicky looked at him. "Michael had taken recordings himself on other nights on his own phone. He was sure that you were going to be really impressed with the results they could get with Charlene's new camera. That text was the l-l-last I heard from him." She sobbed into her tissue and Brenda comforted her.

"Was there anything worrying Michael?" Isobel asked. "Did you notice any change in him recently?"

"No."

Isobel noticed that Brenda frowned slightly but then resumed a sympathetic look.

"You're sure there was nothing at all that had given you cause for concern about him?" Isobel asked.

Brenda's face again reacted and Isobel stared briefly at her before averting her gaze.

Nicky shook her head. "No, nothing."

Isobel looked around and said, "Sorry but all this coffee, I must go to the toilet. Can you tell me where to go?"

"Yes," Jack said and turned around in his seat. "It's . . ."

Brenda stood up. "I need to go too – why don't I show you?"

Isobel stood and followed Brenda through the café and along a corridor past a sign for the toilets, to the end of the corridor where it was quiet.

Brenda turned to Isobel. "Look, I probably shouldn't even be doing this. Nicky just wants to forget all the bad stuff but, well, Michael has been murdered. I'm a law student and I just feel that I have to tell someone."

"Go on."

Brenda took a deep breath. "Actually, things with Nicky

and Michael hadn't been as good for the last six months. Towards the end of last year Michael got really stressed out about his exams."

Isobel nodded.

"But it never really improved. When he came back in September he was still the same – more irritable, moody, just not himself."

"What did you think it was?"

Brenda looked away. "Nicky was worried. We talked a lot about what could have caused this change in him."

"Well, normally, with a change in mood, in personality in a young person, you would be wondering if they were being bullied or if they –"

"Or if they were taking drugs."

Isobel nodded.

"Nicky knew he wasn't being bullied."

"So Nicky thought that Michael had started taking drugs."

"Yes, that's what she was afraid of. When Michael first was stressed about the exams Nicky tried to help. She suggested a counsellor, meditation, those sorts of things. Michael thought that they didn't work because he didn't feel better immediately. Then, after a while he seemed to calm down. He started to say things like, 'Oh, we all need a little help sometimes. There are things that can take the edge off.' Nicky tried to talk to him. She asked him if he was taking drugs but he denied it." Brenda looked miserable.

"How involved in drugs did she think he was?"

Brenda looked at the floor.

"Brenda?"

She looked up. "Michael had more money this year than last year."

"Did Nicky think that he might be dealing? Is that it?"

"She didn't know."

"But she wondered?"

"Yes. She wondered."

Brenda rubbed her hands on her face. "God, I feel so awful even mentioning this. I feel as if I'm besmirching Michael's name. It may not even be true."

"Yes, but as you rightly pointed out Michael was murdered and Charlene is fighting for her life, so anything that sheds light on what might have been going on is important."

Brenda looked up. "You think I need to tell the police?"

Isobel exhaled noisily. "Yes, I do. They're trying to find a killer. They need all the information they can get."

Brenda closed her eyes. "I knew you were going to say that."

"Brenda, you'll feel better when you do the right thing, you know that. And whether she knows it or not so will Nicky. Looking back with regrets, wondering if not opening your mouth let a murderer go free is not a good thing to have hanging over you. Just tell the police your concerns."

Brenda rubbed her eyes roughly. "I know."

Isobel touched her shoulder. "I know you do."

"Nicky will be mad with me."

"Or she'll be relieved that you told them, so that she didn't have to."

Brenda nodded. "Yeah. You're right. Thanks."

"It's OK."

"We'd better get back."

Isobel nodded. "I can give you the name and number of one of the detectives involved in the case."

"Do." Brenda took out her phone.

Isobel passed on Doran's number.

Brenda touched Isobel's arm. "Thanks. I mean it. I do feel better."

Isobel smiled. "You'll feel even better after you talk to Detective Doran."

They walked in silence back to the table.

Jack and Nicky had their heads together, looking at Nicky's phone.

Jack sat up straight when Isobel and Brenda arrived. "Nicky was showing me some of the recordings that Michael had made of the alley. Charlene's camera definitely made a huge difference."

Isobel stayed standing. Jack stood up.

"We'll be thinking of you, Nicky, and Michael and his family," Isobel said.

Nicky nodded. "Thanks."

"Nicky, can you send me the footage that Michael had recorded in the alley?" Jack said.

"What? You can't be thinking about making the film at a time like this?"

Jack shook his head.

"For God's sake, if Michael hadn't been making that recording he might be alive now!"

Jack gasped.

Brenda reached out and touched Nicky's arm. "Nicky,

that's not why Jack wants the recordings, it's not about the film." She looked at Jack. "Is it?"

He shook his head. "No. It has nothing to do with the film."

"Send the recordings on to Jack, Nicky," said Brenda. "Maybe he can help find who did this to Michael."

Nicky bit her lip, then nodded.

Jack gave her his email address. "Thanks, Nicky."

She rubbed her eyes. "I'm sorry. I shouldn't have said what I did. It's not your fault."

"It's OK. Sometimes I blame myself too."

Nicky lifted her head, her eyes wet with tears. She looked Jack in the eye and shook her head. "No, honestly, the film was a good thing. It seemed to give Michael some real interest and happiness. He was excited on Monday night about getting the footage to show you all."

She folded in on herself and Brenda hugged her.

"Thank you for talking to us." Isobel looked at Brenda and gave her a nod.

Hastily, Jack and Isobel left the coffee bar.

In the corridor Jack stopped and faced Isobel. "You know I wasn't asking for the recording because I was thinking about the film, don't you?"

"Of course. I was going to ask for it myself."

"You know, I thought about what you said about being in a fog. That's a good description of how I feel but I have a better one."

"Let's hear it."

"I think it's more like playing a game of pin the tail on the donkey. You can't see anything but you know that the perfect fit or solution is nearby. I'm done wandering in a fog. I'm going to pin the tail on the donkey."

Isobel put her arm around him. "I can see what you're saying. It's certainly more hopeful. If it works for you, then, that's fine with me."

"You never know, we might see something in Michael's footage that helps."

"Maybe. I suppose even if it's not from the day of the attack there might be something. Maybe the alley was a meeting place and Michael had other images of people there." She paused. "You know, everyone seems very committed to your film, Jack – what was it about?"

She was surprised to see the stricken look that passed over his face.

He looked away from her and then back. "Yes, Aunt Isobel, it's high time I told you about that." He heaved a deep sigh. "Could we go back to your hotel? To your room? I'd prefer to talk about it in private."

"Sure."

They walked back to the hotel in silence, Isobel wondering why Jack was so disturbed about the content of the film.

Chapter 11

Room service brought soup and sandwiches and they sat at the small table in Isobel's room looking out on the city. The soup was tasty and Isobel tucked in.

"OK. Tell me about this film."

Jack fiddled with his spoon. "When we started brainstorming about the film we were thinking of doing a mini crime story. The alley was one of the possible scenes of the crime. It was going to be an attack on a woman." He put a hand to his forehead. "I can't believe that that is what happened. It's like a nightmare. Like our story has come true and now we are living it." He took a ragged breath and shook his head, his eyes focused on the table. "The more we talked as a group the more we came around to the idea of maybe looking at the aftermath of an attack and how it affects the people involved. We were thinking of calling it *Impact*, as in 'victim impact'." He covered his face with his hands and sobbed. "And now here we all are, dealing with the impact of a crime, of a death. It's horrible. It's like we made it happen."

"No, Jack, *no*."

"I keep going over things in my head. How can our made-up story turn into reality? Why did that happen?"

"I don't know why it happened yet but we will find out. It had nothing to do with your movie. Either it was an opportunistic theft, or there were drugs involved or someone had a problem with Michael or Charlene or both of them. You can't torment yourself like this. Your story was about a made-up crime but crime happens every day somewhere. I don't know why Charlene and Michael were attacked in the alley but you are not responsible. The person who did it is. You know that, don't you?"

He shook his head. "I can't help feeling guilty. I wish that we hadn't been making the movie."

"No, Jack. You wish that Michael and Charlene hadn't been attacked, that Michael hadn't been killed, that Charlene wasn't so badly injured, that is what you really wish. Your movie didn't create this, someone else did. I don't know why but we can try and find out and, even if we don't, you and your friends making a movie did *not* make this happen. The attacker made this happen. Charlene and Michael were just going about their business, being students, doing research."

Jack looked at Isobel for a long moment. "OK."

"Good. Let's get back to looking at the facts. So, a lot of people were interested in the movie?"

"Yes. We thought so. That's why that last meeting was so acrimonious. The rest of us, Noah, me and Rachel, couldn't understand why Michael and Charlene were dragging their heels with the footage. Of course, now I understand." He pulled out his phone. "Let me check and see if Nicky has sent on the footage. Yes, yes, she has. There are lots of recordings of the alley. Here. Look at this one."

Isobel took the phone. "Oh, yes . . . you can see the difference Charlene's camera made." She handed the phone back.

Jack studied some of the others. "They're not very good."

"Any sign of people in the alley?" she asked.

"No."

"I had a vain hope that they might have hung out there regularly and that Michael had caught a closer shot of them."

"It was worth a try."

"Oh well." Isobel shrugged.

"What now?"

Isobel told him what Brenda had related to her.

"So Michael may have been into drugs and may even have been a dealer," said Jack. "That's a bit of a shock."

"I know. I would like to talk to a friend of Michael's to get his take on things. If Michael was involved in drugs then that opens the possibility that the attack was related to that."

"And Charlene was collateral damage?"

"It's a possibility. I think that would break Tony's heart and I can't imagine what Michael's parents would feel. I suppose it's another attempt at pinning the tail on the donkey, but it could be way off. I hope it is."

Jack nodded. "Let me ring Tom. He's a friend of Michael's. He might meet us."

He wandered to the far corner of the room and Isobel

looked out the window. She felt drained. No wonder Jack had been so upset. She hoped that they could find out who had committed this crime for Michael's sake, and for Charlene and their families – but also for Jack's sake so that he could attribute responsibility to the criminal and relinquish it himself.

In a few minutes he was back. "Yep, we can meet him now."

Isobel groaned. "Not another cup of coffee!"

Jack smiled. "That's what I thought. He wants to meet in the Crown for a pint of Guinness."

"It's always like this."

"Like what?"

"Well, to get someone to reveal stuff you need to create a relaxed atmosphere, hence the beverages, but it's hard work on the kidneys." She reached for her phone. "Before we go, I'll ring Tony and see if there's any word on Charlene."

Jack nodded. "Good idea."

She dialled and Tony answered immediately.

"Hi, Isobel. I'm at the hospital. There's no change but that apparently is good."

"That's great, Tony."

"I'm sitting with her all afternoon while Joan has a rest. Could I meet up with you this evening?"

"Yes, of course."

"I'm at the Europa. I'll see you in the bar at six o'clock."

"See you then."

Chapter 12

The Crown Bar dated back to 1826 and, with its carved mahogany booths, etched glass and gas lamps, retained some of the atmosphere of a Victorian gin palace. The shelves behind the bar were well stocked. Jack ordered a pint of Guinness for himself and Isobel gave in to temptation and had one too. It seemed the appropriate homage to this famous Liquor Saloon.

Jack led the way to one of the booths where a young man with shoulder-length dirty-blond hair sat hunched over his pint.

"Hi, Tom. This is Isobel."

Tom jerked his head. "Nicky told me that you'd been asking her questions. I suppose you're here to do the same to me."

Jack arched an eyebrow at Isobel who sat down calmly.

"We can ask you questions or you can tell us what you know," she said.

Tom snatched up his pint and took a long swig, the glass showing satisfying rings of cream as the Guinness disappeared. "What makes you think that I know anything and, more importantly, that I'm going to tell you? What right have you to be asking questions anyway?"

Isobel took a drink herself. The Guinness was good. "I'm only asking questions in the hope that I can find out something that would help the police find Michael's killer."

"Why don't you just leave it to the police?"

Jack said, "My aunt has helped in other –"

Isobel squeezed Jack's arm and he fell silent.

"I could leave it to the police but in my experience not everyone is honest with them about what's going on. I'm a psychotherapist. I'm used to people talking to me about their secrets."

Tom made a face and then downed the rest of his pint. "I need another." He got up, took his glass and went to the bar.

"He isn't going to tell us anything," said Jack.

Isobel shrugged. "He's getting another pint, not leaving."

"Well, his attitude is very antagonistic."

She smiled. "True. He might not want to tell us, but, for his friend, he feels he has to. He's just working himself up to it."

Tom was on his way back from the bar. He sat down once more and sipped his pint.

"Were you and Michael friends long?" Isobel asked.

He shook his head. "No, I met him when I came to college but . . ." he swallowed, "we were good mates."

Isobel nodded. "I'm sorry that he died."

Tom winced at the last word. He hung his head again and swiped at his eyes.

Isobel rested her arms on the table. "Brenda told me that Nicky had been worried about Michael, that she thought he might have been taking drugs."

Tom swallowed. "Do you think drugs have something to do with his death?"

"Honestly, Tom?" She waited until he looked up at her. "I don't know. What I do know is that it's important to consider every angle."

He moved his pint between his hands. He took a drink. "You're right. I would find it hard to tell the police this but if it helps them find Michael's killer . . ."

Isobel nodded.

Tom took a deep breath. "Michael was taking drugs."

She stayed still and waited.

Tom studied his pint once more. "He got stressed out coming up to our first-year exams. We were all a bit stressed but he definitely was very bad. He started going out to the pub more and after a while he seemed to calm down. He got very focused on his studies. He was handling things better. I was a bit stressed myself and one day he offered me a pill. He said that he'd found them good. I took it. It did help."

"What was it?" Jack asked.

"It was a Xanax."

"Oh." Jack looked at Isobel.

Tom looked at his hands. "I started with those but within a few weeks I was trying other things that Michael had. I got through my exams by taking a combination of things."

"Did you get them all from Michael?" Isobel asked.

He nodded. "Then term ended. I went home to my summer job. It was hard being at home after living in Belfast for the year and I got stressed. I rang Michael and we met up and I got some more Xanax from him. Basically I found that I was getting anxious if I thought that I might not be able to get more tablets. I just seemed to be getting more and more uptight. Eventually my mum and I had a huge row about how I was behaving and my attitude. She accused me of having changed, of being moody and withdrawn and she asked me if I was on drugs. I was shocked that she suspected and I suppose at this stage I could see myself that I was going down a slippery path and I admitted it to her, thank God." He looked up at Isobel.

She nodded encouragingly.

"Mum made me go to an addiction counsellor. I saw him all over the summer, sometimes a couple of times a week. I had only been taking drugs for a short time but it was scary to think about not having anything for my anxiety. The counsellor helped and by the end of the summer I had been a few weeks drug-free. Mum didn't want me to come back to college. The only reason she let me was that I promised to continue to work with a counsellor at the university. His name is Ben Jameson. He has a lot of experience with addictions – in fact, he was an addict himself. He knows all the dodges. I really like him and I've been doing well." He lifted the pint and looked at it. "Until now, that is. I've mostly been off drink too but with what happened to Michael . . . That's why I agreed to talk to you. I thought that if I told someone about Michael and the drugs that I would feel less upset."

"You know that I have to tell the police about this, in case it's in any way linked to Michael's murder?" Isobel said.

Tom nodded. "I kind of expected that."

"Are you going to be alright?" Isobel asked.

"I'm seeing Ben tomorrow."

"That's good, Tom," Jack said.

Tom looked sadly at his pint. "When I came back to college this year I talked to Michael about him getting help. I wanted him to go to Ben too."

"And did he?" Jack asked.

Tom shook his head. "He said that he didn't have a problem."

"Was he still using?" Isobel asked.

Tom shrugged. "I never saw him taking drugs but I think he was."

"Do you think he was dealing?"

"Because he gave me drugs, you think that he might have been giving them to others?"

Isobel shrugged. "I don't know. I'm just asking."

He shook his head. "I don't know. I don't think so."

They all sipped their drinks.

"Is there anything else that you think might be helpful?" Isobel asked.

Tom studied his pint. "No."

"I'll tell Detective Doran about what you've said. He may want to speak to you."

Tom sighed and nodded disconsolately. "I've got it off my chest now." He downed the last of his pint. "I must go."

"Are you sure you're alright?" Isobel asked.

"I'm meeting a friend and we're going to see a movie. Don't worry, he'll keep me right."

Isobel nodded. "Thanks for telling us, Tom."

"Mind yourself," Jack added.

Tom nodded and moved away, his shoulders hunched and his head down.

Isobel sat back in her chair. She still had half a pint to drink. Jack was a bit ahead of her.

"So the reason Michael and Charlene were attacked could be drugs?" Jack said.

"Could be."

"And the motive may not have been robbery."

Isobel exhaled. "If Michael had drugs on him, it may not have been phones and personal cash that they were after."

"God."

"I know."

"This could be an important finding, couldn't it?"

"It could be."

"I'll ring Detective Doran now," Jack said. "Remember he said that I would need to make a statement? We can fill him in on everything."

Isobel nodded. Jack went outside the pub to use his phone.

Isobel sat back in the booth. She felt tired and sad. All of these young people trying to find their way in the world . . . it was so easy for things to get messed up.

Chapter 13

Detective Doran wanted to see them in the Grosvenor Road police station. Isobel was glad that they could walk there. It gave her a chance to burn off the Guinness with some exercise and the fresh air might clear her head. As they moved along the Grosvenor Road she found herself pausing to study the murals. Some were advertising a local car wash. Another showed a woman in green with Celtic symbols and encouraged the viewer to remember the Ireland of old.

"The artwork is amazing," she said.

Jack stopped beside Isobel. "I know. Come and see some more."

He led Isobel on to Sandy Row. There was a mural of King William commemorating the Battle of the Boyne on 12th of July 1690. The artwork was equally skilled. Through the murals the historical loyalties were displayed. Isobel felt the weight of the past and the divides it had created and maintained. Here she was investigating a young man's death and the murals reminded her of all the young people on either side of the Northern Ireland conflict who had died. So much loss. Her heart felt very heavy. She said little and Jack, sensing her mood, led her back to the Grosvenor Road.

As they approached the police station Isobel saw a seven-or-eight-foot wall topped by the same height again in fencing. It was a far cry from her local Garda Station where the building resembled a house. The contrast was stark and at the same time sobering. The entrance to the police station was a gate. They had to give their names. They were checked off a list. Then they were searched. When they had passed these tests they were led from the lodge at the gate across a parking lot and into the main building.

Doran met them in the main foyer. He said little and led them upstairs to an interview room. It was minimalist, with a table and four chairs. In the corner, suspended from the ceiling, was a video camera. It had no light on but Isobel wondered if they were being recorded.

Isobel sat quietly beside Jack while Doran took Jack's statement concerning the pictures Charlene had sent to the joint account.

After Jack had read and signed it, Doran said, "Inspector Williams wants to speak to you. I'll get him."

"Before you do we want to give you some more information that we've found," Isobel said.

Doran sat back in his chair.

Isobel nodded at Jack to continue.

"We spoke to one of Michael's friends and he told us that Michael was involved in drugs."

Doran abruptly leant forward. "Who is this friend?"

"His name is Tom Smith."

"We'll need to speak to him."

Jack nodded. "He knows that. I can give you his number."

"Why didn't he come forward with this information himself?"

Jack shifted in his seat and glanced at Isobel.

"Let me guess," said Doran. "He's involved in drugs himself."

Jack lifted his chin. "He was but he's clean now."

"Maybe. We'll check it out. But if Michael's murder is related to his drug use, believe me, it's going to be difficult to get information about who's involved. No one wants to be a snitch and people who are taking drugs obviously don't want their supply line compromised." He sighed. "There are drugs everywhere. Last night we had two deaths in the city from overdoses – dealers."

Jack glanced at Isobel.

Doran straightened up. "We'll look into it and see where it leads."

Isobel nodded. "What about the footage of the people in the alley? Is it going to be possible to identify them?"

"No word on that so far. I'll get Inspector Williams." He left the room.

"I thought that finding out Michael was taking drugs was a breakthrough," said Jack. "Detective Doran seems very negative about it being helpful."

Isobel shrugged. "He does seem jaded. I guess he has some experience of how hard it is to get information."

Jack was silent for a few moments, then said, "I feel a

bit better now. Talking to people, finding things out that might relate to what happened is helping me. Talking to Tom helped me see that the film may have only been coincidental to what happened. If drugs are involved then making the film had very little to do with what happened."

"That's the truth, Jack."

He nodded. "I feel less to blame and I suppose," he paused, "less powerless."

Isobel nodded. "I'm glad, Jack. But just remember there are no guarantees. Drugs may be involved but that remains to be seen. We'll do what we can, find out as much as possible, but we may not find who did this."

"I know but I'm not ready to give up yet. It sounds to me like Detective Doran is jaded and Charlene deserves –" He stopped.

They heard voices outside the door.

Doran entered first then stepped aside to let his superior officer precede him.

Isobel studied Inspector Williams. He was the same height as Doran, but older, maybe fifty, and bald. He was dressed in a grey suit and had a paunch.

He sat down and looked at Isobel and Jack.

Jack shifted in his seat. Isobel sat very still and looked back at him.

After a minute of silence, he turned to Jack. "So you're the young man who helped at the scene and then found footage from the alley?"

"Jack McKenzie, sir," Doran supplied.

Inspector Williams ignored him.

"Yes," Jack said.

More silence.

"It took you a day to find this footage?"

Jack moistened his lips. "Yes. I was at the hospital all day yesterday. Then I was with some friends. I only checked my media accounts this morning."

Isobel thought that despite Williams trying to rattle him, Jack was doing well. "Is there any possibility that the people can be identified from the footage?" she said.

Williams turned his gaze on her.

Isobel sat very still and kept her face neutral.

"It's with the labs. Obviously they will do their best but with the distance involved, well . . ." he shrugged, "it might take a few days."

Isobel was disappointed to hear this.

"Who have you shown the video to?" Williams asked Jack.

"My aunt, this morning, and then we contacted Detective Doran – that's it."

"Well, keep it that way. I don't want it popping up on the internet."

Jack frowned. "Of course not. I wouldn't do that."

"See that you don't." Williams folded his arms.

"And I've told the other students with access to the account the same thing."

"Get their names, Doran. I want the recording protected."

"My friends are not stupid," said Jack. "They wouldn't do anything to jeopardise the case."

Isobel felt proud of Jack.

Williams pulled a face and waited while Jack gave the names and phone numbers.

"Detective Doran tells me that you've brought more information about Michael and his activities," he then said. "It sounds like you fancy yourself as a detective."

"Jack spoke to some students, people he knew that were also affected by this terrible event," Isobel said. "They have shared thoughts and information with him. He has every right to do that."

"And you, Ms. McKenzie. You like playing Sherlock Holmes too. You were involved in that case in Limerick."

"I found a body –"

"Oh, I think we both know that it was a bit more than that."

Isobel folded her arms too.

"I don't want you interfering here. Whoever killed Michael and attacked Charlene is dangerous and I want you two to stay out of the investigation."

Isobel could feel her temper rising. "So, in future, if we discover anything, we should just keep it to ourselves?"

Williams leaned forward in his chair and rested his arms on the table. "No." His voice carried an edge. "But I don't want you searching. And you don't fool me with your 'talking to Michael's friends' – you were pumping them for information. Stop it."

"Is there anything else, or are we finished here?" Isobel said.

Williams stood up. "You're finished here." He strode out of the room.

There was silence.

Isobel could feel a hot flush coming on, this one triggered by temper.

Doran stood up. "Thank you for the information that you've given us. I will speak to your fellow students Rachel and Noah, Jack. Inspector Williams is concerned for your safety. Please follow his advice."

Isobel raised her eyebrows and looked at him. He blushed.

"Come on, Jack. Let's get out of here."

Doran escorted them to the entrance of the compound. No one spoke while they walked. He paused with his hand on the door.

"You have my number."

Isobel gave a curt nod.

He opened the door.

Isobel and Jack stepped out onto the street and the door closed behind them.

"What was that about?" Jack said.

Isobel muttered, "Not here. Let's walk back to Queen's."

They set off. As Isobel walked she did her best to burn through her anger.

As they passed through Shaftesbury Square, Jack said, "Inspector Williams sure doesn't want us to show that video footage to anyone."

Isobel grinned at him. "I know, which makes me so want to do just that."

"Who would we show it to?"

Isobel turned to him and he halted. "Maybe Williams is right, Jack, and it would be better, safer, if you didn't get involved in talking to people."

Jack shook his head. "No way. I feel better that we've contributed to trying to find who did this and I want to keep doing that. And Mr. Griffiths wants us to find out all that we can."

Isobel nodded. "I know. And, so far, we've helped. But they're trying to frighten us off."

"Inspector Williams sure is an intimidating police officer."

"He is."

"What next?"

"If we're going to continue then I think we should go and talk to the counsellor Tom mentioned, Ben Jameson."

Jack frowned. "I thought that Michael hadn't been to him."

"No. But Tom seemed to think that this Ben Jameson was on the ball and so he might be able to give us some general information about drugs on campus, and that might be helpful."

"I suppose it might be. Should we ring and see if he's free to see us?" He started walking.

Isobel fell into step beside him. "No. I think it's much better to surprise him. I'm sure he'll be able to manage a few minutes for us."

Chapter 14

On campus, Jack led the way through a myriad of corridors to the counselling suite. They arrived into a waiting room where two students sat scrolling through their phones. Isobel and Jack approached the receptionist.

She greeted them with, "Hello, how can I help you?"

"We were hoping to see Ben Jameson," said Jack.

"Have you been a client of his before?"

"No, I haven't but he was recommended to me."

"Things are really busy today."

Isobel spoke up. "Actually, I'm a colleague, a psychotherapist, from Limerick. I was hoping that I could have a quick word with Ben, just a professional courtesy." She pulled one of her old cards out of her shoulder bag and handed it to the receptionist. "Perhaps he has a break, or can spare a few minutes to see us?"

The receptionist studied the card and then Isobel. "I'll check with him." She stood and made her way down the corridor where she entered one of the rooms, closing the door.

Isobel looked at her watch. It was half past four. She grimaced. "We might not be able to talk to him until he finishes for the day."

Along the corridor the door opened again and the receptionist beckoned to them.

"Oh, we're in luck," said Isobel.

They walked down the corridor.

"Ben had a cancellation. He says that he will talk to you now."

The room she showed them into was a staff room with a kitchenette. There were a number of comfortable armchairs and in one of those sat a man with long grey hair tied back in a ponytail, nursing a cup of coffee.

"Help yourselves to coffee," he said, gesturing towards the Nespresso machine.

Jack made a beeline for it.

"I'll just have some water, Jack." Isobel approached the man. "Isobel McKenzie," she said, holding out her hand.

"Ben Jameson," he said, grasping her hand with definite strength.

Isobel gestured. "This is Jack, my nephew."

"How can I help you?"

Isobel studied the man as she sat down. Ben Jameson might look like a hippy but there was nothing laid-back about him. His blue eyes were clear and held the unmistakable look of someone who was astute. Isobel wasn't sure what the best approach was. She knew that he wouldn't betray a client's confidence but she hoped that he could give her some insights into the drug scene among the students.

"Jack knew Michael O'Neill and Charlene Griffiths." she said. "He arrived shortly after they were found and helped with the CPR."

"Oh." He turned to Jack. "How is Charlene doing?"

"She's out of surgery and stable."

Ben shook his head. "A terrible business."

Jack placed a glass of water on the side-table beside Isobel's chair and sat down with his coffee.

"We've been talking to Tom, one of Michael's friends." Isobel saw a flicker in Ben's eyes but his face remained impassive. "He told us that you were his counsellor. He agreed that we should tell the police about Michael's drug-taking." She detected a slight relaxation in Ben's face. "We've informed the investigating officer and they will probably interview Tom. He told us that he was seeing you tomorrow. He seemed fine when we left him and he assured us that he had someone to help him this evening."

Now there was definite relief on Ben's face. "While I'm glad to hear that, I'm at a loss to know why you're here talking to me. You know I can't talk to you about any student I'm seeing."

Isobel sat back, resting her arms on the chair arms. "The police, when we gave them the information, were less than enthusiastic."

"Oh, so they don't think that drugs have anything to do with the attacks?"

"They don't know. I suppose you could say it's a possible line of enquiry. But what they do know is how hard it is to get information about drug activities anywhere."

Ben nodded.

"I realise that you can't betray any confidences but I thought that you could talk about what you've learned about drugs on campus in a general way."

Ben studied her.

Isobel maintained her relaxed posture.

"Is that all or has Tom told you that I am an ex-addict so you think I have a hotline to what is going on?"

"No. He did mention that you were involved in drugs but he just said that made you hard to fool."

Ben tipped his head in acknowledgement.

Isobel sat forward now. "The police think that the attack could have been a robbery. There is evidence that there were two people in the laneway just before the attack. They may be the perpetrators or they may be witnesses who haven't come forward. The laneway has a back door to the pub, the Muse, and a derelict paper-factory entrance, which is padlocked. I just wondered if you had any knowledge of whether this laneway was used for drug-taking or dealing. I suppose I hoped that in talking to the students you'd picked up some useful information." She hurried on. "Not betraying any confidence but general information about locations, movements, patterns, anything that we could follow to get some more information to help the police find who did this."

Ben raised his eyebrows. "And who appointed you an investigator?"

'Mr. Griffiths, Charlene's dad, asked us to help," Jack said.

Ben frowned at Jack and then looked back at Isobel.

She said, "I've helped in a couple of investigations

92

before, in London and in Limerick. Mr. Griffiths was hoping that I could do the same here."

He picked up her card. "A psychotherapist turned detective."

The way he said it, it didn't sound good.

Isobel lifted her chin. "No, someone who was in a certain place at a certain time and whose skills professionally proved useful in another context." She felt herself calm at the truth of her words.

Ben met her eyes and nodded in acknowledgement. "And you're wondering if the two people in the alley were doing a drug deal?"

"Yes. They may have nothing to do with the attacks but be afraid to come forward because they were doing drugs in the alley."

Ben looked thoughtful. He tapped Isobel's business card on the arm of his chair. "I was a student here about twenty years ago."

Isobel realised that Ben was about her age. "Oh."

"Poor Lorraine."

Isobel was mystified. "Who?"

"The owner of the Muse."

"Oh, yes." She remembered that Jack had mentioned her. The woman in black she had seen in the pub, no doubt.

"She was a student here when I was. The attacks have happened on her doorstep. She's bound to be upset."

"She is," Jack said.

Ben looked into the distance. "I know the provost, Sam Prince, from my student days too."

Jack looked very impressed. "Really?"

Ben laughed. "Yes. Don't tell anyone but because he studied law we called him 'The Crown Prince'."

Jack laughed.

Isobel smiled and felt grateful to Ben. For a moment Jack seemed carefree and childishly gleeful. She could feel herself relaxing a bit too. Ben's reminiscences were reminding her of being a student herself.

"It sounds like you knew Lorraine and Sam well," she said.

Ben breathed a deep sigh. "I did, not that I see too much of them these days." He looked slyly at Jack. "Lorraine is gorgeous, don't you think?"

Jack blushed.

Ben grinned. "When I was a student I fancied her something crazy. Ah, well!"

Jack laughed, charmed by this admission.

"There were drugs around then," Ben went on. "I got into them and, unfortunately, I kept taking them and progressed to harder drugs. I suppose I was the classic addict and by my third year I was on cocaine. Unfortunately, one day I overdosed. I was lucky that the Prince had arranged to drop round that evening. He found me and saved my life."

Jack paled. "Oh my God!"

Ben nodded. "I know. I was very lucky. I survived. When I was well enough I went to rehab. Thank God it stuck. I went back to college and did my Master's in Counselling and then some extra training in addiction. When the job came up here I really wanted it. It felt like completing a circle." He took a deep breath. "I suppose what happened to Michael has brought back some of my own student times. Lorraine dropped out shortly after my overdose. It was seven or eight years later that she bought the Muse and she has been there ever since."

Isobel glanced at Jack who was clearly enthralled by these reminiscences.

"Is the Muse a drug pub?" she asked.

"No, not at all," said Jack.

"Generally, what I hear is that the pub is pretty clean," Ben said. "Lorraine runs a fairly tight ship and the Muse has a good reputation. She has a good relationship with the students, I hear, but doesn't put up with any nonsense."

"Exactly," said Jack.

"Drugs are quite prolific in Belfast – uppers, downers and the harder stuff, and prescription medication too. And I have some students who've ended up doing a bit of pushing because they need the money."

"And do you have any idea who is responsible, or where the drug handovers are happening?" Isobel asked.

Ben shook his head.

"Is that alley involved?"

"Not that I know of."

"Is there any other information you've gleaned about drugs that might help us?"

"Not really. The students I deal with are nervous about divulging that kind of information and it's not my business to press them."

"If you think of anything, will you contact me?"

"I will." He held up her card between his fingers. "I

probably shouldn't have told you all that I did. I guess Michael's death reminded me of my own brush with it. But I got a second chance, thank God."

"We appreciate you telling us," Isobel said.

"I like the nickname you had for the Provost – the Crown Prince," Jack said. "That's really good. Did anyone else have nicknames?"

Ben grinned. "Yeah."

"Did you have one?" Jack's eyes sparkled with fun.

Ben paused a moment and then grinned back. "I did."

"What was it?"

"Neat."

"Neat?"

Isobel laughed. "Neat Jameson!"

"Got it in one!"

Jack laughed. "What about Lorraine? Did she have a nickname too?"

"Yes."

"What was it?"

"The same as her pub."

"The Muse?"

"Yes."

Isobel thought of artists and their muses, the source of their inspiration, and wondered if it fitted the woman she had seen.

There was a knock on the door and the receptionist entered. Your last appointment is here, Ben. I've put her in your room."

"Thanks."

The receptionist withdrew.

He stood up. "I have to go." He moved over to rinse his cup in the sink.

"Of course." Isobel went to rinse her glass too. "Thank you for talking to us."

"I doubt that anything I've told you has helped."

Isobel wasn't sure if it had.

Chapter 15

They walked in the direction of the Europa, where they were to meet Tony.

"Well, what do you think about everything that we've learned today?" Isobel said.

Jack frowned. "I think we got lots of information but I don't know if any of it is going to help us."

Isobel reached out and touched his arm. "I know."

"Sometimes it's so hard to believe that it really happened, that Michael is dead and that Charlene is . . . is . . . When we're asking questions and talking to people, sometimes I forget what's happened, or I'm so focused on trying to find information that I almost forget the reality of . . . the awfulness. " He shook his head. "And then it all comes back to me."

"Maybe talking to everyone isn't a good thing for you to be doing after all?"

"No, no, I still think it is. It reminds me that so many people have been affected by what has happened and that's important to remember. And despite everything, I suppose I feel that we have helped and that's good."

Isobel nodded. "I know. I think it's the same for me. Helping the police, finding the truth and, hopefully, some justice, feels like a way of honouring the person who has died or suffered, a way of acknowledging their pain and doing something, however small, to ease it."

"Is it the same when you're working as a psycho-therapist?"

"Yes, I think it is." Isobel often was amazed at the insight and understanding of her nephew. She found her eyes sparking with tears. Somehow he had brought her to a truth within herself that she had temporarily forgotten.

She hooked her arm through Jack's and they walked on.

After a bit he said, "I have to confess that I did think that investigating would be different. I thought it would be easier and more exciting. I thought that finding the bad guys would be more linear, that it would be easy to know what to do. At the moment my head feels like it does when I'm writing an essay: I have loads of information but I'm not too sure what is actually relevant."

"What do you think about the person who was attacking Charlene online?"

"I'm not sure. I suppose I've always thought of trolls as being people who hide behind their keyboards. They want to be anonymous, hidden, secretive and so less likely to hit you over the head. That may be a misperception but . . ."

"I kind of agree with you," said Isobel. "We could get in touch with Nathan Knight and see if he found out for Charlene who it was. Then we could check the person out to see where he or she was when the attack happened."

"Good idea."

"Nathan must be very good with computers if Charlene thought he could help with that."

"Tony's company is called Techsol. I presume the company does exactly what it says on the letterhead. Nathan would just have to track the IP address."

"I think he's definitely worth talking to."

They walked a bit further before Isobel spoke again.

"Doran seemed hopeful initially when he got the footage today but when we saw him at the police station he seemed very subdued about it. And Inspector Williams was the same."

"I hope to God the police experts can do something with the video."

"Yes. But I was wondering if it might be worth getting Mr Tech Solutions to see what he could get from it."

"That's a great idea! We should do that." Jack's phone rang. "It's Dad. He wanted me to keep him up to date with how things were going." He stopped to answer his phone.

Isobel walked on a few paces. As Jack talked in the background, she walked around in a circle surveying the streets. There were groups of students all going about their business. She thought of Charlene lying in a hospital bed with God knows what ahead of her and Michael in the morgue. She shivered and thanked God that Jack was safe. The fragility of life – how quickly it could go from wonderful to tragic with no warning! She rubbed her hands up her face and into her hair. She knew all about it.

It was almost two years since she had been diagnosed with breast cancer. One minute she was going about her normal life and the next she didn't know if she was going to survive. While she was fine now, the experience had left its mark. No one knows how long they have, she thought, the future isn't guaranteed. She shivered. She needed to be less morose. Somehow the age of the people involved had got to her. All these young people with their lives ahead of them but also with dangers all around, like drugs and violent people. Talking to the young people today, then listening to Ben Jameson and thinking about his work in therapy with the students, and finally her reflections with Jack, had stirred something in her. For the first time since she had been diagnosed with cancer and received her treatment she felt a spark of interest, of inspiration, the stirring of the desire to go back to her psychotherapy work. Recovery had taken so long. She had begun to wonder if she would ever feel like going back to work, or feel that she had something to give. The two cases that she had worked on had helped. They gave her a sense that she could do something, that there were options out there, new interests, new areas she could work in and that had helped. But to feel that what she had done before might be at an end had been a worry that she hadn't shared with anyone. Now, with this flicker of interest, she felt some relief. Maybe she could go back to psychotherapy again.

She could hear Jack laughing with his dad as he said goodbye. She knew that she needed to stay focused on what they were doing right now, not worry about her future career path.

Jack came towards her.

Isobel smiled. "Well?"

He grinned. "Dad couldn't believe that Charlene had uploaded the piece of film from the alley. He was teasing me that detection runs in the family. Yeah, suddenly he's gone all Sherlock Holmes. He thinks we found out loads today."

Isobel rolled her eyes.

"I know, I know," he said.

"Did you mention Techsol and the video?"

"Yes. He thinks that Nathan Knight might be able to do something with it."

Isobel felt her shoulders relaxing. "That would be great. I definitely think that is the most important lead we have."

Jack nodded and resumed walking, his lengthening stride reflecting his enthusiasm.

Isobel struggled to keep up. "Slow down, Jack."

"Sorry."

Isobel grinned. "Oh, to be young and fit!"

They proceeded at a more sedate pace.

"I think we need to find out more about the drug scene on campus," Isobel said.

"Yes, we do."

"Or, it could be that Charlene's troll went postal, and Michael was collateral damage. It's a possibility and I think it would be a mistake to rule anything out at this stage. We've found some interesting threads and we need to see where they take us."

"Too many threads."

A little further on, Isobel said, "There's one thing I want to get out of Tony Griffiths tonight."

Jack glanced at her. "What?"

"I want to meet Nathan Knight . . . in person." She stopped. "I don't want to send him the video and have him work on it. I want to give it to him. And I want to ask him what he found out from looking at Charlene's online stuff."

They were almost at the gate into the Europa.

"OK. I'll let you do the talking," said Jack.

Isobel shook her head. "No, you found the video. You're the main man."

Chapter 16

The Europa stretched up over ten floors and was built in a curve as if embracing the city spread out before it. Isobel found herself pausing outside and looking up at it. This was known as the most bombed hotel in Europe, if not the world. It had been bombed thirty-six times during the Troubles but had endured. Somehow that past added to its noble appearance.

Isobel and Jack went through the doorway and into the foyer. The ceiling was high, creating a feeling of airiness. Lots of people were moving around.

Jack led the way upstairs to the first-floor bar.

Isobel's impression was of golden décor, large windows, table lamps and the hushed sound of class.

Jack looked around and over by the window a man raised his hand. Jack threaded his way through the chairs, Isobel following.

As they approached Tony Griffiths, Isobel was surprised to see another man at the table. The second man was younger by maybe a decade, making him around forty, the same age as Isobel. His hair was mid-brown, wavy, shoulder-length and not cared for. His skin was pale. He had his arms on the table and was picking at his hands, his manner agitated.

"Hello," Jack said.

Tony Griffiths stood up, smiling. "Jack, Isobel, sit down, sit down. Good to see you both." He gestured to the seats opposite and then turned to attract a waiter's attention.

Isobel ordered a glass of Sauvignon Blanc and Jack a Jawbox gin and tonic.

Tony gestured to his companion. "This is my business partner, Nathan Knight."

Isobel raised her eyebrows and Jack said, "Oh!"

Nathan Knight shifted uncomfortably under their scrutiny.

"Nathan and I have been in business together for fifteen years. He is the computer wizard. He keeps us ahead of the competition." He grinned. "And I'm in charge of the business side of things."

Nathan Knight kept his head down so that they couldn't make eye contact with him.

Tony, sensing his discomfort, hurried on. "Nathan has known Charlene since she was five or six. When I rang him to tell him about what had happened he was really shocked." His voice wavered. "He told me about the person who has been trolling Charlene and that Charlene had asked for his help with it." He shook his head. "I never knew any of this."

"She didn't want to worry you," Nathan said. "She knew you had a big deal going on."

Tony closed his eyes for a second, his face etched with pain. "She is more important than any deal. She should know that." His voice shook. He swallowed then looked up. "Nathan wanted to be here to tell you about what he'd found out."

"Before we get into all of that, do you have any further news on Charlene?" Isobel asked.

Tony smiled. "The surgery went very well and Charlene is stable. The pressure on her brain has been released. She is doing well, still unconscious but stable."

"That's great, a huge relief," said Isobel.

"Yes. My wife Joan is with her at the moment. And now that the immediate crisis is past I'm determined that we're going to find out who did this to her."

His face darkened and Isobel felt the barely suppressed rage.

"We've managed to find out a few things," said Jack.

"Good, good. I knew that you would. But first let's talk about the troll."

"Yes, we found out about the troll too, from Charlene's friends," said Jack. "In fact, we were going to ask you about meeting Nathan."

Tony nodded. "Over to you, Nathan. What can you tell us about this troll?"

Nathan looked up. "Well, the first thing is that the troll is sending the messages from the computers in Queen's University Library."

"Oh!" said Isobel. Then it could be anybody."

"The culprit is trying to cover their tracks," said Jack.

Nathan nodded. "Yes, they had the sense not to send

the messages from their own phone or computer."

Isobel said, "Does that mean we can't find them?"

"It makes it difficult."

"Maybe they know a lot about Charlene."

Nathan snapped, "Of course they do!"

Isobel ignored him. "I mean, they may know her well enough to know about you and what you could do. Or, at least, they knew that Charlene might ask her dad's company for help and they took some precautions."

"Ah yes!" said Tony. "I see what you mean. They hadn't just met her casually – they actually knew details about her life." He looked at Nathan.

Nathan nodded. "Obviously, the troll hasn't posted since Charlene was attacked and probably won't so . . . "

"So we need to trace them from their previous visits to the library," Isobel said. "We'll need a printout of all the times when a message was sent to Charlene. There may be a pattern. That might help."

"Oh yes," Jack said. "If you're in a lecture hall then you're not in the library sending a nasty message."

"There is a pattern," Nathan said. "The messages were sent either on a Tuesday morning at eight-thirty or a Thursday evening at about ten. I can forward you a list of the contact times and the messages that were sent."

"To me too," said Jack.

"We can read through them tonight, Jack," said Isobel. "There may be a clue in them, something the troll let slip that would narrow our search."

Nathan pulled out his phone and Jack and Isobel gave their email addresses and phone numbers to him. "I'll set up a group chat for the four of us so that we can communicate easily."

"Good idea, Nathan," said Tony. "That's great."

Jack cleared his throat. "I've found something else. We'd like to talk to you, Nathan, about it."

"Oh?" Tony said.

"Charlene sent me some video that she recorded in the alley the night she was attacked."

Tony gasped. "Does it show her being . . . ?"

Jack sat forward. "No, no. It was before she was attacked, but it shows some people, in the distance, in the alley."

Tony rubbed his hand over his mouth. "When did you find this out? Why didn't you contact me immediately?" His voice had risen, his tone angry.

"You needed to concentrate on Charlene today," said Isobel, "and we knew that we would be meeting you this evening."

His eyes focused on her slowly. He took a deep breath. "Have you told the police? What did they say? Can they find the people?"

Isobel nodded at Jack who said, "We have. We gave the police a copy of the video this morning."

"And is there any news? Did they get anything from it?"

"Not yet," said Jack.

Tony pulled out his phone. "I can ring and ask them."

Isobel reached over and put her hand over his phone. "They were less than confident about whether they would be able to get anything from the video. The alley is dark and the figures are some distance away."

Tony's face fell. "How did you get these pictures? I thought everything was stolen?"

"Charlene uploaded the video to a cloud account that we shared," Jack said. "She must have done it from the alley."

Nathan sat forward. "She captured the recording with her new camera?"

"We think so – that was certainly her plan for the evening. Michael had taken some preliminary shots of the alley and definitely Charlene's footage is much clearer than his. So, yes."

Nathan turned his lips in and muttered, "With the number of megapixels . . . I'm sure . . . maybe . . . if I use . . . or contact . . ."

"Nathan?" said Tony.

No response. Nathan had his phone in his hand and his fingers were flying over the keys. "I need a copy of the video."

"Of course," Jack said.

"Nathan?" Tony's voice had risen.

"Send it to my phone," Nathan continued. "I've messaged you, Jack, so you have the number."

"Nathan!"

"Got it." Nathan opened the video.

"Nathan!"

"Yes, maybe if I combine some programs . . ."

"Nathan!"

Nathan looked blearily at Tony. "What?"

"Maybe I should see the video."

Nathan looked bewildered. "Oh yes, yes."

Jack worked on his phone. "Here you are," he said, passing it to Tony.

Tony took a deep breath and then watched the video in silence. After a few moments he handed it back to Jack. "It's fairly dark and the people are a good distance away. They must be the perpetrators."

"Maybe or they could be witnesses," said Isobel.

"But why wouldn't they have come forward?"

"Maybe they were doing drugs in the alley," said Jack, "and therefore were reluctant to identify themselves."

"Oh yes. Of course." Tony sounded deflated.

"This is how important surveillance is." Nathan made eye contact with Tony.

Tony looked at Isobel. "It's a bone of contention between us. Nathan wants the company to branch out into surveillance but I'm not keen." He swallowed.

"It's a million-dollar industry already and growing – and," Nathan looked at Tony, "in a situation like this, where a crime has been committed, it can be a great help."

Tony nodded.

"I can definitely do something with the footage. There are some great new advances in distance surveillance. I can look at that and then find a way to –"

"Really, Nathan? You might be able to get something?" Tony's voice caught. "Oh my God, that would be great."

Nathan nodded slowly. "I'll get working on it immediately."

"I can get you a room and you can stay –" Tony said.

"No. No. I want to go home. I work better from my den with all my stuff around me."

110

Tony nodded. "I understand. Go, go. Please get something."

Nathan stood up. "I'll work on it tonight."

"Whatever it takes. And, Nathan, if you need to buy new software or hire one of your friends online to help you get this done, or grease some palms, or whatever you need, do it. I'll pay. No expense spared."

Nathan nodded. "I'll be in touch."

Tony watched Nathan as he threaded his way through the tables and out of the room. "He's a computer genius. I don't know half of what he does but if there is a way he, or some of his online pals, will find it." He took a deep breath. "You've done a lot today and made great progress."

Jack said, "There's a vigil on tonight and I would like to go. Are you going, Tony?"

He nodded. "I feel either my wife or I should go and Joan isn't up to it."

"What time is it on?" Isobel asked.

"Eight o'clock at the Students Union," said Jack.

Chapter 17

It was seven-thirty when Isobel, Jack and Tony left the hotel. It was a clear night, cold but dry. Tony seemed slightly revived after a light meal. They walked along Great Victoria Street, heading towards Queen's and the Students Union, each lost in their own thoughts.

It was almost eight o'clock when they arrived outside the Students Union. There was a large crowd. Tony seemed overcome. Jack linked him on one side and Isobel on the other. Slowly they made their way through the people. At the front there were pictures of Charlene and Michael placed on stands. In front of these on the ground were a host of tea-lights and artificial candles forming a carpet of light.

Isobel saw Nicky with Brenda and also saw Fiona, Anne and Bernadette. When Fiona caught sight of Tony she came over. She escorted him to the front, finding a place for him beside Nicky and another older couple. Isobel guessed that they must be Michael's parents. The woman was holding a tissue to her eyes.

Someone from the Students Union said a few words

then an official-looking gentleman led prayers. After that some young people with guitars stepped forward and performed a number of songs both religious and popular. The crowd joined in.

Isobel hung back. She sang along and said her own prayers for Michael's soul, for Charlene's recovery and for the parents of both young people. She also sent up a prayer that they would find who did it. She could see Tony rubbing a white handkerchief over his face and Fiona talking earnestly to him. Looking around she saw that many of the young people were upset. Isobel could only imagine the shock it had been to them all and the fear and anxiety they now felt.

At the end of the vigil people started to filter away, many going into the Student Union.

Isobel waited, wanting to speak to Jack. Tony caught her eye and waved her towards him.

"Isobel, this is Mr. and Mrs. O'Neill, Michael's parents. This is Isobel, Jack's aunt. Jack was in the film group with Michael and Charlene."

Isobel shook hands with each of them. "I'm so sorry."

Tony said, "I understand there is tea in the Students Union, why don't we go inside?"

As they moved forward, Jack appeared at Isobel's side.

"How are you doing?" she asked.

Jack made a face. "Some of my friends are getting together in one of the houses. I was thinking of going along to that."

"Of course, of course. You go off with your friends."

"Will you be alright?"

Isobel smiled. "Of course. I'm going to have a cup of tea with Tony and Mr. and Mrs. O'Neill and then head back to the hotel. Where are your friends?"

Jack pointed over to a group of three lads. They waved over at him.

"You go on. See you in the morning."

"There's a Mass tomorrow at noon – the Chaplaincy of the University has organised it."

"Oh, right."

"I'm going to go to that. What about you?"

"Yes, I will."

"Good."

Isobel hugged him and watched him join his friends.

Isobel hurried into the Students Union after Tony and the O'Neills. She saw them with a group of young people. Tony waved Isobel over, finding her a chair at a table. Mrs. O'Neill was beside her. On the table were some cups of tea and a plate of biscuits.

Fiona was again talking to Tony. She acknowledged Isobel with a wave of her hand but remained talking to him. Isobel sipped her tea and was glad of the warmth.

She turned to Mrs. O'Neill and proffered the plate of biscuits.

"No, thank you, love. I'm just glad to get a cuppa."

"I'm so sorry about Michael, Mrs. O'Neill."

Mrs. O'Neill nodded in acknowledgement and sipped her tea. "Your nephew, Jack, knew Michael."

"Yes."

"I can hardly believe it . . . that I'll never talk to him again or hear his voice or hug him . . ." Her voice broke on the last and she pulled a tissue from her pocket.

Isobel gently touched her arm. "I know."

Mrs. O'Neill wiped her eyes a number of times as her tears refused to be stemmed. Eventually she said, "And on top of that I had the police round, telling me that Michael was into drugs. It's too much to bear."

"I'm so sorry. That must be upsetting but I'm sure the police are doing their best to find who did this and they have to explore every possibility."

Mrs. O'Neill looked at her sharply. "Do you think they're as bothered by my Michael's death as they are by that poor girl lying in the hospital? I don't think so. My son isn't important to them."

Isobel felt her heart go cold. Could that be true? Her own impression had been more of a general discouragement than any preferential attention.

"I'm sure that's not the case. They were both victims of the same perpetrator, so the investigation covers both of them."

But Mrs. O'Neill was hardly listening. "Do you know what they asked me? They asked me if Michael was dealing in drugs."

Isobel felt guilt bite into her stomach. This poor woman had so much to deal with and Isobel knew she had been instrumental in uncovering the drug angle. She couldn't shy away from this.

"Mr. Griffiths has asked me to see what I can find out that would help the police."

"Why you? Are you a detective?"

"No, no, I'm a psychotherapist and in that role I have

been involved in a couple of cases." She felt that was the best way to put it. It was hard to explain how she fell into her detective roles quite by accident.

"But why would he do that? Why does he think the police need help?" She stared at Isobel. "Does he feel like I do, that the police are not taking enough of an interest?"

"I think he wants to make sure that everything possible can be done. He knows that I have helped the police before with cases and he asked me to see if there was anything I could do. Sometimes people find it hard to talk to the police."

"Is it because of you that I'm answering questions about Michael and drugs?"

Isobel returned her look. "Do you think it's possible that Michael was dealing drugs?"

They stared at one another. Isobel wished she was somewhere else but waited for an answer.

After what seemed like an eternity of scrutiny, Mrs. O'Neill said, "I don't know. I just don't know." She shook her head and then looked down at the tissue which she was tearing in her hands, the remnants falling onto the floor in front of her.

"I'm sorry to ask you that, Mrs. O'Neill. I promise you all I am trying to do is find out what happened. All of the young people I've spoken to are really upset about Michael and Charlene. You saw how many of them were here tonight. For Michael's sake, for Charlene's, for Jack's, for all of the students, it's so important that we find out who did this."

Mrs. O'Neill's eyes filled with tears and she bent forward to hide them.

After a few moments she lifted her head. "I hate to admit it but maybe he was. He had more money. We thought it was money he made over the summer when he stayed in Belfast to work but maybe . . . I don't want to believe it, but he had changed. We were worried. He wouldn't tell us anything. There seemed to be nothing we could do."

"I'm sorry."

Mrs. O'Neill tilted her head in acknowledgement. She grasped Isobel's arm. "But he wouldn't have put Charlene in danger. No matter what he was into, he wouldn't have been with her in the laneway if he thought anything would happen to her. He was always a kind boy – he would never have done that."

Isobel squeezed her hand. What could she say? She knew that drugs changed people. It changed their moods, their priorities, their relationships, what they were prepared to do. Drugs polluted until often the person bore very little resemblance to what they had previously been.

Tony came up behind Isobel. "Oh great, Isobel. I see you've been talking to Mrs. O'Neill." He shepherded Mr. O'Neill forward then brought a chair for him and found one for himself.

The four of them were now grouped around a small table.

Mrs. O'Neill said, "I was just telling Isobel that I don't think the police are doing enough to find Michael's killer."

"I agree," Tony said.

Mr. O'Neill said, "You do?"

"I don't think they're paying enough attention to what happened to either of our children. What I do know is that nobody cares about my little girl more than me and her mum, and it's the same for you. I'm determined that our children get justice."

Isobel could feel herself relaxing. Suddenly, in a moment, Tony had swept away any concerns of preferential treatment and had turned the situation into two sets of parents fighting for their children. No wonder he was a businessman and, no doubt, a very successful one.

He continued. "Because I'm concerned, I've found a private investigator. I've asked her to look into what happened. Obviously, any information will be passed on to the police but she is working for us."

"Yes – Isobel," said Mrs. O'Neill. "She was just telling me."

"Good."

Mr. O'Neill said, "But what can she do that the police can't?"

"Well, number one, she is focused on our case, not juggling numerous others. And number two she is a psychotherapist and so she is used to talking to young people. Already she and Jack have found some footage that Charlene took in the alley just before she and Michael were attacked."

Mrs. O'Neill reached out for her husband's hand.

"There are some people in the background of the footage," Tony continued. "We've handed it over to the police."

"Oh my God!" said Mr. O'Neill. "The killers?"

"Perhaps – or maybe just witnesses."

"But can they be identified?" asked Mr. O'Neill.

"The footage is dark and unclear but they'll try."

Clearly he didn't want to raise the O'Neills' hopes too high by mentioning Nathan and his expertise, Isobel thought – or perhaps he just didn't want that information to get back to the police.

Mrs. O'Neill turned to Isobel. "That's wonderful. Thank you!" Tears rolled down her cheeks.

Her husband took a folded white handkerchief from his pocket and handed it to her. "It's alright, love. I know you were worried that nobody cared about our Michael but they do. Isobel will find who did this."

Isobel felt tears spark in her own eyes. "I can only promise you that I will do everything that I can."

"Of course she will," said Tony.

"Promise me that you'll keep me updated," said Mrs. O'Neill.

Isobel met her gaze. "I will."

Mrs. O'Neill stood up and everyone else got to their feet. "Thank you, Tony. I appreciate what you've done. You've put my mind at ease. Isobel, I'll be praying that you find the man."

The O'Neills walked away arm in arm.

Isobel closed her eyes for a moment.

Tony said, "Mrs. O'Neill was worried that Michael didn't matter."

Isobel bit her lip. "I know."

"That doesn't make sense – it's one and the same investigation – but I understand that hers is an emotional reaction."

"Yes, it is." Isobel was again surprised at his insight.

"You'll have to find whoever did this."

Isobel knew that somehow this was true. The pain of the situation was so intense that only that outcome would suffice. She wasn't sure if she could accomplish it, if that was even possible, but for tonight she accepted it.

"I need to get back to the hospital," Tony said. "Are you heading to your hotel?"

"No, I think I'll go to the Muse for a drink."

"By yourself?"

Isobel laughed. "Yes. To ask some questions of the bar staff about Monday night."

"Isobel, you don't have to do that now."

"I know but it's too early for sleep so I might as well talk to some people. You never know what I'll find out, and the Muse is closed tomorrow night."

"I'll walk down with you and get a taxi to the hospital from there."

Outside the Muse, Tony said, "Are you sure you'll be all right by yourself?"

"Absolutely."

"You're going inside now, aren't you? Not going near that alley."

"I am."

"And promise me you'll get a taxi from here back to your hotel."

"I will."

"OK, then."

"I'll be thinking of Charlene and of you and Joan."

"Thanks, Isobel."

Isobel stood outside the Muse, watching Tony walk away. She would do all she could – and hopefully it would be enough.

As she stood there, she looked around. Along the street were lamps, but rather than lighting the way they had the effect of creating areas of brightness and then darker more shadowy places. Across the street obliquely was the Red Rose Café, wreathed in shadows. All of the buildings were in darkness either permanently, or closed for the day. The lights outside the Muse cast a halo around it, an island of illumination in an otherwise dark sea. Despite the pub lights, the entrance to the alley alongside it was dark. Isobel shivered at the thought of going down there. She turned towards the pub entrance and went inside.

The contrast could not have been greater. The pub was warm and immediately Isobel took off her coat. It was well lit. There was a general buzz of conversation with occasional bursts of laughter along with crescendos, as voices emphasised their points before lapsing back into the general hubbub. Isobel wondered if some of the students had come here after the vigil.

She hesitated at the door, then seeing a seat at the bar she threaded her way through the tables. As she took a seat at the bar, a young barman approached her.

Isobel said, "It's busy tonight."

He shrugged.

Isobel asked for a glass of Sauvignon Blanc.

When he brought it, she said, "Why don't you take one for yourself too?" She handed over a twenty-pound note.

"Thank you, that's very kind. I'll have a pint when I finish if that's OK?"

Isobel nodded. "Do, do."

The young man returned with Isobel's change.

"Were you working the night that Charlene Griffiths and Michael O'Neill were attacked?" she asked.

He glanced along the bar. No one was looking for his attention. "Yes, I was."

"My nephew is a student in Queen's. He was working on a film project with Charlene and Michael – he arrived on the scene very quickly and tried to help."

"A shocking thing to have happened."

"Yes. Did you see Charlene and Michael that night?"

"I served Charlene but I wasn't talking to her except for her order."

"Did anything unusual happen?"

"Like what?"

"Was anyone bothering Charlene? Did you hear or see anything in the alley?"

"You're taking a powerful interest in it?"

Isobel chided herself for pushing too hard. "I'm sorry. I've just come from the vigil and I'm probably a bit upset."

He nodded. "Lots of them here were at that."

"I suppose it's hard not to worry about my nephew, Jack being out at night when something like this has happened."

"Of course. We're all shocked. It seems unreal. It was just a normal night, nothing unusual, no one messy or really drunk. And there's never been any trouble around here, nothing major like."

"I saw a door from the pub opening into the alley. Is that where you get your deliveries?"

"No, the alley is very narrow for a truck. We carry

everything in the front door. That door to the alley is only used to access the bins we have out there."

"*Jamie!*"

Isobel jumped. She hadn't noticed a woman move behind the bar.

Jamie turned. "Lorraine?"

"Will you clear that table by the door and take their order?"

He nodded. "Sorry. I was just talking to this lady – she's the aunt of one of the students who tried to help Charlene and Michael – Jack, did you say?"

Isobel nodded. "Jack McKenzie."

"She was at the vigil," Jamie said as he left.

Lorraine, the owner of the Muse, was again dressed in black.

"I'm Lorraine McNally. This is my pub." She held out her hand.

Isobel took it, noting the expensive rings. "Isobel McKenzie. I'm visiting from Limerick."

"I do know Jack. I saw you last night with him and I did wonder who you were. It's unfortunate you came just now," she hesitated, "at this sad and traumatic time."

"Oh, actually, Jack's dad asked me to come. I'm a psychotherapist. I think he thought I might be a support and comfort to Jack."

Lorraine gave a sad smile and gestured to the room. "I think all of the young people want to spend time together and talk. We're all a bit shocked."

Isobel nodded her head in acknowledgement.

"Are you meeting someone?"

Isobel felt herself blushing slightly. "No, no. I just called in for a drink."

"Perhaps you wouldn't mind if I joined you?"

"Not at all."

Lorraine poured herself a sniffer of brandy and then made her way out from behind the bar. As she made her way towards Isobel she said hello to some of the young people at the tables. Isobel noticed that she knew them by name and they addressed her very familiarly too.

There was no doubt that Lorraine was an impressive figure. She was about five foot ten with a slim, athletic figure. Her hair was in an elaborate up-do and she was wearing a long straight black skirt, with her black blouse and black patent ankle boots.

She sat up on the barstool beside Isobel.

Isobel sipped her wine. When she had decided to come here she hadn't thought that she would be sharing a drink with the owner.

Lorraine looked around the pub. "It's busy tonight. I think a lot of people have come here after the vigil." She sipped her drink. "We're closed tomorrow as a mark of respect."

"I saw that."

Isobel felt a little uncomfortable. Maybe it was hearing about Lorraine's younger days from Ben. It was a little disconcerting to know so much about someone when they were right in front of you and you've only met them for the first time.

"It must be upsetting to have that happen right outside your premises," she said.

"Yes. I can hardly believe it. I hope Charlene recovers."

Isobel stayed silent.

"It's the last thing you expect. After all these years, to suddenly have such a tragedy on the doorstep." Lorraine's voice tightened. "I can't believe that it happened, that someone would do such a senseless thing."

"Is there generally much trouble in this area?"

"Not at all. Just the usual, really. Every now and again someone has too much to drink but mostly it's fine."

"And what about drugs?"

"Drugs?" Lorraine looked a little hostile at this. "I can assure you that I would report anything suspicious of that nature. I don't want to attract that sort of a crowd here or have that sort of a reputation for my pub."

Isobel felt this was a somewhat defensive reaction. She figured Lorraine must be well aware that there would be speculation about a possible drug connection to the assault on Michael and Charlene. And also would assume that she, Isobel, was there *in loco parentis* and likely to report everything heard and seen to Jack's dad.

"Oh, I just wondered if there was the usual student dabbling in drugs," she said casually, looking around the pub.

"Oh, undoubtedly they dabble – but not on my premises."

"But is it possible the alleyway is used for drug-taking or dealing?"

"Not that I'm aware of. I would have called the police if I thought it was."

Isobel wondered if Lorraine's own experience as a student informed her attitude now. She seemed anti-drugs and yet Isobel knew that she had given Jack an anti-anxiety tablet, which was a drug if not a hard one.

"I don't know why everybody wants to make everything about drugs," Lorraine said. "I heard that Charlene and Michael were in the alley because of something to do with a film project." She looked at Isobel. "Maybe it was from Jack I heard that?" She frowned.

Isobel had the distinct impression that she was being pumped for information. In a way, that was fair enough as that was exactly what she herself was doing.

"I suppose what has happened is bound to have generated lots of speculation and gossip." Isobel didn't want to talk about the filming as it could raise the question of whether the perpetrators were caught on film. "What else is being said? You must get all the gossip here?"

"I hear a good bit. The students like to talk. Jack was here last night. He seemed upset. He told me that he looked around the laneway to see if he could notice anything that might help the police but he didn't find anything."

"I suppose everyone wants to help find who did this, if they can." Isobel paused. "Do people hang around in the alley?"

"Generally speaking, no. I've heard other people saying that the attack was thieves looking for easy marks and unfortunately . . ."

"Do you think that's likely?"

"It could happen."

"It's hard to believe that a young man lost his life and a young woman is fighting for hers for the price of their phones and cards." She didn't mention the camera.

Lorraine shivered. "I know. And, if it is theft, the police may never find who did it."

"I know."

"And such young people, with their whole lives ahead of them. All that potential."

"Yes. It's very sad."

Lorraine looked off towards the back of the bar, not really focused on anything. "Having potential is one thing – lots of people have potential – but being able to harness that potential, that's the difficult thing."

"True."

Isobel wondered if Lorraine was speaking about herself and her own potential.

Lorraine smiled. "Some of the students here are destined for great things – you know, the future leaders of tomorrow."

"Yes, I suppose so."

"The people my age, some of them have gone far. It's strange to see when you knew them as students and they were young and impressionable."

"I'm sure."

Lorraine was certainly reflecting on her own past, her missed opportunities. It sounded as if she had regrets. After all, the people she had known, like the Prince, had reached great heights.

"But people don't really change," Lorraine continued. "We all have the same drives and vulnerabilities that we had as students."

"Do you think so? I think people can change."

Lorraine smiled. "Maybe not the people I know."

Isobel thought of Ben and the changes he had made.

What was Lorraine referring to? Maybe tragedy caused everyone to explore their own past.

Lorraine glanced around at the room. "I had better get back to work."

Isobel smiled. "Sure."

"Call in again for a chat. Hopefully the news about Charlene will be better in the next few days. Tell Jack I said hello."

"Will do."

Lorraine moved towards a table at the back to speak to some students. Isobel saw her sitting down and chatting with a young woman.

Jamie approached and wiped the bar top near her.

"Thanks for the drink."

Isobel wasn't sure if he was angling for another. Suddenly she felt tired. "You're welcome." She smiled and drank off the last of her wine. She got down from the barstool. "Goodnight now."

Back in her hotel room, Isobel lay in bed, thinking. This case differed from the other two cases that she had been involved in. In London she knew who the perpetrator of the crime was and it had been more about discerning the extent of his crimes and proving it. In the second case, in Limerick, she knew the extent of the crime and she had been searching for someone capable of that. In both cases there was a clear focus. Here it felt so different. It was still unclear what the motivation for the attacks was. Was this a robbery that had got out of hand? Yet to kill one person and seriously harm another to steal phones, a camera and some cash and cards seemed excessive, as Detective Doran had said.

Could the same not be said about the troll? That it was a step too far? She then remembered she had to go through the messages that Charlene had received. She opened her email and read them.

There was no doubt that the troll knew a lot about what Charlene was doing and saying. And there was a level of hatred and jealousy and viciousness in the phrases and the names directed at her. But was it really possible that an online attacker would transmute their words of hate and vitriol into a physical attack? An attack so violent that Charlene was in hospital fighting for her life and her companion that night was dead? Isobel wasn't sure.

And what about drugs? Could the attacker have been a drug addict looking for some money? Was Michael involved in drugs again? Had he got in over his head, angered some people and Charlene was just collateral damage?

Lorraine was adamant that she would report any drugs in her establishment. But then she had given Jack a possibly addictive drug. Was that misguided kindness? There were so many questions and no answers.

Isobel had no real sense of the perpetrator. The three possibilities suggested very different individuals. She had no idea what sort of person she was looking for.

She knew that Jack was going to be very disappointed if they couldn't help solve the mystery. Not to mention Tony and now the O'Neills. None of them realised how hard it was to solve a case. She felt that her past successes had given everyone an unreal picture of the challenges involved and the likelihood of success. She felt daunted.

She slid down in the bed. This wasn't helpful. Tomorrow she and Jack would follow up on the troll and see if they could find him or her and rule them in or out. That would bring them a step closer. She hoped that Nathan could do something with the video.

Turning off her bedside lamp, she settled down to sleep.

Her errant thoughts followed her into her dreams. She was in a dark world. She turned in a circle. All she could see was black. Suddenly a figure dressed in a long white robe appeared in front of her. The white robe had black writing on it. Some of the words were in bold and had drops of blood dripping from them. The figure moved towards her, closing the distance. As it reached her the words flowed off the white robe. She watched in horror as the letters got bigger and bigger, growing, strengthening, threatening her. The ground shook. She saw a capital letter C arching over her and bending forward, closer and closer to her head. She raised her hands to protect herself as she feared she was going to be crushed.

Suddenly the scene changed. She was standing and she was holding a bag. The handles were plastic and they were cutting into her hand with the weight inside. She opened the bag. Inside were gold coins and a bejewelled phone. Two dark figures came towards her. One figure reached for the bag. She tried to pull it away. The other figure reached out to grab her. She shrugged away from its hands and then turned and ran, leaving the bag with its contents.

The scene changed again. In front of her was a

structure as tall as a house. It looked like a large, brown-plastic medicine bottle. She saw a doorway. People were entering the building while others waited outside. One of the figures saw her. It studied her. Then it raised its arm and pointed at her. All the figures turned towards her and Isobel felt fear uncurl in her stomach. They were angry. One of the people left the queue and moved towards her After a moment, more people from the line walked in her direction. She turned and ran.

Once again everything changed. She was in a room which had very little light. There was a strand of some material coated in a sticky substance. She followed the strand to where it bent upwards and joined a net suspended in the air. She explored its lattice with her fingertips. It seemed to be all around her. She tried to move back, the way she had come, but the net seemed to be everywhere. Above her head she heard a noise. It was a whistling sound. Slowly she raised her eyes. Above, watching, was an enormous spider. She tried to move her feet but she couldn't free them from the sticky substance. She couldn't move. She was caught, a captive in a huge spider's web.

Chapter 18

Thursday 26th October

Jack arrived when Isobel was finishing her breakfast and enjoying her coffee. He asked the waitress for coffee too.

Isobel asked, "Did you sleep?"

"Yes, I did actually. And you?"

"I slept OK but I had some awful dreams. I was chased by a large figure dressed in paper covered with words. The letters were trying to kill me, in particular the letter C."

Jack frowned. "What was that about?"

Isobel raised her eyebrows. "I had lots of mixed-up dreams, thieves stealing jewels and gold, vicious letters, a giant tablet bottle and a big spider."

"Sounds awful."

"I think I'm dreaming about the case, trying to figure it out."

Jack nodded. "Oh yes, drugs and thieves, I see. And I suppose you read the troll messages that Charlene had been sent, hence the murderous letters."

Isobel nodded.

"The posts were really bad," he said. "Wishing Charlene

was dead, saying that the world would be a better place without her. I was shocked."

"And so detailed, describing things Charlene had said and then verbally attacking her."

"Poor Charlene. I can't imagine what it must have been like to receive those things a few times a week. She never said a word. In fact, considering what was going on she was always so upbeat and positive. When you read them all together you do wonder if the writer could have attacked Charlene."

Isobel shook her head. "Maybe. The more I think about what they wrote and the venom in it, the more I wonder."

"Tony sent me a text message this morning. Charlene is stable and he and Joan are meeting with the consultant later today."

"That's good. Hopefully they'll know a lot more after that."

"Are you still coming to the memorial Mass that the Chaplaincy has organised? Most people I know are going."

"Noon, you said?"

"Yes."

"Yes, I'll come – but you go with your friends."

"I'm meeting Rachel and Noah, the other members of the film group, outside. I can introduce you. They would like to meet you."

"OK. How are they doing?"

Jack inclined his head. "Alright. I told them that Mr. Griffiths doesn't blame us and they were relieved. The memorial today is upsetting but I think it is good for all of us to go and all be upset."

"Yes, it is. Do you want to go and spend some time

with your friends? I can go to the library myself."

"No, I want to go."

Isobel stood up. "OK. Let's go and see what we can find out about the troll."

It was a cold but bright day as they walked down the Malone Road, towards the university, the sunshine a contrast to the dark figure they were hoping to identify.

As Jack led the way, Isobel found herself looking at the buildings, marvelling at their beauty.

Jack stopped outside the library. "Wait here." He walked in through the outer door.

Isobel waited a few minutes, admiring the modern sculpture outside the library. Over two metres tall, it represented the reflection of a head refracted in water. She heard the door open and Jack reappeared.

"I've spoken to the lady on security. She has agreed to let you in as my aunt."

"So no one can get into the library without a card or authorisation? That should make our job easier."

Jack led the way through the doors and scanned his card.

Isobel showed identification and signed a form. When all the paperwork was completed, she said, "Could I please see the person in charge?"

The young woman with long blonde hair and pale skin looked anxious. "Can I help you with something? What is it in connection with?"

Isobel smiled a tight smile. "It's in connection with security and the use of a library computer for online bullying. I need to speak to someone in charge."

The young woman fidgeted with her hands, looking more agitated. She picked up the form Isobel had just signed.

Isobel guessed that she regretted allowing her into the library. "I believe that the head of the library will be able to help me prevent any further unpleasantness but I assure you that this needs to be dealt with."

The young woman studied Isobel for a few seconds, then nodded and reached for the phone on the desk. After a brief explanatory call where she mentioned Jack by name, she said, "She'll be with you now."

Isobel smiled. "Thank you."

The young woman gave a small smile and then busied herself with some paperwork.

Isobel and Jack waited for five minutes. In that time three young people entered the library and used the card-scan system, passing through the next set of double doors into the library.

Eventually the double doors opened from the inside and a woman of about Isobel's height with grey hair in a bun, wearing a pale-grey dress and dainty black shoes, appeared. She had glasses perched on her nose and looked imperiously at Isobel. For a moment she said nothing.

Isobel was sure that many people withered under her stare.

"Thank you, Tabitha, I'll handle this." She opened the door she had just come through and gestured towards Isobel and Jack. "Perhaps you would like to follow me?"

She led them along a corridor into the depths of the

library. Jack looked a little overwhelmed. Isobel rolled her eyes at him and he grinned.

Their guide entered a room.

As Isobel passed the door she glanced at the name on it: *Ms. Gladys Pritchard, Head Librarian.*

The lady in grey sat down behind the desk which was heavy wood and very large. On it was a slim silver computer. She gestured to two seats on the opposite side.

Isobel and Jack sat down.

"I am Ms. Pritchard. Mr. McKenzie, this is your aunt, I believe?"

"Yes."

"And you are a second-year student."

"Yes," said Jack. "English and Film."

"What's the problem?" She sat back in her high-back chair, her hands resting on the arms.

There was something almost theatrical about Ms. Pritchard and how she was orchestrating the situation and yet Isobel could feel the authority and the dignity of the woman.

Isobel spoke up. "You may have heard of the two students who were attacked a few nights ago. Michael tragically was killed and Charlene is in hospital where she has been critical but is now stable. Jack was in the same film group as Michael and Charlene."

"Yes, of course." Ms. Pritchard frowned and waited for enlightenment.

"It has come to light that Charlene was being trolled before the attack, from the second week of term. With the help of a security expert," Isobel felt sure that Nathan would be pleased at this title, "we have obtained the messages sent, the times they were sent and the IP address of the computer where the messages originated. It is one of the computers in the library."

"I see."

"And we were wondering if there was any way we could identify the person who sent the messages."

Ms. Pritchard remained very still, a slight tightening of her fingers on the armrest the only sign of the impact of what she had heard. After a moment she said, "We have a number of security measures, some of which you have already experienced. For example, I can print out a list of everyone entering and leaving the library and the times at which they did this."

"Yes, that would be helpful but I was hoping that you might have security cameras so that we could look at the people who entered the library around the times in question. Obviously if there are no cameras and what you have is a list we will have to work from that."

"I didn't say we had no security cameras. I merely drew your attention to the system you had already experienced."

Despite the pedantic statements and almost obstructive responses, Isobel could feel that Ms. Pritchard was someone who dealt only in accuracy and that was what was needed now.

Isobel waited.

"There are no security cameras in the library, except in the rare book section."

Isobel felt her heart sinking. "Oh."

"You have the times, you say?"

"Yes."

"What times?"

Isobel looked at Jack.

He pulled up the email that Nathan had sent him. "The last message was sent at ten o'clock on Thursday last week. There was also a message sent at half past eight on Tuesday morning last week and the week before."

Ms. Pritchard tapped her fingers on the arm of the chair, her brow wrinkled. After a few seconds, she sat forward.

"The library closes at half past ten in the evening. Lots of people are leaving then who may have been in the library for hours. We open at eight o'clock in the morning. Eight thirty is a relatively quiet time in the library. There are security cameras in the hallway outside the library which show everyone entering and leaving."

Jack sat forward in his seat. "We can look at the footage and see who went into the library when it opened on Tuesday last."

"Yes, and cross-reference it with other Tuesday mornings when a message was sent," Isobel added.

"Or check who left the library after the message was sent on the Thursday night."

"True, that would work too." Ms. Pritchard smiled at Jack. She glanced at her watch. "It's after nine so all the staff should be in now. Jack, can you ask the young woman you spoke to when you came into the library – her name is Tabitha – to bring us some tea and biscuits, please."

"Absolutely." Jack stood and left the room.

Ms. Pritchard looked at Isobel. "Given what has been happening with the death of one student and another seriously ill, I am going to share with you the footage from the camera outside the library but I will have to inform the Provost that I have done that."

"Of course. And thank you."

Ms. Pritchard pulled her silver computer towards her and began to work on it.

Isobel relaxed back in her chair and waited. After a few minutes she heard the murmur of voices and Jack opened the door, allowing Tabitha to enter with a tray.

Tabitha set the tray on the table and quickly left.

Isobel poured tea for everyone. She and Jack added milk to theirs and Isobel set a cup of tea, the milk jug and sugar bowl convenient to Ms. Pritchard.

Eventually Ms. Pritchard sat back and added a little milk to her tea. "Alright. I have Tuesday morning from last week ready to look at."

Isobel went to stand to the side of Ms. Pritchard's chair. Jack stood at the other side. Ms. Pritchard clicked and the footage began to roll. Isobel could see the librarian herself arriving and going into the library. She also saw Tabitha. Some more people arrived.

Ms. Pritchard said, "Those are all staff. I doubt it is any of them, but I can give you their names."

The next person was an older man in a long black coat.

"That's Professor Clarke," said Ms. Pritchard. "He comes in every Tuesday morning and collects some books."

Isobel looked at the time bar on the footage. "It's ten past eight already. The person has to arrive soon or he or she won't be in time to send the message."

A red-haired boy carrying a green plastic bag came

into the frame. Isobel recognised him – she had seen him in the pub last night. He entered the library. Five minutes passed and then he trudged out, head down.

"Look!" said Jack.

A young woman had appeared in front of the library door. She was thin and was carrying a rucksack.

"Isobel! It's Anne, the girl who lives with Charlene!"

Anne entered the library.

It was now twenty past eight. A young man in a black puffa jacket appeared. He disappeared into the library.

Some minutes passed with no new visitors. Then the young man in the black jacket came out.

Isobel checked the time. It was eight twenty-seven. "It's not eight thirty yet so he couldn't have done it, could he?"

Ms. Pritchard said, "No. He must have been collecting a book."

A few more minutes passed then Anne hurried from the library.

"She was definitely in the library at the time when the message was sent!" Jack said.

Isobel rubbed her hand over her mouth. "Anne? Charlene's flatmate? Oh my God, surely not?"

Ms. Pritchard said, "We need to check some of the other days and times."

"Yes," Jack said. "What about Thursday 19th? A message was sent at ten o'clock in the evening."

"Let me bring up that evening. From what time do you want to start watching the footage? Don't forget that someone could go into the library at any time during the day and stay to send the message."

"*Hm*," he said. "Let's watch the people leaving the library after ten o'clock when the message was sent and see if we recognise any of them."

Ms. Pritchard clicked as she selected different options. "Here we are, from five to ten on Thursday 19th." She set the footage moving.

Jack pointed. "*There's Anne!* She's leaving at ten past ten."

"Let's just watch and make sure that none of the other people who showed up on the morning footage leave," said Isobel.

They watched until the library closed.

"No one else," said Jack.

Isobel felt sick.

Ms. Pritchard said, "Give me another Tuesday morning date, Jack."

Jack supplied the date: Tuesday 10th October. Once again they watched as the library staff came in. Professor Clarke arrived and left again carrying his books in a plastic bag. Isobel saw the red-haired boy again and also the guy in his black jacket collecting another book.

And then Anne, once again.

Ms. Pritchard stopped the footage. "So this girl, Anne, seems to be present in the library each time a message has been sent."

"Poor Charlene," Isobel said.

"Given what has happened to Charlene, you'll have to tell the police what we've found," Ms. Pritchard said. "But surely this young woman, Anne, didn't savagely attack Charlene? And kill Michael!"

Isobel could feel her distress. "We'll have to inform the

police," she said miserably. "They may have to look at the footage too."

"Of course."

"Thanks for your help, Ms. Pritchard. We really appreciate it."

"If there is anything else I can do to help, let me know." Isobel smiled. "We will."

Jack and Isobel left the library.

"What now?" said Jack. "Do we go to the police?"

Isobel shook her head. "No. First we talk to Anne."

Jack made a face. "Are you sure?"

"Yes, I'm sure."

"She'll be at the memorial." He looked at his watch. "It's a quarter to ten. I'll tell Rachel and Noah to meet us outside."

"Good idea. We'd better hurry. And, Jack, you can't say anything to the others about what we've found out. You can't mention this to anyone yet."

Jack swung around to look at Isobel as he hurried off. "I know that."

Isobel felt sick as she headed to the hotel to get ready for the memorial. To think that Charlene had been living with the woman who was trolling her. How would she feel if she knew? The pretence, the two-faced nature of it, the betrayal. Everyone felt jealousy at some point. Isobel knew that herself. But online people said things that they would not have shared in person. She didn't envy any of these young people the digital world that they inhabited.

Chapter 19

Noah and Rachel were waiting with Jack outside the Chaplaincy on Elmwood Avenue when Isobel arrived. Jack introduced her to them.

Noah shook her hand. "We think that you and Jack investigating is great. We hope you find who did this."

Rachel nodded. "It has given us something positive to focus on."

"Good," said Isobel. "And you know you can't reveal anything?"

"We know," said Noah. "If you need any help we would be glad to assist."

"Thank you."

Young people were passing into the hall.

"Why don't you go in and sit with your friends, Jack?" Isobel said. "I'll see you later."

Inside, the chapel was full of flowers and crowded with young people, many of whom were extremely upset and were being supported by friends. She saw the O'Neills near the front. Beside them were a young man and woman who bore a resemblance to them. Both read during the service and Isobel guessed that they were Michael's siblings. She hoped that the family was comforted by the number of people who had turned up to honour Michael. It was a small comfort but a comfort none the less.

When the service was over the crowd made its way outside. Jack, Noah and Rachel found Isobel in the crowd. Rachel stood, huddled into her coat, shivering. Noah reached out and put his arm around her. Rachel leaned against him and cried softly. As Isobel looked around at the devastated and shocked young people, she could feel a rage burning in her gut. Who could have done this? It was monstrous. She could feel her determination rising despite all the difficulties with the case. They had to find who had done this, *they had to*.

As people started to leave, Jack said, "Isobel and I need to speak to one of Charlene's friends."

"Of course," said Rachel. "We'll go. Ring us later. And good luck with your investigating."

After they left, Jack turned and faced Isobel. "OK. Let's go and talk to Anne," he said.

They made their way through the people standing in groups. As they did, Isobel heard her name called.

Turning, she saw Mrs. O'Neill beckoning to her and making her way towards them.

"I'm so sorry," Isobel said, reaching for her hand.

"Thank you for coming. I was hoping I would see you today. Hello, Jack."

"Hello, Mrs. O'Neill."

"I lay awake all night. I was thinking about Michael

when he was a little boy. He was so funny, so . . ." Tears sparkled on her lashes as words failed her. She reached up and wiped her eyes. "I feel as if the police with all their questions and insinuations want to take the memory of my son away from me too." She reached into her pocket and handed Isobel a piece of paper. "That's my mobile number. Ring me day or night if you find anything. I won't be sleeping much."

Isobel nodded. "I will."

"Mum, are you alright?"

The young man who had read at the memorial came towards them.

"Yes, yes. I'm coming. Talk to you soon, Isobel. Goodbye, Jack."

They watched the O'Neills walk away.

"Poor woman, poor family," Jack said.

For a moment they stood in silence, pausing before the demands of the present and the investigation took over from the reality of the tragedy that had befallen Michael's family.

Jack heaved a sigh. "We'd better have our talk with Anne."

"Are you sure that you wouldn't like some lunch first?"

Jack shook his head. "Not right now. I think I would be sick."

Isobel nodded. They set off walking, towards the house Charlene had shared.

Isobel and Jack rang the doorbell.

Fiona answered. "Oh, hi." Her voice held no welcome.

"Hello, Fiona. Could we come in for a minute?" Isobel asked.

Reluctantly Fiona stood back to let them enter. Isobel led the way into the sitting room. There were a number of wine bottles on the table and some beer bottles under a couple of the chairs. There was also the smell of stale alcohol.

"Is Anne back from the service?"

Fiona looked uncomfortable. "She's up in her bedroom again." She gestured to the bottles. "We had a few drinks last night. She had a good few too many. She was crying and in an awful way. It was really late when we got to bed. She wasn't fit to go to the memorial today. It was the last thing I needed with the memorial on and worrying about Charlene and all." She hung her head.

"Why don't you make a cup of tea and we can have a chat?" Isobel said.

Fiona nodded and wearily left the room.

Isobel opened a window to get some fresh air circulating. Taking some perfume from her bag, she sprayed it into the air.

"What are you doing?" Jack asked.

"Changing the atmosphere. Will you get me a bin bag from the kitchen? I'm sure they have some."

When Jack returned, Isobel put the wine bottles and beer bottles into it.

"Put that out in the hall, Jack. They can recycle later."

Fiona came in with mugs of tea, milk and sugar on a tray.

"That's better," she said, looking around the room.

"I've had lots of practice." Isobel sat and picked up her tea. "What happened last night, Fiona?"

Fiona shook her head. "We were sitting here chatting, having some dinner. I was talking about Charlene and what a good friend she has always been to me. I was saying how worried I was about her. Anne wasn't saying much, just the odd comment about how Charlene had it easy."

"And?"

"And I got a bit mad at her and told her that she didn't have a clue about how hard this term has been for Charlene, with the troll and everything."

"What did Anne say?"

"She asked how I knew that Charlene had a troll and I told her she had confided in me."

"Did you mention that Nathan was trying to find out who sent the messages?"

"Yes, I did. I was so upset."

"What happened then?"

"Anne dismissed Nathan. But I told her how good he was at computers. She said it was too late now, that because Charlene had been attacked the troll would probably stop. I told her the troll could have been the one who attacked her. She thought I was crazy. She said there was a big difference between a keyboard warrior and the psychopath who killed Michael and injured Charlene. We ended up having a row. She didn't believe me when I said that anyone who could send messages like the ones Charlene had received was capable of bashing her head in and killing Michael. After a while she went to the shop for more wine. Later on she was crying and saying that she was going to leave college. It was horrible. I know she's upset – we all are – but it was awful."

"I'm going to need to go up and talk to Anne. I think that you should come with me."

Fiona shook her head. "I don't know if I can listen to all of that again."

Isobel grimaced. "It won't be the same. But you need to hear it."

Fiona shrugged.

Isobel said, "Sorry, Jack. You'd better leave it to me now."

Jack nodded. "Actually, I have stuff to do. I can meet you again later."

"OK. I'll message you when I'm finished."

She nodded to Fiona. "Come on."

They climbed the stairs.

Isobel waited for Fiona to point out Anne's room.

She knocked on the door. She heard a groan from inside and pushed open the door. The smell of stale alcohol was strong. She walked over and opened the curtains. Light streamed in and Anne groaned.

Isobel sat on the edge of the bed. Fiona sat at the desk.

Isobel said, "Anne, sit up. I want to talk to you."

Anne groaned and pulled the duvet over her head.

"It's about Charlene. She had a troll who sent her messages from a computer in the library. The messages were sent on Tuesdays at eight-thirty in the morning and Thursdays at ten o'clock at night."

Anne shifted in the bed and with difficulty sat up with her back to the headboard.

"And guess what? The library has a surveillance camera outside it. Ms. Pritchard let us see the footage and who do you think is going into the library before eight-thirty on the days Charlene got messages?"

"*Who?*" said Fiona eagerly. "You've found out who the troll is?"

Anne groaned again and put her hands over her eyes. "I never touched her."

"What do you mean?" Fiona looked at Isobel. "What's going on?"

"Tell Fiona, Anne."

Anne started to cry. "I can't. I'm so ashamed. I can't believe this is happening."

"*Believe it.* You did touch Charlene. You sent horrible, vicious messages to her as often as twice a week. You *did* touch her, you *did* harm her."

Anne buried her face in her hands, sobbing. "I'm so sorry."

Fiona stood up. "*You're the troll? You did that to Charlene?*"

Anne put her arms over her head. "I'm sorry. I'm sorry. It never seemed to affect her and so I sent worse messages." She gulped and looked up, her face stained with tears. "But, I swear, I never attacked her in the alley, that wasn't me. I never laid a hand on her."

"*You bitch!*" Fiona exploded. "*You tormented her. She couldn't believe that someone could hate her so much. You poisonous, two-faced bitch! How could you do that to my friend? How could you do that?*"

Anne once again covered her face with her hands. "I'm so ashamed."

"Anne, where were you on Monday night between ten o'clock and midnight?" Isobel said.

Anne dropped her hands. "You can't really think that I attacked Charlene and Michael!"

"*Where were you?*"

"I was – I was – let me think. I was with Bernadette. Yes, yes. We went for something to eat and then called in to Josh's house and stayed there. We only left his house when we got the messages about the attack on Charlene and Michael. Josh can vouch for us. Hold on! Hold on!" Anne reached for her phone on the bedside locker. "Josh took some pictures that night and posted them." She worked on her phone. "Look at those pictures!"

She handed the phone to Isobel who turned it so Fiona could see. The time stamp showed the night of the attack.

"I had nothing to do with the attack on Charlene and Michael, I swear! When I heard about Michael being killed and Charlene in hospital I felt so guilty about what I had been doing. Fiona, I'm sorry. I was so jealous of Charlene and I let things get out of hand. I sent one message and . . . Charlene didn't seem to be affected at all so I let things escalate. I swear I've learned my lesson. I couldn't believe when Charlene was attacked. It was horrible. That isn't what I wanted at all. It was one thing to write horrible things to her but I didn't want anything to happen to her. I didn't!"

"I don't believe a word you say," Fiona said. "I want you out of this house by tonight."

"The police will want to check your alibi," Isobel said. "If they're happy with it then you will be cleared of attacking Charlene and Michael. You had better get yourself cleaned up and go to the police station."

"It's the least you can do," Fiona said, folding her arms.

Anne hung her head. "Yes, of course."

150

Fiona stamped out of the room.

"She hates me."

"She's worried about her friend."

"I can't believe that I've been so stupid."

"Anne, get yourself some help."

"It's awful that everyone will know but the last few days have been torture – the things I wrote and then what happened. I hated myself. *I hate myself*."

Isobel touched her hand. "I know. Now you need to sort everything out."

Anne nodded. "I'll get ready and go to the police."

Isobel squeezed her hand and went downstairs.

Fiona was curled up in a corner of the couch, crying. "What's happening? College is supposed to be the best years of your life and I'm in the middle of a nightmare."

Isobel sat on the edge of the couch and let her cry. At the moment things were a bit nightmarish. Fiona's sobs eventually subsided.

"I heard that Charlene had a better night last night," Isobel said. "Hopefully her dad and mum will know more tonight."

"I'm praying that the news will be good."

"We all are. Will you be alright?"

Fiona nodded. "Yeah, I'll go and visit another friend. I need some good company today."

"That's a good idea."

Chapter 20

Isobel walked away from Charlene's house and found a quiet doorway. She contacted Damien Doran.

"Hello, Detective Doran. Isobel McKenzie here. We've found out that Charlene had a troll."

"How do you know?"

"One of her friends told us."

"Why didn't they let us know? Did they not think that that would have been useful information to tell the police?"

Isobel was glad that she hadn't said Fiona's name. "I don't think that they were thinking straight. They've been too upset about Michael and Charlene." She wanted to get off this subject. "We managed to find out that it was a girl Charlene knew. Her name is Anne and she is coming in to tell you everything. She seems to have an alibi for the time of the attack."

"So you think that she isn't involved in the attack?"

"You'll have to check it but I don't think so, no."

"So if her alibi checks out we're no closer to finding the perpetrators."

Isobel begged to differ. In her mind the monster dressed in white with the killer words written on it was disintegrating. One down.

"What about the GPS from the stolen phone?" she asked. "Has that revealed anything?"

"No. The phones were turned off immediately and they haven't been turned on since. I imagine the SIM cards are long since destroyed."

"So, if it was thieves, then they knew what they were doing."

"Exactly."

"So there's no news on Charlene's footage?"

"Nothing yet. Inspector Williams isn't hopeful."

Isobel rang off, feeling dispirited. She walked past Queen's and towards the Muse. She kept feeling drawn back to this area. Perhaps she was hoping that miraculously she would be inspired. She walked along Botanic Avenue, past a bewildering selection of coffee shops. Scattered among them were empty premises whose doorways held cardboard and rolled-up blankets, evidence of their night-time occupation.

Seeing the Red Rose Café ahead, she decided she would go in for something to eat. As she passed one of the doorways a heap of material in it moved. She stopped. Had she imagined it? It looked like an old blanket, brown in colour and rather dirty. There were some bins nearby and Isobel could smell rubbish. Her stomach turned. Rats? Then the material moved again. She shuddered. The blanket moved again and she stepped away, her hand to her mouth, her shoulders hunched.

"Back again, I see."

Isobel stepped further back.

The bedding moved again, and a grey-haired man sat up, a sleeping bag around him, the blanket over it. "You can't stay away from the place." He burst out laughing, which quickly brought on a coughing fit. "Just like me."

"Are you alright?"

The man banged his chest a couple of times and coughed, spitting some phlegm into the street. "The wet nights are playing havoc with my chest."

Isobel shifted uncomfortably.

"The nights are starting to get cold. Mind you, I'm luckier than most. Got myself a deluxe suite here." He laughed again, gesturing to his alcove. "And let me tell you, I have to keep an eye on it or those others would have me out and be moved in."

A stream of guilt snaked through Isobel as she thought of her cosy hotel room. "Would you like a sandwich?"

The man grinned. "Don't mind if I do."

Isobel couldn't help smiling. "Cheese?"

He looked up at her. "Chicken?"

Isobel laughed. "Chicken it is. Tea?"

"I'd love a cuppa."

"I'll be back in a moment."

Isobel walked into the Red Rose Café, ordering for herself and also a takeaway for the man outside. When the chicken sandwich was ready she took it outside with a takeaway cup of tea and some sachets of sugar.

He grinned. "Thanks for this."

Isobel smiled. "No problem. What's your name?"

He studied her for a moment, said "Henry," and tucked into his sandwich with gusto.

Isobel went back into the café which was warm and the décor restful. Each table had a red rose in a small vase. As she ate, she mulled over the case. While it was great to have eliminated Anne and the trolling angle, there was very little else going on with the case. What could she do to generate some leads, inject some energy into the investigation? All she could think of was to go to the Students Union to see if there was somewhere else she could find out more about drugs.

Chapter 21

Isobel walked into the Students Union. Facing her on the wall were some words. "*Do something today that your future self will thank you for.*" Isobel smiled. She liked it. What would her future self thank her for? She realised that the answer to that was probably that her future self would want her to do a job that she loved. Unfortunately, she wasn't sure what that was now. She needed to put some energy into finding out. Maybe her therapy work was not for her anymore. There! She had admitted it. Maybe she needed to find a new job. That was daunting but it might be the truth. Or maybe the spark she had felt when Ben Jameson was talking about his students was a sign of her old interest and enthusiasm awakening. It was hard to consider all these things, never mind talk to anyone about it. All her friends and family wanted her to get back to normal but there was no normal. She felt that she was different, that having cancer and treatment had changed her. She could never be carefree and nonchalant about her health again. She no longer felt that time or life stretched ahead, rather she felt doubt about the future and somehow that had intensified her desire not to waste it. She wanted to work but at something that she felt passionate about. She had felt that way about her therapy before, she just wasn't sure if it was still true.

A student brushed past her and Isobel came back to the present moment. Stirring herself, she perused the noticeboard and the posters on the walls around the building. There were numerous posters about drugs. She wondered how she had failed to notice them when she had been here a few days ago. It was clear that someone was staging a strong anti-drug campaign.

At the bottom of the poster was a number. Isobel dialled it.

"Hello. Róisín Magill."

"Hi, my name is Isobel McKenzie. I was wondering if I could talk to you about drugs."

"Are you a student?"

"No, no. I'm not a student. I'm the aunt of a student."

"Yes, you can come and talk to me. My office is in the Students Union, the first floor."

"I'm downstairs. Are you free now?"

"Yes, come on up. Turn left at the top of the stairs and I'm in the last office on the left."

"I'll be right up."

Róisín Magill was the same height as Isobel, five foot two. Her hair was grey and cut in a classic bob and gave evidence to her fifty or so years. She was slim and fit but her eyes were shadowed with a dullness that spoke of pain and sadness.

She reached across her desk to Isobel and shook her hand. "Isobel – isn't that what you said?"

"Yes."

"I'm Róisín." She gestured to a more comfortable area near the window. "Let's sit over here. Would you like some tea or coffee?"

Isobel spotted a cafetiere beside the kettle. "Coffee, thank you."

When they each had coffee in front of them, Róisín said, "How can I help?"

"My nephew was in a project group with Michael O'Neill who was killed on Monday night and Charlene Griffiths who is in hospital."

"That's an awful tragedy, those young lives, their poor families."

"Yes. It's awful. I was wondering if you could tell me about the drug situation among students."

"Who suggested that you come and talk to me?"

Isobel frowned. "No one. I saw your posters on the noticeboard downstairs and I thought you could give me some information, that's all."

"You mentioned the attack on the students and now you're asking about drugs. Do you think drugs were the reason for the attack on them?"

"As far as I know it's one of the possible motives for the attack. Obviously the police are looking into it, but Charlene's father is very upset and he asked me to find out what I could. I'm a psychotherapist and have had some experience of working with the police."

Róisín's eyes darkened, her facial muscles tightening,

giving her face a gaunt and haunted look. "God help Michael's parents." After a few moments she refocused on Isobel. "And Charlene's parents too, of course."

Isobel bit her lip. Róisín identified strongly with Michael's family. Had Róisín had some personal experience of tragedy?

Róisín forestalled her. "Well, if no one had told you about me then I had better fill you in."

"Please do."

"My son Patrick died of a drug overdose almost two years ago."

"I'm so sorry."

"He was only twenty-five."

Isobel waited but Róisín seemed almost to have forgotten her. "So now you try to make students aware of the dangers of drugs."

Róisín refocused on Isobel. "Yes. Although, Patrick's death wasn't just an overdose. It was more complicated than that."

Isobel raised her eyebrows. "What do you mean?"

"Patrick was afraid. Before he died he told me that he was in danger."

"Do you think that someone was threatening him?"

Róisín shook her head wearily. "I don't know. Everyone tells me that Patrick's fear could have been due to the drugs, that the drugs were making him paranoid but I don't know. He was really afraid. He wanted to get out of that world. He had tried to get out of the drugs scene but he told me that he couldn't, that they wouldn't let him out. He said he was caught, that he couldn't escape, like a fly in a spider's web."

Isobel frowned as the shades of her dream were reflected back to her. She shivered. "Why don't you tell me about Patrick from the beginning, Róisín? Then I'll understand better."

Róisín closed her eyes. "I don't know if I can."

Isobel bit her lip. The image from her dream was haunting her. "What did Patrick mean about being a fly caught in a spider's web?"

"My son tried to get off drugs a number of times but he was in over his head. He owed the drug people money and they wanted him to keep supplying drugs."

"Did Patrick tell you who 'they' were?"

"No, not exactly, but he said that the threads of this web were everywhere and went very high."

"Did Patrick tell you anything specific about anyone involved?"

"He said that it all started very innocently. The person who introduced him to drugs – he initially thought that person was helping him. He started with the odd tablet, then more often and gradually he moved on to harder and harder drugs. He used to get so mad. He said that he fell for all the justifications: it won't do you any harm, everyone tries drugs at some point, they're not that addictive, you can give them up at any time. He so wished he could go back and change things but he couldn't. He just got deeper and deeper in. When he completed his degree and left college he thought he could get out. Instead the drug people wanted him to use his position in the law firm to do things for them. It was a nightmare. I think he took an overdose because he just couldn't handle it anymore. He hated it. It wasn't just the drugs, it was the fact that they had their hooks in him, that they wanted to control him."

"I'm so sorry."

Róisín nodded an acknowledgement. "I knew he suffered but he wouldn't tell me about the people involved. He said it would put me in danger."

"In danger?"

Róisín squinted at her assessingly, then took a deep breath. "He said there was a head honcho that everyone was terrified of but no one knew his name. That person had links to people high up, judges, police, everything."

"The police?"

"Patrick said that the organisation was very well run and very influential. That was why he was so afraid."

Isobel pursed her lips. A large conspiracy, with links to the police and the judiciary. It seemed like something out of a book, or *Line of Duty*. Could something like that be happening in Belfast? Was any of it true or was it just the nightmare of a drug-addled mind believed by a grieving mother? Was any of this useful in finding Michael's killer and Charlene's attacker?

"Did Patrick contact the police or anyone else about this?"

"No, of course not. I told you the police were involved. He was too afraid."

Isobel bit her lip. What could she say?

"But *I* did. I went to the police after Patrick died."

"Did you? What happened?"

"It was a complete waste of time. They treated me as

if I was exaggerating, as if I was making up some elaborate scenario to somehow absolve my son from what he had done."

"I'm sorry."

"I went to the Provost of the University too, to tell him the danger that his students were under."

"That was brave."

"He treated me as if I was unstable, as if I was deranged with grief. He wasn't going to do anything. I thought about everything for a while and came up with my drug awareness programme to alert students to the dangers of drugs. The Students Union was very supportive. They decided that my awareness campaigns, my myth-busting about drugs was a helpful programme for students and they encourage students to take it when they come to college."

"That sounds good."

Róisín smiled at her. "I am proud of it and hopefully it's helped protect some of the youngsters from what my Patrick went through."

Isobel felt a lump in her throat. There was no doubt in her mind as to this woman's courage and the usefulness of what she was doing.

"Is there anything else that you can tell me about drugs in college?"

Róisín frowned. "I don't think so. Would you like to see a picture of Patrick?"

"Yes, please."

Róisín lifted a photo frame from her desk and handed it to Isobel.

Isobel smiled. The picture showed a young man with dark hair and a wide smile. He was laughing.

"That's a lovely picture."

"Yes. He was so happy," there was an ominous pause, "before the drugs." Róisín reached for her phone. "He sent me some pictures in the days before he died. I actually thought he was looking happier. I was so hopeful that maybe . . ."

She handed her phone to Isobel. On the screen was a picture of Patrick outside Queen's. Roisin swiped the screen to the right. Another picture showed Patrick outside the Muse. A final picture showed him outside a shop. The name *Org* was above the door and Patrick was holding up his plastic bag of the same name.

"I think Patrick must have gone to visit places that were important to him, or significant in some way, or maybe reminded him of where he had been happy before his life started to unravel, before he got sucked into the drug scene."

Isobel nodded. "Thank you for showing me."

Róisín took back her phone and darkened the screen.

Chapter 22

Isobel left the Students Union. Hearing about Patrick's life and death and listening to the story of drugs taking over his world had made her feel depressed. Unfortunately, the story was all too common. She thought about the pushers, the people who supplied the drugs and how they got others started on this path. She thought of the myths about drugs not being addictive and she realised how easily one could fall into that world. Patrick had spoken of a presence that was behind everything, drawing people into the world of drugs and then using and controlling them. She shivered.

Without realising it, her steps had led her back to the alley at the side of the Muse. She walked down the alley again. Somehow she felt drawn back to the source, the starting point of the case. She saw the bins where Charlene and Michael had been found. She brought out her phone and looked again at Charlene's footage. Charlene had filmed Michael walking past the bins further into the alley. Isobel mimicked his steps.

She looked again at the end of the alley, taking in the

double gate and the old pillars. There was nothing to see. Everything seemed closed off: the pub doors, the entrance to the paper yard. It all looked old and deserted and unused. It was eerie. She shivered. That was why the group had wanted to use it in the film. It was so atmospheric. She moved further down the alley.

The old entrance to the yard was dramatic. The stone was weathered. The arch over the gateway was from an older era but it had stood the test of time. The only damage it appeared to have sustained was the pillar cap that was misaligned. At some point something must have knocked against it and moved the capstone. Again, Isobel saw the marks in the stonework where something, presumably a vehicle like a van, had scraped the pillar and in the deepest marking the line of green paint.

Standing back again, she surveyed the gate as a whole. There was no doubt but that it would make a good backdrop to a film.

"What you looking for?"

Isobel jumped. "*Oh!*"

She turned. It was Henry.

"You scared the life out of me."

"What you looking for?" he said again as he shambled up to her.

Isobel relaxed slightly. Henry wasn't frightening, more lonesome.

"I don't know, Henry. I was just thinking about the students who were attacked here."

"Very sad. That young fella – the one who was attacked – he was always taking pictures here."

"Was he?"

"Oh yes, lots of nights. I don't know why he was so interested. There was never anything happening when he was here."

"He and the girl, Charlene, were hoping to use the alley in a short film."

"Oh, was that it?"

"Yeah, they were checking the lighting for the film."

"Oh. I hope she recovers."

"Me too, Henry."

Isobel turned and walked back out of the alley, Henry accompanying her.

She stopped and turned to him. "Henry, you say you've seen Michael taking pictures in the alley recently. You must have been here the night he was killed?"

He suddenly looked alarmed. "I had nuthin' to do with that!"

"No, no," Isobel hastened to say. "I know you didn't. I just wondered if you had noticed anyone besides him going into the alley? Either before or after him? That's all."

"No, I was asleep until the crowd gathered so I didn't see nuthin' until then. I must go now." He gestured towards his doorway.

"But, Henry, other nights – did you ever notice any strange goings-on in there late at night?"

"No, no, I wouldn't be goin' near the place. I know how to mind my own business."

"But, from your doorway, you may have seen something like a van going in there? Even sometime in the past?"

"No. Minds my own business, I do. I keeps my head

down." He gestured again towards his 'deluxe suite'. "I must go now or someone will move into my space or rob my things."

"Sure, Henry. Nice to talk to you."

He shuffled off and then turned around.

"Don't you be coming here at night all alone, like this," he said. "It's not safe."

Isobel nodded. "No. It's not. And you be careful too, Henry."

"I will. I know how to take care of myself."

At the next corner Isobel checked with her phone for the location of the shop 'Org'. It was on the street behind and parallel to where the Muse was. As Isobel walked the route she wondered if 'Org' actually backed onto the paper yard. She went to have a look at it.

The shop had a large frontage with a green 'Org' sign above the door. Along the front window were the words: "*For every minute spent in organising an hour is earned.*" *Benjamin Franklin*. Isobel remembered her own student days and files and pages of notes and essays. However, she wondered, in the modern day of the computer did people still use files and stationary? Judging by how often she had seen the Org bags in students' hands, they did.

Isobel pushed open the door. The shop was full of merchandise. All manner of office supplies and art supplies were stocked. There were a number of young people in the store perusing the shelves. Isobel wandered around too, disappointed to see that there was no back window or door through which she could see what lay behind the shop.

There were three students waiting to buy things. Isobel felt nosy but moved closer to observe what they were purchasing. The first student bought some coloured Post-its and some firm card and left toting a blue Org bag. Behind him was a young man who was buying a flip chart and some pens. The man at the till was tall with dark hair and a quick, nervous manner. He rolled up the chart, securing it with some tape and placed the packet of pens in another blue bag.

Isobel realised that the last person queuing was familiar to her. It was the red-haired young man from the pub who she had also noticed on the library footage. He was holding a file block and some pens. He exchanged a few words with the server.

"You're on the till today," he joked. "Have you been demoted?"

"No, Robin, I'm still the manager," said the man with a laugh. "But a couple of the staff are out sick." Efficiently, he put the purchases in a bag, this time green in colour, and the red-headed Robin left.

The manager looked at Isobel. "Can I help you?"

Isobel smiled. "I'm just looking."

He inclined his head.

More students entered. They seemed to know what they wanted and left with their colourful bags. Isobel selected a small notebook and some sheets of card that she thought might be useful for making notes of her ideas about the case. She added a selection of coloured pens and brought them all to the till.

"Did you find everything you need?"

Isobel smiled. "Yes, thank you. You're very busy."

The man caught her eye. "Well, we are near the University."

Isobel almost blushed. "Yes, yes, of course."

"Are you a student?"

"No, no. Just visiting my nephew. He's a student."

The man quickly placed her purchases in a blue Org bag and Isobel paid and left.

Out on the street, Isobel turned back the way she had come. Her phone rang.

"Jack?"

"Yes. I'm finished lectures but that's not why I'm ringing. The Provost wants to see both of us. We have an appointment at four o'clock."

"The Provost?"

"Do you think this is about the library?" Jack sounded nervous.

Isobel was walking quickly now towards Queen's. "Probably. Ms. Pritchard did say she would be telling him what we had found."

"Oh no." Jack sounded nervous.

"So we're going to meet the Crown Prince."

"Yes."

She could hear an easing of Jack's tension and her own smile deepened.

"I'm walking towards Queen's now," she said.

"I'll meet you at the entrance to the main building."

"See you in five minutes."

Chapter 23

Isobel followed Jack through the building to the Provost's office. A secretary at a desk guarded the entrance to the last piece of corridor.

Isobel glanced at her watch. It was five minutes to four. "Isobel McKenzie and my nephew Jack McKenzie. We have a four o'clock appointment to see the Provost."

The suit-clad woman with her hair swept up in an elaborate plait nodded. "Take a seat. He's with someone now. He'll see you as soon as possible."

Isobel and Jack sat down in chairs provided for waiting. Jack took out his phone and started to play a game.

Isobel checked her phone. She answered a number of messages. She glanced at her watch. Time was passing. She wondered if this was a power game. Keeping them waiting was a classic way of making it clear that his time was more important than theirs. It was a way of ensuring that they were already at a disadvantage when they met him, simple but effective, tried and tested.

Isobel's phone rang. She walked away from the

secretary in the direction she had come until she was out of earshot.

"Isobel, it's Tony again."

"How did it go with the doctor? Is there any news?"

"Yes, some good, some neutral."

Isobel felt relieved. No absolutely bad news, thank goodness.

"I'll tell you everything when I see you. And Nathan is here. He has something to show us."

"What is it?"

"He worked his magic on the footage. You need to see this. How soon can you get here?"

"Jack and I are supposed to be meeting the Provost but . . . We'll be as quick as we can."

"We'll be waiting in the bar at the Europa."

Isobel walked back to the waiting area. "Jack, let's go." She lowered her voice. "That was Tony. He and Nathan are waiting for us at the Europa."

She swung her bag over her shoulder and approached the secretary.

"We have to go," she said.

"Go? What about your meeting with the Provost?" the woman asked, pressing a button on her phone.

"Obviously he's very busy. He can reschedule for a time when he is available." Isobel pulled a business card from her bag and handed it to the secretary. "Ask the Provost to contact me if he wants to reschedule."

Behind her a door opened. "Miss McKenzie?"

Isobel turned to see a heavy man with a receding hairline dressed in an expensive dark suit.

"I can see you now."

Isobel could feel her temper rising.

"I'm sorry," he said. "I had a phone call with the police that overran."

Isobel stood where she was. "Charlene's father just called. He wants to see us. He has some news of Charlene's condition."

"Of course. Perhaps a quick word, I won't detain you long." He gestured with his hand towards his office.

Isobel hesitated a second then nodded and followed the Provost into the office, Jack coming in behind.

"My name is Samuel Prince."

Isobel shook his hand. "Isobel McKenzie."

"And you must be Jack." He shook Jack's hand. "I believe you were a great help to Charlene on the night she was attacked, helping with the first aid and also going to the hospital with her. I want to thank you for your actions. You are a brave and kind young man."

Jack blushed.

Prince sat behind his desk and gestured to the seats across from him. Isobel and Jack sat down.

"Not only that, I hear from Ms. Pritchard that you both are involved in identifying someone who has been trolling Charlene. It seems that now you have turned your attention to investigating." Samuel Prince smiled but it didn't reach his eyes.

Jack said, "We . . . "

Isobel reached out and squeezed his arm. "I'm sure you agree that helping the police with their enquiries is our civic and moral duty and, given that Jack knows Charlene and knew Michael, absolutely essential."

The Provost inclined his head. "And you seem to be doing that very enthusiastically. I understand that you have talked to some friends of Charlene and Michael, God rest him, and spoken to the staff at the Muse, to Ben Jameson in the counselling service, and to Róisín Magill in the Students Union about drugs on campus. You have been taking your civic duties very seriously." The smile was skin-deep, his eyes cold and his manner clipped.

"And you are keeping a very close eye on what we're doing. I wonder why that is?"

"I keep a close eye on everything that happens on this campus."

"But why this focus on us, when there has been a murder and an attempted murder and the police are struggling to come up with any suspects and are unclear as to the motive? Is there a problem about us trying to help?"

"Any information that helps find the person or persons responsible is important."

Isobel nodded. "Of course. But?"

"But I have concerns that you are putting Jack in danger."

"How so?"

"Well, if there is someone who has already attacked two students, killing one and seriously hurting another, I hardly think that pursuing them is a good idea. That's a job much better left to the police. I don't want any more hurt or . . ." he hesitated, "anything to happen to Jack."

"Neither do I!" Isobel snapped.

Prince shifted in his chair. "Despite Ms. Pritchard being a little premature in showing you the footage from

173

the library, I hope that identifying the person responsible for the trolling puts an end to the matter. I have spoken to Superintendent Bernard Taylor and he assures me that they are looking into her movements. Hopefully then we can all get back to education."

"But the person who is the troll was somewhere else when Charlene and Michael were attacked," Jack said.

Prince frowned at him. "I understand from Superintendent Taylor that they are confident that this is a significant breakthrough. And while I am delighted about that, Ms. Pritchard has not followed our policy on disclosure."

"So the police think it's likely that the troll is the attacker?" Isobel asked.

"That is not my business – it's a matter for the police, as I am making clear to you. But it seems highly unlikely that one student would have so many people wishing her harm, don't you think?"

"The police were also looking into theft as a motive, and maybe drugs," said Isobel.

"That's ridiculous. The Muse has never been associated with drugs."

"So we've heard."

"Well, there you are then. I hope now that you will get back to your studies, Jack, and that you, Ms McKenzie, will go home."

Isobel stood up. "I think you have made yourself very clear."

Jack rose to his feet also.

The Provost stood. "Thank you both for your contributions to the case but it is a matter for the police

174

now. For your own safety you need to get back to your normal lives."

"Thank you for the warning," Isobel said.

"It's not a warning, Ms. McKenzie, more an expression of concern."

Isobel led the way out of the office. They passed the secretary and continued until they were out of earshot.

"That wasn't a warning, it was more like a veiled threat," Isobel said.

Jack frowned. "You think that the Provost was threatening us?"

"He was certainly making it clear that he wants us off the case, one way or the other, either by using fear, or concern, or by blaming the wrong person."

"Why would he care what we're doing? Surely if it helped find out what happened that could only be a good thing?"

Isobel shook her head. "I don't know. Politics maybe but it seemed more personal than that. We'll have to find out a bit more about the Crown Prince."

Jack made a face. "He makes me nervous."

Isobel smiled at him. "He was trying to make you nervous."

"It worked."

"Something we've done has riled him, or has riled someone who can influence him to warn us off, which means we've found something important."

Jack looked doubtful. "You think?"

Isobel started walking. "Yes. Tony said Nathan has 'worked his magic on the footage'! So here's hoping!"

Jack's face lit up. "Great!" he said.

Chapter 24

Isobel and Jack joined Tony and Nathan in the Europa.

Jack leaned forward in his chair. "What did the doctor say?" he anxiously enquired of Tony.

Tony smiled around at them all. "The doctor is very happy with how Charlene is doing. She had a good day today and if tonight she remains stable then maybe tomorrow they can reduce the drugs and see how she does." He looked more troubled. "It's only when she comes round that they can be sure if there is any residual damage." For a second he looked desolate.

Isobel glanced at Jack who swallowed noisily.

"Did the doctor say anything else?" she asked.

Tony shook his head and looked up from the spot on the table that he had been concentrating on. "Just that she is happy with how everything has gone and is hopeful, but can give no guarantees. I suppose they have to prepare us for all eventualities, just in case."

"Please God she's as well as the doctor hopes," said Isobel.

Tony nodded. "Exactly."

"How is Joan doing?"

Tony smiled slightly. "She is a little fearful but determined that everything will progress well and Charlene will make a good recovery. I don't think she can consider any other outcome at present."

"That's understandable," said Isobel.

Tony turned to Nathan. "Now, tell them what you have."

Nathan sat forward. "I've had some success with the images Jack found on the cloud."

Isobel hardly dared to hope.

"The camera I gave Charlene was a Canon DSLR."

"Really?" Jack said. "That's a professional camera."

Nathan nodded.

"No wonder Charlene was excited," Jack said.

"The good news is that the camera had a high-speed lens and could take images in poor light. The camera also has about 20 million mega pixels."

Jack whistled. "Wow! That's impressive."

Isobel could feel her eyes glazing over. She looked at Jack but he was concentrating on Nathan. She could feel herself shrinking inside. She knew very little about technology.

Nathan nodded. "It means that we have loads of detail and we can zoom in on parts of the picture and still retain lots of definition."

This Isobel understood. This sounded promising.

"I also bought Charlene a wireless transmitter." Nathan looked around and, seeing Isobel's frown, said, "Like photographers for newspapers would have so that they can send pictures from the scene immediately to the newsroom."

Isobel nodded.

"Charlene could use her phone as a Wi-Fi source and so send pictures from the alley straight to the cloud account she had created for the film group."

Isobel's patience gave out. "So what could you see?"

"I was able to really zoom in on the two men in the background."

Jack gasped. "You were?"

Nathan nodded. "And I have some quite clear images of them."

"Fantastic!" Jack said.

Isobel's heart was beating fast. "Let's see them."

Nathan brought up an image on his phone. It showed a man with close-cropped brown hair and a sharp face. The man was in the act of raising a cigarette to his mouth, the front of his hand clearly visible. And there Isobel saw the image of a bird.

"A tattoo!" She looked at Nathan. "That's going to really help in identifying him!"

"Yes. I hope so."

"I can't believe that you were able to zoom in so close," Jack said.

Nathan nodded. "If Charlene had been using her phone camera we wouldn't have anything. It would be too far away and too unclear to get anything. I thought I might need a special computer package, but in fact I was able to use an app. It helps with enhancing grainy pictures and with it I was able to get the images I am showing you."

Nathan took back the phone and brought up a second image. He handed it to Tony who studied it before passing it to Isobel.

The second man had a shaved head and a thick neck. His eyes were small and he had a cruel look. Isobel shivered. Even from the picture she felt an aura of threat emanating.

Jack reached out and Isobel passed on the phone. As he looked at the picture, he made a face.

"Do you know him?" asked Isobel.

Jack shook his head. "No. But he looks like a bouncer."

"Yes, he does, doesn't he?" Tony said.

Jack sat back in his chair. "I don't recognise either of them."

"We need to get these to the police," Isobel said.

Tony nodded. "Yes. They might know who they are."

"Can you send me all of the photographs you have of the two men, Nathan?" Isobel said.

"Yes, and to me too," said Jack. "I can ask around among my friends and see if anyone recognises the men."

Isobel looked at Jack. "But before we show them to anyone else we'd better share them with the police."

"Yes, good point. We should contact Detective Doran."

"Yes, yes. Call him now."

Isobel looked around. They were sitting in a corner of the dining room. Around them the tables were empty with the closest people being, Isobel estimated, out of earshot. She pulled up a phone number.

"Detective Doran. Isobel McKenzie here."

"Yes, Ms. McKenzie. What can I do for you?"

"I'm ringing about the photographs from the alley that we gave you yesterday."

"We've nothing new to report. The lab has the photographs but we are up the walls. Three middle-level drug dealers died last night."

"What? And two the night before?"

"Yes. It could be a new drug or we might be in the middle of some sort of turf war or drug coup. With all of that going on I would say that the lab hasn't had time to process the photographs yet."

Although Detective Doran wasn't on speaker phone Tony had heard what he had said. His face grew red and he gestured for Isobel to give him the phone.

"I have an update for you," Isobel said to Doran.

Tony leant forward and gestured again for the phone.

Isobel said, "I am giving the phone to Mr. Griffiths now."

Tony grasped the phone and stood up, his face red. "My daughter is a priority. How dare you make drug dealers more important than her and her murdered friend!"

"Mr. Griffiths, I'm sorry, that's not what I meant at all."

"I should bloody well hope not. My daughter is fighting for her life and her friend is lying in the morgue –"

"I'm sorry."

"I can't believe that they are not a priority. There's a killer out there. Other young people could be in danger."

"Please –"

"How can you possibly suggest that–"

"Mr. Griffiths! Of course Charlene and Michael's case is

important, very important. I am merely explaining that we have a number of cases at the moment and the lab is overwhelmed. I meant no disrespect. Of course the photographs will be looked at as soon as possible. My colleagues and I are doing everything that we can, I assure you."

"I hope so. Fortunately, I have my own means of having the photographs enhanced." He handed the phone back to Isobel and waved for her to continue.

Isobel said, "Nathan Knight, an expert at Mr. Griffiths' firm, has done some work on the photographs and has managed to get some very clear images of the two men."

"Are you serious? Send them to me immediately."

"I will. No doubt you have a database that you can go through."

"Yes, of course. If you send me the enhanced pictures I will get them checked against it. Just be aware they may not be in it."

"OK. Let us know the results, please."

"I most certainly will. Send on the images. I'll be in touch with you tomorrow."

"Thanks. We'll be waiting to hear from you." She finished the call.

Tony shook his head. "Charlene is not a priority to the police. My daughter is fighting for her life, Michael has lost his and the police are tied up with some drug dealers." He rubbed his hands across his face. After a moment he caught Isobel's eye. "That's why I wanted you on the case, Isobel."

Isobel handed the phone to Nathan. "Can you go ahead and send Detective Doran the pictures in the best way?"

Nathan nodded and tapped at Isobel's phone. After a few seconds he handed it back to her. "He has them."

"What now?" Tony asked.

Isobel tapped her phone against her lips. An idea had occurred to her. Should she? Three pairs of eyes were focused on her, aware she was considering something.

"I know some gardaí in Limerick," she said. "I don't know if they have access to the same data base as the police here, probably not, but I can contact them and see what they can do. Maybe they have contacts and can –"

"Do it," said Tony.

Isobel stood up and took her phone out to the foyer to a quiet place. She wasn't talking to Detective Inspector Eoin Ryan in front of everyone.

"Hello, Eoin."

"Isobel McKenzie, as I live and breathe, long time no hear. Alanna, do you hear that? Isobel is on the line. "

"Hi, Isobel! Eoin has you on speaker now. We're in his office – you remember it, don't you, as messy as ever?"

Isobel smiled in spite of herself. She had met Eoin and Sergeant Alanna Finnegan when she had found a body while out walking along the River Shannon in Limerick. Despite some initial misunderstandings Isobel had ended up working with Eoin and Alanna to bring a serial rapist to justice.

"Zoe was asking about you recently and saying that we should all go for a meal together," Alanna continued.

"Say hello to Zoe and Daniel too." Daniel was Alanna and her wife Zoe's son. "I'm sorry but this is more of a work call than a social catch-up."

"What have you got yourself embroiled in now?" Eoin asked.

Isobel could feel herself bristling. This is what had happened when they first met. Although she knew that it was Eoin's style and that he was teasing her, she still found herself riled. She took a deep breath.

"I'm in Belfast. Two of my nephew's friends were attacked – Charlene and Michael. One was killed, the other is in the hospital recovering from brain surgery."

"Oh God!"

"Isobel, I'm so sorry," Alanna said.

"I was wondering if you could help me."

"How can we help from Limerick?" Eoin said.

"The police here have five drug dealers dead and they are under pressure. It seems that Charlene and Michael are slipping down their list of priorities."

"I heard about those dealer deaths," Alanna said.

"Yeah, the word is that they aren't sure if they were dodgy drugs or they were in effect executed," Eoin said.

"In effect?"

"One of the easiest ways to get rid of a drug dealer is to give him some really pure drugs. When he takes his next hit, he takes the dose he normally does but of the purer stuff and he has taken an overdose. It looks self-induced, it is self-induced but it's murder . . . Five dealers, all in a few days? It's either a dodgy drug or someone is cleaning house and that could mean a takeover. I'm not surprised that the police are busy. We would be too if that happened."

"That's why I thought of you guys. We have some photographs taken by one of the victims a very short time before she and her friend were attacked. We've had the photos enhanced and are now waiting to see if the police can identify the men. But their lab is overwhelmed at the moment. Do you think you could put them through your system and see if they're on it?"

There was silence on the other end of the phone. Isobel knew that she was probably pushing her relationship with the two gardaí. Maybe they couldn't help her. But, she reassured herself, it was worth a try. She heard a deep sigh from the other end of the phone.

"Isobel, I'm not sure," said Eoin. "I don't think we should be getting involved in a case up North. It could get very complicated."

"Oh . . . I suppose I shouldn't have asked."

There was silence.

Isobel bit her lip.

Eoin then said, "Look, I have a friend working in Narcotics in Dublin. I can reach out and ask him if he can help but I can't promise you. Maybe he can check their data bases."

"That would be great."

"No promises, Isobel. If it's going to cause trouble . . ."

"I understand. Just do what you can. Thanks, Eoin, thanks, Alanna."

"Send the pictures on to me and I'll let you know," said Eoin.

"And when you're back in Limerick give us a call and we can have that meal," said Alanna.

Isobel smiled. "Will do."

"And watch yourself out there," Alanna said. "You do seem to be a magnet for trouble."

It was true. During the case they had shared Isobel had been attacked by the rapist and it was only by using her walking poles and some self-defence that she managed to escape.

"I'll be careful."

"Do. Bye."

"I'll be in touch," said Eoin.

Isobel rang off. She was pleased. She knew that they would do all that they could.

She went back to the others. "I've sent the photos on to my Garda friends. They'll see what they can do. They can't get too involved as the situation is very difficult politically but they're hoping to send them on to a Narcotics colleague in Dublin."

"I understand," said Tony. "I've just been telling Nathan that if these pictures help the investigation, then I'm going to let him develop our security and surveillance."

Nathan laughed. "As you know, I've been trying to tell him that it's a million – no, billion-dollar industry."

Isobel could feel her mind shutting down. She wasn't interested in the profits of the industry. She realised rather sadly that she had already given up on the police in the North. Detective Doran seemed very eager, but the news he had given her of the spate of deaths and the attitude of Inspector Williams just didn't inspire confidence. Her only hope now was Eoin and Alanna and the man in Dublin. All in all, it seemed a rather depressing situation.

Jack stood. "I might head home then. It's been a long day."

"I'll go too," said Isobel. "Let us know how Charlene is. We'll talk to you tomorrow."

Isobel and Jack made their way out of the Europa. Isobel arranged once again to meet Jack for breakfast at her hotel and he quickly took his leave, going off to meet friends.

Isobel glanced at her watch. It was seven o'clock. She realised that she was hungry. She walked back towards Queen's, keeping an eye out for somewhere to eat.

Chapter 25

When Isobel reached the gates of Queen's she realised that she had been so deep in thought that she had walked up University Road. She stopped and pivoted on her heels. She hadn't been attracted to any restaurant she had passed and she was very hungry now.

"Isobel! Isobel!"

Isobel swung round. Hurrying towards her was Róisín Magill.

"Hi, Róisín. Are you just finishing work now?"

"Yes, yes. And you?"

"Oh, I was just looking for somewhere to have a bite to eat. Can you recommend somewhere? I'm a vegetarian."

"Yes, of course. In fact, if you wouldn't mind I'll join you."

Isobel smiled. "That would be great."

"I know a great restaurant on Botanic Avenue, not far from here. They do lovely artisan food and the vegetarian options are good."

"It sounds ideal, lead the way."

Róisín led the way down University Square, past Queen's Film Theatre. At the end of the street they passed the Muse. They turned left there. The restaurant was further down on the right-hand side. It was called Sate.

Róisín seemed to know the waitress and she found them a table at the back where they had some privacy to talk. Isobel looked at the menu and ordered a mushroom risotto, one of her favourite dishes. Róisín ordered a chicken dish.

Róisín looked at Isobel. "A glass of wine?"

Isobel nodded. "Yes."

They both ordered.

"Charlene has had a good day today," Isobel said. "The doctors are hoping to reduce her sedation tomorrow."

Róisín nodded. "That's great. Please God she'll be OK."

The waitress brought the two glasses of wine.

Róisín raised her glass. "To Charlene's recovery!"

"To Charlene's recovery and to catching the people who did it!"

After her first sip Isobel set her glass down and watched as Róisín played with the cutlery in front of her.

"Is everything all right, Róisín?"

She looked up. "Yes, yes." She dropped the fork she had been fiddling with. "Sort of." She grimaced. "I was just wondering . . ."

Isobel sipped her wine. "Why don't you tell me what's on your mind?"

Róisín sat back in her chair.

"I've thought a lot about how young people get drawn into drugs and there is a process. A grooming process that they go through." Róisín leant forward. "In the same way

188

that a child is groomed by an abuser, young people are groomed into drugs."

"Yes, I see the correlation." Isobel's interest was piqued.

"I actually know of young women who have managed to get off drugs and some of the dealers actually put drugs through their letterboxes, trying to get them back to a life of drugs and prostitution."

Isobel shook her head. "That's shocking."

"I know. It's like the dealers own people, can control their lives." She picked up her fork and started fiddling with it again. "Patrick said some things. I'm convinced that the network operating in Belfast is ruthless like that. They wanted to control my son. They got him hooked on drugs and took over his life."

Isobel sipped her drink and waited for Róisín to continue.

"I think there are people who are on the lookout for vulnerable young people, unhappy, overwhelmed, lonely young people."

"That probably describes people who are vulnerable in general."

"Being around a campus there are loads of possible victims. I think someone from the drug web earns that person's trust and then starts feeding them a drug that seems to help. And, the young person being helped and supported and feeling calmer, or freer, or more confident, trusts the drug person, the pusher. They fall for all the usual myths. Everyone needs a bit of help sometime. Everyone tries drugs. You can give up any time. The pusher becomes a more and more influential person in their world. They get the young person to trust them.

Imagine being a student encouraged to study, to do well and at the same time relying on the pusher and the drugs they are supplying. By the time the student has finished college they have an established drug pattern and they are also either in financial debt, and so at the mercy of the drug pusher, or there are photos of them engaging in illegal activities and any future they might have is under threat, and that is how they get drawn deeper and deeper into the web, where their life isn't their own."

"Isn't that how any addiction works? With drinking or gambling it starts out as a social thing, a bit of fun and gradually becomes a dependency."

"I know, I know. But the difference is that this is a deliberate process. Literally young people are identified and then they are groomed into a life of drugs, through addiction, through manipulation because they owe money or because there are photographs of them doing something illegal. With this network they don't just want people addicted to drugs, they want people in their power. They want people who are in positions that might be useful to the network – solicitors, judges, politicians, policemen. I think they particularly target young people who may, in the future, go on to have influential jobs. If they also have drug habits then they are at the mercy of the network. They have to do their bidding or risk losing everything."

"But what you're describing is a process that needs years to be realised. When young people leave college they aren't in positions of power, they're only starting out in their careers."

"I know but this system, this process, this web, has been operating for a while."

"How do you know that?"

Róisín rubbed her face with her hands. "Please believe me. There are people now who were inducted into this drug web twenty years ago. They're in positions of power and they are influencing what is going on."

Isobel put her elbows on the table and clasped her hands together.

Róisín leant back in her chair. "I know, I know. I can only imagine what I sound like to you. Over the top, maybe even a bit mad or obsessive."

"No, no. You're talking about someone who thinks very long-term."

"Why not? Drug dealing is a business. Why wouldn't they plan for the future and plan to protect themselves?"

Isobel shrugged. "Maybe my perception of drug dealers is naïve."

"Believe me, the head of things here in Belfast is a planner, is organised and is ruthless."

Isobel took a deep breath. "Is this what you believe happened to Patrick?"

"Yes." She paused. "Before he died Patrick was working for a firm of solicitors, Markham and Young. They work mainly on criminal cases. To be honest, I think it was someone from the network who suggested that Patrick go for the job there."

Isobel sipped her wine.

"Needless to say we were delighted when he got the job. Patrick was enjoying his life, he had a good job, he was doing well. We were thrilled. And then came one of the cases he was the junior on, someone from the drug

191

web contacted him and they wanted him to do something, something he wasn't happy about."

"Like what?"

"I don't know. He wouldn't tell me. He was very stressed, off-the-scales stressed and he wouldn't tell me anything and then he overdosed."

Isobel bit her lip. "I'm so sorry."

"Patrick felt under pressure and so conflicted. They were influencing his job and he couldn't escape the hold they had on him." She paused. "He just couldn't see a way out."

"Oh, Róisín!"

"I know. A Catch-22. I think Patrick did what he thought was best. Or I tell myself that anyway. I believe that in the end he did the only honourable thing he felt he could."

The waitress brought their food. Isobel, despite feeling very disturbed, was hungry. She grated some black pepper on her meal and started to eat. Róisín paused a moment and then also started eating.

"So who was pressuring Patrick?"

"I think someone at the law firm was involved but they're in the same position as Patrick, just a cog in the wheel."

"Who do you think the head of the organisation is?"

Róisín shook her head. "I don't know."

"Patrick didn't tell you or give you any hint?"

"I'm not even sure if he knew their identity." Róisín chewed her food and swallowed. "But I've worked with a lot of young people and I have heard whispers."

"Like what?"

"Whispers that the head of the organisation, the boss of this drug web, is someone legitimate."

"Legitimate?"

"Someone who seems respectable. Someone you wouldn't suspect. But someone very ruthless. Patrick was terrified for his life. Believe me when I say that he was afraid to tell me anything in case it got me killed."

Isobel frowned and sipped her wine. The food was excellent but the story she was hearing was leaving a bad taste in her mouth.

"That might be what happened to Michael and Charlene," Róisín continued. "Maybe they got too close, or knew too much about the drug scene. Perhaps it has backfired. The attacks on them mean that people are asking questions. There's a chance that more information will come out. That's why I've told you what I know."

"Yes –"

Róisín held up her hand. "You have to be careful who you share this information with. I'm warning you that it could put you in danger. I don't want anyone's blood on my hands. I don't know who you can trust. Just be careful."

"If you suspect members of the police then who can I talk to about this? Who can help?"

Róisín paused with her loaded fork halfway to her mouth. "I don't know. But I thought you should know more about what's going on and what you're up against. A mastermind in drugs who has people doing their bidding everywhere."

"And if that is true . . ."

"Then attacking two students has drawn attention to them and put the operation in danger. It can't have been a decision from the top. It must have been a rash move by underlings. The deaths of the five drug dealers . . ."

"Oh, you heard about them."

"Yes, I heard. That's a sign that things are shifting and, again, all I can hope is that in the shifting something or someone, preferably the boss, is exposed. They can say that the attacks on Charlene and Michael were robbery but that's not the case. I'm convinced it's drug-related and that someone made a mistake. I can only hope that they make some more, enough to get them all caught."

Isobel had stopped eating.

Róisín lapsed into silence and picked at her food.

Isobel studied her but she seemed to have closed down and said all that she was going to on the subject.

"Is your food good?" Róisín said then.

"Excellent." Isobel took another mouthful and chewed slowly.

"I'm glad you like it. " She hesitated. "It's been good to share with you what I know." She lifted her glass. "To finding the attackers and the boss!"

Isobel raised her glass and touched Róisín's in a clink. She wondered what Róisín would think of the fact that they had photographs of two men in the alley where Michael and Charlene were attacked. For now she was going to say nothing to Róisín about that. She would be mindful of her own, and Jack's safety, and she would pay attention. If there was a boss, the spider at the centre of the web, a groomer of young people into a life of drugs and crime, a destroyer of lives, then she would love to catch him.

Chapter 26

After dinner Isobel bid Róisín goodbye and walked down Botanic Avenue towards the Muse. The streets were busy with people walking along, mostly in groups or couples. There was a buzz of energy. Isobel passed a pub lit up with colourful lights and with seating on the street. It was busy with young people talking, laughing and enjoying themselves. Many others walking by hailed friends, were drawn into conversation and ended up joining the party.

Isobel walked past the outside area of the Muse. It was in darkness, its lifelessness reflecting the sombre day Isobel had had and the heaviness she felt inside. The alley looked dark and unwelcoming.

Isobel wondered what she was doing back here again. Did she think that repeatedly coming back to the scene of the crime would somehow enlighten her? Ahead she could see a supermarket. She walked towards it.

As she passed the Red Rose Café she glanced into the doorway beside it. She could see a figure lying there rolled in a sleeping bag. Henry, no doubt.

At the shop Isobel looked around for buckets containing flowers. There were a few bunches, some white and yellow chrysanthemums and a couple of bunches of carnations in pink and peach. Isobel chose the pink carnations, paid and left the shop.

She felt a little self-conscious. Many times, driving along the roads, she had seen flowers laid at places where accidents had happened and people had lost their lives. Maybe it was talking to Róisín about Patrick, maybe it was thinking of all the young people caught in the snare of drugs, but tonight she felt a weight of sadness, sadness for all the pain and all the losses. She wanted to acknowledge that, acknowledge the tragedy of it all.

She walked back towards the Muse and paused at the entrance to the alley. She looked around. No one was paying any attention to her. Everyone was getting on with their lives.

Isobel took a deep breath and entered the alley. It was dark. She felt the cobbles uneven beneath her feet. Once again she was struck by the atmosphere. Even so close to Botanic Avenue with all the people – just a couple of steps into the alley – she felt alone. It was dark. She stepped forward carefully. She could see the two bins ahead of her. The lamps cast very little light. Two people had been attacked here. She had better keep her wits about her.

She glanced back at the entrance to the alley and saw the bright lights of the street. She looked again at the bins. It was only a few more steps and she could lay the flowers behind the bins where Pat had said he found Michael and Charlene. She wondered if she should take out her phone.

But that was only going to prolong things. She hurried forward another few steps.

Passing the two dumpsters, Isobel stepped towards the wall, her body now behind the bins. She laid down the flowers against the wall and said a little prayer that Michael would rest in peace. Here she felt closer to him that she had at the memorial. Maybe that was why she had wanted to come.

As she turned she heard a noise. Her heart raced. She gulped in shock and panic, her hands flying towards her mouth. Her bag slid off her shoulder. She lifted it up, knowing it was the only possible weapon that she had. Reassuringly, it was heavy.

"It's all right, it's all right. It's only me."

Isobel saw a figure, not tall, stooped, coming towards her, his hands moving in a calming gesture.

"I never meant to scare you. I just wanted to make sure you was alright."

"Jesus, Henry, you scared the life out of me!"

"Sorry, miss. I thought it was you going into the alley. You was kind to me and I just wanted to make sure that you was safe."

Isobel breathed out in relief. "I appreciate that, Henry."

Henry nodded. "This is a bad alley. Bad things happen here. Those two youngsters shouldn't a'been here and neither should you."

"You're right."

Henry stepped forward. "You was leaving flowers for that poor young fella, God love him."

"Yes."

"I hope that wee girl makes it."

"I hope so too, Henry."

"Maybe she'll remember what she saw and tell the police and the bad men can be caught and bad things won't happen here no more."

"True." Isobel started walking out of the alley.

"You best keep away from here. It ain't a safe place."

"No, it isn't. And thank you."

"No problem."

They had reached the end of the alley. Isobel was relieved to see the bright lights of the street and people passing by. It was amazing that twenty steps brought you to a dark and isolated world which felt so threatening.

"Maybe I'll see you again tomorrow," Henry said.

"Maybe."

"I helped you cos you was kind to me." Henry wandered away.

Isobel could hear him muttering to himself.

She watched him as he made his way back to his doorway.

And what he'd said earlier was true. If Charlene regained consciousness she might remember what had happened. Isobel sent a silent prayer that Charlene would have a good night and that tomorrow the doctors could reduce her sedation.

There were no messages from Eoin yet. Patricia, a friend Isobel had met on her first case, had sent a WhatsApp message with a photograph. Patricia and her partner Peter were on a beach in Lanzarote sipping cocktails. Isobel smiled and answered: **Looks like you're having a great time. Enjoy the sun and rest.**

Patricia had helped Isobel on cases in London and in Limerick. Isobel really missed talking things through with her but Patricia needed a holiday and Isobel was determined that she was not going to distract her from her romantic break by telling her about the case.

Isobel looked around – what now? She glanced at her watch. It was nine o'clock. It had been a very busy and harrowing day. It was time to go back to the hotel.

Isobel walked onto the Malone Road. Queen's was beautifully illuminated. She walked the short distance on to her hotel. She was tired and her head was full of snippets of conversation. She rode the lift up to her floor and opened her room door.

Her mobile rang.

Isobel dumped her bag on the bed and fished out her phone.

It was Eoin.

Heart speeding up, she answered.

"Hi, Eoin. Have you got news for me?"

"Yes, Isobel. Can we meet tomorrow?"

"Yes, but what news?"

"Let's meet tomorrow. Can you come to the Dale Hotel? It's just on the southern side of the border. It's about an hour for you to travel. I'm coming up from Limerick."

"Can't you tell me now?"

"No, Isobel. And you need to come alone. Can you meet me at the Dale at nine o'clock?"

"It sounds like you have important information."

"Yes. Can you make it? For nine?"

"Yes."

"I'll be in the restaurant."

"See you then."

"And Isobel –"

"Yes."

"Don't mention our meeting to anyone."

Isobel contacted the front desk and asked for a seven o'clock wake-up call. She messaged Jack and told him that she would meet him later in the day. Having done that, she sat down at the window and looked out over the city lights. What had Eoin found that necessitated him travelling to meet her? It must be important. One or other of the men must be known to the gardaí – otherwise why would he be coming? Why didn't he want her to say anything about the meeting? What was going on?

Isobel gave a heavy sigh. She felt exhausted. She undressed and slid under the bedclothes. Before she knew it, she was asleep. She slept heavily. When she woke the only dream she could remember was of Henry. In the dream he was holding a baby and rocking it.

Chapter 27

Friday 27th October

It was raining as Isobel left the carpark of the Park Hotel and crawled through city traffic until she could filter onto the Westlink. The traffic here moved more quickly. On the opposite side, cars were bumper to bumper as commuters queued to get into the city. It was raining and Isobel had her wipers permanently on. She shivered and cranked up the heat, turning on the fan to keep her windows from misting up.

As Isobel left Belfast behind the traffic lessened. She followed the M1 to Sprucefield, then the dual carriageway towards Dublin. She focused on her driving, noting the speed limit changing from seventy to sixty regularly, and adjusted accordingly as she kept an eye out for speed cameras.

She thought about Eoin Ryan. Initially when she met Eoin he had been antagonistic and Isobel would have been glad not to see him ever again but, as the case unfolded and Isobel got drawn more and more into it, she came to know him better. She realised that his initial antagonism was driven by his upset at what the victim had suffered.

Indeed, as the case progressed Isobel came to appreciate how much he cared for the victims and their families and also how committed he was to finding the perpetrator. Patricia had also been involved in the case and she felt that the brown-eyed, brown-haired, six-foot-two Eoin was attractive and would make a great match for Isobel. Isobel did wonder if she had really needed to contact Eoin to identify the men. Surely Detective Doran and Inspector Williams would have come through for them? Was that what she had really wanted? An excuse to talk to Eoin?

Isobel was surprised that Eoin had wanted to meet and was travelling all the way up from Limerick, a three-hour journey. And at short notice too. He would have to be up early to be at the Dale Hotel for nine o'clock. The M50 around Dublin was always busy and in the mornings especially so. Eoin must have identified the men and there must be something of concern in what he had found. Nothing else made sense.

She crossed the border. Her exit came quickly and ahead she saw the hotel. It was still raining. She pulled into the carpark and found a space as close to the entrance as possible. It was ten minutes to nine. She slipped on her coat and ran towards the hotel.

The foyer of the hotel was large with sofas and chairs grouped to allow areas for congregating. To the right was a restaurant and to the left the bar area. Isobel saw a sign for toilets and made her way there. She used the facilities and, as she washed her hands, she looked in the mirror. She fluffed the ash block at the front of her hair with her fingers. Her brown eyes were wide-set. She had a slight flush on her cheeks. Her stomach had butterflies. She pulled a face at herself. She had to admit that she was looking forward to seeing Eoin. Taking a deep breath, she hoped that she could hide all of that from him.

Isobel asked at reception and was directed to the restaurant area where breakfast was being served. As she entered the room she looked around the tables. At the very back of the room Eoin stood up and signalled to her.

She walked across the ocean of carpet towards him. He stood watching her as she approached.

"Isobel."

"Hi, Eoin."

"You can't stay out of trouble for a moment."

Isobel smiled. "No."

A man seated at the table stood up. He was as tall as Eoin but, where Eoin was slim and athletic, this man had the broad chest of someone who worked out regularly.

"Isobel, this is a friend of mine – Aaron McGuinness."

Isobel held out her hand. His handshake bore testament to the gym.

"Sorry the meeting is so early, Isobel, but I have a lot on today," said Aaron.

He had blond hair which was short and well cut. Isobel knew he had hair product shaping the front of it. In contrast Eoin needed a haircut, his brown hair starting to curl at the ends as it grew.

"Mr Important here and I went through training together at Templemore," said Eoin as they sat down, "before he headed off to the bright lights of Dublin."

Aaron's blue eyes twinkled at her. "Not so much bright lights as a higher crime rate."

Eoin laughed. "He thinks that I'm buried in some backwater, not handling serious criminals like he is."

"Well, the serial rapist that you caught in the summer, that was something – a case I would have liked to be in on myself," said Aaron. "It certainly helped your careers – yours and Sergeant Finnegan's – she got promoted to Inspector and I hear there is talk of a Sexual Crimes Unit in Limerick. I thought for sure you would be heading that but I hear the new Inspector Finnegan is going to head it up. You missed the boat there, mate."

Isobel was pleased for Alanna. She glanced at Eoin. He was frowning.

"How did you hear about the new unit?" he asked. "That was supposed to be under wraps until everything was decided."

"You know me. I traffic in information. That's why I'm a valued member of the drug squad."

"True."

Aaron turned to Isobel. "I believe you were involved in that case, Isobel. You found the first body, didn't you?"

"Michelle. Yes, I did."

"And I think you were attacked as well?"

Isobel felt her insides churn at the memory. The rapist had attacked her when she had been walking and tried to strangle her. Only that she had her walking poles and knew some self-defence she might not be here. The experience on top of her diagnosis and treatment for cancer had created anxiety. She had sought support from a psychotherapist and it had helped. All of this passed through her mind.

Aaron seemed a bit invasive, one of those people who liked to know everything, who bombarded you with questions, seeking whatever information that they could get. Ruefully Isobel admitted to herself that when she worked as a psychotherapist and also when she was involved in cases she also sought information. Maybe she and Aaron weren't that different . . . but she hoped that her style was gentler than his.

"That's right."

"But the criminal came out worse in that confrontation," said Eoin. "That was his biggest mistake, taking on Isobel. Not only did she escape but she was quick-thinking enough to get his DNA."

"Oh, I didn't realise that."

"Absolutely, and that is what started us on the road to really identifying him."

Aaron looked at Isobel. "I didn't know that you were so involved in the case."

Eoin opened his mouth to speak but Isobel cut in. "I helped out the gardaí as best I could, as any citizen would."

"It sounds a bit more than that. Is that what you're doing now in Belfast? Helping out the police?"

"Yes, but in this case one of the parents asked me to see what I could find out. My nephew knew the two students. They were in his film group. He arrived on the scene and helped to give the girl, Charlene, CPR."

"How is she?" Eoin asked.

"She's unconscious – just out of surgery."

"And your nephew? How is he?"

Isobel sighed. "It's hard to say. I think he's coping very well with all that has happened but . . ."

"How did you get these pictures?" Aaron asked.

Isobel frowned.

Aaron made a face. "I had to contact the PSNI because of jurisdictional issues. I've already spoken with Superintendent Taylor briefly. But I would like to hear it from you."

Isobel was overwhelmed that so much had already happened.

Aaron continued. "Superintendent Taylor said that the two students were attacked in an alley near a pub, the Muse, a pub frequented by students."

Isobel nodded. "Yes."

"And the pictures? When and how did they surface?"

"My nephew checked some cloud account that he shared with his film group. Charlene had uploaded the pictures before she was attacked. Do you know who the men are?"

"Yes," said Eoin. He lifted an envelope from the seat beside him and pulled out some printed pictures.

Isobel looked at the photos.

"Superintendent Taylor was surprised to hear from me," Aaron said. "The lab in Belfast had not had time to work with the pictures. He told me that the photographs of the men were taken from a distance away and there was some doubt as to whether the lab would be able to get clear pictures. But you seem to have been ahead of the lab. How did you manage that?"

"I know someone who works in computers and is very good at what he does."

"I hope he hasn't been showing the photographs around."

"No!"

"And I hope that he won't be selling them to the newspapers. That's the last thing that we need."

"I'm sure that Isobel understands the importance of keeping information confidential," said Eoin, "and I'm sure that anyone she has involved is equally trustworthy."

Aaron shifted uncomfortably. "I'm just worried about the situation and I suppose worried about Isobel getting too involved. I wouldn't want a repeat of what happened in Limerick, when she was attacked."

"Perhaps you could tell me who the men are," Isobel said sharply.

"Yes," said Eoin. "This man . . ." He pointed to the man with the cropped brown hair and the bird tattoo on his hand. "I recognised him as soon as I looked at the pictures. His name is Tim Tanner. He's a major drug dealer from Dublin known as Tim-Tan."

"A *suspected* major drug dealer," Aaron cut in.

Eoin rolled his eyes. "A *suspected* major drug dealer. A real bad guy."

"Which means what?" Isobel said. "You know he's guilty but can't prove it?"

"Exactly," Aaron said. "We've been trying to get the goods on him for ages."

"And no luck," said Eoin.

Aaron shook his head. "Just when we think we've got

a case, suddenly a witness withdraws their statement or disappears."

"Disappears?" Isobel said.

Aaron nodded somberly. "Yeah." He waited for that to sink in. "The drug world is tough and dangerous. These men are ruthless. They will do anything to protect themselves and their business. That's why I'm concerned about you, Isobel, and your nephew." He locked eyes with her. "I mean, it's great that you've found these pictures but you need to leave everything to us now."

Isobel felt a small shiver. She gestured to the pictures. "Who is the other man?"

"We suspect the baldy fella of being very high up in the biggest drug gang in Belfast," Aaron said.

"What's his name?" Isobel asked.

Aaron looked uncomfortable.

"Come on, Aaron," Eoin said. "Surely Isobel has a right to at least know that, after she brought you a picture of the two men?"

"The second man is George Simpson, called Geo."

"As in the world?"

Aaron rolled his eyes. "Who knows? He's certainly an egotistical gobshite. He's ex-paramilitary, suspected of up to ten murders, none of which can be proved." He looked away and shifted in his seat.

"What is it?" Eoin said. "Come on, Aaron, don't hold out on us."

Aaron looked at the table. "We had an undercover guy from Dublin who infiltrated Geo's gang. He was collecting evidence. We thought we were close to having a case and then suddenly our guy was gone. No one saw him again. We suspect that he was killed."

"Oh, my God!" said Isobel.

Aaron looked miserable. "He was convinced that Geo wasn't the boss."

"So who was?" Isobel asked.

Aaron shrugged. "He didn't know. We still don't know."

Eoin frowned. "And these two men meeting? What is that about? A deal? A takeover?"

"Something not good," said Aaron. "We didn't know that they were so cosy. It's definitely a worry."

"So there could be something big happening if Tim-Tan is liaising with this major player in the North?" Eoin persisted.

"There could be."

"Why would Tim-Tan be meeting with Geo? Why wouldn't he meet with the Number One, the boss?"

Aaron shrugged. "As I mentioned, getting information is virtually impossible. The identification of Geo as a major player was down to our undercover man. When he died – I mean disappeared, we lost any chance of getting more information. The gang in the North – they're running their drug-dealing like a type of pyramid selling. They're making lots of money and they have lots of power, influence even."

"You sound almost admiring," Isobel said.

Aaron shrugged. "Maybe I am a bit. Number One has taken the cell idea of the paramilitaries and has brought it into the drug world. Cells operate separately with no cross-information about each other – answerable only to the top dogs. It works. It's successful. We don't know who they are. We have no idea. Our man on the inside thought he was going to get to meet the top dog but instead he's gone." He clicked his fingers.

"So, if you could get Geo on a possible murder rap then you might get information from him about Number One," Eoin said.

"The photo certainly gives us possibilities. I need to wait and see what the task force decides is the best way to proceed but certainly there are possibilities."

There was silence for a moment as that sank in.

"There's a lot going on," Aaron continued. "Superintendent Taylor told me about the five deaths from drugs in Belfast."

"Yes, I heard about them," Isobel said. "Is that because of a takeover?"

"What makes you say that?" Aaron regarded her keenly.

"Oh, I heard someone talking. I think the police in the North are worried."

"So are the gardaí," said Eoin.

"What do you think is happening?" Isobel asked.

Aaron shrugged.

"Are gangs from the North and South amalgamating?" Eoin asked.

"That's a possibility or they could be in competition for drugs."

"So it could be a friendly meeting or an unfriendly one," Eoin said. "Either the gangs are doing a deal together or they're feuding."

"True. We're not sure. I probably shouldn't even be telling you this much."

"Alanna talked to one of the gardaí she knows," Eoin said. "This friend said that one of the biggest problems at the moment is that they think there's a leak."

"Jesus, the cat and his mother know everything!" said Aaron. "Here they are talking about a leak while at the same time revealing to another officer, someone not involved, private information. We've little chance of finding the leak with every piece of information floating around for all and sundry, including the person we're looking for, to hear it!"

Eoin said coldly, "Hardly, Aaron – this is my mate Alanna, the new inspector, we're talking about. She is not all and sundry."

"No, I didn't mean . . ." Aaron ran his hands through his hair. "OK, you're right. It's true. It looks like there is a dirty cop tipping off the drug dealers."

"*Shit*. Do you have any idea of his identity?" Eoin asked.

"We think it's someone in the North."

Eoin sat back in his chair. "What do they say?"

"The usual shit."

"Don't tell me! The North think it's one of our gardaí. And with all the political bullshit and finger-pointing, the leak doesn't get found and even if it is no one is going to admit it."

"A classic Catch-22," Aaron said.

"And in the meantime the drug dealers continue with impunity," Isobel said.

"No," Aaron said. "We're doing everything we can, I promise you that. OK – part of coming here today to meet you was to thank you for the photos."

Isobel nodded.

"But also to warn you. Drugs and drug dealers are dangerous, these ones in particular, and I want you and your nephew to stay out of it."

"I'm worried too, Isobel," Eoin said. "There's already one student dead with a second one critically ill. You've done everything you can. Please stay out of this now."

Isobel chose to ignore the issue. "So what you know is that a senior member of the gang in Belfast had a meeting with a prominent drug dealer from the South and within a day or two there were five dead dealers in Belfast. That's what you know. It also sounds like these men are guilty of killing Michael and attacking Charlene."

"We don't know that," Aaron said.

"But it's likely, given that Charlene was taking pictures of them."

"It's possible that they were responsible for the attacks."

"The murder and the attack."

"But whether we could prove that or not remains to be seen. The lad, Michael, is dead and Charlene is in hospital and, well, who knows? Is she likely to recover? Proving they were in the alley isn't proof that they were the attackers. They can say that they saw the students but that they were both fine when they left the alley. As I understand, there are no witnesses."

"Unless Charlene recovers," Isobel said.

"Often with head injuries people don't remember what happened to them and, even if Charlene did see something, getting her to testify could be difficult."

"So we most likely have found the killer or killers and now nothing is going to happen?" Isobel said.

"No, something is going to happen. The drug squad is going to follow this up and do its best to build a case. I'm meeting with Superintendent Taylor later today with a view to setting up a cross-border task force."

Isobel sat back in her chair, slightly mollified.

"I've trusted you because Eoin vouched for you. I've told you as much as I can. I beg of you, say nothing about what I've said about the leaks to anyone. This is a fraught situation but I promise you I'm doing my best and the drug squad is doing everything possible to nail these people. Maybe when we catch them we can find out what happened in the alley to Charlene and Michael. Do you understand how delicately we have to progress?" He turned to Eoin. "You understand?"

Eoin gave a slight nod of his head.

"I have to go now," Aaron said. "I need to meet up with the Superintendent and see what we can do. Please, please, not a word to anyone, and treat everything that I've told you as confidential."

Isobel nodded.

He left, stopping at the till. Then he waved and was gone.

Isobel watched him leave, feeling a weariness descending on her. She really did not know what to say, or what to do. The information she had received felt like a weight pressing her into the seat, making it impossible to move, or shift or act. What a mess!

Eoin signalled to the waitress and ordered coffee and croissants.

"I'm sorry, Isobel," he said. "I know you were hoping for more progress."

Isobel kept her head down. "I thought that we had found the attackers."

"You probably have. But they're tied to a much bigger picture. If this is a new drug alliance forming then the repercussions for a more organised and wide-spread dissemination of drugs is huge. Lots of lives are at risk."

"I do realise that, Eoin!" Isobel snapped. "But, at the same time, I don't want Michael's murderers and the men who left Charlene in a coma to get away with what they did. What happened to them could disappear in the bigger picture. That isn't right either."

Eoin nodded. "I know, Isobel, I know. But organised crime isn't like other crime. We have to trust Aaron. He knows the drug world. He knows the best way to use the evidence you've given him."

Isobel shook her head.

"You don't like him?" Eoin said.

"That's neither here nor there."

"I think it is. I can sense that you don't like him."

"It's not that I don't like him. I just don't trust him."

"Why not?"

Isobel looked towards the window. It was true. She hadn't liked Aaron and she definitely didn't trust him. Why was that? What had he said or done that had alienated her so quickly? What was it? There was a cockiness there that grated on her but . . .

She turned back to Eoin. "OK, you're right. I don't like him and I don't trust him."

Eoin nodded. "Why?"

Isobel looked away again. "I think it's because when he mentioned the rape case it felt like he wanted to be part of it, not to catch a criminal who needed to be stopped, but because he would have liked some of the publicity and the promotions. I know you and Alanna wanted to catch the rapist too, but you actually cared about the women who were being attacked and victimised. He doesn't. He wants to catch criminals to make the news and advance his career."

"Well, so long as he catches them, does it matter?"

Isobel shrugged. "Maybe it doesn't but you asked me why I had a problem with him and that's why. If it came down to it, Aaron would sacrifice justice for Michael and Charlene for a bigger career coup."

"But if the outcome is criminals in custody, I ask again, does it matter what the motivation is?"

"Maybe not but, in the rape case, if you and Alanna hadn't been the people you are, then you wouldn't have listened about the women who had been attacked and not reported it, and we wouldn't have found a way to use their information, and ultimately we wouldn't have caught him." She looked at Eoin fiercely. "You know that's true."

"OK. Yes, I can see your point – in the rape case, indeed with sex crimes in general we have a more victim-centred approach. But that's why I'm doing what I'm doing and Aaron is in the drug squad. He's very successful at what he does. He's good at it. His skill set is what makes him effective. You may not like that but that's his skill and it's valuable."

Isobel gave a small nod. "OK. I don't have to like him

or even trust him. I just want him to do his job well."

"And he will, not least because he will probably get promoted to Superintendent."

Isobel laughed. "So long as he puts away the men who attacked Michael and Charlene, I'll be happy."

The waitress arrived back with a pot of coffee and croissants, and for a while Isobel and Eoin concentrated on drinking and eating. The coffee was excellent and the croissants fresh and warm, accompanied with butter and jam.

After a while, hunger sated, Isobel asked, "Are you going to be on this drug task force?"

Eoin shook his head. "No."

"Even though it was you who brought the photographs to Aaron?"

"Yeah. I would like to have stayed in the loop but Aaron didn't think it would work."

"But if there's a leak in the North or the South, would it not be sensible for him to go for someone like you, someone he can trust, and someone who is clean?"

Eoin grinned at her. "I made that very point to him but at the moment no go. He's going to talk to the Superintendent in the North. He thinks the task force is going to be very small and very elite to stop any leaks."

"Oh, yes, I see."

"I told him to keep me in mind and he said he would let me know after the meeting in Belfast. In the meantime, he has sworn me to secrecy. And, Isobel, the danger from drug dealers is real. You heard what Aaron said about that undercover officer and you know what happened to

Michael and Charlene. You're messing with serious criminals here. They would have no qualms about killing you or your nephew. You've done enough now. You've found a link to a major drug deal. You have photographic evidence of it and it places those men in the alley with Michael and Charlene. You have most likely found the murderers. The Garda and the PSNI have all of that information now. Let them take it forward. I'm deadly serious. I want you to stay out of the investigation. Leave it to Aaron and his task force. I don't want anything happening to you."

Isobel felt her cheeks flush slightly. She wasn't sure but Eoin's concern seemed personal. She felt a little flame of excitement in her tummy.

Eoin shifted in his seat. "Aaron wanted me to make it very clear to you about the dangers inherent in the situation."

Isobel felt the flame flicker and go out. "Aaron asked you to warn me off?"

Eoin shifted in his seat again. "Yeah. He thought you might listen to me because we know each other. He doesn't want any more civilians killed or injured."

Isobel gulped at her coffee. "No, of course not. It would look bad for him."

"It's not just him. Alanna also asked me to speak to you."

Isobel stared. "Why would Alanna warn me off?"

"She saw the picture of Tim-Tan. She knows about him too. When she saw him, she told me to get you out of the situation and that was before we even knew who Geo was. She wanted me to emphasise the dangers to you. We all want you to be safe. Collette too."

Collette was Eoin's sister. She and Isobel had some good conversations during the last case, some about the case and some about more personal issues.

"Collette suggested that when you get back to Limerick we all get together to celebrate Alanna's promotion. She even suggested that Patricia and Malcolm should come over from England."

Isobel felt a pang of longing to be surrounded by all of those friendly faces. "OK."

"OK, you won't get involved?"

Isobel nodded.

"Good. When are you back in Limerick?"

"I'm not sure. Jack is doing alright, I think. I'll probably hang on for a few more days to make sure of that and also to see how Charlene is."

Eoin nodded. "Give me a ring when you get back and we'll set up the celebration. And, Isobel, you've done good on this case too. Getting the photo, you know, you've done a lot."

Isobel nodded miserably.

"I had better be going." He stood up.

Isobel rose. "Me too."

"It was good to see you, Isobel."

Isobel searched his face but could only see the concern of a friend.

"You too, Eoin. See you in Limerick."

He smiled. "Soon."

"Soon."

Isobel stopped off in the toilets once again as she left the hotel. She looked in the mirror. Her eyes were dull, the dullness of realising that while you like someone a lot they see you as an acquaintance, a colleague. The day which had started out with so much excitement and promise felt flat.

Chapter 28

Isobel drove along the motorway back towards Belfast. There was a steady stream of traffic in both directions. As she drove along she felt the weight of all that she had heard. There didn't seem to be anything more that she could do.

She definitely had not warmed to Aaron. He seemed to be moving in a dangerous and treacherous world and he seemed to relish that. He was also, he had admitted, somewhat admiring of the drug organisation in the North and the mysterious Number One. Who were they? She thought of Róisín Magill. She had hinted at a drug organisation that was far-reaching and ruthless. Aaron had said a similar thing – an efficient gang with a mysterious leader. What more could Isobel do in the case?

Back in Belfast, Isobel met Jack for lunch at the Red Rose Café. She ordered the roast red pepper soup with sourdough and Jack had carrot and lentil soup.

Despite her misgivings and the warnings of confidentiality,

she felt that she owed it to Jack to be fully honest with him. She recounted all that she had heard along with her impressions. They sat in silence for a few moments.

Isobel said then, "Why on earth would these two major drug dealers meet in that laneway?"

"The only reason I can think of is that the drug gang might be centred around the student area and that is a quiet place where nine times out of ten no one would see them or pass any remarks."

"True. There was very little chance of anyone seeing them and even if they were seen what would a bunch of students know about a Northern paramilitary and a Dublin drug dealer?"

"Exactly."

"But what if, as Róisín Magill said, the drug gang has a particular interest in students? What if this Number One is extending his particular style of dealing into the South? There are plenty of campuses."

"You mean the meeting was like a business takeover or more like a franchise sale – here's how we do it, it works well for us – so why don't you buy our business model?"

"Very funny but what if that isn't so far from the truth? I actually think that you're on to something there, Jack. I was so blown out of the water by Aaron's talk of leaks and of task forces that I missed something very important." Isobel nodded. "The location."

"You mean Michael and Charlene were in the wrong place at the wrong time."

"Yes. And, if the Muse is so squeaky clean, what were two major drug dealers doing so near it?"

Isobel could feel her heart pounding. She knew there was something important here, something that she couldn't fully see. Her mind started to riffle through all the facts and information that she had. She saw Jack sitting looking at her, his face intrigued and very much interested. In an instant she wished that she had told him nothing. She could feel the weight of what Eoin, Alanna and, she reluctantly added Aaron, had been saying to her about danger, about keeping herself and her nephew out of it. She looked at Jack's face and wished with all of her heart that he was not involved and was safe in classes or in the library. But then she realised that that wouldn't keep him safe. Michael and Charlene had been just doing a project and had stumbled into something. Jack wasn't safe, nor were any of the students.

"Jack, you have to keep everything I've told you completely confidential."

He nodded. "I know that. I do understand all that you've told me. I know how dangerous all of this is and I know not to say anything."

Isobel shook her head. "Sorry."

"I have to get back to lectures."

"Of course. Can you just send me on all the pictures from the alley that Nicky gave you? I want to have another look at them."

"Sure. No problem." Jack worked on his phone. "You have them. What are you going to do?"

Before Isobel could reply her phone rang. She glanced at it. "It's Detective Doran." She answered.

"Isobel, could I meet up with you? I'm not sure what's

going on. I want to talk to you about the photographs you gave us."

Isobel could feel her heart starting to accelerate. Was Damien Doran a possible source of the leak? Was it a good idea to meet him? How could she know?

"Isobel, are you there? Please, can we meet up for a chat as soon as possible?"

"Just a second. I can't talk here. I'll ring you in a few minutes." She finished the call. "It's Detective Doran. He wants to meet about the photographs."

Jack frowned. "Why?"

"Could he be the leak? I don't know if meeting him is a good idea."

"It will look stranger if you don't meet him. We've always sent him on any information. Meet him. See what he wants and say very little."

Isobel nodded. The meeting with Aaron seemed to have driven her a bit crazy. She took a deep breath. She needed to act normally.

"Meet somewhere public where there are lots of people," Jack suggested. "That will make you feel safer."

Isobel nodded. She called Doran back.

She cleared her throat. "Sorry about that. I can meet you now if you want. I'm in a coffee shop on Botanic Avenue, the Red Rose Café."

"That would be great. I'll be there in ten minutes."

She hung up.

"You look a bit spooked," Jack said. "Do you want me to stay?"

Isobel smiled. "No, no. I'm fine. You're right, I am

spooked but I need to calm down. I'll be fine. I'll meet him. You go to your lecture."

"Are you sure?"

"I'm sure. Temporary panic. All gone now."

Jack smiled at her. "You'll be fine. Ring me later and let me know what he wanted."

Isobel grinned. "I will."

Jack left and Isobel ordered a fresh coffee. This was her fourth one today. If she wanted to sleep tonight then this needed to be the last one.

Chapter 29

Doran appeared in the doorway of the coffee shop and looked around. His movements were jumpy and agitated. Isobel waited for him to notice her. He walked towards her, looking around him as he did. He ordered a coffee and Isobel indicated that she didn't need anything. He said nothing but checked his phone and then turned it off. The waitress delivered his coffee. He added sugar and milk and sipped it. Eventually he looked at Isobel.

"I shouldn't even be here. I'm not sure why I am."

Isobel could feel his distress, his agitation, his fear. "What's wrong? What's happened?"

Doran sat back and shook his head. "I'm not sure what's going on and I don't know what to do."

There was no doubt about his genuine upset. "Do you think that I can help you in some way? Is that why you called me?" Despite her own earlier misgivings and anxieties, she could feel herself calming in the face of his distress.

Doran rubbed his face with both hands. "I suppose I thought I could trust you because you brought the enhanced photograph of the men in the alley to us. I believe you're genuinely trying to find out who killed Michael." He fell silent.

Isobel could feel her anxiety going up. Only this morning she had been talking to Eoin and Aaron about leaks and they were telling her to stay out of the investigation and now here was a police officer on the investigation drawing her back into the case. What was going on? She could feel a light film of sweat starting at her hairline. She needed to stay calm and see what he wanted.

"Have you found out something about the men in the alley?"

Doran looked at her sharply. "I don't know who to trust anymore."

Isobel did not know what to say. She knew that all that Eoin and Aaron had told her was confidential. She needed to forget that she knew anything about drugs and dealers and leaks.

"I don't know what to say to you. Something has obviously upset you. Do you want to tell me what it is? I presume that's why you asked to meet?"

Doran nodded. He took a deep breath. "When you gave me the enhanced pictures last night I immediately called Inspector Williams. I couldn't reach him and left a voice mail for him about the photographs. I also sent a text message. I received no immediate answer. I waited a while and when he didn't get back to me I decided that time was of the essence and I took the photographs to the lab myself. I wanted them put through the program for facial recognition. Before we did that I happened to mention that the lab had the hazy photographs that you had given us." He paused. "And the lab guy was adamant that they didn't. I asked him to check and when he did there was no record of Inspector Williams passing on the photographs from Charlene's camera."

He looked up at Isobel and she nodded to him to continue.

"I asked if there might be another lab where they could have been sent and he said that sometimes there was a private lab that did specialist work and also helped out when they were busy. That lab is called SpeedAn. I realised that they probably sent the photographs there and apologised to the lab technician. He knew that I had made a bit of a balls-up and assured me there was no harm done, and that he would say nothing."

Isobel nodded.

"I checked the computer to see if there was anything connected with the case at the SpeedAn lab and I couldn't find any reference. I didn't know what to think. It was late and so I went home. Inspector Williams rang me at nearly two this morning. I didn't hear the phone. He left a message telling me to tell no one about the photos and to bring everything to him this morning." He shrugged. "I met him and gave him everything. He told me that he recognised George Simpson immediately. He also said that Superintendent Taylor had been on to him. He wanted to know how officers in the South got the photographs?"

Isobel blushed.

Doran looked at her. "No, I think it's good. A Southern drug squad officer is meeting with the Superintendent.

Inspector Williams told me a task force would be taking over and that I was to forget about everything to do with the case as they wouldn't welcome any interference."

"Oh."

Doran shrugged. "Yes. It sounded almost like a warning. And maybe if I had left it alone . . . but something didn't feel right."

Isobel nodded.

"I contacted SpeedAn and asked about the photographs submitted to them and when they checked their records they hadn't been. There was no record of the police submitting anything to them. I made the excuse that it must have gone to our own labs and got off the phone but . . ."

Isobel felt her heart skip a beat. "So what are you saying?"

"That as far as I can tell the photographs weren't submitted for analysis to any lab by us, which means that –" he put his hand to his forehead, "which means that there's a cover-up, which means that more than likely my boss, Inspector Williams, is corrupt. And if he is, and has got away with it, then there may be others. I don't know what to do and I don't know who I can trust."

Isobel certainly knew about that. Right now she didn't even know if she could trust Detective Doran.

"Was it you who gave the photographs to the officers in the South?" he asked.

Isobel bit her lip. "I don't know if I really want to answer that."

"Well, if it was you, I'm grateful to you. George Simpson,

or Geo, is a dangerous man. I'm sure that he or his companion killed Michael." He shook his head. "I really don't know what to do. This was important evidence and it was suppressed. If you hadn't had someone work on the pictures and then sent them to someone in the South, this information wouldn't even be known and these two men would have got away with it."

Doran seemed to be saying all the right things and, unless he was a consummate liar, Isobel believed him.

"I'm not even sure why I'm telling you all of this."

They sat in silence. Isobel could feel a struggle inside her. She wanted to believe him, to trust him, but something held her back. She hated this, not knowing who was trustworthy. It was so much easier when there was a villain and you were trying to catch him. The good guys and the bad guys were easily and clearly defined. But here things were different. Everything felt murky and grey. The lines weren't clear. There were people in the police North and South of the border in disguise, masquerading as catchers-of-villains but actual villains themselves. She was glad that she had people like Eoin and Alanna to turn to, to trust.

She looked at Doran. He seemed sad, drained, diminished, the shadow of betrayal had dampened his enthusiasm and his energy.

"I think you should take Inspector Williams's advice and be really careful," she said. "If he, or someone else, is suppressing information you may be in danger by just knowing about that. I don't want something to happen to you. Please be careful."

Doran nodded sadly. "I know." He pulled a piece of paper from his inside pocket. "I've written down everything I've told you and signed it."

Isobel went pale.

"Just in case something happens to me," he said.

"Oh God."

"I want you to keep this. In fact, you could share it with whatever gardaí you know if you judge it the right thing to do."

This was serious. "Detective Doran –"

He sat up straighter. "I'm not giving up or anything. I'm just being careful."

Isobel nodded.

He stood up. "Thanks for all your help. You've done a real service to Michael and Charlene."

"Keep in touch, detective."

"Damien, please. And I will."

"Maybe the task force will find out what happened to the photographs."

Doran shrugged. "I doubt it. Now that the men are identified no one will be interested in how the pictures were suppressed – that will all be covered over."

"I see."

"Bye, Isobel."

"Bye, Damien."

She watched him walk away, his head down, his footsteps slow, a forlorn figure.

Isobel sat a few moments and then walked out to the street. The whole day had made her weary. She caught a taxi back to her hotel.

Chapter 30

Upstairs in her hotel room Isobel sat on the bed. She thought about Inspector Doran – Damien – and the piece of paper he had given her. He believed he was in danger.

She thought for a minute then picked up her phone.

"Eoin, hi, are you back in Limerick?"

"Almost. Is everything alright?"

"I've just had a meeting with Detective Doran. He's the junior officer we have been liaising with. We gave him a copy of the enhanced photographs yesterday, before I contacted you. He took them to the police lab to go through their system. While he was there he asked about the originals and it turned out that the police lab never got them. They suggested that maybe the shots had been sent to a private lab that the police sometimes use. He checked with them and again the photos weren't submitted. He thinks his boss, Inspector Williams, might have suppressed the pictures. I met him and he's distraught."

"Are you saying that Detective Doran thinks that his boss Inspector Williams is corrupt?"

"He's beginning to wonder about that, yes."

"Did anyone else know about the photos? Did Doran or Williams show them to anyone else?"

"I don't know. They're the only ones I know about."

"It might be worth asking Doran if anyone else knew about the pictures. There can't be many but it's best to be sure before you jump to any conclusions."

"OK, I'll ask him."

"I suppose I should let Aaron know about this. He might be able to keep an eye on things, or find out something about it when he's up in Belfast."

"I don't know about that. I worry about putting Damien in danger."

"Damien?"

"Detective Doran."

"Oh, it's Damien now, is it?"

"He was really upset, really frightened and very disillusioned. I feel sorry for him. He seemed to care and he was doing his best to solve the case and now he's in the middle of a cover-up. He even gave me a signed statement of all that he told me in case something happens to him."

"God, that is serious. Isobel, what a mess you've landed into. I wish you were miles away from all of that. Drug dealers are dangerous but bent cops are lethal – they have everything to lose."

"I'll be careful but I agree that this is awful. I thought it was bad when Aaron started talking about organised crime but this corruption is worse."

"Unfortunately, Isobel, they often go hand in hand." Eoin took a noisy breath. "OK. Find out from Damien who else knew about the photographs. I'll ask Aaron why Belfast was so slow to identify the men."

"Don't mention Detective Doran or, I don't know, maybe the labs and what Damien found. It might put him in danger or draw attention if Aaron asks too many questions."

"I won't mention any names or talk about the labs, just a general query about how tardy Belfast was and see what he can find out. OK?"

"Yeah. OK. Thanks, Eoin."

"Where are you staying, Isobel? I hope you're safe."

"I'm in the Park Hotel. It seems safe."

"OK. Keep your eyes open, alright?"

"Yes."

"Bye."

"Bye."

Isobel paused a moment then dialled Damien's number. "Hi, it's Isobel again."

"I can't really talk now."

"No problem. I spoke to Eoin, the garda in Limerick, and he asked who else knew about the photographs. Was it just you and Williams or did anyone else know? I suppose it's a way of narrowing down who could be involved. But please, please, be careful."

"Got it. I'll bring the milk when I'm coming off duty. See you later."

Isobel laughed. "Careful, like that."

"Bye."

Isobel hung up and leaned back against the headboard. Obviously, Damien felt in danger. The signed statement showed that but if the call they had just had was anything to go by, he was taking precautions. She hoped they would be enough.

She felt completely out of her depth. Maybe she was in over her head this time and it was time to think about leaving it to Aaron and his task force. She looked out of the window. At least here in her hotel room she felt safe and secure.

She let her mind float for a while as she calmed down. Then, remembering the pictures she had asked Jack to forward to her, she opened her phone. He had sent her lots of pictures that Michael had taken. She pulled out her computer and looked at Michael's emailed pictures on the bigger screen. He had certainly spent time checking out the alley.

Isobel flicked through the different shots. Some of them were much brighter than others. Why was that? Had he tried other phones or a camera? That seemed unlikely if he knew Charlene was getting a special camera. Surely he would have waited. So what was the difference? Isobel went back to the first pictures again. She checked the date. The pictures were taken on a Saturday night and the alley was very dark. Moving forward, there were photos taken the following Friday night and again the pictures were dark. More nights and pictures followed, then there it was, a picture where the light seemed brighter. Isobel studied the photo. At the back, a penumbra illuminated the alley. She checked the night, a Monday, the 9th of October, two weeks before Michael was killed.

She scrolled on. Michael had taken pictures on

Tuesday and Wednesday night and they were dark. She kept scrolling through the weekend. Michael seemed to have been out taking pictures in the alley every night. That seemed a bit strange, a bit intense. Why would he suddenly have gone to the alley every night?

Isobel scrolled on to the night of Monday 16th. Again Michael had taken pictures of the alley and once again they were brighter with the same halo of light. For the next week Michael went every other night to the alley. The additional lighting was absent. He died on Monday 23rd.

Isobel stood up and paced around the room. It seemed that Michael had noticed the light in the alley on a Monday night. He had then gone every night and there was no additional lighting until the following Monday. Obviously the light was significant. It only seemed to be there on Mondays. Obviously Michael thought that the light would help their filming hence he went with Charlene to the alley on Monday night. Or was it that he had noticed something else on those Monday nights? She swallowed.

She knew this discovery was important but now, apart from Eoin and Jack, she didn't know who she could tell. There seemed no one to trust. One thing was sure though, she needed to look at the alley again.

Chapter 31

Isobel decided to walk to the Muse as walking always cleared her head, reduced her stress and improved her mood. It was four o'clock and the evening was getting cooler. Students were rushing to and from Queen's and their cheerful and exuberant chattering seemed so alien to the dark deeds that had brought Isobel to Belfast and the murky miasma of drugs, crime and betrayal that had taken over her world.

Her mobile rang.

"Tony here, Isobel."

"Hello, Tony. Is Charlene doing OK?"

"Yes, she is. No dramatic improvement but the doctors are still hopeful, thank God. Can you and Jack meet me at six in the Europa bar?"

"Yes, that's fine. I'll text Jack."

"See you then."

Isobel stopped in the shop on Botanic Avenue and bought another bunch of flowers. She hoped this would act as a cover for being in the alley. She searched her phone and found the torch app.

She made her way past the Muse entrance and into the alley. There was still some daylight but it was fading. There seemed to be no one around. Isobel looked behind to see if she could see Henry but there was no sign of him.

She made her way down the alley. She passed the two dumpsters and the area where she and others had placed their tributes. She held on to her fresh bouquet in case she encountered anyone.

At the door in the pub wall she checked for an outside light but there was none. Looking back up the alley and thinking of the pictures, the light seemed to be behind the men. She continued towards the gate at the end. There were no street lamps down here. She looked at the old wall and gateway. There was no light over the gateway. Stepping back, she looked into the yard behind and saw there was an old pole with a dilapidated spotlight on it. It looked like it had come out of the Ark. Isobel turned through three hundred and sixty degrees. There seemed to be nothing else that could act as a light source. She took out her phone and photographed the old spotlight. That seemed to be the only possible source of light in the pictures. And if it was, then maybe while the light looked defunct it wasn't, and maybe the derelict yard wasn't so derelict.

Isobel moved back to the gate. She remembered the green paint on the gatepost. She shone the light from her phone on it. The shade of green was like sage. She looked up along the alley again. It was getting darker but she could see no one. She rummaged in her bag and found an old envelope. Taking out her nail scissors, she used it to scrape off some of the paint, catching it in the envelope. She almost laughed at herself. Who did she think she was, Kay Scarpetta?

Hastily she tucked the envelope into her bag and, cradling her flowers, moved back up the alley. She gently laid the bouquet and said a quick prayer for Michael and another for Charlene's recovery. Ahead she could see the lights of the street and she hurried towards them.

Once again out on Botanic Avenue, she turned towards the city centre and started walking.

As she passed the Red Rose Café she heard a voice: "Can't you leave that place alone?"

Isobel jumped. "Henry, is that you?"

Henry sat up in his doorway. "You're as bad as that boy Michael – coming here every night. Bloody fool. Can't none of you leave well enough alone?"

"Henry, let me buy you a cup of tea. I want to ask you something – to do with that light at the end of the alley?"

He stared and then frowned. "Don't you go getting interested in no light."

Isobel could feel a stir of excitement. "I'll get you a cup of tea."

"And some fish and chips?"

Isobel smiled. "OK. But I don't think the café does that?"

Henry stood up. "This way."

Isobel let Henry direct her down the street to a takeaway. There was a picnic bench outside. Henry sat down and Isobel went inside and ordered the fish and chips. She brought him out a cup of tea then went back in to wait for the food. It seemed as if Henry knew something about the light. The challenge would be getting him to talk.

Isobel carried out the fish and chip supper and a cup of tea for herself. From her pocket she withdrew sachets of salt, vinegar and ketchup.

Henry smiled happily. "This is great. A real treat."

Isobel felt ashamed. Henry was experiencing such pleasure in this meal and she was doing this to get information. She sat at the picnic table and sipped her tea while Henry enjoyed his food. It didn't take him long to finish. He pulled out a roll-up, lit up and sighed happily.

Isobel let the silence lengthen. Henry finished his tea.

"More tea, Henry?"

He nodded.

Isobel brought more tea.

She sat down again. She decided on a direct approach.

"Henry, I'm wondering what Michael was looking for when he kept coming back to the alley. It started out about his film project but it may be he realised something was happening, maybe in that yard at the back."

Henry shifted uncomfortably in his seat. "He shouldn't have got involved. And that poor girl he dragged into it. He didn't know what he was messing with."

"What do you mean, Henry?"

"I mean there are things that go on, things that you shouldn't meddle in."

"What things?"

"I dunno."

Isobel was sick of warnings from everyone. She wanted information, information about what the hell was happening. "Henry, I am so sick of everybody talking about the danger and no one doing anything about it. Jesus, one boy is dead and Charlene almost died and nobody is saying or doing anything."

"Do you think that anyone would listen to the likes of me? Do you think that anyone would take seriously anything that I reported?"

Isobel was brought up short. That was true. "I would listen. I want to know. Something is very wrong. Please help me."

"Why d'you think I been watching you? I can see that you're interested and you care. But that's not enough. That's no good against the people doing all of this and the police, well, I could'ne trust them."

He *did* know something was going on.

"Doing all of *what*, Henry?"

"Oh, I couldn't be sayin'."

"Just help me understand, Henry, and then I can see what we can do."

"If I tell you, you might be in danger like Michael. And I don't want anyone to know what I know and what I sees because then I might be found dead in my sleeping bag."

"I understand that, Henry. Please tell me and I won't tell anyone where I got the information. I swear."

Henry cradled his cup of tea. "I'll tell you what I know but it won't do any good. It's too late for Michael and . . ."

"Just tell me."

Henry focused on a patch of the pavement. "I've been sleeping in my doorway for a few years now. I watch everything that happens." He looked up at Isobel.

She smiled. "I believe that."

He grinned. "It took me a while to figure things out but most Monday nights, during the night when the pub is closed and shut down, a van drives down that laneway and the gate is open and it goes into that ol' yard."

Isobel could hardly breathe. This was tremendous.

Henry glanced up at her again.

She nodded encouragingly.

"Those nights, the Monday nights, that's when that light goes on. It's usually on by ten, ten-thirty, but no van comes 'til the pub is closed and there ain't anyone about. It stays an hour and then it leaves."

"But there was no delivery at the time Michael and Charlene were attacked."

"Like I said, it was too early for the van to come. That wouldn't be until the pub was closed."

"What about the men in the laneway? Had you seen them before?"

Henry stilled. "What men?"

"I know there were two men in the alley just before Michael and Charlene were attacked. In fact, those were the men that probably did it."

"Why you asking me about men? You got someone who saw them, why are you talking to me 'bout this? I don't want to get involved with no bad men."

"Henry, had you seen men in the alley before?"

"Do you know who you're messing with? I'd be like Michael if they thought that I see'd what they were doing."

Isobel leaned forward on the picnic table. "Henry, just tell me what you know – for Michael."

"You can't tell the police, not anyone."

"No one will know that you've spoken to me. Come on, tell me about the men."

"Well, one of them men is a big baldy bastard. He's from Belfast and he's dangerous. You don't want to draw him on yeh. He's been coming to that yard off and on since I ever been sleeping in my place. The other one, I heard him, he's got a Southern accent. I only see'd him a few times. And only recently."

"How did you see so much, Henry?"

"There's no one pays much attention to a man in a doorway."

"But how could you see them from your doorway?"

"Sometimes I be ramblin' around or pokin' in that bin in the alley to see if there's anythin' useful or food still fresh – or I stagger around like a drunk and they just think I'm some silly old man. But I see'd 'em, that big baldy fella from Belfast and that Southern fella. They usually come everybody's gone, but poor Michael and Charlene was in the alley at the wrong time. They didn't even know they were in danger, just fussing with some silly pictures and then . . ." Henry covered his eyes with his hands. "Too late, nothing I could do."

"But you know what happened, Henry."

"It don't make no difference, girl. I can't go to the police. I can't be in court. You know that would never happen. I'd be dead long afore it made any difference."

"Tell me which of the men hit Michael and Charlene."

"I'm never making no statement to anyone."

"Just tell me."

"It was that other fella, the Southern one. He saw them two with the camera and he went up to them and it was all over in a second. The baldy fella he was real mad with the Southern fella. They carried them kids behind the bin and I scuttled back to my doorway. I watched but I didn't see 'em come out of the alley and after a while I went back and looked but there was no sign of 'em."

Isobel felt a cold weight in her stomach. There it was, what they had suspected, but she felt no relief. Henry himself had told her clearly the dangers physically and legally. She thought of Aaron's fellow officer who had disappeared. She might know the truth of what happened but justice seemed far away.

"Only that the young guy went for a pee and saw them and then the other students came, I reckon the two bad bastards woulda got rid of the kids. But I don't know where they were by that time. Maybe they'd slipped into the yard or maybe they just scarpered."

"You're probably right – they would have got rid of the evidence."

"Course I am. I'm glad I told you but that's all I'm doing, you hear me?"

Isobel nodded.

Henry rose and shambled off into the night, his head down, shoulders hunched forward. He moved along the street close to the buildings, almost trying to melt into them, making no eye contact and drawing little attention.

Isobel remained where she was seated. She felt powerless, sad, overwhelmed and, she realised, afraid. All the warnings about drug dealers had sunk in. What could she do? She felt alone. Tears came to her eyes. Fear, overwhelmed by threat, alone, she knew this place. She had been there before. The only way she knew not to sink into the darkness was to find something that she could do. But what could she do here, in this situation where the threat was external not internal? She might not have evidence, or a statement to bring to anyone but she certainly had new information. How could she use it? Perhaps she could find out more about the old yard and what was going on there, as discreetly as possible. Maybe something that would link Geo and Tim-Tan to something criminal. At least for now that was a step she could take and maybe something else would come to her.

She took a deep breath and glanced at her watch. She realised that she was going to be late and hurried towards the Europa hotel.

Chapter 32

As Isobel arrived outside the door of the Europa she heard a text arrive. **Where are u? We are in the bar waiting.** It was from Jack.

Isobel had hardly time to think. Everything that Henry had told her needed to be thought about before she mentioned it to anyone, so for now she needed to shelve it. There was also, of course, all that Eoin and Aaron had told her confidentially. All in all, it seemed as if she needed to keep her mouth shut and listen.

As Isobel entered Jack raised a hand. He was sitting in a booth with Tony and a woman. Isobel made her way over. As she approached she realised that the woman was Joan. She was beautifully dressed and was smiling. Tony stood out of the booth as Isobel arrived.

"Isobel, Isobel, great to see you. What will you have to drink?"

Isobel looked around at the smiling faces. She could feel her heart lifting. They must have positive news, thank God.

"A glass of Sauvignon Blanc, please."

Tony signalled a waiter and gave the order.

Isobel took off her coat and slid into the seat beside Jack.

"Hello, Isobel. I'm Joan."

"Good to meet you."

Joan reached over and shook Isobel's hand, smiling.

"You have good news about Charlene, I take it?" Isobel asked.

"We have indeed!" Tony said.

The waiter arrived with Isobel's drink.

Tony raised his glass, smiling at his wife. "*To our little girl, Charlene!* She's a fighter, thank God."

Joan leant in towards her husband, raising her glass at the same time. "*To Charlene!*"

Isobel and Jack raised their glasses, echoing "*To Charlene!*"

Isobel waited until everyone had taken a sip and then said, "What has happened?"

Tony gestured to Joan.

"The doctors reduced Charlene's sedation today," she said, "and she is breathing for herself, not on the ventilator."

"And when we talked to her she squeezed our hands." Tony's eyes filled up and he pulled out his white handkerchief to dab them.

"It's still early days but those are good signs, and the brain scans are looking good." Joan's voice was full of relief and hope.

"The consultant is very happy with her progress," Tony said. "She needs to rest and sleep a lot which is normal for a brain injury. Hopefully tomorrow she might open her eyes."

"And please God she will have all her faculties," said Joan. "The doctor isn't sure but is hopeful."

"Oh, that is such good news!" said Isobel.

Joan finished her drink and stood up. "I'm going for a rest. I know Tony wants to talk to you so I'll leave you."

Tony watched his wife leave the bar then turned to Isobel.

"OK, what is the latest on the two men? Are they in the system? Do the police know who they are?"

"Yes, they do," Jack said. "Tell him, Isobel."

"One of the men is a known drug dealer from Belfast, the other is from Dublin."

"They've arrested them?"

"Not yet."

"What?" Tony's face tightened. "Why not? They need to at least talk to them!"

"Well, both of the men are involved in the drug world," Isobel explained, "but the police North and South didn't know that the men were associates. The photograph of the men together has caused a bit of a furore."

Tony frowned.

"And a cross-border task force is being set up. They're investigating now."

"But surely they're bringing the men in for questioning?"

"I'm sure they will. I think they're concerned about what they can prove."

"*What?*"

"They can prove the men were in the alley but they

may not be able to prove that they were responsible for the attacks. They need enough evidence to get a conviction. I'm sure the forensic people are processing everything."

"Are you saying that the pictures aren't enough?"

"I'm saying that they need to *prove* the case, not just know who did it – so the more evidence the better."

Tony nodded but clenched his hands and sat there, brooding.

Isobel glanced at Jack who was frowning, staring into his drink. This was truly difficult.

She thought of Henry who had witnessed the attack. His testimony would be proof. Somehow she needed to get him to make a statement but, as he rightly pointed out himself, he was vulnerable both in court and before it. She wondered if proving the case hung on the evidence of a homeless man. It was possible that if Charlene recovered she might remember the attackers but often with head injuries that wasn't the case. Aaron had suggested that he would have to get one of the men to turn against the other. Maybe that was the best way to go.

Isobel chewed her lip. "There is something else that we need to consider."

"What?" Tony asked.

"While Charlene was unconscious and fighting for her life she posed no threat to whoever attacked her but, if she recovers consciousness and if she remembers the attack and can identify the perpetrator, then she is a very important witness. Her testimony would convict a murderer."

"That's true, Isobel!" said Jack.

"But she may not remember anything," Tony said.

"I know. But best not tell anyone that she's been coming out of the coma. Best keep Charlene's progress private."

"You're saying that she's in danger?"

"I'm saying that these are ruthless men. Certainly the man from Dublin, Tim-Tan, has evaded conviction because witnesses haven't testified or have changed their story. The less they know about Charlene and how she is doing the better. While she is unconscious she is no immediate threat to anyone." Even as she spoke she could see the flaw in her argument: even unconscious, Charlene posed a threat as she could recover and speak at any moment. She quailed at the thought of pointing this out to Tony.

"I think I should contact the police and see if they can organise protection for Charlene," said Tony.

"*No,*" said Isobel.

"*Don't,*" said Jack.

Tony drew back. "Why not? Surely the police can protect Charlene, that's their job."

Isobel chewed on her lip. "Yes but, number one, we don't know if Charlene will remember anything and, number two, the less people who know she is recovering consciousness the better."

"Including the police?"

Isobel swallowed. "I think it's prudent not to trust anyone at the moment."

"Not even the police?" said Tony. "Isn't that a bit paranoid?"

"No, it's not. I'm trying to get you to understand how careful we need to be. Better safe than sorry."

Tony clasped his hands together and leaned forward on the table. "You *know* something. What did your Garda friend tell you?"

Isobel met his eye. "Enough to make me wary, very wary."

Tony rubbed his face with his hand. He started to speak and then stopped. He took a deep breath. "This seems unreal. It's like something out of a book."

"I'm sorry."

"There's no harm in being extra careful," said Jack.

Tony looked from one to the other. After a few moments he asked, "Should I hire protection for Charlene?"

"I don't know if the hospital would allow that," said Isobel.

"But someone should be with Charlene all the time," said Jack. "Either you or Joan or another family member."

"Yes, and it should begin from now," said Isobel. "The more time passes, the more nervous the perpetrators will be – afraid she may at any moment recover consciousness."

"My God, you're right," Tony said, shocked.

"Is there anybody with her now?" Jack asked.

"Yes, my sister is."

"Good," said Isobel. "And you need to make sure everyone is extra-vigilant."

"You're scaring me."

"I'm sorry," said Isobel. "I just want you to make sure Charlene is safe. And for me one of the simplest ways of doing that is keeping her progress quiet."

Tony went pale. The lines of worry on his forehead deepened. "OK. I can see some sense in what you are saying. But if those men were arrested and off the street then she would be safe."

Isobel wished that were true but didn't believe it. She remembered Aaron's stories of witnesses being intimidated and disappearing and the reality of dealing with a crime organisation was beginning to sink in. Even if the two men were arrested, their friends and fellow criminals could act to protect them. It seemed a bit like Hercules dealing with the many-headed Hydra.

"Keep the good news of Charlene's progress to the immediate family," said Isobel. "That means no posting about it on social media. And you need to talk to Joan and make sure that she does the same. To everyone else who asks me I've just said no change."

Tony gave a tight nod. "If that's what it takes to protect my daughter, I can do that. In a way I hope she doesn't remember." He sat, his spirit subdued.

He seemed smaller to Isobel. The strain of what was happening was taking its toll.

"But, Tony, as I suggested ..."

She hesitated.

"There's more?" Tony asked wearily.

"Keep it as vague as possible with the police too."

"You really don't trust them at all?"

"I'm just not sure yet which ones to trust."

"OK, Isobel. But how are these men going to get prosecuted if the police can't be trusted?"

"With difficulty."

"You'll stay on the case. You might be my only hope."

Isobel nodded. "There are still some things to follow up."

"OK. And Isobel, you and Jack need to be careful too."

"Yes."

"I'll be in touch." Tony stood and walked away, his shoulders hunched.

Jack exhaled loudly. "That was tough."

"I know but what could I do? I had to make sure they were careful."

"I know."

Later, as Isobel and Jack walked along Botanic Avenue, they came to the Muse again. Once again it was lit up and there were people sitting outside in the covered area. Isobel felt Jack hesitate.

"Why don't we go in for a drink?" she said.

Jack needed no encouragement.

The bar was crowded. One of the tables was particularly crowded and noisy. The young people appeared to be playing a drinking game with much laughter and downing of drinks. At the centre of the hoopla was a young man with red hair. She remembered that he had been here the last time she was in the Muse. Obviously he was a regular. She heard Jack's name being called. Some people at another table were waving him over.

Isobel said, "Go on. I'll have a drink at the bar."

She made her way through the tables and took a seat at the bar. A young woman she hadn't seen before took her order.

"You're busy tonight," Isobel said when she returned with the drink.

"Every night."

"Are you a student?"

The young woman smiled. "Yes. I work here a couple of nights a week."

"I suppose the money comes in handy for college."

"Yes."

"I'm Isobel."

"Cherry."

"That's a lovely name."

Cherry grinned. "Apparently my mum craved cherries when she was pregnant with me."

Isobel laughed. "It could have been worse."

"How?"

"You could have been called 'Tuna' or 'Biscuit'."

Cherry laughed. "I suppose. Being closed yesterday for the funeral has made it extra busy tonight." She shook her head. "It's just so hard to believe that Michael is dead. It's awful. I hate that alleyway. I always have."

"Were you working that night?"

"Yes, I was."

"Did you see Michael or Charlene?"

Cherry shivered. "I don't remember seeing them."

"What time do you finish at?"

"If there is no late bar we get everyone out by eleven thirty and then clean-up takes about an hour."

"*Cherry!*" Lorraine called. "Will you fill up the fridges with beer and mixers?"

"Sure." Cherry hurried away.

Lorraine smiled at Isobel. "Hello, again."

"Hello, Lorraine." Isobel sipped her wine.

"Is there any news on Charlene? I thought Jack might have heard how she was doing."

"Not a lot of change apparently."

"Oh. So she hasn't regained consciousness?"

Isobel swallowed. "No, no, she hasn't."

Lorraine nodded. "I suppose time will tell."

"Yes."

Lorraine rinsed a couple of glasses and loaded them into the dishwasher.

"I heard that they've found someone who was trolling Charlene and that the troll might be the one who attacked Charlene and Michael."

Isobel raised her glass to her mouth and sipped, taking her time. "Really? Where did you hear that?"

"Oh, in this pub I tend to hear everything. Between students, lecturers and other employees of the college, pretty much nothing is a secret."

Isobel smiled. "I can imagine."

She thought back to their trip to the library and then her meeting with the Provost. Between students, personnel in the library, the Provost's secretary and since he knew Lorraine from college maybe the Provost himself, anyone could have said something.

"The sooner this case is sorted out the better," said Lorraine. "I'm a bit nervous myself with it having happened so close."

"Yes, of course."

"Are you visiting Jack for long?"

Isobel sipped her drink again. "Not for too long."

Lorraine looked her in the eye. "I suppose he's happy to see you but also wants to get on with his student life."

Isobel nodded. "I expect you're right. I'm enjoying seeing Belfast though. It's a long time since I was here."

"You seem to spend a lot of your time around the university."

Isobel raised an eyebrow.

Lorraine laughed. "I bumped into Ben Jameson today. He mentioned that you had visited him. I gather you've been to the library too."

Isobel felt uncomfortable. She had come here probably to ask questions herself, as she had done with Cherry, but she had the distinct feeling that she was the one being questioned and she felt uncomfortable with people being so aware of who she had talked to. It made her feel as if she was being watched. She tried to shake off the feeling and appear relaxed.

"Yes, I called up to see the counselling services. After all, Jack and indeed a lot of his friends have been through a lot. It's always good to know what help there is available."

Lorraine gestured out at the bar. "I guess everyone wants different sorts of help. Sometimes people want to forget, not talk about what happened."

"That's true. We may want to forget but sometimes that's hard to do."

"Jack is going to be fine. He'll get through this."

Isobel fiddled with her glass. "He said that you were very good to him the other night."

Lorraine smiled. "I was just doing my best to be supportive. All of these young people away from home, sometimes they need a little support."

Isobel picked up her glass and nodded.

Cherry left some glasses on the bar. Lorraine started to rinse them.

She added the glasses to the dishwasher. "Is there anything else you want to do while you're here?"

"I'm not sure. Maybe walk around the Botanic Gardens."

"Not so much then."

Isobel finished her drink and stood up.

"Call in any time for a chat," said Lorraine. "I'm here most of the time."

"Yes, thanks. See you again."

Chapter 33

Isobel snuggled into her bathrobe and sat on a chair looking out on the city lights. She had indulged herself with a hot scented bath and felt more relaxed now. She wasn't meeting Jack until lunchtime tomorrow as he expected to have a late night.

Isobel's mobile rang. "Eoin, our third chat today. Has something happened?"

"Isobel, can you go down to the bar of the hotel?"

"Why? You're not here, are you?"

"No. That wasn't an option."

Isobel blushed. "It isn't Aaron, is it? I don't want to talk to him again today."

"No, Aaron is up to his eyes."

"Has he been on to you?"

"Yes, just a quick call to confirm that I wouldn't be on the task force and to say that they're keeping everything very tight."

"Who's here then?"

"Someone you're going to be glad to see, I promise."

Isobel was mystified. She dressed quickly in trousers and a blouse, grabbed her key and took the lift to the bar level.

As she stepped out of the lift a tall muscular black man with white hair stepped forward.

"*Malcolm!*" Isobel ran to hug him. "*It's so good to see you!*" She could hear her voice breaking. She was so relieved. Only now as help was here did she realise how stressed and wound-up she felt.

Isobel had met Malcolm in London when he and Bella, his dog, had helped her with a case. Then, when she had been attacked in Limerick, he and Bella had also arrived.

"Patricia is still on holiday or she would be here too."

"I know. I haven't even told her anything about what's happening in case it distracts her from her romantic holiday."

Malcolm laughed. "Oh, it would distract her. She would be on the phone constantly looking for updates and I'm sure Peter wouldn't appreciate that."

"Where's Bella? Is she here?"

"Unfortunately, no. Having to stay in a hotel ruled that out."

Isobel pulled a face. "Aw, what a pity!"

She felt as if a weight had been lifted off her. With Malcolm here to share everything with, suddenly the situation didn't seem so treacherous and bleak.

Malcolm guided her to the bar. "Come on, let's get a drink so we can catch up."

Malcolm ordered a pint of Guinness for himself and a juice for her then found them a quiet corner.

"I can't believe this. I presume Eoin called you."

Malcolm grinned. "Yeah. He rang me when he was driving back to Limerick from your meeting this morning. He had me and Alanna on the line at the same time and filled us in on everything that he knew." He shook his head. "It sounds a mess. Eoin was really worried. He knew that you didn't like his mate Aaron and, anyway, Aaron is going to be really busy with the task force. Neither Eoin nor Alanna could come up because of jurisdictional issues and they thought of me. It helps that I'm retired. Anyway, they explained everything to me. I sorted out for my neighbour to look after Bella, booked the last flight and here I am. And, Isobel, Eoin wanted to come but he couldn't. And, as I pointed out to him, at least we know we can trust him and Alanna and we might need their help, officially."

"True."

"There's nothing I hate more than a bent copper. That's a weed that needs to be pulled out." Malcolm's shoulders tensed and his face tightened.

"You seem very determined."

Malcolm grinned at her. "I am. Eoin was concerned you'd be mad at him for calling me but he and Alanna were just worried about you."

"Why would I? I'm delighted!"

The waitress delivered Malcolm's pint. He watched it settle fully and then took a deep and satisfying drink.

"Now, fill me in on anything else that has happened."

Isobel sat forward and told Malcolm everything, including what Henry had seen and his reluctance to say anything.

"I can see why he's afraid and he's right to be," said Malcolm.

"What should I do? I haven't told anyone else about him. I'm not sure what to do."

Malcolm frowned. He took another deep drink. "I suppose it will depend on what the task force does. Maybe this guy Aaron will be able to get one of the men to betray the other but I wouldn't hold my breath. What about forensic evidence?"

Isobel shrugged. "I don't know and at the start the police were treating it all as a robbery gone wrong so I don't know how well they looked."

"With the murder, they would have to have processed the scene."

"Yes, I suppose."

"It seems to me that finding the rogue policeman is vitally important to everything. If that was sorted then maybe your witness could be kept confidential and safe."

They sat in silence.

"What's on the agenda for tomorrow?"

Isobel took a deep breath. "I was going to see if I could find out who owned that derelict yard at the back."

"Good idea." Malcolm finished his pint. "OK. I'm staying here too so let's meet in the foyer at eight o'clock."

Isobel climbed into bed, weary and looking forward to sleeping.

In her dreams she found herself in a dilapidated house. She could only see a short distance in front, after that complete darkness.

She inched forward. Something brushed her face. She reached up and wiped her face. It was a cobweb. She looked up. The web above was large but empty.

She ducked her head to avoid the web and made her way slowly across the room to the doorway and out into the hallway. At the end of the passageway she noticed some colours. The colours started to move towards her. They were coloured blobs suspended in the air – pink, blue and green. She saw the green colour move towards her. She crouched down and put her hands up to protect her head. The green blob landed on top of her. She reached up to push it off.

She woke as her arm banged into the headboard.

Chapter 34

Isobel enjoyed showing Malcolm Belfast as they walked down the Malone Road. He was suitably impressed by Queen's and nearby they found a place to have breakfast. Malcolm had an Ulster fry which he thoroughly enjoyed and Isobel had avocado toast. The coffee was good. Isobel searched the internet for land registry in Northern Ireland. The office was closed on a Saturday.

"Don't worry," said Malcolm. "Let's go and look at the alley."

In the alley, he stopped where the flowers were and then walked on towards the stone archway and old gate.

"This is the paint that you mentioned."

"Yes." Isobel rummaged in her bag and pulled out the envelope. "I scraped some off."

Malcolm nodded.

"Let's walk along the street and try and work out which buildings are backing onto the yard from the other side."

They walked out of the laneway and past the Muse.

There was a gift shop. Malcolm went in. "Hello. I'm just checking the buildings in this row to see how far they extend back. Is it possible for me to see out the back?"

"You thinking of buying one, are you?"

Malcolm grinned. "You never know. I'm guessing that they have a big storage area at the back."

"No, no, they don't. That big old yard backs onto all of the properties on the street. I would love more space but nothing doing. A few of us shop owners got together and wrote to the owners but they wouldn't give us more space."

"That's a shame. Who are the owners?"

"The same ones as own that shop Org. It's just further down the street and round the corner."

Isobel said, "I know it."

"There's no point speaking to the people in the shop, they're just employees. They won't be able to tell you anything."

Malcolm smiled at her. "Thanks for your help."

"No problem. It would be great if you were working near here."

Malcolm laughed and he and Isobel left.

"It seems I'm a hit in Belfast."

Isobel grinned. She led the way down the street and up the next road to the right.

Parked in front of Org was a green delivery van.

Isobel grasped Malcolm's arm. "A green van! The same colour as the paint on the gate!"

The door of the shop opened and a man came out, wheeling a delivery trolley.

Malcolm smiled. "We were just admiring your van."

"Yes, I love that shade of green," said Isobel.

The man grinned back. "That's the company colour. All our vans are that colour."

"I would love that shade for my curtains," she said. "What's it called?"

The man rolled his eyes at Malcolm. "I don't know. My wife's the same with her colours and her swatches, always changing the curtains and carpets. Never-ending!" He smiled good-naturedly as he spoke.

"Do you mind if I take a photo to see if I can match it?"

"You go right ahead."

Isobel took some shots of the van as Malcolm wandered round the far side of it.

Malcolm wandered back to Isobel's side of the van. "It's a busy city. It must be hard sometimes doing deliveries, finding a place to pull in. Is there no delivery access at the back of the shop?"

"No, not that I know of. We always park here at the front. I'm never long anyway, not at any of the shops."

"Are there many stores?"

"There's ten. And every one near a college. I suppose that's where their market is. Got to go. Saturday is a busy morning. Bye."

Isobel took Malcolm's arm and walked on past the shop. She stopped outside a convenience store, looking back at Org.

"I would swear that the van is the same colour as the paint on the pillar in the alley!"

"Your man seems like a regular delivery man. He didn't

mind chatting to us. He seemed like he had nothing to hide."

"I agree." Isobel gestured towards the door of Org. "That guy going into Org – he's a student. I've seen him before – I'll tell you about that later."

"The red-haired lad?"

"Yes. His name is Robin. Let's follow him."

"Why? He's just some student getting supplies."

"On a Saturday morning?" Isobel said. "He must be keen."

"Oh, yes. Good point."

Malcolm stepped forward. Isobel pulled him back.

"I thought we were following him."

"I've been inside. Let's wait until he leaves and then follow him."

They stood and waited, feigning interest in the convenience store window.

"If the shop has its deliveries through the front entrance then why was there paint from one of their company vans on the pillar in the laneway?" Isobel said. "Why would one of their vans be using it? Unless the shop is a front for something else?"

Malcolm nodded. "I see what you're thinking. Are you guessing drugs?"

"I am."

Malcolm looked pensive. "I had a case before I retired. There was a chipper and when you got your takeaway you got your drugs in with your fish supper."

"It could be a similar thing here. What better way to collect your drugs than when you get your paper and pens?"

"I see what you mean. There he is. "

Robin emerged from the shop, carrying his stationery supplies in a plastic bag.

"He's off," said Malcolm. "Let's go."

Isobel and Malcolm stayed well back from the red-haired young man as he walked out onto Botanic Avenue and then turned into the Holy Land.

He walked along Bethlehem Street, stopping at Number 13. The door was opened by another man, dressed in jeans and a T-shirt.

"Alright, Adam. Good to see you, man."

They shoulder-bumped.

"Come on in."

Robin followed Adam into the house.

"He's just visiting his mates," Isobel said.

Malcolm smiled, typing the number of the house into his phone. "I got a picture of the two of them. Be patient, Isobel."

All of the houses had small front yards and opened onto the street. It was Saturday morning and there were few people around. Strewn around were takeaway food boxes and empty cans, the detritus of a sociable Friday night.

Malcolm touched Isobel's arm and led her back to the corner of the road. They stood out of sight of Number 13 and watched from the shelter of the wall.

"Tell me about this Robin," he said.

"I saw him in the Org shop before, the time I nosed around there and spoke to the manager. Then I also saw him on a video at the library when we were looking for

Charlene's troll who messaged her from the library every Tuesday morning at eight-thirty. Robin was in the library early on each Tuesday morning."

"So he gets up early. Maybe he's a committed student?"

"There is something that is bothering me about him. I'm sorry. I can't join up the dots for you but it's something. Let's hope it comes to me."

"OK. We'll just follow him. No harm done if we find nothing." Malcolm hunched forward. "There he is. He's on the move again. Come on."

Robin walked away from them and turned right. Malcolm and Isobel walked after him. They turned the corner into a similar street. Robin was standing at a black door. It opened and he went inside.

Malcolm led the way past the house, Number 5. The street was Angel Street. He made another note.

They once again lurked at the street corner. Isobel stamped her feet in the cold. Malcolm pulled a cap out of this pocket and put it on. He looked at Isobel. "Take your scarf and put it outside your coat."

Isobel looked down at her turquoise wool scarf tucked in under her navy puffer jacket.

"Go on, open it out and wrap it around the top of your coat. It will make you look different."

Isobel rolled her eyes but complied.

"Surveillance one-o-one. Small changes make you look like someone different."

"Fine."

Ten or fifteen minutes passed. Malcolm remained in position. Isobel walked in small circles to keep warm.

"And we're off again!" Malcolm said.

Robin had emerged onto the street and turned back the way he had come, moving away from Isobel and Malcolm.

They followed at a distance as Robin led them into the Botanic Gardens. He took a seat on a bench.

It was now about ten-thirty and there were a number of people in the park, some walking dogs, parents with children and some students.

Isobel and Malcolm sat on a bench some distance from Robin but where they could clearly see him. A young man dressed in the student garb of jeans, runners and a sweatshirt sat down on the end of Robin's bench. They chatted a few minutes. Malcolm discreetly took a photo. Robin handed the young man a notebook from his Org bag. The young man shook Robin's hand and then slouched away.

Malcolm indicated that he wanted to move bench. They walked arm and arm and sat on another path which provided them with some cover of trees but still an excellent view of Robin on his bench. Over the next half hour ten different young people, both boys and girls, strolled up and spent a few minutes on the bench, each leaving with a notebook.

Malcolm took pictures of each interaction. "You see. This is dealing in action."

"And the two house visits?"

"Maybe a party tonight, maybe he lives in one of them and was dropping some of the drugs home."

Robin slid his Org bag into another plastic bag and then sauntered off.

"That's a bit strange, isn't it? Why would he put the green Org bag into another plastic bag?"

Malcolm nodded. "All I can think of is that the first bag is a sign that he has drugs. That fits with what we have just seen. Green bag for drugs and we have a line of people coming. Then business is done and the green bag disappears."

Isobel frowned. "When I saw him in the library both mornings I don't know if he was carrying a bag."

"Let's go and look at that library footage. I don't believe that this guy is an early-morning learner. He's a drug dealer. And Tuesday is the morning after the Monday night when the light is on. Maybe that's delivery night in the back gate."

Isobel felt her blood run cold. It was the chill of exposing something harmful, something sordid, something that Michael may have been killed to protect.

Chapter 35

They left the Botanic gardens by the gate nearest the Queen's library at the back of the quadrangle. Isobel led the way towards the library.

Malcolm said, "It sure is beautiful round here."

Isobel nodded.

They passed the sculpture outside, Malcolm lagging behind to study it as Isobel hurried inside.

He caught up with her. "What's the hurry?"

"Oh my God! I can't believe I missed this on the library tapes. Would you believe last night I was dreaming about coloured blobs floating at me, green and blue and pink?"

"Oh?"

Tabitha wasn't on reception today. Isobel smiled at the receptionist. "I spoke to Gladys Pritchard a few days ago about a security issue. I wonder if she is here today?"

"Ms. Pritchard always works on Saturday morning."

"Perhaps you could let her know that Isobel McKenzie would like to see her."

The woman picked up the phone and murmured into

it. Then she tuned to Isobel. "She's on her way."

Isobel paced around, knowing that Ms. Pritchard might have been in trouble with the Provost because of their last meeting.

"Ms. Mckenzie, more security issues?"

Isobel turned. "I'm sorry but –"

"Come this way." Ms. Pritchard turned, leading the way to her office.

Malcolm raised his eyebrows at Isobel. She frowned at him and followed Ms. Pritchard, with Malcolm bringing up the rear.

Inside her office Ms. Pritchard seemed determined to take her time seating them and then offering them beverages.

"No Jack today?" she asked.

"No. This is Malcolm Carr. He's a friend of mine."

"Mr. Carr."

"Please, call me Malcolm."

Ms. Pritchard inclined her head graciously.

"I'm sorry if the Provost berated you for letting me look at the library footage," Isobel said.

Ms. Pritchard's eyes sparkled behind her glasses. "Don't worry about it. A student was dead and another grievously injured. I did the right thing and no one can tell me otherwise."

Isobel smiled.

"Good for you," said Malcolm.

"What's the worst they can do? Make me retire? I can tell you that when I leave it will take two people to replace me."

Isobel's smile grew wider. "I don't doubt it."

Malcolm grinned. "It took two people to replace me as well."

Ms. Pritchard laughed. For a woman near retirement she had a vibrant, musical laugh. "So what can I do for you this time?"

"We need to have another look at the footage from those Tuesday mornings."

"Did we miss something?" She frowned.

"No, this isn't anything to do with the trolling. But I missed something else on the footage that might be even more important. I need to see it again."

Ms. Pritchard moved towards her keyboard and typed efficiently. After a minute or two she said, "I saved all the footage we looked at into a folder in case it was needed."

Isobel nodded. "That was a good idea."

Isobel and Malcolm walked around the desk to stand behind Ms. Pritchard.

She played the first video.

As the video played they saw a tall man in black enter the library.

"Professor Clarke to collect his books, as regular as clockwork," said Ms. Pritchard.

Next they saw the red-haired young man, Robin, entering the library carrying his green Org bag.

The footage continued and they saw Robin leave the library.

Isobel pointed at the screen. "No bag now."

"He left it in the library," Malcolm said.

"Someone would have handed that in," Ms. Pritchard said. "Or maybe he realised and came back for it." She paused. "Here's the young woman who was trolling Charlene coming to send her emails."

The video continued.

"There's Professor Clarke leaving," Ms. Pritchard commented.

Malcolm pointed. "And he has a green Org bag!"

Ms. Pritchard looked round at them. "He probably had that in his pocket to carry his books. In fact, I'm sure he always has a bag to put his books into."

"Or, maybe he picks up a bag that someone else has left," Isobel said.

Malcolm nodded. "Could be."

Ms. Pritchard swung round. "What are you suggesting?"

Isobel didn't know what to say.

"We're searching for behaviour patterns," Malcolm said.

Ms. Pritchard stared at him. "One incident isn't a pattern. Professor Clarke is – is . . ." She exhaled loudly. "He's a very respected man."

"Can we look at the footage for the next Tuesday, please?" Isobel said. "Let's just see what it shows before we jump to any conclusions."

Ms. Pritchard nodded and clicked on the keyboard. "Here it is. The following Tuesday."

The video played. Robin duly arrived with his Org bag. Anne arrived also. As they watched Robin left the library.

"No bag," Malcolm said. "Again."

After a few minutes Isobel said, "And here's the Professor."

They watched as he left the library once again with a green Org bag.

273

Ms. Pritchard stopped the video. Her hands shook slightly and she clasped them together. "The same thing." She took a noisy breath. "You were expecting that." She put her hand to her head. "What's going on in my library? What are they doing?"

Isobel glanced at Malcolm. He made a face.

They both sat down, facing Ms. Pritchard.

Isobel waited for her to look up and then said, "Ms. Pritchard, I suppose once again I need you to trust me. We're not sure but we suspect that there is . . . we think that there might be . . ."

Malcolm came to her aid. "We suspect the red-haired boy, Robin, of being involved in drugs."

Ms. Pritchard's hand moved to her throat. "*Drugs!*" It was a whisper but there was agony in her voice. "*In my library!*"

"We're not sure," said Malcolm. "That's why you can't say anything to anybody."

Isobel nodded. "Not even the Provost."

"But, if you suspect drugs, you have to notify the police."

Isobel rolled her eyes. "True, but things are complicated at the moment."

Malcolm cut in. "That's why I'm here. I used to work at The Met. and Isobel needed some help, so I came over last night."

"You can trust Malcolm. He'll make sure this gets handled properly and discreetly." Isobel bit her lip. "Ms. Pritchard, you need to listen to me. You can't tell anyone about this. I promise we are handling it."

Malcolm added, "This may be related to Michael's

murder. You have to keep everything completely confidential until we figure out what to do."

"You're serious."

"I'm deadly serious."

"Oh my!" Ms. Pritchard moistened her lips. "I heard the news this morning. A prominent drug dealer was found dead, shot and dumped in the Lagan. They haven't released his name yet."

Isobel gasped and pulled out her phone. "I put it on silent earlier when we were in the Botanic Gardens watching . . . There's three missed calls from Damien."

Malcolm nodded, standing up.

"What can I do to help?" Ms. Pritchard asked.

Malcolm looked at her. "You want to help?"

"Yes, yes, of course I do."

He nodded. "OK, if you want to help, here's what you can do. You need to go back through all the footage of Tuesday mornings and see if what we have observed on these two Tuesdays happens every week. Can you do that?"

Ms. Pritchard frowned at him. "Of course I can."

"And," Malcolm said, "not a word to anyone. Literally, not a single other person."

"I think I understand the English language well enough to know what you are saying."

Malcolm grinned at her and she smiled back.

"I'll call Isobel and let you know what I find," she said.

Isobel stood too. "Thank you. We've got to go."

Isobel and Malcolm hurried from the library.

Once outside Isobel called Damien.

She said "Hello, Damien" and then fell silent, listening. "In my hotel room would be best. I'll meet you in the foyer."

"What's happened?" Malcolm asked when she had finished.

"He wouldn't say. He wants to meet us. He sounded very fearful so I said we'd meet in my hotel room. It will be private there and we can talk."

Isobel started walking back up the road towards her hotel. "I'm going to text Jack and tell him to meet us there."

Malcolm fell into step beside her. "Busy day. I'm glad I had that big fry this morning."

Chapter 36

Isobel left Malcolm in her room and went to reception to meet Damien and Jack.

Jack arrived first. They waited, saying very little until Damien arrived and then they went up in the lift.

In the room, Damien sat at the table by the window with Malcolm. Isobel sat against the headboard of her bed and Jack perched at the foot of it.

Isobel introduced Malcolm as a friend from England but said nothing about his previous employment.

Jack said enthusiastically, "Oh, you met Isobel when she was in London that time –"

"That's right," Isobel cut in. "When I went to visit my friend Patricia. Malcolm's been a good friend ever since."

Jack took the hint and said nothing more.

"What's going on, Damien?" Isobel said. "What's happened?"

"Did you hear the news about the prominent drug dealer found in the Lagan this morning?"

"Yes, someone mentioned it to us."

"Well, it's Geo, George Simpson. They're going to release his name this afternoon."

"One of the men from the alley!" Jack said.

Damien nodded. "The Superintendent thinks that he was killed because of what he did in the alley."

"You mean killing Michael?" Jack said.

Damien nodded. "Yes, they think his own crowd took him out for drawing attention to them."

"On the other hand," said Malcolm, "that's a handy solution for the police. It means they can close the investigation into Michael's death."

Damien looked at him and Isobel judged he was already aware of that possibility. She thought of what Henry had told her. "But how do we know it was Geo who killed Michael? It could have been the other man – Tim-Tan."

"The Superintendent has been contacted by an informant who confirmed that Geo was responsible for what happened to Michael and Charlene. The informant says Geo acted alone."

Isobel gasped.

Damien looked at her questioningly.

Isobel glanced at Malcolm who gave a little negating shake of his head.

"So the case is over then?" he said.

"And the pictures that you gave us, Isobel, turned up in the lab," Damien said. "Apparently there was some sort of mix-up."

"Funny that," Malcolm said.

Damien shot him a glance.

"Malcolm knows all about what's been going on, Damien," said Isobel. "You can trust him."

"It's all a bit convenient," Malcolm said.

"I know," Damien agreed.

"It sounds to me like someone is cleaning house," Malcolm said. "With Geo dead, the case is closed. The lab had a mix-up and now everyone can go back to business as usual."

Isobel felt miserable. According to Henry, Geo wasn't the killer. The informant had lied. He was determined that Geo would take the blame. Malcolm was right. It all seemed too fortuitous, designed simply to shut down any further investigation.

"Superintendent Taylor wants you, Isobel, and you, Jack, to come to Grosvenor Road this afternoon at five o'clock," Damien said. "I think he might be asking the O'Neills and the Griffiths too. He wants to tell you all in person that Geo was responsible for the attacks and is now dead. He's then having a press conference to tell the public and it will probably make the *Six O'Clock News*. He asked me, since I knew you from the investigation, to make sure that you got the message and would turn up."

Isobel looked at Malcolm.

"Of course Isobel and Jack will be there," he said. "They'll want to be there for that announcement. Don't you, Isobel?"

"I'll certainly go," Jack said. "Mr. Griffiths is going to be relieved that the perpetrator has been found. And I suppose at least there won't have to be a trial now which means they can move on and concentrate on Charlene's recovery and now, well, now she's safe." He looked at Isobel. "At least we helped."

Isobel nodded at him.

Damien finished his tea. "There is something else."

Isobel raised an eyebrow.

"I bumped into the guy from the police lab again – the one I asked about the pictures."

"Is there a problem?" Isobel asked. "Did he tell someone that you'd been asking questions?"

Damien hurried on. "No, no, not at all. He was really pissed off. He said that the Superintendent himself came down and blamed the lab for the mix-up. Brian, the lab guy, defended himself, saying that they never got the pictures. The Superintendent claimed that he had assigned someone to hand the pictures in."

"So you think it's Inspector Williams? You think that he never passed on the information to the lab?"

"I did think that but then I wondered why he'd told the Superintendent about the pictures at all. He could just have kept telling me that there was no luck with the pictures. I would've probably accepted that but for the fact that you were able to get resolution on them."

"So what are you saying?" Malcolm asked. "You thought the snitch was Inspector Williams and now you're not sure?"

Damien grimaced. "Brian told me that in the end the Superintendent said that they would accept that there had been an administrative foul-up but, since we had the pictures and the perpetrator was dealt with, then there was no harm done."

"You're right. Why did Williams show the pictures to the Superintendent at all?" Isobel said. "If he was trying to suppress evidence, why would he?"

"True," Jack said.

"I'm wondering if maybe he showed the Super the pictures and the Super said he would deal with them and now he's covering his own ass," said Damien.

"Oh, you're saying that now you doubt Superintendent Taylor and think he might be the dirty cop?" Isobel said.

"It's possible."

Isobel frowned. "This is enough to drive anyone mad. It's impossible to know who to trust." She paced up and down the room. "And what scares the shit out of me is that you could be in a very dangerous position, Damien, because we passed on information to you. What if Brian said that you had been asking questions?"

"I know. But Brian definitely said nothing about me. Don't worry, I asked him. He told me that he knew there was shit going on when the Superintendent came to the lab and he basically said that he didn't know what had happened. He didn't want to get involved and he played dumb. Superintendent Taylor seemed happy with that."

"Damien, be careful," said Malcolm. "A man has just been killed to clean up this mess and if you draw attention to yourself you could go the same way."

Damien looked at Isobel. "I know you asked me to find out if Inspector Williams had passed on the photos to anyone but I have to confess I've been afraid to. I haven't done anything but, well, it seems that Superintendent Taylor did know about the photographs so . . ."

"That's it, Damien," she said. "You're not to ask. You're not to draw attention to yourself in any way."

"She's right," said Malcolm. "Don't ask anyone anything. It seems both men knew about the photos but someone suppressed them and it isn't clear who. Do nothing."

"I hate this," Damien said. "Officers covering up for a paramilitary drug lord. They're destroying the force and my belief in it."

"Don't let that happen," said Malcolm. "You're doing your best but you have to be smart here." He turned to Isobel. "Maybe we need to talk to Eoin and Alanna."

"The gardaí in Limerick?" Jack asked.

Isobel nodded. "Yes, Inspectors Ryan and Finnegan. Yes, I think we need to talk to them about a number of things." She looked at Damien. "Maybe you need to take a leaf out of Brian's book and play dumb for now. I'll talk to Eoin and Alanna and see what they say."

Damien nodded. "OK. I guess I'll see you at the meeting then."

He left and as he closed the door behind him a message pinged on Isobel's phone.

I need to speak to you urgently. Come to my office in the students union. It's very important. Róisín

My God, what next? Isobel thought.

"So there is a traitor in the PSNI then," Jack said.

"It seems so," Isobel said. "The North blamed the South and vice versa. Neither one wanted to be the one to have the problem. It's a political football but it seems now that Damien has found the leak."

She messaged Róisin back: **I'll be there within the hour.**

"Isobel!" Malcolm said.

"Sorry," she said, startled. "What is it?"

"I'm not disputing the political situation but, given how serious things are, with Geo being killed, I don't like it. I think we need to be very careful."

"Of course."

"It's too late to go back and be more careful when someone innocent has been killed. Remember that undercover garda that you told me about, who was killed?"

She nodded.

"I don't like it at all," he went on. "We have Geo killed in Belfast to protect Tim-Tan."

"What do you mean to protect Tim-Tan?" Jack asked.

Malcolm looked at Isobel. "I mean Geo's death means that Tim-Tan is in the clear. The other evidence we've found is potentially explosive. If the people involved found out that we knew then other people could die."

"What other evidence?" Jack asked.

"Jack, I don't think that I should tell you for the very reason that Malcolm has just explained," said Isobel. "This whole situation is out of hand."

"But I want to know. I've helped you all along. I was the one who found the photos of Tim-Tan and Geo."

Isobel nodded. "I know, Jack. But I don't know who we can trust. I'm terrified for you, for Damien. Jesus, if anything happened to you I would never forgive myself. And Dave would kill me." Isobel sat down hurriedly in a chair, her head down, her hands running through her hair.

"We all need to calm down," said Malcolm. "We do

know people we can trust." He pointed to himself. "You can trust me, Isobel, you can trust Jack."

Jack smiled at him.

"And we can trust Eoin and Alanna."

Isobel nodded.

"Most likely we can trust Damien."

Isobel opened her mouth.

"Do you think he could be a plant, Malcolm?" said Jack. "Trying to find out what we know?"

Malcolm smiled. "No, not really. I think he is genuinely scared."

"And, he was only doing his job," said Jack. "He passed on the pictures to Inspector Williams."

"Exactly. He put the photographs in the system which is what has caused someone to suppress them. In fact, he's done very well at inadvertently drawing the corrupt officer out."

"What other evidence have you two found?" Jack said. "Come on, tell me. I want to know."

Malcolm nodded at Isobel.

"Not a word, to anyone," she said.

Jack nodded impatiently.

Isobel filled him in on all they had found out.

"But you're not going to tell me who the witness is who saw Tim-Tan kill Michael and attack Charlene?" said Jack.

"No," Isobel said.

"I don't know either, Jack," Malcolm said. He looked at Isobel. "You need to persuade that person to make a statement."

"I can't see it happening and anyway they'd not be considered," Isobel made hand quotes, "'a reliable witness'. And who could they make a statement to? Who could we trust? Once the witness made themself known, their life would be in danger."

"I think we need to discuss all of this with Eoin," Malcolm said. "Is there any chance we could meet him like you did the other day, Isobel?"

Isobel shrugged. "I don't know. It's a three-hour drive for him up to where we met."

"We need to tell him all we suspect about the drug-dealing although we don't really have proof, just some suspicions." He pulled a piece of paper from his pocket. It was folded over on itself many times. He slowly opened out the folds and held it out towards the others.

Inside the paper were some green flecks.

"What's that?" Jack said.

"Paint from the Org delivery van. And Isobel has some flecks of paint from the back entrance to the yard in the alleyway."

Isobel nodded, reaching into her bag for the envelope.

"And if the paint is the same then that at least puts an Org van going through the gates at the end of the alley. And Michael's pictures show a light on in the yard on Monday nights late. And we have a student coming out of houses and meeting people in the park and giving them stationery."

Jack laughed. "That is suspicious!"

"Stationery with drugs in it. But I think the cover of studious students is deceptively good. Who would question it? In fact, I think it could be a model spread out over the country. Ten shops, near ten education establishments, an endless supply of vulnerable young people. It sounds like a good plan to me."

"When you put it like that!" Jack said.

"Isobel, we've more than you think. I want to go to that lab, that private one Damien told you about."

"SpeedAn."

"Yes, SpeedAn, and see if they can look at the two paint samples. Maybe they will live up to their name and do a quick job for us. That would be a help. We also need to see if Ms. Pritchard has found more episodes with the bag left in the library."

"I could check with her," Jack said.

"We also need to get pictures of students from the years in college when Ben and Lorraine and the Provost were there," Isobel said. "There are too many people from that time all hanging around."

"That's the North for you," said Jack. "It's a village."

"*Hmm*, less of a village and more of a syndicate – and we need to see who the members are," said Isobel.

Malcolm shrugged. "It couldn't hurt."

"I can do that as well," said Jack.

"I'll go with you but first you can take me to the lab," Malcolm said.

Isobel stood up. "I have to meet my friend."

"The one who messaged you? Is that your informant?"

Isobel smiled. "No, it's someone who has a window into the drug scene here. I don't know what they want."

"Jack and I have some things to do. Let's get together later. By the way, I'm going with you to your meeting with

Superintendent Taylor and Inspector Williams."

"But –"

"No, Isobel. I am not letting you and Jack meet those men alone, no way. And besides I'm looking forward to making my own assessment of them."

"You can't just get in, your name –"

"Make sure Damien gets my name on whatever list. The two of you aren't going on your own. If they really want you there they will have to make room for me."

Isobel sent a text to Damien.

"I'll text you the name of a coffee shop near the police station we're in, Isobel," said Jack.

Isobel smiled. "Do."

"Or pub," said Malcolm. "It might be a pub. I might need a pint of the good stuff to fortify me."

Chapter 37

Isobel was glad to leave the hotel and walk towards the Students Union. It was a bright, sunny day with a cold nip in the air. Normally she enjoyed days like this but today the beauty and freshness of the day contrasted sharply with the murky world she was dealing with. Could Damien be right and it was in fact Superintendent Taylor who was involved with the drug gang and Inspector Williams was innocent or, worst of all, could they both be involved? Isobel felt sick. The very people charged with finding who had killed Michael could be corrupt and working with the men who had done this. No wonder they had wanted the attack to be a robbery. She dreaded the thought of meeting them this evening. Malcolm might want to get the measure of them but she wondered how she was going to manage.

She also wondered what Róisín had thought was so important that she had to see her. She felt sure that Róisín had told her everything she knew about the gang when they'd had dinner together. Maybe Michael's death had stirred things up for her about Patrick and she wanted to talk. Isobel was glad to have a respite from thinking about corruption and wondering who she could trust.

The Students Union was busy. Isobel made her way up to Róisín's office.

As she came through the door, Róisín looked up. Open on the desk was a photo album.

"Thank God you came so quickly."

Isobel closed the door and sat down across the desk from her. "What is it?"

Róisín leant forward across the desk. "Remember I showed you those pictures Patrick sent me a few days before he died?"

"Yes."

Róisín worked her phone and handed it to Isobel. The picture on the screen was Patrick outside the Org shop holding up a bag. Isobel could feel herself tense. A green plastic bag. Knowing what she knew now, she wondered was Patrick trying to communicate something with this photo.

"Do you notice anything?"

Isobel didn't know what to say. She didn't feel that she could tell her what they now suspected.

Róisín was growing impatient. "What do you think about this picture?"

Isobel grappled for a reply. "Obviously you feel there's something important here so why don't you tell me what it is."

Róisín sat back in her chair. "I have always thought that Patrick went to some of the places he loved when he was a student to take these pictures. I assumed they were selfies because by that time in his life he was a loner. His old friends had tried to help him and when they couldn't they had gradually drifted away. He was into drugs and was becoming more depressed and anxious. He was hard to be around." She made a face. "I found that and I was his mother. He had no one he was close to. I imagine he had people who supplied him but I hardly think that they went with him on a nostalgia trip."

Isobel nodded. "OK." She wondered where Róisín was going with this.

Róisín reached out for the phone. "Look at the photographs. I don't think they're selfies. The distance is wrong for that. I think someone else took the picture."

"Maybe he asked a passerby."

"He could have. But look at these." She turned the album towards Isobel.

Isobel glanced down. She saw Patrick in the picture, smiling at the camera, and alongside him was another boy, dark-haired with blue eyes. He was broader and taller than Patrick. Isobel looked at another photo. It was of Patrick in his graduation gown and the same boy, in the same colours, was smiling beside him.

"Who's that?"

"That's Gareth Short, his friend. He and Patrick were in the same class and were good friends for a while. Gareth wasn't into drugs at all. He hated what Patrick was doing to himself. He tried to help but ultimately they lost touch. He came to Patrick's funeral. He was very upset."

"What's so important about all of this, Róisín?"

"I think Patrick had someone with him who took the pictures and if I had to guess who I would say Gareth."

"I thought you said that they lost touch."

"I know."

"Did Gareth say anything at the funeral about having seen Patrick recently?"

"Well, no."

"Surely he would have mentioned it to you if he had seen him, what, less than a week before Patrick died? Surely he would have spoken to you about that, to tell you how he felt Patrick was."

Róisín sat back in her chair. "I know. But the three photos from that day, I don't think any of them are selfies – the distance between the camera and Patrick are too great and the pose is wrong – it's too relaxed. I thought we could go and see Gareth and ask him if he was with Patrick. Maybe he knows something about how Patrick was feeling or what was going through his mind. Maybe he told Gareth something."

Isobel bit her lip. Had she time before the meeting?

"Please come with me. I just want to see if Gareth was with him. I know he wasn't alone and Patrick wasn't the sort to go asking strangers to take his picture. He just wasn't. Someone was with him."

Isobel nodded. "OK. I'll go with you – as long as I'm back for a meeting at five o'clock. But please don't get your hopes up. I find it hard to believe that if he had seen Patrick he wouldn't have mentioned it to you."

"Thank you, Isobel."

Isobel could feel the weight of grief Róisín carried and her hope. She prayed she wouldn't be disappointed.

"Where is Gareth?"

Róisín relaxed a little. "I phoned his mother. He has his own law firm based out in Holywood."

"How long would it take?"

"We'll definitely have time."

Isobel gave a heavy sigh. "OK. But I can't be late for my meeting."

Róisín jumped up. "Great. I have my car parked nearby."

They went at almost a run to Róisín's car.

As they sat into the car Isobel said, "So Gareth didn't stay in the city?"

"No. His mum said that he left the city firm around the time that Patrick died. She said that he was very upset about Patrick."

As Róisín negotiated her way through the streets, Isobel found her mind wandering. That was the thing with drugs. It ended up not just affecting the person who was taking them but everyone around them, everyone close to them. She could only imagine how hard it was for old friends of Patrick to deal with his death, his overdose. Róisín's work obviously helped her and indeed helped other young people but nothing could take away the loss or answer the questions.

She turned and looked out the window. They were leaving the city behind. As the intensity of buildings and cars gave way to a more open road she could feel some of the tension leave her. The sky seemed higher here, there was more space, more light. She knew it was just a notion but she could understand why Gareth might have chosen to move out of the city.

Holywood was near the edge of Belfast Lough. The main street was busy, the shops had some class about them. Róisín found a parking space on the main street and went to the machine for a ticket.

Isobel climbed out of the car. The streets were busy with people passing. They were talking and calling to each other. Life here seemed so normal, so innocent. Isobel felt a tug on her heart. Searching as they were for answers had drawn them all into a dark, murky world. And, as so often happened when you had cause to be near that world, you felt tainted by it. She was glad that she had come, if for nothing else than to remember what it was like to feel clean, unsullied.

"It's this way." Róisín led the way along the main street.

Isobel fell into step beside her. At the side of a chemist shop Róisín gestured to a sign: *Woods and Short*. She pushed open the door and led the way up the stairs.

At the first landing there was an open area. A young woman with auburn hair sat behind a desk. She was pale-skinned and had clear blue eyes.

"Can I help you?"

Róisín smiled. "My name is Róisín Magill. I would like to see Gareth, please."

"Let me see if he's free."

Isobel turned away as the young woman spoke into the phone. The reception area had a cream carpet. A large window onto the street made the area very bright. To the right was a wall covered in paper featuring trees. Beneath it was a cream sofa. On a low table were magazines and a pot with an orchid. The effect was extremely relaxing.

She heard a door opening. A man appeared at the end of the corridor near the reception desk.

"Mrs. Magill, is everything alright?" He stepped forward, his face creased in concern.

Compared to the young man in the photos, Gareth Short looked ten years older. His dark hair had shots of grey but they added distinction. His face had more lines. He still looked solid but gone was any hint of youth. Instead he had an air of experience.

"Come through. Tell me what I can help you with."

Gareth led the way along the corridor to his office. It too had a large window. The walls here also were cream.

Róisín said, "This is Isobel McKenzie."

Gareth shook Isobel's hand and then sat behind his desk, his back to the window. He gestured to the two seats in front of the desk and Isobel and Róisín sat down.

"You moved out of the city then?" Róisín said.

"Yes, I wanted a change."

"Your mum said that it was around the time that Patrick died."

Gareth's face tightened. It was almost a wince. "Yes, it was." He paused. "How are you doing, Róisín? You look well."

"Thank you."

The silence lengthened.

Isobel wondered if Róisín had lost her nerve or just didn't know where to begin. She said, "Róisín was showing me photos of Patrick, old ones of when you graduated and before."

Gareth almost smiled.

"You and Patrick were in the same class and graduated together."

"Yes." He frowned.

Isobel looked at Róisín. Her hands were clasped around her handbag, her knuckles white with strain.

"We were also looking at more recent photos – in fact, ones taken a very short time before Patrick died."

She spotted a muscle tremor in Gareth's face. He seemed to grow paler. He clamped his lips together.

Isobel looked again at Róisín. Her eyes were fixed on Gareth.

"Róisín, perhaps you could show Gareth the pictures we were looking at earlier?"

"Oh. Oh yes." Unclenching her hands, Róisín opened her bag and brought out her phone. Her movements were jerky. She made two attempts to unlock her phone and eventually managed to bring up the photograph of Patrick in front of the Org shop. She handed the phone to Isobel.

Isobel reached the phone across the desk to Gareth. He looked at it for a moment. Isobel studied his face. For a moment she saw desolation in his eyes and then he tightened his face into a mask. He passed the phone back to Isobel.

Isobel glanced at Róisín but her eyes were fixed on Gareth. What should she do? Maybe Róisín wasn't up to this? Maybe she'd changed her mind? She wondered if she should just let it go and then remembered the enthusiasm that had possessed Róisín in her office. If they left without finding out if Gareth had been with Patrick the day the photos were taken then it would torment Róisín – another unanswered question.

She cleared her throat. "Róisín was saying that the photo of Patrick outside Org isn't a selfie. It had to be taken by another person, someone who was with him." Isobel studied Gareth's face.

Gareth tensed. Isobel could see it in his shoulders and his hands resting on the desk. She could feel it in the increasing tension of the room.

"Maybe Patrick asked a passerby to take the picture?" Gareth's voice shook slightly.

Isobel continued as if he hadn't spoken. "Róisín thinks that he may have asked an old friend to join him that day. She says that he seemed happy in the photos. It may well have been his last happy day."

Róisín gulped. She rummaged in her handbag and brought out a tissue. Isobel kept her eyes on Gareth. He swallowed.

Isobel lowered her voice. "Were you with Patrick that day, Gareth? Did you take this photo?"

Róisín sat forward in her chair. With her movement, Gareth dragged his eyes from Isobel and looked at Patrick's mum.

"*Were you with him, Gareth?*" Róisín's voice was almost a whisper.

Gareth's eyes looked shiny with tears. In a strangled voice he said, "Yes."

Róisín made a sound, almost a whimper.

No one spoke. Isobel held her breath. Róisín had been right. Why hadn't he told her that when Patrick died?

Surely it would have been a comfort to her? Why keep it a secret? Could it be that Patrick had shared something with Gareth that was private? It was a strange photo, outside a stationary shop, holding one of their plastic bags. Did Gareth know something about the importance of the green bag, the nefarious use of the shop? Had Patrick called his old friend to meet, not just to share some time and memories with him, but also to share some information with him, information that he was afraid to share with Róisín?

Róisín spoke, bringing Isobel's focus back to the office. "How was Patrick that day?"

Gareth eyes shone with tears. "He was very anxious."

"I know, his anxiety just got worse and worse. I'm sure spending time with you helped him."

Gareth swallowed noisily.

Isobel could see torment in his eyes.

"Did he talk to you about the significance of the Org bag?" she asked.

Gareth gasped. His mouth fell open.

Róisín looked over at Isobel. "What?" Her voice faltered. Her brow wrinkled.

Gareth shifted in his chair. Isobel felt her stomach knot. Gareth knew something, she was sure of it. The shock tactic of them turning up, the photo, asking about the Org bag had almost broken through the silent wall he'd erected. How could she get him to reveal what he knew?

"I know about the shop and I know about how the coloured bags signalled that the Org dealers were carrying drugs. Did Patrick tell you anything else that day, anything about what was going on, anything about why he was so afraid?"

Isobel heard Róisín inhale sharply.

Gareth looked at Isobel. He had almost a vacant stare, as if he were miles away.

Isobel lowered her voice. Softly she said, "What was Patrick afraid of?"

Gareth's voice shook. "He didn't want his mum to know anything. He was trying to protect her. These people are too dangerous."

Isobel reached out and squeezed Róisín's hand. She could feel an answering squeeze. "I know. I understand. He wanted to protect his mum but she wants to know, that's why she came here today. Anything you know, anything you can tell her, she wants to know."

Gareth glanced at Róisín. She nodded to him. He turned back to Isobel. "He swore me to secrecy."

"I know, Gareth, but young people are dying. Please, now is the time. Please tell us anything else you know."

Gareth ran his fingers through his hair. "It won't make any difference. I can tell you what Patrick told me but they're all dead."

"Please. Tell us. You'll feel better. If everyone is dead, what harm can it do?"

Gareth shook his head. "You have no idea. Patrick knew stuff about people, important people. That may be why he's dead. He didn't want his mum to know anything in case it put her in danger."

Róisín let go of Isobel's hand. She sat forward in her chair. "*Gareth, I want to know. Please.*"

Gareth looked away and then got up and walked to the window. He looked out, his hands in his pockets. "OK, I'll tell you."

He sat down at his desk again, his clasped hands resting on the table.

"Patrick called me and asked me to meet him that day. I had to get the afternoon off from work. I told them I had a toothache. We went round some of our old haunts taking pictures. We went back to my place and had a takeaway and a few drinks. He had a difficult situation at work. There was a problem with one of the clients."

"That's right," Róisín said.

"Basically, a client of the firm, Joe, was being charged with a drug offence."

"Yes, he told me about that. The firm wanted Patrick to do something illicit."

Gareth shook his head. "No, that wasn't it. Joe was a dealer. He worked for one of the drug groups. Patrick got to know him. Joe was really anxious, really scared. He was convinced that he had been caught and was facing prison time because of something he knew. Eventually Joe trusted Patrick enough to tell him what was bothering him. One night Joe and another dealer mate of his, Leon, had a meeting with a man called Richard. The meeting was at the back of an old warehouse along the Lagan. An off-duty policeman came to the meeting. The off-duty policeman said that there was an informer among them."

No one spoke. Isobel could almost visualise the scene. She could feel the tension in her body.

"They all denied it. Obviously Joe was petrified. The

off-duty policeman said that he had a tip from a very high-placed source. He called him 'The Prop'. One of them – Joe, Leon or Richard – was apparently an undercover garda."

Isobel gasped and raised her hand to her mouth. Could this be the garda that Aaron had mentioned to her? The one who had gone missing?

Gareth paused.

Isobel swallowed and gestured for him to continue.

"They all denied that it was them, of course. Then the off-duty policeman pulled out a gun and shot Richard dead. Then they disposed of the body."

Róisín turned to Isobel. "I *told* you the police were involved!"

"The policeman told Joe and Leon to keep quiet and they would be fine. A few weeks later Leon died of an overdose. Joe was suspicious. He thought that Leon had been silenced. Then Joe was arrested for dealing. He was afraid for his life. Patrick wanted him to make a statement revealing all he knew. Joe didn't want to do that. He said that he wasn't safe. He was right. He was found dead, also of an overdose, a few days later. Patrick was convinced that the shooter was getting rid of the witnesses to the murder. He was nervous for himself too. He was sure that they suspected that Joe had talked to him . . ."

"And within a few days Patrick was dead as well," Róisín whispered.

Gareth nodded and hung his head. "Yes."

"So there's a policeman in the North who is a murderer," Isobel said.

"Yes."

"Do you know who he was? The off-duty policeman?" Isobel persisted.

Gareth nodded.

"Who?" Isobel said.

"I don't think that I should tell you. Everything I've told you is what Joe told Patrick. It's third-hand at this stage. I can't be sure it's true."

"I need to know. You may have heard about the two students attacked near the Muse in Belfast. I'm helping with the investigation and have been co-ordinating with the PSNI."

"Yes, I heard about that."

"In the course of that investigation we've realised that there's a corrupt policeman. It would be good to have confirmation of who it is so that we can be careful."

Gareth studied his hands. "There's nothing that can be done now. All the witnesses are dead."

"I heard you. But it would be safer for me and my friends if we knew who not to trust."

Gareth rubbed his hands over his face. "I'm serious, this guy is lethal. You can't let him know that you know any of this. And you can't let him know that I told you this."

Isobel nodded. "I understand completely."

"Right." He took a deep breath. "It was Superintendent Taylor."

Róisín's mouth fell open. "Superintendent Taylor? *Oh my God!*"

Isobel took a shaky breath.

Gareth was studying her. "You knew?"

Isobel nodded. She clasped her hands together in her lap. "Not one hundred per cent but his name has been mentioned."

"Is there any evidence to prove his corruption?"

"I'm not sure. There may be something. But it might not be enough."

Gareth studied her. "If you think that you have something, come back and talk to me."

Isobel raised her eyebrows. "I thought that you were disinclined to get involved."

"I am but I'm prepared to advise you legally."

Isobel inclined her head in acknowledgment. "Thank you."

She pondered all that she'd heard. "And the person who alerted Taylor – you called him 'The Prop' – do you know anything about who that is?"

Gareth looked off into the distance. "Not really. From something Joe said Patrick suspected that it might be another garda."

"A corrupt garda as well as a corrupt officer in the North?"

"Patrick wasn't sure but that's what he suspected, or what Joe suspected."

Aaron's words came back to Isobel. The North and the South suspected each other. Maybe they were both right.

"The man who got shot – Richard, the undercover garda – do you know the rest of the name he was using?"

"Castles. That's all I know. I don't know what his real name was."

302

"Thank you for telling us all of this."

They fell silent, then Róisín said, "Can you tell me more about how Patrick was that day you were with him?"

Gareth swallowed. "He was fearful, as I said, but after he told me all of this we had a few drinks and a bit of a laugh about old times. That was good. We both enjoyed it. He was worried about you. He didn't want you to know anything about all of this. He didn't want anything to happen to you."

Róisín was crying now.

"I'm sorry I couldn't help him more." Gareth strangled a sob. "I tried to think of something. When we were saying goodnight, Patrick told me that he wished he'd steered clear of drugs but that now he was in so far he knew he couldn't get out. He just regretted all the pain he'd caused you."

"Thank you, Gareth. You were a good friend. I'm glad Patrick had a good evening with you, just like old times."

Gareth nodded. "I couldn't tell you I'd met Patrick that day in case . . . I'm sorry."

She mopped up her tears. "It's alright, Gareth. You've told me now." She put her tissue away. "We'd better go, Isobel. You have a meeting and traffic might be bad."

"Yes – but one last thing – the bags. Why was Patrick holding up the Org bag in that photo?"

"I think he wished that he could reveal all he knew. He felt that there was no safe place – the police were corrupt – if he said anything he felt he would be killed. I think he wanted to make some sort of a statement even if no one understood it, even if it was never heard. Except, you did understand – maybe not from the pictures he left but you figured out about the drugs, the bags." He bit his lip. "His statement wasn't completely in vain. He'd be pleased about that."

He stood and came around the desk.

Róisín stood up and hugged him. "You were a good friend."

Gareth stifled a sob. He shook Isobel's hand.

As Isobel closed the door behind them she saw Gareth seated at his desk with his head in his hands.

They drove back to the city in silence, each alone with her thoughts.

As they neared the city, Róisín said, "Where's your meeting?"

"The Grosvenor Road police station."

The wheel jerked slightly in Róisín's hands. "The Lion's Den. Is *he* going to be there?" She spat out the word 'he'.

Isobel nodded. "Yes, he is."

"What will you do?"

"I can't do anything now. I have a retired police officer from London working with me. I'll tell him everything when I can and we'll see if we can do something."

"*It's not fair!*" Róisín snarled.

"No, it's not but please realise how dangerous this man is."

"How did you know already?"

"A young policeman told me about his suspicions."

The car moved a little sideways on the road and then

straightened up again. Isobel wished they were sitting having coffee to discuss this – the height of traffic was not the best place or time.

"I'll warn this young man so he doesn't put himself in danger and we can see if there's anything we can prove. *Please, please*, don't do anything now."

"Will you keep me informed?"

"Of course. You've helped tremendously. We weren't sure who the corrupt officer was so this is an enormous step forward."

"Thanks for coming with me, Isobel. It's good to know that Patrick . . . well, that . . ."

"He had a good friend and a mother who loved him."

Róisín nodded. "Thanks."

Isobel rang Jack.

"Isobel, wait until you hear what we've found out. It's a huge breakthrough."

"I've got news for you too. I'm running late. I'll meet you at the police station. Let's get that over with and then we can catch up."

Malcolm's voice came over the phone. "Yes. Let's get this meeting over with quickly, we've a lot to talk about."

"I'll be there soon. See you."

Isobel rested her head against the seat and worked to compose herself. Her head told her she had to be sensible and use the meeting as an opportunity to meet and observe Superintendent Taylor but her heart wanted to have him locked up in a cell. However, she had the sense to know that she needed to be careful not to give anything away or cause him to have any suspicions. Malcolm had wanted to meet the men, to get their measure. Isobel could see the wisdom in that. She hoped she was up to the task of playing her part.

As she looked out of the window it started to rain. She watched the droplets running down the window and wondered if she would ever believe that things were clean again.

Chapter 38

Róisín didn't stop outside the Grosvenor Road police station but instead pulled up down the road a little. Isobel could see Jack and Malcolm standing outside the main gate. Jack was sheltering them under an umbrella.

Isobel got out, waved goodbye to Róisín and walked towards the men.

"Not a word, Jack," said Malcolm. "Not here. Nor you, Isobel. Whatever we need to discuss will have to wait until this is over."

"I wish I didn't have to do this now," she said, "and that you didn't –"

"Well, I want to be here. You need to let the dog see the rabbit."

Isobel couldn't help smiling. "You're missing Bella."

Malcolm nodded. "I sure am. But to continue my metaphor, this rabbit needs to continue to think that it's not a rabbit, so be careful and don't give anything away."

Isobel raised her eyebrows. "Graphic and clear."

Earlier today it had seemed that Inspector Williams

was corrupt then Damien had questioned that. She wondered who Malcolm thought the rabbit was. She wondered what he would say when she told him her news. Obviously he and Jack had also found something important.

"Everyone on your best behaviour," Malcolm said. "Act natural. Now, show me the rabbit!"

He led the way up to the gate.

Isobel smiled at Jack who grinned back as they followed.

Isobel gave their names to the guard on the gate. Damien had put Malcolm's name on the list so there were no problems as they went through all the security checks. They entered the main building and Damien stepped forward to greet them.

He led the way through the well-lit corridors to a conference room. Tony and Joan were already there talking to Inspector Williams.

Williams stepped forward. Their previous meeting had been particularly fraught but, given what Gareth had told her, Isobel felt more disposed to him now.

"Ms. McKenzie." He shook her hand. "And, Jack, it's all thanks to that footage you found that Michael's killer and Charlene's attacker have been revealed."

Isobel gestured towards Malcolm. "This is a friend of mine. Malcolm Carr."

Williams looked at him assessingly, then shook his hand. "Mr. Carr."

Williams seemed less abrasive today. Isobel wondered what had changed.

She saw Michael's parents approaching. Mrs. O'Neill looked upset.

After greetings were exchanged, Mrs. O'Neill pulled Isobel to the side. "I thought you would have phoned me."

Isobel felt guilty. "I'm sorry."

"I trusted you."

Isobel felt sick. "I will ring you."

Mrs. O'Neill studied her face. "When?"

Isobel stepped in close so she could speak almost into her ear. "I can't say anything other than the fact that I will phone you. Please say nothing."

Mrs. O'Neill gave a nod.

Joan and Tony joined them.

Isobel whispered to Tony. "Who's with Charlene?"

"Don't worry. She's safe. Nathan is with her. "

Isobel nodded.

"I know the man's dead but after what he did to Michael," Joan reached out and touched Mrs. O'Neill's arm, "and Charlene, I can't say that I'm sorry. I'm glad we won't have to go to court. I would hate that."

"And you never know what happens in court."

Everyone turned towards the speaker. A tall man, about six foot, stood in the doorway. He was broad-chested and muscular, with white hair and dark eyes

Inspector Williams said, "This is Superintendent Bernard Taylor."

He introduced the O'Neill's and the Griffiths.

Then he said, "This is Isobel McKenzie."

Superintendent Taylor focused intensely on Isobel's

face. He shook her hand, his grip too tight. "Ah yes, Ms. McKenzie. I've heard a lot about you."

"And this is Jack McKenzie," Inspector Williams added.

Jack shook hands with the Superintendent.

"Oh yes, the young man who recovered the pictures from the alley. I expect the assailant thought he had escaped with the evidence. If you hadn't found those pictures, things might have turned out very differently. We might still have thought that it was a robbery gone wrong and never found the perpetrator."

Knowing what she knew now, Isobel wondered how much he wished that was the case.

Williams continued. "This is Malcolm Carr, a friend of Isobel's."

Malcolm and Taylor shook hands. Malcolm and he were much of a height and Malcolm was just as muscular but not as broad as Taylor.

"Where are you from?" Taylor asked.

"London."

"And what do you think of Belfast?"

"I haven't done much sightseeing yet."

Inspector Williams cut in. "I suppose not." He turned to the O'Neills and the Griffiths. "Have you any questions before we have the press announcement?"

Tony asked, "What about the other man? Is he going to be arrested too?"

Taylor answered. "The second man is from Dublin and is most likely back across the border. And, according to the informant, Geo acted alone." He swung back towards the door. "My colleague from Dublin, who is on the drug task force with me, should be here any minute. He'll be able to answer any questions for you. How is your daughter?"

Isobel cut in. "Yes. How is she? She was still unconscious the last I heard." As she spoke she reached out and caught Tony's arm.

Tony said, "Oh yes, yes . . ."

Isobel increased her grip on his arm.

"It's a slow process," he said.

"I know," Isobel said. "And head injuries can be so unpredictable."

Joan stammered, "That's right, very unpredictable . . ."

Tony took his wife's hand. "We just have to keep praying."

Joan nodded. "Yes, and hope for a miracle."

"So Charlene is still unconscious?"

The voice was loud and they all turned to the door.

"This is the colleague I mentioned," said Taylor. "Garda Inspector Aaron McGuinness."

"Hello, Isobel."

"Oh, you know each other."

"Yes, we do. Hello, Aaron. Yes, Charlene is still unconscious."

When all the introductions were completed, Taylor said, "Tony and Joan were asking about what would happen to the other man and I'm sure Michael's mum and dad want to know too whether you're going to arrest him?"

Aaron nodded. "We will, of course, be interviewing him."

Mrs. O'Neill said, "Is he likely to be charged with being an accessory to murder?"

Aaron shifted. "That may happen but he may claim that, though he was in the laneway, he played no part in the attack."

"No! He can't get away with that!" Mrs. O'Neill cried. "If he was there he must be involved as well!"

"Unfortunately we can't prove that."

"But how do you know the man who is dead was the attacker then?" Tony asked.

"We know because he was killed. A confidential informer has come forward and stated that George Simpson, Geo, was killed for attacking and killing the students," Taylor answered.

"I see . . . but –"

"We have no reason to doubt this informer. He's always given us accurate information before."

"And rest assured, Mr. and Mrs. O'Neill," Aaron said, "Tim-Tanner is on our radar and we will be watching him like hawks."

Isobel shivered, more animals, more hunting references.

"Tony, I'm sure they will do everything they can," Joan said.

Isobel felt her stomach lurch. She felt sick at the games and the lies. She wondered if Aaron had any idea of who he was working with. Maybe she needed to warn him. But she needed to talk everything through with Malcolm and Jack first. At least she could trust them implicitly.

"Yes. We better get organised," Taylor said. "I've prepared a short statement, basically saying that Michael's killer and Charlene's attacker has been killed. Aaron will be at the table with me, as will Mr. and Mrs. O'Neill. Williams and Doran, you stand behind us with Mr. and Mrs. Griffiths and Isobel and Jack. There are going to be no questions as enquiries are ongoing."

Isobel said, "No, I'd prefer not to be on television." She couldn't take much more of this. "You all go ahead. I think Malcolm, Jack and I will head away. Is that all right with you, Jack?"

"Yes, of course."

"You have to meet us later at the hotel for a celebratory drink," Tony said.

"Do," Joan added.

"OK," Isobel said. "I'll phone you to arrange things."

Mrs. O'Neill grasped Isobel's arm. "I look forward to hearing from you, soon."

Isobel nodded.

Aaron came up to Isobel. "Thanks for all your help, Isobel. If you're talking to Eoin, tell him I'll be in touch."

Isobel nodded. "Sure."

Aaron fussed with the hair at his ears. "Do I look OK?"

"Yes, fine."

He walked up to Taylor and they stood shoulder to shoulder. Isobel guessed that this would make a good news item: North-South co-operation. Once again the duplicity of it sickened her. She really needed to talk to Jack and Malcolm. She swung around to find them.

Jack was talking to Joan and Tony. Malcolm was deep in conversation with Inspector Williams.

Isobel spoke quietly to Damien. "When you're finished can you ring me to meet up. I have information for you."

"Yes. I'll be an hour or so here. I'll call when I'm finished."

Taylor called the others for the press conference.

Isobel, Jack and Malcolm made their way out of the police station.

The journey to the Park hotel led past the murals on the Grosvenor Road and Sandy Row. Malcolm marvelled at the colourful and political messages. All Isobel could feel was a weight in her heart. The paramilitaries of the past had become drug dealers. The victims were as numerous, the wounds were different but the lives lost and ruined, the families tormented and grieving, were the same. Drugs were a worldwide problem and the only agreement seemed to be that no one had found a solution.

Chapter 39

Isobel let the three of them into her room. She was wound as tight as a drum with stress and anger.

"Jesus, that was so hard. I feel dirty pretending –"

"Let's get some food up here," Malcolm said. "We need to talk." He picked up the room-service leaflet and passed it to Isobel. "Calm down, Isobel. We have good news for you. Helpful news."

Isobel felt drained, weary, but she knew eating would help. She ordered a vegetarian pasta dish. Malcolm ordered a steak with all the trimmings and Jack had chicken.

"I'm having a pint of Guinness," said Malcolm. "I deserve it after the day I've had and the breakthrough we've made, eh, Jack?"

Jack grinned. "It's so good."

Isobel couldn't help but feel easier. "OK. I'll have a glass of Sauvignon Blanc. Jack?"

"I'll have a Guinness."

Malcolm phoned the order for food and asked the bar to send up the drinks immediately.

While they waited, Isobel went to the bathroom. She brought a fresh top in with her. She washed her face and freshened up. That helped. She heard a waiter arrive and leave. She came out of the bathroom.

Malcolm passed the drinks out.

"*To success!*" Malcolm said, raising his glass.

"*To success!*" Jack clinked pints with Malcolm.

Isobel toasted with her wine, then sat against the headboard of the bed with her drink on the bedside locker. Malcolm and Jack seated themselves at the table.

"OK," Isobel said. "Enough suspense. Let's hear what you've found out."

Malcolm took a deep drink and sat back in his chair. He looked over at Jack. "When you left, Jack ordered a taxi to take us to SpeedAn. I was paying for the taxi at the gate when Jack noticed a man in the car park." He gestured to Jack.

"It was Inspector Williams," said Jack. "Because we were suspicious of him, I didn't want him to know that I was at the lab so I stayed in the carpark."

"But he hadn't met me at that stage so I followed him into the lab," said Malcolm. "When I entered he was at the counter. He was asking for printed receipts showing when he had left in pictures and when he had received them back. I heard him saying that they were left in under his wife's maiden name of Collins."

"His wife's name? For official business. Why?" asked Isobel.

"Wait," said Malcolm. "All will become clear. Well, some of it!" He leaned forward. "I pulled out my phone and pretended to be absorbed in reading messages but really I was recording him. I thought that this might relate to him suppressing the pictures. The man behind the counter was telling Williams that another officer had come in asking for the photographs. I swear, Williams went as white as a sheet. He looked like he was going to faint. Even the guy behind the counter asked him if he was alright." He grinned. "I got all of that on tape, and I was thinking, oh God, we have to warn Damien that Williams might suspect him." He paused, looking at Isobel. "And then Williams pulled out his phone and asked if the man on the screen had been in asking questions." He shrugged. "I couldn't see the picture, of course. But the guy behind the counter said no, he knew the Superintendent and it wasn't him. Well, William's looked so relieved!"

Isobel raised her eyebrows. "So Williams is afraid of Taylor?"

"Terrified." Malcolm continued. "Williams had the guy check the receipts. I recorded him reading it out. Williams left the pictures in on Wednesday before lunch."

"The day we gave them to him, Isobel," Jack added.

"So almost immediately he received the information."

Jack nodded. "He left them in as soon as Damien gave them to him."

"Which is a bit strange, if you want evidence to disappear."

"Exactly," said Jack.

"That's what I thought," said Malcolm. "The lab man reminded him that he had said forty-eight hours. Williams collected the pictures on Friday morning."

"When we had already contacted Eoin and he had identified the men," said Isobel.

"Yes," said Jack.

Malcolm nodded.

Isobel looked at Jack and back at Malcolm. "So?"

"So it seemed to me that Williams might just be a policeman trying to do his job. I thought about what Damien had told us about Taylor going down to the lab and raising hell. And I thought about how scared Williams looked when he thought that Taylor might have checked up on him . . ."

Isobel nodded. "And?"

"And I reckoned that Williams might be one of the good guys and Superintendent Taylor might be the dirty officer."

Isobel nodded.

"You don't seem surprised," said Malcolm.

"I told you that I'd found out some things too. But continue . . ."

"I texted Jack and asked him to delay Williams when he came out until I got my business done."

"You left the two samples of paint in?"

Malcolm nodded. "Yes. If this is a drug front we need to start getting some sort of evidence."

Isobel nodded.

"Obviously, I didn't know what was going on inside," said Jack. "I was shitting myself wondering why Malcolm wanted me to delay Williams. All I could think to do was start asking him about a future with the police."

Malcolm burst out laughing. "It was so funny. By the

time I came out, Williams was desperately trying to get away and Jack was actually holding on to his arm."

Jack laughed too. "I know. He must have thought that I was an idiot."

Malcolm wiped his face with his hand as his laughter subsided. He took another slug of Guinness.

There was a knock at the door. Isobel moved to go but Malcolm quickly stood and opened the door. Two waiters were outside with trays of food.

Malcolm smiled. "Excellent." He gestured to the table and told them to set up two places there.

Isobel kept one of the trays to balance her food on, and remained sitting on the bed.

Malcolm signed for the food. "My treat," he said. "And, another round of drinks."

"I was going to pay for this," said Isobel.

Malcolm shook his head as he sat down. "No way. This is the most fun I've had since the case in Limerick."

Isobel acknowledged that with her fork. She had already tasted the pasta dish and it was good. She was really hungry.

Malcolm and Jack tucked into their meals and for a few minutes there was only the sound of cutlery on plates.

When the first pangs of hunger had abated, Isobel said, "Go on. What happened next?"

Malcolm swallowed his mouthful of steak. "Well, I introduced myself to Williams as a retired Met officer, and a friend of yours and Jack's."

Jack raised his finger in acknowledgement but kept eating.

"Anyway, I asked if we could talk and the upshot was we sat into Williams' car," Malcolm said. "I suppose I took a risk but I said that I had heard which day he had left the pictures in the lab. I told him that we knew there was someone in the police working for the drug gang but that it seemed unlikely to be him." He shrugged. "He was shocked. I asked him if he had any proof that Taylor suppressed the pictures."

"He didn't want to tell me initially. But I think the fact that I was ex-police myself helped – and I suppose maybe he needed someone to trust too."

Jack said, "Wait 'til you see what he showed us. It's great, Malcolm, isn't it?"

Isobel raised her eyebrows.

"It's something. I can see why he wanted the receipts. They proved that he had submitted the pictures for resolution, albeit using his wife's maiden name. He was doing his job. But exercising extreme caution. And that combined with the video he showed us . . ." He picked up his phone, worked on it and then handed it to Isobel. "Just press play."

Isobel studied the screen.

Inspector Williams pointed the camera at himself and then turned it towards a closed door. Superintendent Bernard Taylor's name was on the door. The screen then went blank and Isobel heard a knock. She heard a door open.

"*Ah, Williams. You needed to see me about something important.*"

"*Yes, sir, superintendent.*"

"*What is it?*"

"*It's about the case in the alley beside the Muse, the two students, one dead and one in intensive care.*"

"*A bad business. I thought that was a robbery gone wrong. I've already spoken to the Provost about it, a sad and unfortunate business.*"

"*Yes, sir. I have a development. I think it could be very important.*"

"*What is it? Spit it out.*"

"*Charlene, the young woman in intensive care, sent pictures from the alley to another student and he has turned them over to us.*"

"*I see.*"

"*There are two figures hazy in the background.*"

"*Let me see.*"

There were a few moments of silence.

Then Taylor said. "*I can see two people in the background but not clearly at all. They could be anybody.*"

"*True. I was hoping, sir, that the lab could clean up the pictures for us – maybe enhance them.*"

"*I suppose it's possible but I wouldn't hold out much hope.*"

"*But it's definitely worth a try.*"

"*Yes. Have you shown these around, inspector?*"

"*No, sir. Jack McKenzie found the pictures this morning. He contacted Detective Doran who met with him and received the pictures. That's Doran's phone actually.*"

"*Yes, good. Good. It's probably best to keep this on a need-to-know basis. Nothing may come of it. No point causing a furore. I presume Detective Doran is discreet.*"

"Of course, sir."

"OK. Tell Doran to send that footage to me. I'll pull whatever strings I can to get the lab to work their magic. Of course we'll hope for the best, just don't be too disappointed. I'll get back to you if I have any news."

"Thank you, Superintendent Taylor."

Isobel heard chairs scrape and a door open and close, then the recording stopped.

"So Inspector Williams can prove that Superintendent Taylor knew about the pictures," she said.

"And that he took charge of them. But there's more." Malcolm brought up something else on his phone and again handed it to Isobel.

Once again she saw Inspector Williams' face.

He said, "Thursday 26th October, five o'clock pm." Once again Superintendent Taylor's name on the door flashed up then again the screen went blank and Isobel could hear a knock and a door opening and closing.

"Ah, Williams."

"Superintendent Taylor."

"I just wanted to let you know that I had the pictures looked at and the lab cannot get anything from them. I'm sorry. You'll just have to forget that line of enquiry and move on."

"That's a shame, sir. I was hopeful about those pictures."

"Can't be helped. Thank you, Williams."

"Taylor must have been anxious when we produced such clear pictures," said Isobel.

"Yeah," said Malcolm. "Williams, unfortunately, couldn't record that conversation. Apparently, Taylor pulled Williams aside in the corridor on Friday and made some comment about the private sector and funding, implying that that was the problem, more money, better labs. I would say he thinks he's covered his tracks."

Jack said, "It's good, Isobel, isn't it?"

"Yes, but while all of this is something, it probably isn't enough to make a case against Taylor," said Malcolm. "The recordings may not even be admissible in evidence."

"Oh." Isobel felt deflated.

Jack had finished his meal and now sat forward eagerly. "What did you learn today, Isobel?"

Isobel told the story she had heard that afternoon.

"*Oh my God! Taylor killed someone!*" Jack was horrified.

"Maybe more than one," said Malcolm.

"I'm not sure what to do now," Isobel said. "Everything seems so messed up."

No one spoke for a while.

Then Isobel said, "I suppose the only thing I can think of is to tell Eoin what we know."

"What can he do?"

Isobel threw up her hands. "I don't know. This case seems too big. I just wanted to find out who killed Michael and put Charlene in a coma. And now we seem to be dragged into dealing with drug dealers and gangs and corruption!"

Malcolm stood up and walked to the window. "Isobel, the two cases you worked on before involved a crime with an individual who was responsible but it isn't always like that. In this case, it's true that someone killed Michael – Tim-Tan – and of course I want him to go to jail for that but we've found more crimes here. Michael died and Charlene ended up in a coma probably because they inadvertently saw some drug dealers. They were harmed to protect the drug dealers. Geo died to protect the continuation of drug dealing. But the effects of drugs, the prostitution it leads to, the thefts, the violence, the deaths, those aren't over. They're going to continue. Of course I want to catch Tim-Tan but, honestly, if we have any chance of making inroads into the drug dealing and the corruption that upholds it, supports it, then I'm sorry but I want to take it."

He turned around to face the others.

"Sometimes I lie awake at night and wonder how many lives have been ruined by the men that I couldn't put away, all that suffering that I couldn't stop. I know this is awful. It's scary. It's overwhelming but, believe me, we actually have a chance here to do something."

"I agree with Malcolm," Jack said.

Isobel nodded. "OK." She took a deep breath. "Sorry. You're right. But it is overwhelming."

"Organised crime is but I don't think that we can just pretend we haven't found what we have, or bury our heads in the sand. That doesn't help."

"No. I suppose not." Isobel put her hands up to her face. "I'm glad you're here, Malcolm."

Jack said, "Me too."

Malcolm smiled and shook his head. "You always manage to get embroiled in something big, Isobel."

Isobel laughed. "True but this time I think it's too big."

He walked over, pulled Isobel to her feet and draped his arm around her shoulders. "That's why you have friends like me."

Isobel laughed and pushed him. "Go back to what you were saying about the case."

"Where was I?"

"It was about Taylor," Jack said.

"Right. We have Taylor on tape with possible conspiracy charges. We suspect he may have shot the undercover garda. We need to know who that is and also who tipped Taylor off about him. You say that Patrick thought the snitch was Southern."

"Yes. He did. But I don't know what the basis for that was."

Malcolm looked out of the window. "Why don't we see if Eoin can find out about this missing garda? Maybe knowing who he is will help us identify who could have betrayed him."

"That's a good idea. Should I warn Eoin's friend Aaron that we are suspicious of Taylor?"

Malcolm shook his head. "No. We don't want to tip our hand yet and Aaron is working with Taylor. That would put him in a very difficult and dangerous position. We know how ruthless Taylor is. Tell Eoin to say nothing to him yet. See if Eoin can find us some information very discreetly."

Isobel frowned. "OK, that makes sense. Though he might find it hard to keep this quiet as he knows Aaron."

"He'll have to cope. It's safer for Aaron not to know anything at the moment. And we need to be very careful about information. There are leaks everywhere. The less people who know what we're doing the better."

"Eoin will understand. Let's ring him now."

It took some time to tell Eoin about all that they had found out.

When they were finished the call, Malcolm said, "Eoin is worried about our safety. He's going to be very circumspect in what he does and that's a good thing. I feel a bit relieved."

"Malcolm, in all the excitement we forgot to tell Isobel our other piece of news," Jack said. "You know, what Ms. Pritchard found."

"What did she find?"

"That the Professor has been doing the bag pick-up every Tuesday for nearly a year," Jack said. "Ms. Pritchard has it all saved on tape and has emailed me the file."

"Great. And back to the drug case," Isobel said. "We didn't tell Eoin about the distribution system that we think we've found."

"I know but he has enough to deal with," said Malcolm, "and, anyway, I don't want the system closed down. If they do that we're going to miss out on identifying and catching the major players. They're going to cover their tracks. There might be another way of revealing everything that helps us catch everyone." He looked pensive.

Isobel's phone rang.

"Damien?"

"Hi, Isobel! Inspector Williams and I are downstairs in the hotel. Can we come up?"

"Sure. Room 417."

"We're just collecting a drink first. We'll be up then."

"OK. See you then."

Isobel clicked off her phone and it rang again.

"Hi, Tony."

"Isobel, when are you coming to the hotel to meet me and Joan? Charlene is doing so much better. We wanted to tell you earlier but I realised that you didn't want me to say anything. She came round and recognised us. We couldn't be happier, everything is working out. The guy is caught, Charlene is conscious. It's all great."

"Does Charlene remember anything?"

"We haven't started down that road yet. I wondered if the police might want to be there for that."

"That's a good point, Tony. You haven't spoken to any of the police yet?"

"No, no. I was waiting to talk to you because you were so insistent on secrecy. Only Joan and I know."

"That's good, Tony. Keep it that way for now."

"Even though they've got the man who did it?"

"*Yes, Tony. Please. I'm begging you.* Another day. Just keep it all quiet for now. I'm actually meeting with someone now. I'll discuss it with them and let you know. I don't think we can come over tonight. I'm really tired – maybe tomorrow evening."

"OK, Isobel. I understand. We're tired ourselves and relieved."

"You must be. That's the best news I've had for a long time. I'll let you know tonight or in the morning about talking to Charlene."

"Sure thing. Bye."

Isobel clicked off her phone and turned to Malcolm. "You heard?"

"Yeah, Charlene has come round."

"Tony is wondering about the police being there to see what she remembers. I need to tell them that there's a witness who says that Tim-Tan committed the murder and the attack on Charlene."

Malcolm frowned. "Maybe. Or you could speak to Charlene first and see what she remembers. You can always tell them about your witness later, to substantiate what she remembers. It would be a stronger case if Charlene remembers without prompting."

"I see what you mean."

Malcolm paced up and down. "Something has struck me. Halloween is coming. There will be customers looking for drugs. I think the drug gang will want to go ahead, business as usual."

"But surely after Michael's death they will have to stop what they're doing," Jack said.

Malcolm shook his head. "The murder is solved. The bad guy is dead. People will still want their drugs and the gang won't want to risk losing their custom."

"But they won't go ahead with the delivery on Monday night as usual," Isobel said. "That would be too risky after all the publicity."

"I think the big press conference was to tie everything up, job done, bad guys caught, it's all over, nothing to see here. No more investigating needed. Let's get on with our lives."

"What do you think is going to happen?"

"I think that since Michael was killed the dealers have been working on a new plan. While the investigation was ongoing and the focus was still on the laneway they wouldn't have risked moving drugs into the area but now the case is over and no doubt they have an alternative plan. I think Monday may still be the night. It's quiet. It has worked for them before."

"But how are we going to find the new distribution system?" Jack said.

"That's what I have been trying to figure out."

"And?" said Isobel.

"I think we need to watch that guy Robin because we know he's a seller. Somehow he is going to get more drugs to dispense."

"OK. That is a possibility," said Isobel.

"Yes, and I think we should watch the manager of the Org shop. He must be involved and he may get the drugs to the shop another way now."

"Look, Damien and Williams are on their way up. Do you want them to do the surveillance?" Isobel asked.

"No. I don't think they could do it officially without Taylor knowing and that would defeat the purpose. What we want is enough evidence to bust the supply chain, really cause damage."

"So what are you thinking?"

"I was thinking more that Jack and I could do it. Jack, you could follow Robin and I could keep an eye on the manager of the shop."

"Yeah, I can do that."

"Just take pictures on your phone and if we see a transfer then we can let Williams know."

"But the drug handover could be anywhere in the city. You'd need cars."

Jack perked up. "I know who could help us."

Isobel held out her hand. "Wait, Jack. Malcolm, do you really think that this is the best way to go?"

"Yes, Isobel. I do. We have suspicions about a delivery using the Org vans and the laneway which backs onto the Org shop. We have some questionable behaviour with Org bags in the library and in the Botanic Gardens. We have a theory about what was going on but that will all be changed now. I'm just suggesting that we wait a day or two to see if we can use who we think is involved to find the new delivery system. If not, then we can still pass on our suspicions to Williams and Damien. A few more days, that's all I'm suggesting."

"OK. Maybe Eoin will have found something by then too. Should I mention anything to Williams about Taylor and the shooting?"

"What we could do with is some evidence tying Taylor to the crime. There seems to be no body and no witnesses. It's very hard to prove a crime with all of those things absent. Maybe Eoin will find something." He pursed his lips. "Tomorrow, Isobel, I think you should go and see Charlene and, Jack, you should go with her. Charlene knows you, Jack, and that will help. And Isobel, at least you have some training in talking to people who've experienced trauma. If anyone can get her to talk, I think you could."

Isobel felt a rush of pleasure that Malcolm thought so

highly of her skills. She felt it was another vote of confidence for her going back to work.

Malcolm smiled. "OK, Jack – who is it you think can help us?"

"My dad could help you watch the Org shop guy, then if you need transport he can drive you – and Noah can drive me – he has a car."

"No, Jack," Isobel said. "I don't want any more young people involved and I have a car myself."

"With a Southern registration, too obvious."

"Good point."

"And Noah is involved – he has been from the start. He and Rachel knew about the film and I warned them to say nothing about it and they didn't. They told you that they wanted to help. They felt as bad as I did about giving out to Michael and Charlene. They're delighted with all that we are doing. They would do anything to help. And watching that red-haired guy, Robin – we're all students so that would be easy for us. Noah can keep his car nearby in case we need it."

"It sounds like a plan to me," said Malcolm. "We're only talking about observing and photographing, Isobel."

There was a knock on the door.

Jack went to open it. Williams and Damien were standing there with pints of Guinness in their hands. Jack stood aside to let them into the room.

"Sorry we were so long," said Williams. "The bar was busy."

"And you didn't think to bring us a drink," Malcolm said.

Damien blushed.

Williams grinned. "I knew you would have yourselves well sorted."

Damien saw the glasses on the table, all with something in them, and laughed.

Malcolm grinned at him. "I had you going there."

Williams sat at the small table with Malcolm, and Damien settled on the floor with his back to the wall. Isobel was on the bed and Jack joined her there.

Initially, all conversation centred on the press conference and how credible Taylor had been.

Damien said, "Thank God, I at least know who I can trust now."

"I know," said Williams. "That's something. Damien has told me about his friend Brian who works in the lab. I'm going to get a statement from him that no pictures came to the lab. We can probably prove that Taylor didn't hand in that evidence but I would prefer if we had something more."

Malcolm made a face at Isobel.

She said, "I have a solicitor whose friend, now dead, told him that a client of his, also dead, named Taylor as the killer of an undercover garda."

Williams shook his head. "Honestly, I don't find it hard to believe that he has killed someone but it's all hearsay and all of the people are dead. I don't remember hearing about a garda being killed."

Isobel looked uncomfortable. "They disposed of the body."

"So nothing then," said Williams. "Any witnesses?"

"Taylor got rid of all of the witnesses."

"Right. Well, we need the body and we need a way to tie Taylor to it." He glanced at Malcolm.

"We're working on finding out more," he said. "We'll let you know if our sources turn up anything."

Isobel felt stupid. What could she do but go back and press Gareth for any other information? "Well, we know how potentially dangerous Taylor is and what he's prepared to do, which is something."

"Isobel is right," said Malcolm. "Inspector Williams, you and Detective Doran need to be very careful."

"Yes, I realised what Taylor was doing a while ago. I've managed to acquit myself OK while collecting some incriminating evidence, so I think I'll cope." Williams gestured to Damien. "And Detective Doran is learning fast. He shows great aptitude and I'm keeping an eye on him, so he'll be fine."

"I have the name the garda was using when undercover," said Isobel.

Williams raised his eyebrows. "You do?"

"Richard Castles."

Williams nodded at Damien who typed the name into his phone.

"And something else I need to tell you," Isobel continued. "Charlene is waking up."

"Oh, thank God! That's great news," said Damien.

"I think it would be good if Isobel and Jack talk to her tomorrow," said Malcolm. "Maybe Damien could go too in case Charlene does remember anything from the night of the attack."

"But," said Isobel, "no one else must know that Charlene is conscious. It might endanger her life."

"If the attack has been claimed and the culprit has been punished, is that really necessary?" Williams asked.

"Yes." Malcolm glanced at Williams. "Not that I'm telling you your job."

"Like hell you aren't!"

"I don't mind going to see what Charlene has to say," said Damien.

Williams rolled his eyes. "Go on then, I suppose it's the least we can do after the debacle with the pictures." He turned to Malcolm. "Have you any other information?"

"Not at the moment."

Williams squinted at Malcolm. "Why do I get the feeling that I'm getting the run-around?"

"We're checking out some things. I promise if any of those bear fruit you'll be the first to know."

Williams finished his pint. "Fine. I'm going home to have a good night's sleep. Come on, Doran, you need your beauty sleep too before you go to the hospital."

Malcolm closed the door after them. "Are you sure about giving them the name of Richard Castles? If they go poking around, Taylor might get wind of it."

Isobel sighed. "No, I'm not sure. But somehow we have to find a way to corroborate this story. I'm sure they'll be careful, especially when they know he's committed murder. I'm just hoping that somewhere someone will find something that can help us. I might go and see Gareth again after the hospital. Maybe he has remembered something else."

Malcolm nodded. "OK. We all have a busy day tomorrow so I'll say goodnight."

Isobel hugged Malcolm and Jack and they left. She was tired too.

In her sleep Isobel found herself in a dark place. As she looked around she could see that ahead it was brighter. She stepped forward in the direction of the light until she was standing under it. The light was coming from a golden gun as big as a canon. The gun started to turn. After a number of its revolutions Isobel moved forward. She felt something beneath her feet. She reached down. They were bullets. She stood paralysed, her hearting hammering in her chest, a cold sweat breaking out all over her body.

Chapter 40

Sunday 29th October

At breakfast Isobel reflected on her dream. She needed to find a way to tie Taylor to the death of the garda. With that information they could send him to prison for murder and hopefully conspiracy too. She was quiet as she mulled all of that over.

Malcolm was tucking into another Ulster fry. "I could get used to this, all the different types of bread."

Isobel smiled. Malcolm's enthusiasm was a balm.

"Patricia messaged me," she said. "She wants to talk. I said I could speak to her this morning at nine."

Malcolm paused in his eating. "Funny. I'm talking to her at a quarter past nine."

"She must have news."

"She's pregnant?" Malcolm suggested.

Isobel rolled her eyes. "I was thinking more along the lines of an engagement."

Malcolm grinned. "Oh yes, I get it, a romantic getaway, a sandy beach, a ring. I can see how that would work."

Isobel smiled. "You're not a detective for nothing."

"I'm not a detective, I'm retired and on holiday visiting a friend. But let me tell you, engagement or no engagement, Patricia is going to be so annoyed that she's missed all of this."

"Well, I miss her too. And make sure you act surprised when she says that she's engaged."

"Or pregnant."

Isobel laughed. "Or pregnant." Her good humour faded. "I have missed her. She's so good to talk to during a case."

Malcolm made a face. "Are you suggesting that I'm not up to the job?"

For a moment Isobel wondered if he did feel slighted then she saw his eyes sparkling at her. "Stop winding me up. I've enough to be thinking about today."

Malcolm shook his head. "All the more reason for a bit of light relief." He stood up. "Come on, let's go and hear this news."

Isobel sat waiting on her bed.

Patricia called at exactly nine.

"Isobel!"

"Hi, Patricia. How are things?"

"I've got news for you."

"Tell me!"

Peter appeared beside Patricia.

"*We're engaged!*" they chorused together.

"Congratulations! I'm so glad! But, wait, I have a surprise as well."

Isobel ran to the door and opened it. She pulled Malcolm into the room and closed the door.

"They're engaged," she told him.

Malcolm stepped up behind Isobel so he could look into the phone too. "*Congratulations!*"

"*Malcolm!*" Patricia said. "What are you doing there?"

"That's great news – I'm delighted for you both," he said.

"Thank you!"

"Have you set a date yet?"

Patricia grinned. "Not yet. But it won't be too long. Anyway, we can discuss all that when we get back and make plans. Right now I want to know what you're doing in Limerick? Is it another case or are you over fishing?

"It's not Limerick," Malcolm said. "We're in Belfast."

Patricia glanced at Peter then at the phone. "Belfast? What's going on?"

"Right," said Isobel. "Settle down and we'll tell you. It's a long story."

Between them Isobel and Malcolm told them everything that had happened as succinctly as they could, with occasional requests for clarification from Patricia and Peter.

At last they reached the end of the story to date.

"Jesus," Peter said. "That's a Gordian knot."

"What a mess!" Patricia said.

"Any thoughts? Any ideas that might help?" Isobel asked hopefully.

Peter rubbed his hands through his hair. "Not off the top of my head. Patricia?"

"Not immediately. Leave it with us and we'll talk it through and get back to you."

Isobel smiled. "Thanks. I'm going to the hospital now to see Charlene. I'll be free in a few hours. We'll talk to you later. And congratulations! Have a wonderful day today. Don't let what's going on here dampen your celebrations."

Patricia grinned. "We won't. Bye."

Isobel met Jack and Damien outside the hospital. They contacted Tony and he came down and escorted them up to the ward where Charlene was. At the entrance to the ward the Sister stopped them.

"Mr. Griffiths, I thought that we made it clear – although Charlene is improved and is out of ICU she still can't have many visitors."

Damien stepped forward, pulling out his badge. "Detective Doran. Investigating Michael O'Neill's death."

"I thought the killer was dead. Why do you need to speak to Charlene?"

"We need to see if Charlene remembers anything from that night." He indicated Isobel. "This lady is a psychotherapist. She's here to mind Charlene and make sure that she isn't too traumatised."

The Sister gestured to Jack. "And who is this?"

Tony put his hands on Jack's shoulders. "This is the young man who performed CPR on Charlene that night and who came with her to the hospital and waited until my wife and I got here. He's her friend."

"Oh, very well. But you can't push Charlene. She may not remember anything."

"I know," said Isobel. "And if she doesn't then that's

fine. We won't force it. Detective Doran is here so that if Charlene does remember anything she doesn't have to repeat it or go through everything again."

The Sister frowned. "All right. But be careful."

Isobel nodded.

Tony pushed open the door of Charlene's room. Joan was sitting at the bedside but got up as they came in. Tony led Jack forward to the bed. Isobel and Damien hung back.

Charlene had a bandage on her head and was propped up slightly with pillows. She was very pale and her lips were dry and drained of colour. She frowned, her eyes taking in Isobel and Damien before coming to rest on Jack.

"Do you know who this is, Charlene?" Tony asked.

Charlene licked her lips. "Jack."

Jack smiled slightly. "It's good to see you. Are you in pain?"

Charlene moved her head slightly. "No, the pain is OK."

"The tablets are doing the trick, thank God." Tony looked at Isobel. "Joan and I will go for a cup of tea." He patted Charlene's hand where it lay on the covers. "We won't be long, pet."

"OK."

Tony and Joan left, Joan looking somewhat anxious.

"Charlene, this is my Aunt Isobel and this is Damien," Jack said. "He's a policeman."

Charlene frowned.

Jack looked worried and glanced at Isobel. She gestured for Jack to sit in the chair Joan had vacated. She moved forward and sat in the chair on the other side of the bed. Damien stood in the corner, taking out his notebook.

"Would you like some water?" Isobel gestured to the cup and straw on the table.

"Yes."

Charlene's voice was hoarse and Isobel guessed that her throat was tender from having tubes to help her breathe. She held the cup and straw so that Charlene could take a drink.

"Thank you."

"I'm glad you're not in pain."

"Yes."

"Fiona is very worried about you."

"Fiona, yes."

"She says that she was talking to you on Monday about teatime. She said that you got a new present that day. Something Nathan got for you." She paused.

Charlene licked her lips again. "The camera. Yes. The new one. The Canon." She looked at Jack. "I sent you the pictures."

Isobel could feel herself tensing up. Jack looked over at her. She said softly, "What pictures did you send Jack?"

Charlene kept her eyes on Jack. "I was waiting for the camera so the pictures would be really good." She took a ragged breath. "I was taking the project seriously."

Jack reached out and squeezed her hand. "I know you were, now. I'm so sorry that we gave out to you."

Charlene frowned. "Michael wanted to tell you but I wanted it to be a surprise." Her eyes filled up with tears. "Poor Michael."

Jack looked at Isobel with panic in his eyes.

"Do you remember Michael being with you when you sent the photos?" Isobel asked.

Charlene looked over at her. A tear slid down her face. "Yes."

Isobel reached for a tissue from a box on the locker and wiped the tear off Charlene's cheek. She could see Jack biting his lip. She glanced at Damien. He was taking notes but also had set his phone on the windowsill and she assumed was recording everything.

"What else do you remember, Charlene?" she asked.

Charlene looked deep into Isobel's eyes and Isobel could see terror there.

"The men." She reached out with her other hand towards Isobel.

Isobel pulled her chair closer to the bed and grasped Charlene's hand, never breaking eye contact.

"The men?" she asked.

Charlene stared at her. "They were smoking."

Isobel nodded. "Yes, they were."

"They saw us."

"I know. Do you remember what happened next?"

"Yes." There was a long pause. "One of them shouted."

"Did he?"

"Yes. Then he ran towards us." Charlene's grip tightened painfully on Isobel's hand.

"One of the men ran towards you."

"Yes. I was sending the pictures to our cloud account. I didn't realise what was happening." Charlene's breath was more laboured. "Michael stepped in front of me."

A part of Isobel wanted to intervene and stop Charlene. She did remember. She was reliving a terrible trauma but stopping her from talking about it was not going to eradicate the experience.

"He hit Michael. Michael fell to the ground." Charlene's face crumpled in tears. "I knew he was going to hit me. I don't remember anything else."

Isobel rubbed her hand. "You've remembered a lot."

"I'll never forget it."

Isobel offered Charlene another sip of water.

When she was settled again she said, "No one has mentioned Michael to me."

"Haven't they?" Isobel said.

"No. I know what that means."

"You do?"

"It means he's dead." Charlene looked at Isobel with challenge in her eyes. "He is dead, isn't he? I heard the sound of the man hitting him." Her eyes filled with tears.

Isobel squeezed her hand.

"Why did I survive?"

Isobel shook her head. "I don't know. It might have been where he hit you, or your skull was stronger."

Charlene kept her eyes on Isobel but didn't say anything.

"Michael stepped in front of you."

"Yes. He was trying to protect me."

Isobel could feel tears welling in her own eyes. "Do you think so?"

"Yes."

"I'm glad you remembered that. Michael's mum will be proud of her son."

343

Charlene cried for a few minutes.

Isobel gave her a tissue and she wiped her face.

"Will you tell her?"

"If you want me to."

"I might be here for a while. You tell her."

Isobel nodded. "I will." She waited but Charlene said nothing for a minute.

"Could you describe the man who hit you, Charlene? Can you remember anything about him?"

"He had a tattoo on his hand."

Damien spoke up. "Are you sure of that? That he had a tattoo?"

"Yes, it was a bird. I saw it when he raised his . . ." She broke off and sobbed for a minute.

"It's alright. You're doing really well." When her sobs subsided, Isobel said, "Just a few more questions and then we'll be done. OK?"

"OK."

"Do you remember what colour his hair was?"

"A browny colour." She paused. "I only saw that when he got closer."

"Are you sure that his hair was brown?" Damien asked.

"I saw him as he came near me. The light from the street lamps in the alley shone on his face."

Damien said, "Would it be too much for you to look at some photos for me, Charlene?"

Isobel hadn't realised that Damien had come this prepared.

"You don't have to, Charlene," she said. "You can do that another day if you want."

Charlene moistened her lips. "No, I'll do it now. I want you to get the man who attacked Michael," she paused, "and me."

Damien pulled an envelope from inside his jacket. He spread out six photos on the hospital bed-table. "Take your time," he said. "And if you don't recognise anyone that's OK too."

Isobel saw that there was one of Geo and two other men who were also bald and there was a photo of Tim-Tan and again two men with similar hair colour. Isobel wondered if this was too hard for Charlene's bruised brain. Wouldn't Charlene mentioning the tattoo on the hand be enough to identify Tim-Tan?

The silence lengthened.

"It's fine, Charlene, if this is too much," Isobel said. "You've done a lot today in talking to us."

As she finished speaking Charlene glanced over at her, her face tight, her eyes stormy. She looked back at the photos then lifted her hand and pointed. "That's him." She pointed at one of the photos.

"Are you sure?" Damien asked.

"Yes, positive."

Isobel looked at the photo Charlene was pointing at. It was Tim-Tan.

Damien glanced at Isobel. He raised his eyebrows.

Isobel broke eye contact with him. "You've done really well, Charlene. You've been a great help to the police. You need to rest now and get your strength back."

"You did so good sending the pictures, Charlene," said Jack. "That really helped."

Charlene smiled at Jack. "Good."

Her face relaxed a little and Isobel could see that she was exhausted.

"We'll tell your mum and dad to come back," she said.

Isobel stepped away. Jack leaned in to say something which Isobel could not hear.

Damien leaned towards Isobel. "You knew it was Tim-Tan."

Isobel didn't answer. She rang Tony. "Tony. Charlene has done great. She's tired now."

"We'll be right there."

Isobel turned to Damien. "Later, we'll talk about this later."

"We will indeed."

Tony and Joan arrived very quickly. Charlene's eyes were heavy.

As Isobel said goodbye, Charlene said, "Tell Michael's mum."

"I will."

Isobel drew Tony out of the hospital room. "Charlene has identified the second man, not the one who was killed, as the attacker."

"*What?*"

"You need to tell no one that and you need to keep it quiet that she is conscious and has remembered anything. Make sure that Joan knows that."

"What happens now?"

Isobel took a deep breath. "I'm not sure. I need to talk to a lot of people. I'll let you know. You focus on Charlene. And don't leave her alone at any point."

"Don't worry, I won't."

They walked in silence out of the hospital.

Damien said abruptly, "Let's talk in the car," and stalked off through the grounds to the car park.

Jack raised his eyebrows at Isobel and she shrugged.

Damien unlocked the car and sat into the driver seat. Isobel sat into the passenger seat and turned to face him. Jack sat in behind Isobel, closing the door with a click.

"What the hell was that? I know Malcolm has been saying that Geo being killed was convenient, tactical even, but when Charlene identified Tim-Tan as the killer, you knew that. Don't lie to me." He put both hands up to his head. "Jesus, what is going on? Even the people I think are trustworthy are lying to me."

Isobel could see the confusion and hurt in his eyes. "That's not it. Are you just going to condemn me or do you want to hear what I have to say?"

Damien gave a laboured breath and crossed his arms. "Go on then."

"No, Damien. I'm not going to sit here and justify myself. I'm prepared to tell you but if you've already written me off as a liar then I'm not going to waste my breath."

Damien shifted in his seat but some of his anger had leaked away.

"Tell me. I'm listening."

"Malcolm and Jack know that I found someone who identified Tim-Tan as the killer. When Geo was put forward as the killer we knew that a major cover-up was going on. In fact, it would be worth checking who dealt with the informer who said that Geo killed Michael. I wouldn't be surprised if Taylor received that information."

Damien nodded. "You're probably right."

"Accepting Geo as the killer was bringing the whole case down the wrong track. And Malcolm did his best to raise the issue about how convenient it all was. The witness didn't, and probably still doesn't, want to come forward because, firstly, he would be easily discredited in court. Secondly, because he knows that if his identity was known he would be killed. And, believe me, it would be easy to do it and pass it off as an accidental death. The witness believes his life would be in danger and he doesn't trust the police – as we now know, with very good reason."

Damien uncrossed his arms and rubbed his mouth with one hand, rasping his hand over his emerging stubble.

"I completely understood and agreed with the witness's assessment of the situation," Isobel went on. "His testimony wouldn't have stood up in court. But, I thought there was value in knowing what really happened and not letting, let's call it, the accepted story overshadow the truth. I couldn't prove the truth but at least I knew what the truth was."

Damien frowned. "OK. I see where you're coming from."

"Now, of course, with Charlene's statement and his as corroboration they have a much better chance of being believed. The defence lawyers could have used Charlene's brain injury to question, or try to throw doubt on what she said. Which makes both of the witnesses vulnerable witnesses, but perhaps together they could make a case, if I can persuade him to make a statement."

"You don't think he will?"

"He wants to survive and people who know anything don't seem to live that long around here."

"True."

"You see the difficulty?"

"I do."

Isobel took a deep breath herself. "Look, the man is homeless."

Damien nodded. "Oh right, yes."

"Charlene identifying Tim-Tan is more than I hoped for. It gives us a possibility. Right now, I'm more concerned with keeping her safe. She's a threat to Tim-Tan. Obviously Tim-Tan was considered to be more important in the scheme of things than Geo, as Geo was sacrificed to protect him. Charlene's life could be in danger now."

Damien shook his head. "Are we any further forward?"

Isobel smiled slightly. "Who knows?"

Her phone rang. She pulled it out of her bag and glanced at it.

"It's Patricia, a friend of mine. She said she would get back to me if she had any ideas. Her ideas are usually good. I want to take this."

"OK. Go ahead."

"Patricia, hi. I'm here with Jack and Damien – Detective Doran."

"Is now not a good time?"

"No, no, it is. Have you got an idea?"

"Peter and I have been talking things through. It's a bit of a string of ideas but it could be something. It might give you something to look into."

"Great."

"Are you sure you don't want me to whatsapp you later?"

Damien reached for Isobel's phone. "Patricia, hi, this is Damien, Detective Doran. I assure you I'm trustworthy. Isobel has been a great help."

Isobel laughed. "A minute ago we weren't in this good a place." She took the phone and turned it towards Jack. "This is Jack, my nephew."

"Hi, Patricia."

"Hi, Jack. I'm sorry about Michael. How is your friend Charlene doing?"

"We've just been to see her. She's conscious, thank God, and seems herself."

"That's great. Peter's here with me, Isobel."

Peter cuddled in beside Patricia.

Isobel held her phone out in front of her so that she and Damien could see it. Jack slid across the back seat so he could see better.

"OK, let's hear it," she said.

Peter said, "We were talking about Geo, the man who was shot and turned up in the river."

"OK?"

"That's the problem with water," Patricia said. "You never know when a body might reappear. When the policeman shot the garda he wouldn't want that body to turn up ever. It would cause a major incident and lots of investigation."

"Especially if he was killed undercover in Northern Ireland," Peter added.

"That's definitely true," said Damien.

Patricia continued. "While if someone disappeared, with no body, that creates a very different situation."

"And here's where we're making a bit of a jump," said Peter.

"The off-duty policeman shot the garda in front of the two drug dealers, right?" Patricia said.

Isobel nodded.

"We reckon that he would have used the two drug guys to help him dispose of the body and as a way to ensure their silence."

"Possibly, probably even," said Isobel.

"So they knew where the body was."

"I know, but they're both dead."

"Yes, but the only information they had that was worth anything was the location of the body," Peter said. "Trust me, people in the system know things like this. I think that the guy who spoke to the young solicitor –"

"Patrick," Isobel said.

"I think to try and prove his innocence or confirm the story he was telling, to make Patrick even *consider* believing him, he would have told him the location of the body. That was the only fact he had that would lend any credence to his story, the only piece of information he could use to even ask someone to believe him."

"That's also why he needed to die," said Damien.

"Exactly. That's why he posed a danger to the policeman, probably what got him killed – but if he shared his story with Patrick then there's a chance he also shared the location."

"So, if we can find the body of the garda, based on this drug guy's information," said Damien, "then we have to consider that the other things he alleged were also true – that the murderer was an off-duty policeman."

"Exactly," said Peter. "Then you would need to find evidence maybe from CCTV cameras that they were all at that warehouse on the docks and left together. And I suppose you have to hope that either the body can tell you something more or, if you ever get the policeman, that producing the body scares him so much he makes a mistake. It's not great but there's definitely a possibility here."

Jack had pulled out his own phone and, after scrolling a bit, said, "The dock area has loads of cameras and has done for years."

"True," said Damien, "but a shooting, a killing, would take place where there isn't camera coverage."

"I know," Peter said. "But an off-duty policeman in the vicinity of a number of drug dealers meeting and leaving around the same time links him to the meeting."

"True but he could say that he spotted them and followed them."

"Also true. But did he report it?"

"He could say that he thought there was nothing suspicious."

"Also true. But if the drug guy claims this is the night the shooting happened and on his word you can produce a body, that's something. I know you need more but all I'm saying is it's a start."

Patricia said, "Peter thinks that Patrick's friend – Gareth, was it? – might have that information and didn't reveal it. Go and see him again, Isobel, and ask him."

"To sum up," said Peter, "the drug guy was terrified. He ended up dead a few days later. I think he told Patrick everything, including where they buried the body and I am hoping that Patrick told his friend Gareth."

"And, as far as I'm concerned," said Patricia, "the fact that both of those drug guys are dead supports his story too."

"Patrick's dead too," said Jack.

"Exactly. The only person still standing is the policeman who the drug guy claimed committed the crime. He cleaned house."

"You're right," said Damien. "God, I would love to get him, the bastard! I can look at the footage from the dock." He flicked through his notebook. "Do we have a date?"

"I can get an approximate date from Patrick's mum," Isobel said.

"Do. I'll see what I can find. There's nothing to lose."

Isobel smiled. "Well done, you two! Getting engaged, solving crimes, you have it all going on. OK. I'll ring Róisín and we can go and visit Gareth again and see what we can turn up."

"Let us know what happens, do you hear me?" Patricia said.

Isobel grinned. "Of course we will. Thanks a million. I'll talk to you later. Bye."

They hung up.

"Do you think that Peter is right, Damien?" Jack asked.

"There's definitely something in what they're saying. How come they're so on the ball about cases? Are they police too?"

Isobel smiled. "Peter is a solicitor and Patricia is a private investigator."

Damien nodded. "You can tell."

"Let me ring Róisín and then you can drop me wherever is handy for her. What about you, Jack?"

"I'll talk to Malcolm. You can drop me off too."

Chapter 41

Róisín drove again out towards Holywood. The roads were quieter. It was a clear day once again with blue skies and a sharp, fresh nip of cold in the air.

"Does Gareth Short live in Holywood, as well as work there?" Isobel asked.

Róisín glanced at her. "No. He's meeting us at the office again."

"Was he working yesterday?"

"No, I don't think so. When I rang his mum she rang him to see what would suit him and he suggested the office."

"It was Saturday. Most solicitors don't work on a Saturday." Isobel shook her head. "I never even thought of which day it was."

"Can't you tell me why you want to go back?"

Isobel rubbed her forehead. Keeping all the pieces of this jigsaw in play and keeping everyone safe and on a need-to-know basis was a struggle. She needed a chart up on the wall that she could refer to.

"We think Gareth might have held back some information yesterday."

Róisín took her eyes off the road and looked over at Isobel.

Isobel broke eye contact to encourage her to watch where she was driving. "We might be wrong but I wouldn't forgive myself if I didn't check it out."

"I was glad that we went to see him yesterday. I slept so well last night."

"That's good. Róisín, on the way back, could we drive out to Antrim? I'd like to see Michael's mum for a few minutes. Is that too much of an imposition? There's something I want to tell her that might help her sleep better too."

"It would be my pleasure."

It was easy to find parking on the main street in Holywood today.

The bottom door to the office was closed.

Isobel rang the buzzer. She heard a click and, when she pushed, the door released.

Today the secretary wasn't at her desk. Gareth himself appeared and escorted Isobel and Róisín to his office.

His secretary was sitting in a chair on the other side of the desk, beside his chair.

"This is Audrey, my office manager and my fiancée." He gestured to the women. "Isobel, Róisín."

Audrey smiled and they sat down.

"I was going to ring you tomorrow, Isobel," Gareth said.

"Oh?"

"Yes. After you left I talked to Audrey. We had some big decisions to make." He reached out and took Audrey's hand. "Obviously, yesterday when you called I told you what I thought I could. I was shocked that you were here asking those kinds of questions and hinting at knowing more. I never really thought that anyone would come to me looking for information."

"What didn't you tell us?" Isobel asked.

"Why did you think there's more? That's why you're here, isn't it, to see what else I know?"

"Friends of mine, one a solicitor, one a private investigator, figured it out. I guess my friend Peter, being a solicitor, knew the way you and Patrick might think, legally."

"Audrey had to be in agreement because revealing any more information could put us in danger, or that's what Patrick warned me. I had to be sure that she could cope." He smiled at Audrey. "And was willing to take this last step."

"And I am," said Audrey.

The light through the window lit up her auburn hair. It was rich and beautiful. Her blue eyes were clear and direct. More than anything, Isobel was struck by her calm, quiet strength. She understood who had decorated the office, why it all felt so peaceful. This woman had an inner world like that and one of her gifts was to create that feeling, that ambience around her. She smiled at Audrey who returned it.

Taking a deep breath, Isobel said, "OK, let's hear it, what's the additional information?"

Gareth opened the drawer beside him and pulled out two A4 size envelopes. "I have here a statement signed by

Patrick and witnessed by me where he outlines the information that I gave you yesterday." He tipped the envelope up and three photographs slid onto the table. "These are the pictures Patrick and I took that day, which you've already seen and which brought you here."

Isobel nodded.

Gareth picked up the second envelope. "Here I have a statement that I gave to my partner in the firm, Brendan Woods, about everything that Patrick told me and also about the fear for his life he had before he died. There is also a signed statement from Joe, giving his version of what happened the night the policeman shot the man who had infiltrated the drug gang. In his statement Joe identifies where they buried the body of the man."

Róisín gasped.

"This is what my friends suggested that you had," said Isobel.

Gareth nodded. "Patrick advised Joe that the only way to save himself was to disclose everything, although Patrick knew that proving Joe's innocence was going to be well-nigh impossible, especially up against Taylor."

"It still might be impossible," said Isobel.

Gareth nodded. "I realise that but at least the family of the undercover garda would have his body. Joe knew what he did could be interpreted as him being the perpetrator but the fact that everyone associated with the case is dead has to suggest conspiracy. Proving it might be difficult but it is certainly a reasonable interpretation of the facts."

"I need to talk to people I trust about how we use this information," Isobel said.

"Of course."

"My biggest concern is that we don't alert Taylor that we're on to him until we have enough to charge him with. At the moment he's convinced that everything is peachy. I want it to stay that way for now."

"But surely you can do something with all of this," said Róisín. "Patrick died because of what he knew. He overdosed because of the strain of it all."

Gareth winced and Audrey shifted a fraction closer to him.

"I have an ex-Metropolitan police officer working with me," Isobel said. "Also a detective and an inspector from the PSNI who know that Taylor is corrupt. I have two Garda Inspectors who are trying to find out about the murdered man, also without alerting anyone to their search. Patrick thought there was an informer in the South. We have to proceed very carefully. One slip and this house of cards will fall and the big players will cover their tracks and we'll have nothing."

Róisín made a slight sound and Isobel glanced over. Her eyes were huge, her face full of worry.

"Maybe tonight myself and the group can have a Zoom meeting and see if between us all there is a way forward," Isobel said. "My friend Peter, the solicitor, might know a way that we can proceed. He's suggested some things for the detective to look into. All I can say is thank you. I promise we'll do everything we can, everything."

Gareth gave a small smile. "The last thing I wanted to say was, if there's anything I can do to help you, I want to do it. Even now, having told you, I can feel a weight lifting off me and, hearing that you have all of the people around you, I feel some little bit of hope. Anything, I mean it."

Isobel took a shaky breath. The weight of everything was heavy. It always felt easier when she was with Malcolm or Patricia – somehow their presence made it feel shared.

A thought came to her: there *was* something Gareth could do.

"Gareth, I have a witness to the murder, Michael's murder – a homeless man. Just now I've spoken to a corroborating witness. Neither one on their own could carry a conviction but maybe together their eye-witness accounts could. The homeless man knows the danger he would be in if he came forward. If I arranged for him to see you tomorrow, could you take a statement, always assuming I can convince him to give one?"

Gareth nodded. "Absolutely. I'm not in court this week so any time just phone and Audrey will sort everything out."

Isobel smiled. "Thank you, Gareth, and you too, Audrey. You made this easier than I thought it was going to be."

"Even if your witness refuses to make a statement, will you let me know how everything turns out?"

Isobel nodded. "The next few days are crucial. By Tuesday we'll know if we can build a case – more than one actually. I'll let you know."

Chapter 42

Isobel rang Mrs. O'Neill to let her know that she was coming. They drove in silence. Isobel felt as if her mind was empty. So many things had happened, there was so much information to process and yet right now the only thing she could think of was Mrs. O'Neill and her plea to let her son be the boy, the young man, she knew. The anguish in her cry had touched Isobel's heart. She glanced at Róisín beside her. She too was on a journey to deal with her son's death. She had found a purpose in helping other young people and in providing valuable support to them. Understanding the pressure that Patrick had been under and the deep fear that he'd had and why, seemed to have helped her find some ease. She hoped that Charlene's words would bring Mrs. O'Neill a measure of peace.

Róisín pulled up outside a detached house. It was almost dark now. Isobel could see similar houses clustered around a green. Street lamps illuminated the area. Most houses had cars parked in the drive and lights on.

The front door of the house they were outside opened.

Backlit by the hall light, Isobel could see Mr. O'Neill.

Róisín said, "I'll wait here for you."

"It's cold. I'm sure the O'Neills would want you to come in. We won't be long."

"OK."

As they walked up the path Mr. O'Neill swung the door open more widely. "Come in, come in!"

He ushered them into the sitting room where Mrs. O'Neill came to meet them.

"Mrs. O'Neill –" Isobel said.

"It's Stella and Gerard."

Isobel smiled. "Stella, this is a friend of mine, Róisín Magill."

Róisín reached forward to shake hands. "I'm so sorry," she said.

Stella gestured to the couch. Isobel and Róisín sat down side by side. Stella took the armchair nearest Isobel and leaned forward. "What have you found out?" Her husband moved to sit on the arm of her chair.

"Charlene is conscious."

Stella's eyes filled with tears.

Isobel could see the conflict in them, gladness for the Griffiths, and loss for themselves.

Stella swallowed. "That's good."

Isobel reached out a hand to Stella. "I'm here to tell you that Charlene remembers Michael stepping in front of her in the alley when that man launched his attack. She wanted you to know."

Stella's hands gripped Isobel's hand fiercely. "He tried to protect her!"

Isobel nodded.

Tears poured down Stella's cheeks.

Her husband laid a hand on her back. "It's all right, love."

"He was doing the best he could. He was always a kind boy," Stella whispered as she let go of Isobel and turned into her husband's shoulder.

Isobel could feel her heart being squeezed until it hurt. Today alone, the lives she had witnessed decimated by the drug ring! Both of these women had lost their sons. Was there no end to the destruction this drug ring could cause? Even as her heart ached she could feel a rage igniting in her belly. Patrick had left information in the hope that someday someone would have a chance at taking down these villains. Maybe Malcolm was right, maybe they had a chance now and if they had then they needed to take it.

"Did Charlene say anything else?"

Isobel snapped her attention back to Stella. "Nothing more about Michael."

"But there was more?" Stella persisted.

Isobel sat straighter. "Yes, and for that reason Charlene could be in danger if certain people knew that she remembered what had happened."

"So it's not over?" said Gerard.

"I knew it!" said Stella.

"No, it's not over. You cannot say anything to anyone about Charlene being conscious and remembering. This was for your ears only. Absolutely no one else."

Stella sat up straight and took her husband's hand. "We understand. Are you going to get more of them?"

Isobel took a deep breath. "I hope so. We have a window of a couple of days, I think. If we can catch more of the people responsible it's going to be now."

"And when it's over you will come back and tell me everything?"

Isobel nodded. "I will."

Stella nodded back. "Thank you for this. It may not seem like anything to you but it's everything to me. The police suggested to me that my son dealing drugs in the alley is what got him killed and Charlene injured. It may have been just a theory but I couldn't get it out of my head." Her eye filled with tears and she covered them with her hand. She took a shuddering breath and then looked at Isobel. "Now at least that picture is gone and for that I am eternally grateful to you, Isobel, to both of you."

Isobel gave a small smile.

"You look tired," Stella said.

"I'm fine."

"Take care of yourself."

"I will and I'll be back in a few days."

Gerard stood up. "Thank you, Isobel. Thank you both."

As Isobel walked towards the car, her phone rang.

"Eoin?"

"Isobel, we need to talk. I have news."

"I'm with people. I have news for you too. Let me get back to the hotel to Malcolm and the others."

"How long will you be? Are you on Zoom? Can we do a call then?"

"I'll be at least an hour." She glanced at Róisín who

nodded. "Let's do a call in an hour and a half. Jack will get me organised for Zoom. Talk to you then."

"Bye."

They sat into the car.

"Is that about the case too?" Róisín asked.

"Yes. Eoin is a garda. He and another friend, Alanna, also a garda, were looking into something for me."

"You'll let me know everything when it's over, won't you, Isobel? If anything Patrick left helps, you'll let me know."

"Of course."

"If there is anything I can do to help – lifts, anything – you only have to ask."

"Thanks, Róisín. You've been a huge help already. I mean it. Right now I don't know what the next step is but I know one thing, we need a miracle – so if you pray, now is the time to pray."

Róisín met Isobel's eyes for a moment. "I will."

Chapter 43

Isobel waved goodbye to Róisín and hurried into the reception area of her hotel.

Malcolm stood up. "Isobel."

"Oh, Malcolm, I was going to ring you. There's a meeting."

"I know. Zoom meeting in half an hour."

"I need to call Jack."

Malcolm raised his hands. "*Whoa!* I've already called Jack. He and Nathan are coming and so are Damien and Inspector Williams."

Isobel took a deep breath. "Oh, good."

"The meeting's in my room, Room 325. You have half an hour. But, Isobel, you need to calm down."

Isobel could feel her anger rising.

Malcolm took hold of her arms gently. "Isobel, I'm not trying to order you around but you do need to take a breath. Everyone is at this meeting because you've brought us together. For God's sake, you even have people across the world chipping in!"

Isobel frowned.

"Peter and Patricia in Lanzarote. It sounded better the way I said it."

Isobel smiled in spite of herself.

"One of your greatest gifts is getting people to work together as a team and whether you like it or not you're pivotal to the team." He gestured with his thumb. "All the officers North and South have had hard things to come to terms with. What have you done today? Talked to a woman who was nearly killed, talked to a solicitor whose friend died a few days later?"

"Talked to Michael's mum."

"Exactly. Harrowing stuff. Take a breath. Reboot."

Isobel took a shuddering breath. She could feel her mind calming, the tension in her body loosening slightly. "You're right. I'll be at your room in time for the meeting."

She took the lift up. Even as she opened the door of her room, she was kicking off her shoes. She might not have time for a bath but she could have a freshen up and that would help.

Twenty minutes later she was pulling on clean clothes when she heard a knock at the door. "*Just a minute!*" She zipped up her ankle boots and checked herself in the mirror. She felt so much better and she looked refreshed.

Malcolm was standing outside.

He stepped in and closed the door.

Isobel knew at once there was something bothering him. She walked back to her bedside table and strapped on her watch.

Malcolm sat on the edge of the bed and waited for her to turn round. "There's one other thing."

Isobel raised an eyebrow.

"Dave's here. He's coming to the meeting,"

"What? I thought he was helping you watch Robin and the manager of the Org shop?"

"He has been but Noah and Rachel are keeping an eye on our two guys until we finish the meeting, then Noah is with me on Manager Man and Dave and Jack are on Robin."

"And they know to just watch?"

"Watch and photograph. Believe me, I've been very clear with them. I'll fill you in on what we have at the meeting. It's good for Dave to see how well his son has been doing and how much he has helped and is helping . . . and I think it's no harm for him to see what you actually do. He's been vocal at times in his lack of support and, if he wants to help now and if he comes to appreciate what you do, I think that's a good thing."

Isobel shrugged.

Malcolm stood up and put one arm around her shoulders. "Come on, let's go and meet your motley crew."

When Malcolm opened the door to his room it was already quite crowded. He had obtained extras chairs and people were also sitting on either side of the bed. Nathan was there with a computer open beside the television.

Jack got up and approached Isobel. As everyone chatted, he said to her, "I hope you don't mind Dad coming to the meeting."

Isobel could see the worry in his eyes. She smiled. "No, it's fine."

Jack breathed a sigh of relief. "He knows only a little bit about everything but he has been helping and he wanted to come. I'm glad he's here."

That was enough for Isobel. She looked over at Dave and smiled. He smiled in response.

Nathan called, "Jack!"

Jack moved over to consult with him and Malcolm followed.

Damien stood up and muttered to Isobel, "I've found something from the archives of CCTV of the docks as Peter suggested. Are he and Patricia on the call?"

"Yes."

"Malcolm, We're ready to go!" Nathan said.

"*OK, everyone!*" Malcolm called out.

Isobel saw the screen of the television move through a number of changes as Zoom set up the meeting. Suddenly she was looking at a screen with three locations. There was the scene of the bed with Malcolm sitting on it, one of Patricia and Peter sitting side by side at a table and another of Eoin and Alanna – Isobel recognised the window behind them: they were in Eoin's office in Henry Street in Limerick.

Malcolm introduced everyone. As he named the people in the hotel room, Nathan allowed Eoin, Alanna, Peter and Patricia to see each person briefly on screen.

"Right," said Malcolm. "We've a lot to get through and many different pieces of the puzzle to fit together."

"And, boy, do we have a tale to tell you!" said Eoin.

Malcolm grinned. "Glad to hear it." He looked over at Isobel. "Where do you want to start, Isobel?"

Isobel only knew Malcolm as a retired officer but she could see his experience shining through. Already he had taken the position of Chair of the meeting and now he was asking her to choose the starting point. She felt herself relax. She was so glad that she had Malcolm for a friend. Already she could feel her mind shift from worry towards clarity.

"Yesterday we gathered information that identified Superintendent Bernard Taylor as a corrupt officer and also as a murderer," she said.

She heard Dave gasp, paused unintentionally and then refocused.

"The source of that information identified the victim, Richard Castles, as an undercover garda. They further suggested that Castles may have been murdered because of information coming from another garda whom he called 'The Prop'. Given that we might have a leak in the South, Eoin and Alanna were going to see if they could find out anything more for us," she paused, "without any other gardaí knowing and potentially being tipped off. I presume that means you didn't tell Aaron, Eoin?"

"No, I didn't."

Alanna added. "Just as well – I heard you never liked him, Isobel – good instincts – he's so arrogant."

Isobel hadn't realised that Alanna wasn't a fan of Aaron's either. "Why don't you tell us what you've found out, Alanna?"

Eoin gestured for Alanna to continue.

She said, "If Richard Castles was an undercover garda then he was most likely one of the drug squad. One of their inspectors, an Inspector Daly, retired two or three years ago. Since he's out of the force now, he seemed like the safest person to talk to."

"Alanna knows someone who helps retired officers. She was able to get his address," said Eoin.

"He still lives in Dublin and Eoin and I went to see him this morning in Malahide."

Dave whispered to Malcolm: "On the outskirts of Dublin, along the bay, about two hours from Limerick."

Isobel frowned at the interruption.

"Thanks," said Malcolm. "I know where Alanna's talking about now. Dublin Bay prawns, I've heard of those."

Isobel had forgotten that Malcolm would be unfamiliar with all of the geography.

"The situation was a bit tricky because Daly retired early, depressed, when one of his officers disappeared and another was killed in a car accident," said Eoin. "He's a shadow of the man he was, grey-haired, thin, as if he's lost loads of weight. His wife was there too and she was very protective. But Alanna played a blinder."

"Hardly a blinder. At the door I asked him if he knew a Richard Castles. I thought the poor man was going to faint. His wife insisted we come in."

"Naturally they were very cagey – to be honest, Daly didn't want to talk at all but Alanna explained about Michael being murdered and Charlene's injury and eventually he agreed to talk."

Alanna took up the story again. "Richard Castles was Darren Kelly, one of Daly's officers. His job was to infiltrate the drug gang in Belfast and find out who the Number One player was. At the time Daly suspected that there was a corrupt PSNI officer but he knew we had a leak in the South also. Only two officers knew what Kelly was up to, himself and Sergeant Wells. Kelly's cover story here in the South was that he was on sick leave. Daly didn't know who the leak was, hence they kept Darren Kelly's undercover work very secret. Before he disappeared, Kelly told Daly that he was getting somewhere. Kelly was sure that very soon he was going to have information about the mysterious boss and then –" Alanna clicked her fingers, "he disappeared."

"Daly spoke to Kelly one evening and he seemed fine," said Eoin. "He wasn't worried, or concerned. And then suddenly he was gone. Kelly seemed to have no inkling that they were on to him."

"Daly blamed himself and he didn't do well after Kelly disappeared," Alanna said. "He was out on sick leave and retired soon after that. He couldn't face the job. He went from being a capable officer to being depressed, anxious, having nightmares and being paranoid."

"I think Darren Kelly was his protégé," Eoin said.

"Been there, done that," said Malcolm. "It's part of the service, the mentoring, the passing on of things. There are always certain younger officers who mean more to you."

Eoin nodded. "You go the extra mile for them."

"We've all done that," Williams said.

Damien glanced at him.

"Basically Darren was like a son to him," said Eoin.

Dave put his arm around Jack's shoulders.

Isobel could feel the sense of loss in the room, not just for Darren but for other officers not named.

After a few moments, Alanna spoke again. "I think one of the things that really played on Daly's mind was that he was at a party the night that Darren disappeared. Daly spoke to him at about seven o'clock. He was fine. Then he went to his sergeant's birthday, Sergeant Gary Wells, the other officer who knew about Kelly's undercover work."

"What date was the night that Darren disappeared?" Isobel asked.

"30th September," Damien said.

"Yes, it was," said Alanna.

Isobel turned and looked at Damien as did everyone in the bedroom.

"It sounds like you have another source of information," said Eoin.

"You go ahead," said Damien. "I'll add what I've found when you're finished."

Isobel looked back at the screen. "Is there anything more?"

Alanna tilted her head. "Oh, yes." She gestured to Eoin to go ahead.

"OK. Here's the thing: Sergeant Gary Wells, whose birthday party was on 30th of September, was killed a fortnight later in a hit-and-run accident."

Isobel shook her head. "God, that's awful."

"And, according to Daly, he had taken Darren's disappearance very badly too. So Alanna got one of her gut instincts. Nothing would do her but that we should see footage of that party. Daly didn't have any but it turns out that Mrs. Wells and her three children live in the row of houses behind the Dalys. The Dalys are very good to them since Sergeant Wells died. So we went round to visit."

Alanna said, "It was awful. The eldest girl is about ten and has long blonde hair like her mum. She's called Trudy. Then there's a younger boy who looks like his dad and a toddler called Connor. The house was festooned for Halloween in orange streamers and fake cobwebs. There are pictures of the family, including the father, everywhere in the house."

There was nothing to say. Isobel knew that Alanna was imagining how her partner Zoe would be if anything happened to her.

"Obviously, Mrs. Wells was very upset," she went on. "She described the party as the last night that Gary was happy. That was a red flag to me. She mentioned that Gary was upset about Darren Kelly going missing but, when I asked her about seeing the video of the party, she nearly lost it. She accused me of stirring things up now and said that Gary was a good officer, that she wasn't going to have anyone blaming him for anything or besmirching his memory." Alanna took a deep breath. "I kind of knew that we were on to something."

Isobel thought about what they all did when they were on a case. It was all about getting people to talk about things in the past that they might prefer to leave alone, searching for new information or a fact that could unlock the case. It was the same when she was working as a psychotherapist: she was helping people to deal with upsetting things, things that it might seem easier to leave alone, working to relieve the pent-up feelings.

"It seems that Gary Wells watched the DVD of his birthday party several times for the last few nights he was alive. And when he was leaving the house the last time he said to his wife, 'I think I've made a terrible mistake'."

"So something important may have happened at the party," Isobel said,

Alanna nodded. "Yes. It did." She looked at her notebook. "Basically, Gary believed that he had done something wrong, something he didn't want the others to know. Mrs. Wells said he was consumed by it before he died. She even wondered if he had stepped in front of the car deliberately."

"So maybe he betrayed Darren Kelly," said Malcolm.

"Yes, that's what we thought," said Eoin.

"And if Gary was drunk at the party and then watched the video several times," Patricia said, "he must have been trying to see who he let the information slip to."

Alanna nodded. "Exactly. "

"So Gary Wells when drunk let something slip," said Malcolm. "Darren disappeared that same evening. When Darren disappeared, Gary worried that he had said something at the party to someone he shouldn't and watched the video to figure out who."

"That is what it looks like," said Eoin. "Malcolm had Jack and Nathan help us, so hopefully Nathan can show you the video. Nathan, Jack?"

"Yes, it's ready," said Jack.

Alanna looked down at her notebook. "We reviewed all the footage but we thought this part was the important bit. Nathan, can you get the video set up for about a quarter to ten that night?"

Jack opened his computer and set it on the table beside the television. The screen was smaller but it was still possible to see the party. As the camera swept around, Isobel could see pictures of a baby and then a small boy and also a young garda in uniform. There were shots of people dancing and then the camera focused on a man sitting at the bar."

Nathan said, "OK. I have the video ready to go from the point you asked."

"The man at the bar is Gary," said Alanna. "He's a bit drunk."

"Yes, we've got it," said Malcolm.

Eoin took a deep breath. "Roll the footage, Nathan." His voice seemed heavy.

The man at the bar had dark hair and a wide smile. He was talking, his face flushed and his gestures exaggerated. The man beside him punched his arm and then stood up and left.

"The man who punches Gary's arm and walks away is his brother-in-law," said Alanna. "He works in insurance."

Gary sat alone for a few minutes and then a man in a black leather jacket joined him. It was Aaron McGuinness.

"That's the garda on the new task force," Damien said.

Isobel glanced at the zoom screen. Eoin had his eyes on the zoom screen, watching them as they watched the recording.

Isobel looked back at the computer playing the video. Gary and Aaron were chatting and laughing. Then the mood seemed to change and Aaron leant in close to Gary. The conversation became more intense. Gary looked behind them and pulled closer. They were deep in conversation. Then Aaron stood up abruptly. He pulled his phone from his pocket and moved away from Gary, looking at his phone. The camera focused on Gary but behind him Isobel could see Aaron moving around the bar away from everyone. His shoulders were tight, his movements staccato and rigid, his eyes darted around. He seemed stressed, wary, hyped-up. He stood in the corner and made a short phone call. Isobel looked at the time stamp on the recording. It was 9.50.

"At 10.15 Richard Castles drives into the docks," said Damien. "Joe Wilson arrives at 10.20. At 10.25 Superintendent Taylor arrives. Obviously, they know the cameras in the docks. I can't place them all together but at 10.40 Taylor leaves and three minutes later so does Wilson, as does Richard Castles' car, presumably driven by this Leon Barr. Castles' car was never found."

Isobel felt as if all the energy had left her body. Her mind was blank. She took a shallow breath. *Aaron?* Surely not? He was Eoin's friend. He was on the drug task force.

Eoin cleared his throat.

Isobel focused on him, her mind still reeling.

Eoin looked around at all the faces and stopped on Isobel's. "I didn't want to believe it. When you said The Prop, I knew that was Aaron's nickname at Templemore but anyone who played rugby could be called that."

Isobel could feel her mind struggling. It couldn't be Aaron. He wouldn't betray the force.

"Your friend Aaron is the leak in the Garda, Eoin?" said Malcolm.

"It looks that way."

Isobel recovered her voice. "I'm sorry, Eoin."

Eoin shook his head. "The witness naming The Prop as the source of information was one thing, I could dismiss that – but seeing Aaron talking to Gary Wells and then making that call. It all fits together."

"But Eoin, you and Aaron weren't buddy-buddy," Alanna said.

"I know, Alanna, but it's hard to believe that someone I trained with, someone I reached out to for help, is in fact the enemy, working against us, having other officers killed." He shook his head. "I'm thinking about other things Aaron said to me and wondering what was really going on."

Malcolm said, "Like what?"

"Aaron said a few things about you, Isobel. He said that you were a threat to the Northern dealers. And, he kept in touch with me, asking if you had told me anything, if you had found out anything else. At the time I thought he had realised from our case in Limerick what a help you could be and he was trying to change. Now, I think he was probably pumping me for information. Thank God you came over, Malcolm, and thank God you didn't like him, Isobel. Because of that I was more reticent about telling him anything that you said. And then you were worried about his safety – that's a joke when he is the one who . . ."

After a few moments, Alanna said, "We think that Aaron is making the call to Taylor. It seems Gary was drunk and let something slip, not for a moment realising . . ." Her voice trailed off and she glanced at Eoin. "Aaron knew that he had to act immediately. As yet, Darren hadn't found out about Taylor or about Aaron but it might be only a matter of time. Aaron called Taylor. Taylor probably needed Joe and Leon to arrange the meeting with Darren. Taylor implicated Joe and Leon in the crime, hoping that would keep them quiet."

"And then later, to protect himself, he got rid of them," said Peter.

Alanna continued. "After Gary Wells was killed, Daly asked the gardaí who were investigating for his phone records. Naturally, as a favour they let him look at them. The last call Gary made was to Aaron. Obviously, when he was interviewed he said all the usual things: Gary was fine, he just wanted to chat about the party, no, he didn't seem upset, I can't believe I was the last person to talk to him. No one had any reason to suspect Aaron."

"Daly did say that he didn't particularly like Aaron," said Eoin. "He felt he was cocky and fancied himself and Daly didn't like the way that he did things. A bit like you, Isobel."

"I may not have liked him but I didn't think he was the leak," said Isobel.

"No, nor me," said Eoin. "I'm sorry, Isobel. I can't believe that I talked to the very guy who was completely untrustworthy." He shook his head. "I don't want to even think about what . . ."

"Good work, you two," said Malcolm. "What about the hit-and-run on Gary Wells? Could that be Aaron tidying up loose ends, making sure that he couldn't be traced back to Darren's disappearance?"

"We started to wonder that too," said Alanna. "By this stage retired Inspector Daly knew there was something up so we had to take him into our confidence a bit. Gary was knocked down by someone who fled the scene. They never found the perpetrator. It happened in a part of the city where there aren't cameras. There was no reason for Gary to be there."

"Unless he had gone to meet someone?" said Williams.

"What about the car that hit him – no garages with suspicious repairs?" Malcolm asked.

"Ah! According to Daly, the car that they suspect hit Gary was found burnt out later that day," said Alanna. "The paint on Gary's body was consistent with that."

"That seems professional to me," said Malcolm. "A great no-questions-asked way to get rid of someone."

Alanna said, "I agree."

"Had Daly any idea who in Dublin might have that sort of MO?" Malcolm asked.

Eoin smiled. "That's just what we asked and you'll never guess whose name popped up . . ."

Malcolm grinned. "Surprise me."

"The Tanners."

"Tim Tanner, Tim-Tan," said Williams.

Alanna smiled. "You better believe it. According to Daly, in his early days before he became the boss, Tim-Tan took out a few of the competition that way. Steal a car. Set the victim up. Burn the car and destroy the evidence. Make sure it happens in an area with no cameras. No evidence, no forensics and get a mate to swear you were somewhere else."

"Tim-Tan in league with Aaron." Although Isobel hadn't liked Aaron, she had thought along the lines of shallow and self-serving. This case was bringing her into a level of crime she knew nothing about. Corrupt police officers chipped at the safety she liked to believe that she had.

Peter cleared his throat. "All of this sounds very credible but we need more evidence. Isobel, did you go back to Gareth Short? Did he have any more information about the shooting? Unless we have something definite there won't be enough for a case."

Isobel pulled her wandering mind together. She straightened up in her chair. "Yes, yes, I did go back. And you were right, Peter. Gareth kept something back, mainly because he needed to discuss revealing it with his fiancée. He knew that revealing it could put them in danger."

"Come on, Isobel, tell us," Malcolm said.

"He gave me the co-ordinates of where the body is buried."

"*I knew it!*" Peter punched the air. "That was all that that guy Joe had, to try and make a case for his innocence!"

Isobel nodded. "And that's why Patrick was afraid for his life."

"Do you think that they killed Patrick too?" Jack asked.

"I don't know. We'll probably never know but it is a

possibility. What do we need to do now, Peter?"

Peter took a deep breath. "We need to dig up the body. At the very least it would help Darren Kelly's family and work colleagues. I suppose I'm hoping that Taylor had very little time. Hopefully he made some mistakes. But how can we dig up the body without Taylor knowing anything about it?"

Isobel looked around the room until her eyes settled on Williams.

He closed his eyes. "I'm thinking."

Everyone waited.

"All I can think of is that we speak to the head of the lab," he said at last. "We tell him that we have a report of a buried body, that we don't want any publicity in case it's false but we have to follow up. He won't want news cameras, in case it's a false alarm. We swear him to secrecy until we see if there is anything there. Maybe Damien's friend in the lab – Brian, is it? – could do the recovery for us and he'll definitely say nothing. He can bring whoever else he trusts. I think that might work well here."

Malcolm frowned. "Really?"

Williams explained. "There are bodies here that have never been found because of the prolonged conflict. It's a very painful issue in the North. Recovering those bodies is very important."

Malcolm nodded slowly.

"What do you think?" Williams asked.

"That could work," said Peter. "It's official but also necessarily secret."

"I've suspected Taylor for a while," said Williams. "I have

footage of Taylor suppressing the photos from the laneway. When Isobel and Jack brought me the pictures, I gave them to Taylor. I recorded that. Those pictures never went to the police lab or the private lab we use. Taylor sat on them."

"So Taylor tried to suppress that evidence?" said Eoin. Williams nodded. "Yes."

"The recordings may not be admissible as evidence," Peter said.

"I know. And Taylor has already been talking in the lab about a mix-up."

"We'll keep it in mind," said Malcolm. "I'm hoping that Darren Kelly's body can give us something definite."

"What about the other witness to Tim-Tan killing Michael?" Peter said. "Have you persuaded him to make a statement yet, Isobel?"

Isobel shook her head. "No, not yet. I'll do that tomorrow. We have Charlene's statement, but no one else knows about that, just Damien, Jack and I."

"OK," said Malcolm. "There's one more piece of information. We may be onto a drug distribution pathway."

Williams raised his eyebrows.

"A pathway connected to everything that has happened. We'll let you know if we find something definite but we need more time – at least another day. Halloween is coming with parties and that means drugs, so hopefully we'll know soon. For now, Taylor and Aaron need to believe that the case is over. Tim-Tan too. You never know, if we have two witnesses to Tim-Tan murdering Michael and attacking Charlene and then we ask him about Gary Wells, he might be more disposed to drop Aaron in it for a lesser sentence. If Tim-Tan drove the car that killed Gary Wells then he did it on Aaron's instructions. We really need him to turn State's evidence."

"Yes, we do," said Eoin. "We can prove that Gary spoke to Aaron from his records at the time but it's too late to get data from Aaron's phone. In the South, phone companies only have to keep triangulation data for a year. We surmise that they set up a meeting and that Aaron lured Gary to a place where Tim-Tan ran him down. We have the footage from the party and the record of Gary's phone calls. I'm not sure it's enough. I wonder if any of the old traffic footage would show that Aaron was in the vicinity of the hit-and-run."

"We could look into that," said Alanna. "Also, we could look at where the car used to run Gary down was burned out. Obviously, Tim-Tan got a lift away from it. Maybe we can place Aaron's car in the area too. It may not be conclusive but it would certainly be supporting evidence."

Eoin nodded.

"And the drug distribution, what help can we give you?" Williams asked.

"We were thinking that we would tip you off," Malcolm said. "You know, concerned citizens see something suspicious and disturbing. Then you arrive and arrest everyone. We have people who we suspect are involved under surveillance – probably the less you know about that the better – you know, plausible deniability and all that."

Williams made a face. "That sounds a bit vague. If we're going to pick up a number of drug pushers we would need reinforcements."

"I was thinking more of following them and seeing what

that reveals before we pick anybody up," Malcolm said. "Drugs are at the centre of everything that has happened." He counted on his fingers. "Michael's death, Charlene's head injury, Darren Kelly's murder, Gary Wells' death, Joe's death, Leon's death, Patrick's death, and those are only the people we know about. This whole situation is a house of cards. If we pull something, everything will collapse and we won't get all of the players. I want them all. So we're going to need a clean sweep. Everything put in motion at the same time so no one can warn anyone else. Agreed?"

Isobel thought back to Róisín talking about the web of drugs. She also thought about her dream of the spider. It was true. The spider could lose part of its web and replace it. They needed to get the whole web. She pictured a spider sitting at the centre of its web, waiting for any vibration, any stir to suggest that something was happening. They needed to move very carefully.

No one said anything.

"What we need to do is a co-ordinated clean-up," said Malcolm. "All pieces of this puzzle need to be moved at the same time. Does everyone agree?"

They all voiced their agreement.

Malcolm nodded. "We need to keep in touch so we can decide on the best time."

"Let me set up a group chat so everyone is able to communicate." Nathan started entering numbers in his phone.

Isobel took the opportunity to sit back in her chair. Her shoulders were tense and she felt as if she had been tumble-dried. Aaron, part of a drug ring. She couldn't process it.

"If it's OK with everyone," said Eoin, "I would like to

tell our Superintendent Carruthers what we know. You know him, Isobel – he's a great guy and in the next few days we might need to arrest a Garda Inspector and a PSNI Superintendent. He could begin thinking about how we could do it and who would be safe to contact."

Malcolm shifted uneasily in his seat.

"I promise he won't do anything," Eoin said. "He can just be thinking about it. And please, Malcolm, Williams, keep us informed. We need to know what's happening."

"And if we find a body we may need Darren Kelly's dental records," said Williams.

"If that's the case, Eoin and I will speak to Daly and he can sort that out for us," said Alanna.

Williams nodded at Damien. "Let's go," he said. "Good luck, everyone."

Everyone chorused goodbye and Williams and Damien left.

"Right," Malcolm said to the others, "there's one last thing that Isobel and I need to tell you about."

He proceeded to explain about the Org shop and the young student, Robin, dispensing drugs.

"The lab messaged me today," he continued. "The paint on the pillar at the end of the alley is the same as the van that was delivering to the Org shop."

"And that means?" Eoin asked.

"Org has ten shops in Northern Ireland, usually sited near a third-level campus. We think that Org might be a front for drug delivery."

"And we know from Michael's photographs of the alley that Monday night was the likely night of the delivery," said Isobel. "It's also the night that Michael and Charlene were attacked. We think they stumbled into the drug delivery preparations and a meeting between Geo and Tim-Tan. Tim-Tan didn't want to risk that Michael and Charlene had seen too much."

"Geo was disposed of as an attempt to wrap up the case so the drug gang could get back to business as usual," Malcolm said. "They don't know that Charlene remembers her attacker or that Isobel has found another witness."

"And what are you proposing to do?" Patricia asked.

"I've been watching the manager of the Org shop. Jack's friend Noah has been helping me. He's watching him now. Jack and Dave have been keeping an eye on Robin, a student we suspect of being a drug dealer."

"Rachel is watching him at the moment," said Jack. "Robin went to the Org shop earlier today when I was watching him. I followed him into the shop but I couldn't hear anything and it would have looked suspicious if I had hung around too long so I had to leave. Robin was there for half an hour then went back to his house." He looked at his phone. "Rachel says he's still at home."

"We suspect that drugs were delivered to this Org shop on Monday nights," said Malcolm. "Robin then set about dispensing them over the week. We know some of his patterns. They may not deliver them in the usual way now but Robin still needs to supply his customers and, if we follow the two people we suspect of being involved, they might lead us to more of the drug network."

"Do you suspect the other Org shops of also moving drugs?" Eoin asked.

"I do. The only problem is that I don't know anything about the delivery times in the other shops. They may be on a different night. But you're right. If we don't get anything from following these two guys, the next step would be to watch some of the shops. That's a big job and perhaps Williams and Damien may have to do that in the future. In the meantime we'll keep watching for a few days and if we see anything suspicious we'll alert Williams. And, if drugs are delivered, Williams can execute a raid based on 'credible information from a concerned member of the public'."

"Do you think something will happen tonight?" Eoin asked.

"I don't know but supply and demand rule. I think there is demand and I think that there will be an alternate plan to arrange supply."

Eoin glanced at Alanna. "It makes sense to wait and see if there's a delivery."

Alanna nodded. "Especially as in that same time frame Williams and Damien may have found Darren Kelly's body."

"The biggest difficulty is keeping everything quiet," Eoin said.

"We'll talk to our Superintendent and see what he suggests," said Alanna.

"OK. I think that's a wrap," said Malcolm. "Agreed?"

All agreed.

"You have to keep us informed about what's happening," Patricia said. "We'll be on tenterhooks, won't we, Peter?"

Peter nodded. "Of course."

"We will," said Isobel. "Thanks for everything. Talk tomorrow."

With a chorus of goodbyes they all disappeared from the call and Nathan shut down the Zoom.

Malcolm sat back in his chair. "That's everything. If we're lucky we take down a drug operation and also two bent officers of the law. I call that a pretty good result."

Isobel stood up and stretched. She moved over to speak to Dave.

He hugged her. "Jesus, Isobel, you've found out so much, you and Jack."

Isobel grinned at Jack.

"That meeting was intense," said Dave.

"It's good that you're helping."

"Glad to be involved. Let's hope that everything goes to plan."

"Yes." Isobel felt relieved. Her role in the case was nearly finished.

"Dad and I need to go and relieve Rachel," said Jack. "We'll let you know if Robin is on the move."

They said goodnight and left.

Nathan gathered up his things and followed.

"The meeting went well," Malcolm said. "We just have to wait and see how things play out but we did good."

"I know, Malcolm. I just feel really sad."

"Betrayal does that, Isobel. It leaves a bad taste in your mouth and a lot of distrust in your heart."

"You sound like you've been there."

Malcolm folded his arms. "Haven't we all, with someone?"

Isobel thought for a moment. "True."

They were coming hopefully to the last stages of this upsetting and unsettling case.

Malcolm stood. "OK. I'd better go and resume my surveillance of Manager Man. You get some rest. I'll see you tomorrow at some stage."

Isobel said goodnight and went to her room. She ran a bath and slipped into the water. She found herself crying for the mess they had uncovered. Maybe they were on their way to dismantling a drug gang but tonight it felt horrible.

Later she lay in bed, looking forward to the anaesthesia of sleep.

In her dreams she was at a party. People were smiling. When she smiled back the faces in front of her changed into scary Halloween masks, cruel and sinister. Isobel felt wary and unsafe. She felt something dripping on her head. She looked up. Above her was a dense web of white fibres. The fibres shook and Isobel saw a spider with bright yellow eyes picking its way towards her.

Chapter 44

Malcolm joined her for breakfast.

"All quiet last night," he said.

"Is someone watching the manager now?"

"Yes. Rachel slept last night and took over from me at seven o'clock. I'll get some sleep today and be ready for tonight again. I won't need much sleep. I'm all wound up."

"What about Jack and Dave?"

"I think Dave watched until four then Jack took over. Dave thought that he might be needed to drive places so he wanted to get some rest."

"Are you organising everyone?"

"Yeah, kind of. What are your plans for the day?"

"I need to persuade Henry to make a statement."

"Where are we off to then?"

Isobel frowned. "You need to sleep."

"Not yet. Later on today. And Noah is helping too. If anyone gets too tired they know to message me."

"I thought I would go by myself to see Henry. He might be more relaxed that way."

"You can talk to him alone but I'm going to be nearby, no arguments."

"You seem very adamant."

"I am. This ain't over 'til it's over. We need to be careful, all of us."

Isobel and Malcolm walked from the hotel past Queen's and then down onto Botanic Avenue. Isobel went into a shop and bought a cup of tea and a bacon sandwich.

Malcolm waited across the road while Isobel approached Henry's doorway. He was curled up in his sleeping bag, facing away from her, the bag pulled tightly round his neck, his shoulder hunched against the cold, the old blanket thrown on top of him.

"Henry, Henry! Wake up! I brought you some breakfast."

There was no movement from the doorway.

Isobel called more loudly. "*Henry, I've brought some tea!*"

There was no movement, no shift. Isobel studied the blanket, praying for a small rise that showed he was breathing. Nothing. The paper cup wobbled in her hand and some of it splashed on her skin. The pain barely registered. She felt her heart constrict. Inside her head a voice was screaming silently, *NO!*

She reached out with her free hand and tentatively slid her hand under the blanket. The sleeping bag felt cold to the touch. She swallowed and inched closer and touched the sleeping bag more firmly. The chill of the bag matched the chill in her heart.

Malcolm appeared at her side. She looked up at him. She saw him frown. He took the paper cup from her fingers. Steeling herself, Isobel grasped Henry's shoulder and pulled it outward.

Her hand was shaken off. Isobel jumped back.

"*What you doin'?*"

"Henry! Oh God!"

"Waking me up at this hour, disturbing a man when he's trying to sleep." Henry rolled to face her, scowling. "Oh, it's you! My food angel."

Isobel could feel her heart hammering in her chest. "Oh, thank God you're alright."

"O'course I'm bloody alright or I was 'til you woke me up at the scrake of dawn."

Malcolm put his arm around Isobel, helping to steady her. Her heart was still racing. Just for a minute she had experienced the awful feeling that someone's death was her fault. She had a lump in her throat. Now, brutally, viscerally, she realised what ex-Inspector Daly had been going through for two years.

Henry looked at the wrapped sandwich in her hand. "I take it that's not a steak."

Isobel felt weak with relief.

"You frightened the life out of me."

Henry looked past her to Malcolm.

Malcolm said, "Here's a cup of tea."

Henry studied Malcolm but reached out for the tea. "I ain't seen you before."

Malcolm hunkered down beside Isobel.

"Are you some new policeman in these parts?"

Malcolm laughed. "An old policeman, retired, visiting my friend Isobel."

Henry stared at him a moment and then nodded. "Are you ever going to give me that food?"

"Sorry. Here you go."

Henry opened the wrapper and then lifted the bread. "Ketchup, good. I like a bit of ketchup."

He took a bite and munched contentedly. In between mouthfuls he sipped his tea, his eyes flicking back and forward from Isobel to Malcolm.

When the sandwich was gone, he rolled up the paper and put it in his empty cup. He handed the detritus to Malcolm.

He made himself comfortable sitting in his sleeping bag and then turned to Isobel. "OK, what do you want?"

"Charlene has come round."

Henry nodded. "That's good."

"She says that it was a man called Tim-Tan who killed Michael and attacked her."

Henry inclined his head. "Didn't I tell you that myself?"

Isobel nodded. "You did, Henry."

"I ain't making no statement. I told you afore. I don't trust the police one bit."

Malcolm said, "Neither do we."

"So?"

"We want you to make a statement to a friend of mine," Isobel said. "He's a solicitor out in Holywood. The police here won't know about it."

"If that young 'un Charlene can tell what happened, why d'you need me?"

"They've blamed Geo for the attacks."

"I told you it wasn't him."

Isobel nodded. "Two witnesses are better than one, especially if one has had a head injury."

Henry folded his arms. "Maybe."

"Please, Henry, for Michael and to make sure that these people get stopped."

"You don't know who you're messin' with."

"We have a fair idea," said Malcolm. "This is part of a bigger operation to clean things up."

"My brother Dave would take you to Holywood to make your statement. No one would know."

Henry looked at her for a minute then gave an impatient toss of his head. "Fine. But I'm doin' it for that young fella. That was awful."

"*Oh, thank you, Henry!*" Tears sprang to Isobel's eyes.

"Thanks, man," said Malcolm. "You're a hero."

Isobel pulled up a picture on her phone. "This is my brother."

Henry nodded.

"Could you meet him outside the homeless shelter on the Dublin Road? Do you know it?

"O'course I know it. I know this city."

"I can get you a taxi there."

"Don't be silly. I don't want no lift. What d'you think I do all day only walk around?"

"Can you get to the shelter for half eleven this morning?"

Henry nodded. "I can do that. No reason why I wouldn't be up looking at that place."

Isobel smiled. "Exactly. So you'll be there?"

Henry nodded.

Malcolm reached out and felt the sleeping bag. "You could do with a warmer one of these too."

"New bag, that looks suspicious."

"Oh yes, of course."

"But maybe in the next few weeks."

"That can be arranged." Malcolm grinned.

"Thanks again, Henry," Isobel said.

As Malcolm and Isobel walked away Malcolm said, "I'll get Jack to keep an eye on him and down the line replace that sleeping bag. And maybe find some other way to help him."

"Good idea. What now?"

"I'd like to take the bus tour of Belfast. I read that it's very good. I'd like to see more of the city."

Isobel accompanied Malcolm. While he seemed able to lose himself in what the guide was saying, she felt really distracted, her mind jumping from one thing to another, her stomach tight with anxiety. The only sight that made an impression on her was the iconic cranes of Belfast harbour, Samson and Goliath. Isobel equated herself with the smaller crane beside the mighty Goliath. She felt exactly like that in relation to the drug gang they were up against. She prayed that they would emerge victorious. She didn't feel confident, she felt terrified, and she wondered what would be the fallout if they were unable to prove their cases. She was terrified for the future, terrified for Jack, for Henry, for Charlene, for Damien and Inspector Williams. She'd be able to go back to Limerick but all of the others lived here. How safe would they be?

Chapter 45

Isobel's phone rang while she and Malcolm were having a late lunch.

"It's Damien."

Isobel felt her heart start to beat faster. "Damien, any news?"

"Brian found a body."

"Is it Darren Kelly?"

"Impossible to say yet. I've just been on to Dave. Henry made his statement and Dave is on his way to Dublin now. Daly is speaking to Darren Kelly's parents. He knows that everything has to be kept quiet. He'll make sure of that. He'll collect Darren's dental X-rays and meet Dave at the airport to give them to him. Dave is bringing them to us. There can be no mistakes about this."

"Taylor still doesn't know, does he?"

"No. So far Brian has kept everything very quiet. And, if this is Kelly's body, the lab needs to be very sure before they say anything. Trust me – a garda murdered in Northern Ireland – no one is going to breathe a word until there is a positive ID. They may even wait for DNA confirmation before releasing a statement. Nobody is going to let anything slip. There's too much at stake. Brian knows that. We all know that."

Isobel exhaled. "OK."

"There's something else."

"What?"

"One of the bullets is still in the body. There's no exit wound. When we have the bullet we can run it through ballistics."

Isobel could hear the tension in his voice.

"The autopsy should be late this afternoon. Brian hopes that he will have the bullet early this evening. Fingers crossed it gives us something."

"Let us know. And, Damien, be careful."

"I will. Talk to you later."

When he'd heard everything, Malcolm said, "I know what Damien is hoping, Peter too I think?"

"What?"

"That because everything happened so fast, Taylor used his own gun, hence he had to make sure the body was never found."

Isobel made a face. "That's not likely, is it?"

Malcolm shrugged. "It's a possibility. When Aaron found out about Darren he rang Taylor immediately. I would say they were panicking. Taylor had very little time. I think he used his own gun and that's why he then buried the body. He needed it to stay hidden."

"Why didn't he get rid of Joe and Leon that night too?"

"He didn't want any questions asked so he waited a

few weeks and both deaths were overdoses so no questions."

"He'll have got rid of the gun."

Malcolm shook his head. "No, I don't think so. An officer losing or damaging his gun – questions are asked about his competence to have one. Taylor wouldn't have that on his record and again it draws attention. No, I think he banked on Darren's body never being found, therefore no questions to answer."

"That means we could get him."

"Yes, it does."

"I want that to be true but I'm afraid to get my hopes up."

"I know. I think that's why Peter didn't say anything either."

The knot tightened in Isobel's stomach. Her phone rang again. "It's Jack." She answered. "Jack, is everything alright?"

"Isobel, the Provost would like to see us again at two o'clock today. Can you make it?"

Isobel looked at her watch. "Sure. I'll meet you outside the Lanyon Building at a quarter to two."

"OK."

She ended the call.

"Problem?" Malcolm asked.

"I don't know. The Provost wants to meet us again."

"You're not thrilled."

"Not especially. Last time we saw him he was insisting that Michael's death was a result of a failed robbery, information courtesy of Superintendent Taylor."

Malcolm finished up his soup and stood up. "If they're buddies, make sure you don't give anything away."

Isobel snapped. "I know, I know! I could do without this."

Malcolm draped his arm over her shoulders as they walked along. "Take it easy. Days like this are always stressful. You're just waiting for things to happen, waiting for time to pass. But you can't get wound up. That's when mistakes are made."

"I'm sorry. I keep going over things and wondering what the outcome will be. I'm also worrying about Damien and his friend Brian. I hope to God they're careful."

Malcolm grinned. "I know but it doesn't help. They know the score and they'll be careful. You reminded Damien when you spoke to him. We've made a plan. We just need to stick to it now."

Jack saw Isobel and Malcolm walking towards him and rushed to meet them.

"Is Noah watching Robin?" Malcolm asked.

"Yes, and Rachel said she's fine with Manager Man."

"Your dad must be tired."

"I think he slept well for the few hours he got and he's thrilled to be helping."

Malcolm nodded. "Before you go into this meeting I'm going to tell you the same thing that I told Isobel. You need to stay calm, say very little and give nothing away. Apart from that, you're fine, unless you've been up to things that we don't know about, young Jack." He punched Jack on the upper arm.

Jack grinned. "No way!"

Isobel could see that Malcolm had relaxed him.

"I'll wait outside the office for you," Malcolm said. "You have any trouble, you give me a shout."

Isobel grinned.

The secretary greeted them and told Isobel and Jack that they could go straight in.

Jack whispered, "That's an improvement."

Isobel made a face.

As they entered the office the Provost rose from behind his desk.

"Ms. McKenzie and Jack, have a seat!"

It was only then that Isobel noticed that the professor from the library was already sitting in the room. She felt her heart speed up. What was he doing here? What was going on?

"This is Professor Eamon Clarke," the Provost said. "He's an old friend of mine."

Isobel moistened her lips and nodded to Clarke. "Professor."

Professor Clarke was thin with unruly white hair. His face was lined and at the moment seemed full of worry and stress.

"Professor Clarke and I went to college together."

"Did you?" Isobel asked, her throat tight.

There was an uncomfortable silence.

Isobel kept her face neutral. "Perhaps you could tell us why you want to see us?"

The Provost took a deep breath. "Yes, yes. As I said, Professor Clarke and I were at college together. We're good friends, always have been. I was sharing with him the whole debacle about the cyber-bullying and how you had found the person responsible on the tapes and, well, Professor Clarke, well, he . . . he . . ."

"Basically, I realised that you would have seen me going into the library on those same mornings and also maybe noticed, well . . . I need to explain what I was doing in the library."

"Of course, yes, we noticed you on the tapes."

"Yes, and no doubt wondered what I was doing."

Jack said, "We did wonder about –"

"Why don't you tell us," Isobel cut in, "since that's obviously why you've brought us here?"

"Well, Tuesday morning is the morning I collect my cannabis supply. Someone leaves it for me in a bag and I pick up the bag and Bob's your uncle."

"We did suspect something like that," said Jack.

"Who leaves the cannabis for you?" Isobel asked.

"I don't want to implicate anyone else."

"As you said, we've watched the security footage," she said.

He studied her for a moment. "You saw who brought the bag into the library."

Isobel nodded. "What can you tell me about him, apart from the fact that he has red hair?"

Professor Clarke looked at the Provost. "I rather hoped I could behave honourably."

"I can't elaborate," said Isobel, "but, I assure you, sharing with me what you know is being honourable."

"Very well. His name is Robin Tully. He's a student.

When I wanted to find a . . ." he hesitated over the word, "a supplier I was given his name."

Isobel nodded for him to continue.

"I've been collecting cannabis from the library most weeks for about eleven months. In my defence, I will say that the reason I'm doing it is that my wife has chronic bone pain and any tablets that the doctor has given her aren't working. It's terrible to watch someone you love in pain. One of our friends gave Grace a joint one day and it seemed to really help with the pain. It was the only thing that had. My wife was comfortable and so I embarked on my sortie into the drug world. Each Tuesday morning I collect my wife's cannabis for the week. My habit has always been to collect any texts I need for the week on that day. All it required me to do was pick up the bag and put my books into it. I'm not sorry and I would do it again. When Sam mentioned to me that you had looked at footage to find the person who was sending the unpleasant emails and that Tuesday was one of the days, I realised that you had probably deduced what I was doing. I didn't want to embarrass Sam or the university so I thought I had better confess."

"I'm sorry about Mrs. Clarke," said Isobel.

He nodded. "Thank you."

"Is there any significance in the colour of the Org bags?" she asked.

Professor Clarke smiled. "Oh, you figured that out as well. To ensure that I don't have to be seen talking to Robin, he uses a green bag if he has the cannabis and if the bag is blue then I know that he doesn't have any, for whatever reason."

"And does it often happen that Robin can't fulfill your weekly delivery?"

"No."

"Do you get any warning if he can't?"

The professor shrugged. "No. I would go to the library on Tuesday morning and the bag would be blue and I would have to wait." He paused. "I know I need to go and make a statement to the police about what I've done. As I said, I don't really want to reveal anyone else's involvement."

Isobel stood. "I'll step outside and ring Inspector Williams."

Outside, she briefly explained the situation to Malcolm in a whisper.

"I'm with you. You need to let Williams know. This is confirmation of drug-supplying and we have pictures of this Robin handing out stationery to lots of students."

Isobel rang Williams. The phone rang and rang. No answer. She tried Damien.

"Isobel, we can't really talk now."

"I'm in the Provost's office at Queen's. I have a professor who can make a statement that he was being supplied with cannabis by a student. He collects it on a Tuesday morning. It might help the case."

"Let me tell Inspector Williams."

Isobel heard voices in the background.

"OK, Isobel. " Damien was back. "I'm coming to take the statement now. I'll be there in half an hour."

With a thumbs-up to Malcolm, Isobel went back into the Provost's office.

"Detective Doran is on his way to take your statement,

Professor Clarke. Professor, it's really important that you don't tell Robin or anyone that you've spoken to us. I'm begging you. A lot depends on it."

The professor nodded. "I'll make my statement and say nothing."

"Thank you."

"Sam, I'm sorry," he then said. "I know I've put you and the university in a terrible position. I suppose I could end up losing my job. But . . ." Tears came to his eyes. "If you'd seen Grace, the pain she was in – it wasn't human. You know her, Sam, she didn't complain but I knew, I could see it in her face. The pain. I couldn't leave her like that."

The Provost shook his head.

"Grace went to college here with Sam and me," said Clarke. "We've been together ever since."

"Of course, Bernard – Superintendent Taylor – was at college with us too," said the Provost.

"He was?" Isobel felt her heart go cold. The last person she wanted knowing anything was Superintendent Taylor. She flicked a glance at Jack.

"I could, of course, have talked to him about this situation but I don't want, nor does the Professor, to be accused of covering things up or of using acquaintances to circumvent the law. Eamon and I have discussed things and we feel that for the sake of the students and the reputation of the college, he should be treated like anyone else. I thought that one of the policemen that you met while looking into the case for Michael and Charlene could deal with it – no favours, no special treatment – that's why I rang you."

Isobel nodded. "I think you made the right decision."

"Of course this is going to be a media nightmare but it is what it is . . . You can see why I want to be sure that there's no sign of special treatment or anything of that sort. The officers who have been dealing with Michael's death should be the same ones who deal with this situation. They can then refer it on to whoever is appropriate."

"Do you know what will happen?" Clarke asked Isobel.

Isobel bit her lip. "I'm not sure but I imagine Detective Doran will take your statement and then it's up to the police. As I said, it would be most helpful if you told no one for now and the same applies to you, Provost. I'm sure Detective Doran will say the same."

"Enjoy your student days, Jack," Clarke said. "They are over so quickly. It seems only yesterday we were all students running around – me, Sam, Grace, Bernard, Ben Jameson and Lorraine McNally whom we called 'The Muse'."

The conversation lapsed. The Provost glanced at some letters and Jack looked at his phone. Professor Clarke sat with his hands clasped as he waited.

There was a knock on the door and Detective Doran entered.

Isobel stood up and Jack rose too.

"Detective, we'll leave you to it," said Isobel.

The Provost escorted them to the office door.

"Thank you, Ms. McKenzie, for your help with this matter and also with the matter of the attack on our two students. I'm glad that the man who killed Michael has been identified." He shook Isobel's hand then reached out for Jack's. "Thank you too, Jack. I appreciate all you've done."

Malcolm stood as they emerged and they left the building without any conversation.

"Right," said Jack. "I'm going to go back and check on Noah. I'll talk to you later."

"Take care!" Isobel called after him as he headed off.

"Well?" Malcolm said when they were alone.

"It's awful really. Professor Clarke seems quite the wrong person to be caught in our net. He was getting cannabis for his wife who has chronic bone pain, to help her when nothing else could."

Malcolm made a face. "Yeah, that's tough."

"I know. I feel sorry for him, for his wife, for the awful situation they're in. What would any of us be prepared to do to ease the suffering of someone we love?"

"What are you saying?"

Isobel shook her head. "I don't know. I suppose I don't know what I would do if I was in Professor Clarke's position."

"There are other ways to do things, Isobel. I'm pretty sure I read that cannabis for medical use is available in Northern Ireland but it has to be prescribed by a specified doctor."

"I didn't know that."

"Yeah, in a lot of places limited use medicinally is allowed but with strict prescribing protocols. I don't think that the PSNI will take too kindly to Professor Clarke doing his own prescribing."

"No. I guess not. But what threw me completely was when the Provost suggested that he could have contacted his old college buddy Superintendent Bernard Taylor about this today."

"*Oh no!* That would have been a disaster! But why didn't he?"

"Apparently he wanted to avoid any suggestion of special treatment for Clarke because the three of them were buddies in the past. Both he and the professor want him to have the same treatment as everyone else."

"Thank God for that," said Malcolm. "And I'm sure Damien will make sure that they say nothing."

"Yes, he will. God, this waiting around is terrible."

"What do you want to do now to help you pass the time?"

Isobel looked thoughtful. "I want to go and talk to one of the group who knew Taylor from college – Neat Jameson."

Malcolm laughed. "No way! What's his real name?"

"Ben Jameson."

"I think I prefer 'Neat'. In fact, now that I think of it, I have been remiss in not sampling some Irish whiskey. Maybe tomorrow, if all goes to plan, I can remedy that."

"Do you know what the Irish for whiskey is?"

Malcolm shook his head.

"*Uisce beatha* – the water of life."

"How poetic! I definitely need to get some of that."

Isobel grinned.

"Why do you want to see Neat anyway?"

"He might tell us a bit more about Taylor. I just find it so hard to believe that Taylor's a murderer and involved in or maybe leading a drug gang. Why would he do that?"

"You think that Neat will be able to help you understand?"

"I don't know." Isobel looked uncomfortable. "I just

don't get it. I suppose I thought if I understood the man better I might be able to make sense of it in my head."

"Corruption is a slippery slope, Isobel. It can start out as small things and in time become full-blown."

"I know but this isn't just corruption – this is a major drug gang with influence. This is someone who had a serious plan, smart, forward-thinking, patient, careful."

"I know. But the little we know of Taylor he's all of those things. He had to be to get away with it for years. He's covered his tracks and even when things went off the rails he's been resourceful and fast-acting at staying hidden. And he's ruthless."

Isobel frowned. "I think that's what bothers me. He's been quick to act in situations, as you say, resourceful, fast-acting and ruthless. But conceiving of this drug scheme and the building of it over time, is that not a different mentality?"

Malcolm raised his eyebrows at her. "It's the same ruthless disregard for people's lives. I think Taylor is a planner, a strategist, who lucky for him is also good under pressure."

She shrugged. "Talking to Neat isn't going to do any harm and anyway it will pass some time."

"Maybe it's the psychologist in you, trying to understand. Me, I just want to catch him and put him in jail."

Isobel laughed. "That too."

"How are we going to explain our interest in Taylor to Neat Jameson?"

"I don't know," said Isobel.

"I suppose we'll just have to wing it."

Chapter 46

Isobel led Malcolm to the counselling service office. Ben Jameson was free at four o'clock and was happy to meet with them.

"No Jack today?"

Isobel smiled. "No. This is a friend of mine, Malcolm."

The men shook hands.

"It's great news that they found Michael's killer," said Ben.

Isobel kept forgetting that for all those who listened to the news, the case had been solved.

"Yes, yes. It is."

"How can I help you?"

"I'm interested in hearing about the group of you who were students together." She smiled. "You, the Crown Prince, the Muse. I think Professor Clarke was one of your crowd also?"

"Yes, we called him 'The Professor' even then. Why are you so interested in our student days?"

Isobel frowned. She and Malcolm really should have

prepared a cover story. "I believe that Superintendent Taylor was also one of the group. Needless to say, with what happened, I've had occasion to meet him and I just wondered . . ." As she spoke she realised how weak this sounded but she didn't know how to frame things to get Ben to talk.

"He made an impression, then, did he? He always tended to do that."

"When you told me about you as students, I couldn't help being intrigued. The Provost mentioned Superintendent Taylor – it seemed that they were quite close."

"Not a bit of it. There's no love lost there at all. Taylor's nickname was –"

"I can't wait to hear this." Isobel grinned.

"Stitch."

Malcolm laughed. "Stitch Taylor! Oh my God! No wonder he has issues with power and feels a need to dominate."

"You've certainly got his measure."

Isobel couldn't help but laugh.

"Stitch seems such an unfortunate nickname compared to yours," said Malcolm.

Ben grinned. "I know."

"Who came up with that?" Malcolm asked. "In fact, who came up with all the names?"

Ben grinned. "Lorraine started it. You can probably guess we were all crazy about her. The Prince and Stitch were both in love with her. She just had this way about her. She still has. You get pulled into her orbit. It's like a gravitational pull that seems impossible to resist, or it did.

411

I was in love with her too and the professor was besotted until he met Grace. Taylor thought he had the best chance with Lorraine. He had. I was sure that they were an item and then someone new came on the scene and the new guy became number one with her."

"I bet Taylor didn't like that," said Isobel.

"You would think so, but he was so under Lorraine's spell that he just accepted it."

Isobel raised her eyebrows. "Who was this new guy?"

"Taylor actually introduced him. He played rugby against him and they became friends. I think they still are. They certainly work together. I saw them at the press conference on Saturday when they announced who had killed Michael."

Isobel shot a glance at Malcolm.

Ben continued, lost in his reminiscence. "It was actually he who gave Taylor his name. Apparently, when they played rugby, Taylor often got stitches in his side. Everyone thinks he has the name because Taylor is his surname but really it's because of his rugby."

"Weird coincidence," said Isobel, laughing.

"I know. That Southern guy, he had a nickname too – we called him 'The Prop'."

Malcolm said, "So the Prop and Stitch were old friends?"

Ben nodded. "Oh yes. And once he and Taylor got together with the Muse, well, none of the rest of us had a look-in. They sort of formed their own little triumvirate. I tried to hang on to Lorraine. I wanted to be included and found it hard to accept that I wasn't – so I started dabbling in drugs."

"Are you saying that you got into drugs because the 'triumvirate' were into them?" Malcolm asked.

Ben shook his head. "No, not at all. I made that choice and I take responsibility for it. All I'm saying is that it was around that time that drugs came on the scene. After my overdose, Lorraine decided to leave college."

"And are Taylor and Lorraine friends now?" Isobel asked.

"I've no idea. I'm not in contact with them."

"And The Prop, as you call him?" Malcolm asked.

Ben shook his head. "I never see him around, only on the News associated with some case or other. Obviously he and Taylor work together. And, as far as I know, Lorraine leads a quiet life."

There was silence.

"I don't know what else you want to know or even why you're so interested," Ben said then.

"I suppose I've had occasion to meet a lot of your group in the last few days – and when you were kind enough to share some of your memories with me and Jack before – and now having realised that Superintendent Taylor was also there . . ." She stopped, aware she was gabbling.

Ben was looking strangely at her.

"It's just that he makes quite an impression, as you said," said Malcolm.

Ben shrugged. "He always liked to be the big man."

"And still does," Isobel said.

Ben laughed. "Have you had a run-in with him?"

"Not yet," Malcolm said, "but it may be on the cards."

"I would like to get the better of him," Isobel said.

413

"And I would like to see that!" said Ben, laughing.

"Watch this space," Malcolm said.

"I will. I'm intrigued."

"But mum's the word," said Malcolm with a wink.

"My lips are sealed."

Isobel stood. "Thanks for sharing your college stories with us."

"No problem. Silly stuff really, all those old rivalries."

Isobel wanted to say not silly – serious, deadly serious.

As they walked through the grounds Malcolm said, "What's on your mind, Isobel?"

"I'm not sure," she replied, her mind fizzing with ideas.

"Well, let's have some of your Irish stew and you can spell it out for me. We might have a busy night ahead and I want to be prepared."

"Spit it out, Isobel. What's going through that head of yours?" Malcolm said as he finished his plate of stew.

Isobel put down her cutlery. "Do you really think Taylor is the Big Boss? I'm not convinced."

"I knew that what Ben said was running around in your head. Look, you might never know why Taylor made the choices he did. Don't worry about that. The most important thing is that we catch him and end his criminal career."

"You haven't answered my question."

"Isobel, I don't care what they did as students but I do care about the shit he has done since – the murder, the drug-supplying, the gang involvement and the corruption."

"Come on, Malcolm, answer my question."

Malcolm shook his head. "Well, according to Neat, he always was and is an impressive figure. Feels a need to dominate. Likes to be the 'big man'. Fits the profile, in my opinion."

"Well, I feel the Big Boss must be someone more subtle. A manipulator. The spider in the web."

"And is he not? Having played a part skillfully all these years, without arousing the faintest whiff of suspicion? For that matter, Aaron could fit the bill. Don't you think so? Look, to be honest, if we can put both of them away I will count this a huge success, massive."

"I'm just telling you what my instincts tell me."

"I know but, with all we have going on, I don't think the psychology is the most important thing. We have people, friends, in dangerous situations trying to find proof of what we suspect and know. Damien and Williams are in the lion's den and that guy Brian. And Henry is vulnerable. I'm trying to stay calm and focused but it's an effort. Isobel, enough is happening – you need to stay focused. You can't distract yourself, but more especially anyone else. We can come back to this hunch of yours when arrests have been made, if it's necessary." Malcolm waited a few seconds. "You know I'm right. Do you think it's possible, with all that has happened, all that you've heard, all of the betrayals, all of the someone-being-who-they-aren't, that maybe it has got to you and now you're afraid to trust your own logic? Is that not possible? That you're afraid to trust what we have found out?"

Isobel looked at her hands. "That's possible, but . . ."

"Superintendent Taylor and Aaron McGuinness, The Prop, are capable of murder so I think running a drug gang is well within their capabilities."

"True, true." Isobel sighed. "So you're satisfied one of them is the Boss?"

"My money is on Taylor because he's in Belfast. It's his turf."

Isobel frowned. "I suppose."

Isobel and Malcolm were in the lift when Eoin and Alanna phoned at seven o'clock. They hurried through the hallways to Isobel's room and sat at the table with the phone on speaker.

"How has it all been going?" Isobel asked.

"Really good, Isobel," said Alanna. "Superintendent Carruthers sends his regards. He says you specialise in up-scuttling everyone." She laughed. "Things have been a bit hectic."

"We spoke to the Super about everything," said Eoin. "He has a good friend in Dublin, also a superintendent. He's reached out to him and told him to be ready for a call soon. He's given him the heads-up that there is corruption involved."

"That's good," said Malcolm.

"Carruthers is suggesting that Alanna and I go with him to talk to his superintendent friend in Dublin since we know most about the case. We may even help with the arrests just to prevent any leaks. And I hear that Brian found the body. Hopefully the dental records will confirm if it's

Darren. Keep us up to speed with all the developments."

"Will do," said Malcolm. "Talk later."

He hung up and glanced at Isobel. "I'm going to go and lie down for a while and get some rest. This is going to be a long night. Why don't you do the same?"

Isobel nodded. "Good idea."

"I suppose you're going to join the surveillance tonight?"

"Of course."

"I thought you would say that. I think you should go with Jack and Dave. I would feel better if you were with them."

Isobel nodded. "Sure."

Chapter 47

It was eleven o'clock. Isobel opened the door and slid into the passenger seat of Dave's car. He was parked on Carmel Street around the corner from Fitzroy Avenue where Robin lived.

"*Brrr!* It's cold out there."

"Has Jack found a good place to watch from?" he asked.

"Yeah, he has a good view of Robin's house. He's down the street a bit, loitering at a house which is in darkness and has a big bush, so he has some cover. Nothing is happening though. The curtains of Robin's house are closed. Robin definitely was there earlier but I haven't seen him since they closed the curtains. I assume he's still inside. Let me check with Malcolm."

She texted: **Can you talk?**

Her phone rang a few seconds later.

"Well, any news?" she asked.

"No, nothing to report. Manager Man is home in his sitting room and I would say is watching television. I can see the light changing behind his curtains."

"Nothing here either. Jack is keeping an eye at the moment. Robin has been in all evening – very boring."

"Ring me if anything changes."

"I will. Don't worry." Isobel rang off.

There was nothing to do but wait and in truth nothing might happen.

"Are you all right, Dave?" she asked. "You've had a busy day. Do you want to sleep for a bit?"

"Not at all. But if nothing has happened by three o'clock I might go to bed then – otherwise I'm fine."

At midnight Isobel's phone pinged with a message.

"What's happening? Is Robin going out?" Dave straightened up in his seat and his hand hovered over the ignition.

Isobel checked her phone. "No. It's Jack. He wants someone else to take over."

"I'll go," said Dave, reaching for the door handle.

"No, you need to stay in the car to drive. I'll go."

Isobel zipped up her coat and pulled on her hat. She climbed out of the car and walked round the corner onto Fitzroy Avenue. She walked past his house and on towards Jack's hideout. Jack saw her coming and moved to meet her.

"Nothing," was his greeting.

Isobel shrugged. "Get some rest. I'll message you when I get too cold and bored."

Jack grinned.

Isobel took his post, half hidden behind the bush, and

shoved her hands deep into her pockets to keep them warm. Every now and then, when there was no one around, she stamped her feet, all the time watching the front of Robin's house.

At just before one o'clock her phone pinged again. It was Malcolm.

We have movement. Manager Man is in his car and we are following.

Something was happening at last. Isobel wanted to dance for joy.

She heard a noise from down the street. Looking up, she saw that Robin's door was open and a young man was standing on the step. As he turned to close the door, Isobel saw in the light from the hall that it was Robin.

He walked to his gate. Isobel wondered if he would turn in her direction. If he did, she would have to walk on as if she was going somewhere. At the gate he paused and then walked in the opposite direction.

She messaged Jack quickly.

Robin coming your way.

Isobel followed behind at a distance. Robin approached the corner with Carmel Street. Isobel held her breath. Then Robin continued on Fitzroy Avenue.

Isobel paused at the entrance to Carmel Street and sent a text to Jack: **You follow Robin.** A few seconds later Jack waved to her as he pulled up his hood and walked after Robin.

Isobel ran to Dave's car.

"Thank God," said Dave. "Here, hold my phone. Jack

is on Snapchat." He pointed at the screen. "We can track where he is going. If they go too far away I'll have to move the car."

"Oh, that's handy. Malcolm said that Manager Man is on the move too."

Isobel could feel knots of anxiety. Their two quarries were on the move. That couldn't just be a coincidence.

"It looks like Jack might be going towards Botanic Avenue. I'm going to move the car so we are closer."

Isobel held Dave's phone, her eyes on the screen.

Dave started the car and drove slowly.

Isobel's phone pinged with a message. Clumsy in her haste, she set Dave's phone on her lap so she could watch it and opened her own phone. It was from Malcolm.

Heading towards you.

"Manager Man is heading towards us."

"Where's Jack now?"

Isobel studied the picture on Dave's phone. "He's turned onto Botanic Avenue."

Dave accelerated and turned right. "Botanic Avenue is the road ahead of us."

Isobel's phone rang.

"Jack?"

"Robin got into a car. Pick me up. I'm in sight of the Org shop. Are you close?"

"Yeah. Quick, Dave. Org shop on Botanic Avenue."

Isobel's phone pinged another message. Malcolm.

Manager picked up Robin. Following. Not sure where they are going.

Dave drove up Botanic Avenue.

Isobel saw a figure waving. "There he is. There's Jack."

Dave pulled in to the side and Jack ran across the road and sat into the back of the car.

He said, "The car Robin got into, I lost sight of it. There are too many cars – we'll never find them. They could be going anywhere."

"Don't worry, Malcolm was following Manager Man. Hopefully they are still behind him," Isobel said. "I'll ring him and see."

If Robin and the Manager were together, surely something was happening. Isobel could feel the butterflies in her stomach.

"Malcolm where are you? Where are you going?"

"We've made a couple of turns and now we are on a bigger road. Hold on. Noah says we are on Sandy Row. I'll ring back when I know more." Malcolm rang off.

Isobel said, "Dave, they're on Sandy Row."

Jack said, "Go straight on, Dad – I'll tell you when to turn." He leant over the seat. "Maybe they're heading to another shop."

"Maybe," said Isobel.

There was a reasonable amount of traffic. Isobel wondered if it was always as busy as this or if the fact that Halloween was tomorrow was contributing to the cars. She wished Dave would drive faster but she said nothing. She took some deep breaths and tried to relax.

Her phone rang again.

"Malcolm?"

"Noah says we've turned onto the Grosvenor Road."

"They're on the Grosvenor Road, now," Isobel said.

"Turn left here, Dad."

"I'll have to wait for the light!" Dave snapped.

"I know," Jack said. "They might be going to the Org shop at Saint Mary's College on the Falls Road. That seems to be the closest Org shop to the one on Botanic Avenue."

Isobel was almost jumping in her seat. Would the lights ever change?

"Isobel?" Malcolm called down the phone.

"Yes, where are you now?"

"Noah says we're on the Falls Road."

"They're on the Falls Road," Isobel said for Dave and Jack's benefit.

"I knew it!" Jack said with satisfaction.

"*Shush!*" Isobel hissed. "Sorry, Malcolm. Go on."

"We're at another Org shop. We've driven past the shop and have found a place to pull into with a good view. Robin and Manager Man have gone into the shop."

"At this time of night."

"Yes. The shop is in darkness but someone let them in."

"They're up to something."

"Definitely."

"Org shop at Saint Mary's," Isobel whispered to Jack. He gave her the thumbs-up and leant forward to whisper directions to his dad.

"*Oh, oh, we have activity!*" Malcolm said.

"What is it?" Isobel lowered her voice.

"What's happening?" Jack asked.

"*Shush*, I don't know yet. Malcolm, what's happening?" Isobel had her phone pressed hard to her ear in her anxiety to know what was going on.

"Robin and Manager Man are carrying boxes out to the car," Malcolm said. "Another man is helping them. Hold on, Isobel."

Isobel could hear Malcolm telling Noah to get his phone out then some more words she couldn't hear.

"Sorry, Isobel, I was just getting Noah to take photos for me. Can you hurry up and get here? I want you, Jack and Dave to watch the new guy and follow him. Noah and I will continue to follow Robin and Manager Man."

"OK, hold on, Malcolm." Isobel quickly explained that to Dave. He seemed to sense her urgency and the car jumped forward as he speeded up.

Jack said, "We're nearly there."

Isobel could feel her heart racing.

"Malcolm, we're very close. What's happening now?" she asked.

"The three men are putting a second lot of boxes in the car. They're closing the boot. Manager Man is shaking hands with the new guy. Hurry, Isobel."

Isobel turned her face a little away from the phone. "Jack, how long until we get to the Org shop?"

"It's just ahead of us."

"Pull in here, Dave," Isobel instructed.

Isobel spoke into her phone again. "Malcolm, we're here, down the street a hundred metres. Where do you want us?"

"It looks like Manager Man and Robin are leaving. We were watching from outside a nail shop. We'll be leaving in a second. You could pull in here. Try and stay with this new guy and see where he goes. We're leaving. I'm not sure where we're going but I imagine back into Belfast to one of their houses. I'll update you soon." Malcolm rang off.

Isobel said, "Move forward slowly, Dave. We're looking for a nail shop."

Jack said, "I see it coming up on the right."

"Park outside it," Isobel said.

Isobel fixed her eyes to the right, looking past Dave as best she could. She could see a man in dark clothing fiddling with the door of the Org shop. He was tall and thin.

Dave said, "Here it is." He pulled in and parked

"Watch the man at the Org shop, Jack. And get some pictures if you can."

"No problem."

Isobel could feel her heart pounding in her chest. She tried to take a deep breath and calm herself.

"He's leaving. He's walking down the road in the direction we came."

Isobel said, "Dave, you need to swing around. We need to follow him."

"Hold on, Dad!" Jack was looking through the back window of the car. "I can see him. He is getting into a silver Audi."

"Yes, yes," Dave said. "I can see him in my mirrors."

"His car is facing this way. Wait. He might come this way."

Isobel looked back over her seat. "What's he doing?"

Jack said, "He's swinging around."

Isobel could feel her hands clenching with tension.

425

"We'll lose him. You can't do a U turn, Dave. He might see your lights in his mirror."

"Not if I don't have any lights on. There's nothing coming. I can turn now." Dave made a quick U-turn and headed back the way they had come. He reached out and squeezed Isobel's hand. "I have my lights back on."

"Jack, can you see the silver Audi?"

"I can."

Dave said, "Where is it?"

"You've almost caught up. Look, that car is turning off. The Audi's in front of that white car."

Dave said, "This guy in front is going too slow. We're going to lose the Audi. I'll pass this car."

Dave spotted a break in the traffic coming the other way and accelerated quickly.

"Well done, Dad. Get a bit closer so that we can get the registration in case we lose him. Isobel, can you see it?"

"X10 PXP – got it!"

"I'll drop back a bit," said Dave.

"Where is he going?" Isobel asked.

Jack said, "We're on Divis Street now."

"He could be going anywhere." Isobel sighed. "Just do your best, Dave."

"I know. I'll have to stay fairly close to him or I'll lose him."

"He's turning left," Jack said. "This is Millfield."

As they followed the Audi, Isobel found she was sitting forward in her seat with one hand on the dashboard. Dave's hands were white on the steering wheel. Jack was leaning forward through the gap between the front seats.

"He's indicating right."

"Stay with him, Dave."

A horn beeped as Dave turned right.

Jack glanced at his phone. "Great Patrick Street. We're heading towards the Lagan. This is quite a built-up area. Maybe he has an apartment."

They passed a number of complexes with double gates.

"Look, the gates of that block are opening - he's going in," Isobel said.

"Dad, let me out. I'll follow him."

"*No!*" Dave said but, as he slowed approaching the gates of the apartment block, Jack jumped out. "*Jack! Stop!*"

Jack ran towards the gates. He slipped inside as the gates were beginning to close.

Isobel pushed open her door. "Stay nearby!" She ran after Jack, just managing to slip through the gates before they shut.

She heard a car door slam. She paused and saw a tall man in a black top and jeans walk away from a silver Audi. And there was Jack following right behind him to the entrance door to the block of flats.

Her heart pounded as she stormed after him.

Jack swung around and gaped at her in surprise.

"I told you to wait for me," Isobel said crossly.

"Sorry," Jack mumbled.

The man ignored them. He opened the door.

Isobel stepped up close behind him but turned back towards Jack. "*You can never do what you're told!*" she said, injecting anger into her voice.

Jack frowned.

"Thank you!" Isobel snapped as she followed the man through the entrance door.

Jack scurried behind. "You know I hate meeting Dad."

Thank God, thought Isobel. He was playing along.

"He is your father!" Isobel continued.

The man moved away from them towards the lifts.

Isobel grasped Jack's arm and slowed their progress. As the doors opened, they followed the man on. He hit a button and then stepped to the back of the lift.

Isobel checked the display. The light for the third floor was illuminated. She and Jack stood near the control panel.

Isobel said, "Why didn't you do as your father asked you?"

Jack made a face at her. "I don't want to talk about it."

"For God's sake! You're always the same!"

Isobel lapsed into silence, impressed with Jack's contributions to the impromptu domestic drama. In her estimation, nothing made people more uncomfortable than witnessing a family disagreement.

The man in black shifted uncomfortably. When the doors opened, he moved through them and to the right quickly.

Isobel stepped out and turned left, pulling Jack with her. He had his phone in his hand.

"Selfie mode," whispered Isobel.

Jack nodded and held his phone so he could see the corridor behind him.

Isobel walked slowly. "Well, you need to see him.

We've talked about this." She heard a door close.

Isobel and Jack stopped.

"Three doors down, I think," Jack said.

Isobel turned back towards the elevator and walked a little bit past. Jack followed.

"Number 324," he whispered.

Isobel stepped back onto the lift. "Let's get out of here."

As they travelled back to the ground floor the hammering in her heart gradually returned to normal. In the car park Jack took a photo of the silver Audi. Walking to the gates Isobel wondered how they would get out. Jack pointed to a side gate and they slipped through.

Back on the road Isobel looked for Dave. As she turned from left to right a car travelled towards them and stopped.

"Get in," said a tight voice.

Isobel sat into the front seat. She felt weak.

"We got it, Dad. We got his address. Oh, Isobel, that was so funny! He couldn't cope at all with our little drama." Jack burst into laughter.

"*Jack!*" Dave snapped. "*You shouldn't have done that. That man could be dangerous. It was supposed to be surveillance only.*"

"We were fine," Jack said.

"You didn't know that."

"And Isobel was there. I was fine."

Isobel's phone rang. "It's Malcolm."

Isobel pressed her phone to her ear. "Well?"

"Robin and his friend are back at the Org shop, carrying the boxes in."

"I'm going to let Williams know and send on the photos. With your professor's statement about Robin and the videos with the boxes, they probably have enough for a search warrant. What about your guy?"

"Jack has an address."

"*Great!* Tell him to send it on to me and I'll forward everything to Williams. We've done all we can. Go and get some sleep, all of you."

"We will."

Isobel was in bed when her phone rang again. It was Malcolm.

"Just a quick update. Dental records prove that the body found was indeed Darren Kelly."

"That's terrific. Sad but good."

"And ballistics are back. Darren Kelly was shot with a bullet from Superintendent Taylor's gun."

"*Oh my God! I don't believe it!*"

"Williams has been to see the Chief Constable. They're set to arrest Taylor at six this morning."

"Fantastic!"

"Eoin and Alanna have spoken with the Superintendent in Dublin, I'm not sure of his name, and they're going to arrest Aaron McGuinness and Tim-Tan at six also. And, in Belfast, they're going to arrest Robin and Manager Man and search the shop. If they find drugs then the guy you followed will also be picked up. Operation Clean Sweep is set."

"Wonderful."

"Nearly there. I thought you'd want to know."

"Thanks, Malcolm."

"Get some sleep. We need to celebrate tomorrow."

Isobel felt somewhat reassured but until all of the criminals were arrested she couldn't relax.

And that was it. There was nothing more to do. Everything was now in the hands of others.

Chapter 48

Tuesday 31st October

When Isobel woke it was nine o'clock. She grabbed her phone. There were no messages.

She had a quick shower and rang Malcolm's room.

They met in the dining room and ordered breakfast. Malcolm was in good spirits and had an Ulster fry. Isobel had coffee and a croissant.

Jack and Dave arrived. No one had any news. They ordered more coffee and sat and waited.

Isobel glanced at Malcolm. "Is no news good news or is that a sign that things have gone awry?"

Malcolm shrugged. "They're busy. There were a lot of people to arrest and no doubt some serious solicitors to contend with."

Isobel hunched her shoulders. She checked her phone to see if there was any news items relating to last night but there was nothing. She realised how much she hated waiting for information.

Suddenly, there was a ping on all of their phones, a text.

Williams and Doran were on their way to update them.

The minutes dragged by. Eventually the policemen strode into the dining room.

"Well?" Isobel said before they had even sat down. "What happened?"

Inspector Williams grinned and settled himself comfortably in his chair before answering.

"A lot. Early this morning officers raided the Org shop here on Botanic Avenue and found a quarter of a million pounds worth of mixed drugs, all bagged up and ready to go."

"*Wow!*" said Jack.

Dave whistled. "That much!"

Isobel clasped her hands together, relief flooding through her.

"What about Taylor?" Malcolm asked.

Williams nodded. "We arrested him as well. You can imagine how angry he is. He has a solicitor from Markham and Young. We'll be interviewing him shortly."

"Patrick Magill worked for Markham and Young before he died," Isobel said.

"Is there enough evidence to prosecute Taylor?" Malcolm asked.

"It's going to be hard to explain how someone was shot with his gun without his knowledge. It's the gun he still uses. Damien has all the footage from the docks and we have Joe's statement. And, of course, Darren was a garda so I don't think Taylor's going to be able to wriggle out of this. Plus we have the videos of him suppressing the evidence from the alley. I think we have a reasonable case."

"And he might implicate Aaron to get a reduced sentence," said Damien.

"Yes," said Williams. "They may turn on each other. One of them may try to make a deal. Aaron and Tim-Tan were arrested this morning too. Tim-Tan knows that he's in trouble with two witnesses to Michael's killing. He knows that we suspect him of killing Gary Wells also. We can place him in the vicinity of the burned-out car. He is trying to negotiate a deal by giving us Aaron McGuinness which is good because, while we know McGuinness is guilty, the evidence is more circumstantial. So if Tim-Tan gives him up we're elected."

"Oh, thank God!" said Isobel. "That's great news."

Malcolm nodded.

"We're raiding the Org company headquarters," said Damien, "and also the other shops to see if they are also involved in drugs."

Williams stood up. "Yes, really we have to go. There is so much to do. We just wanted to let you know how well everything is going."

"I had heard rumours about this Big Boss here in Belfast," said Isobel. "Is it Taylor? Do you think he's the Boss?"

Williams nodded. "Yes, the limited intel we had was of someone in charge whose identity was carefully guarded. We're confident that Taylor is the one. It's fantastic to think that we've busted open this gang."

"It doesn't get much better than this," Malcolm said.

"And it wouldn't have happened without all of you," said Williams. "We're very grateful. I was hoping that we could all get together for a meal this evening to celebrate."

"We like a celebration, don't we, Isobel?" Malcolm said.

Isobel nodded. "We sure do!"

Williams and Doran left.

"Why don't we get Eoin and Alanna to come up if they can?" Malcolm suggested. "They were involved too."

Isobel grinned. "That sounds like a great plan."

"I'll ring them."

"Can Rachel and Noah come too?" Jack asked. "They helped."

"Of course," said Malcolm. "The more the merrier."

"I'm going to call round and tell them," Jack said, getting up.

Dave rose too. "And I'm going to ring home. We'll see you later." Together Dave and Jack left.

"Is it really all over? I can hardly believe it," Isobel said.

"Yes, it is," said Malcolm.

"I never thought it would end as well as this."

"No, I didn't either," said Malcolm.

Isobel experienced a niggle of doubt.

"You see," Malcolm said, "I told you that Taylor was the Boss."

Isobel nodded. "Yes, yes, you did."

But inside she could feel the niggle gaining power. The idea that had tormented her. Was Taylor really the Boss? A part of her had always felt that he wasn't. He wanted power, he looked like he had power but was he really the one in charge?

"Now it is time to chill out and wait for the celebration."

"Yes. I'm going to take a breath of fresh air and then go up to my room and listen to some music or

435

something," Isobel said.

"OK. See you later then."

Isobel wandered out of the hotel. The day was fresh with blue skies and puffy cotton-wool clouds. She started walking towards the university and then turned down the street towards the Muse.

She stood at the entrance to the alley. This was where it had all started. Two kids checking out a location for a short film. It seemed astonishing that their presence there had led to all that had ensued.

Isobel swivelled on her heel and looked at the front of the Muse pub. Muses were the goddesses who inspired artists with ideas. The artist created, the Muse inspired. It seemed that artists reached their heights through their Muse. Isobel turned and walked along the front of the pub. It was ten o'clock. The door was closed. She listened carefully and could hear movement inside.

What should she do? Malcolm had been unequivocal in his rejection of her doubts and Williams and Doran seemed happy that they had arrested the Boss. But Isobel wasn't happy. What if the spider was out there ready to spin her web again?

Isobel took her phone out of her handbag and took a picture of the front of the pub and sent it to Malcolm then she phoned the group chat.

Jack answered immediately.

Isobel said, "Jack are you with Rachel and Noah?"

"Yes."

"I want you to stay on this line and listen, do you hear me?"

"Yes, what's happening?"

"Just do what I'm asking you."

Isobel slipped her phone into the top of her bag and then knocked on the door of the pub. She heard the lock click. She took a deep breath. The door opened.

Lorraine was standing at the door.

"Oh, Isobel! You're a bit keen this morning. I'm not open yet."

"I know. A lot has been happening."

"Indeed. I've heard that the Org shop near here has been dealing drugs. I'm shocked. First the murder and now this. I don't think I'll be opening today."

"That's a lot to take in, overwhelming. Perhaps one of the staff could open for you? You could take the day off."

"Perhaps. I'll think about it. Would you like to come in and have a cup of tea with me? I find that I'm hot one minute and cold the next and very shaky."

Isobel felt her stomach tighten. She hesitated.

"It's cold. Come on in. I'd like to talk about things."

This was, after all, why she had come. "Sure, I can manage a quick cup."

"Great." Lorraine smiled and, turning, led the way into the pub.

Isobel followed. Once inside, she turned and pretended to close the door but instead locked the snib in place so that the door could not close fully and anyone pushing it would be able to get in.

She followed Lorraine through the smaller swing doors leading into the bar.

Lorraine went behind the counter. "How about a glass

of brandy?" she said. "I think I need something strong for the shock."

"It's a bit early for me," Isobel said as she shifted one of the barstools and sat on it. She took off her coat and hung it on the barstool beside her. At the same time she positioned her bag on the stool with the top open. She could see her phone.

"Oh, I think the day they arrest a major drug boss who also turns out to be a superintendent of police is a day for brandy!" said Lorraine.

Isobel shivered. She had heard this from Inspector Williams only a few minutes ago and Lorraine knew already.

"You know what, that might be worth a decent drink." Isobel ran her eyes along the bottles on the shelf. "How about a Jameson Redbreast for me? That's one of my favourite whiskeys."

Lorraine smiled at her. "No problem." She turned to the shelves, reaching up to get down the bottle.

"I'm looking forward to this actually. It's a long time since I had whiskey this early in the day."

"I'll make it a double then. Ice? Water?"

"No, I'll take it as it is."

Lorraine pushed Isobel's whiskey towards her and then poured herself a brandy sniffer.

She raised her glass. "*Bottoms up!*"

"*Sláinte!*"

Both women took a swallow.

"I feel more relaxed already," Lorraine said.

Isobel nodded.

"So, what do you think about everything?" Lorraine asked.

"Drugs in the stationery store – shocking – and a superintendent arrested as the boss of a drug gang! It's hard to believe."

Lorraine stared at her. "I don't know. It seems to me that you've been sniffing around for a week now. I imagine that you knew quite a lot about what was going on."

Isobel sipped her drink.

Lorraine threw hers back and poured another. "Brandy is reviving, isn't it? I think I need some reviving."

"You also seem to know a lot about what's happening."

Lorraine smiled. "I know some of the solicitors in Markham and Young. I've known them for years. They rang me because of the Org yard being off the alley beside my bar. I can't believe that drugs were being brought in under our noses, so to speak."

"It is hard to believe." Isobel felt her stomach knot more tightly.

"And we saw nothing of what was going on. It seems the deliveries were at night. No one sleeps on the premises so obviously everything happened when the pub was closed."

"Nevertheless, strange you noticed nothing at all over the years."

Lorraine's mouth tightened. "It's amazing that all of this has come to light now. I wonder why?"

"I suppose when you kill an innocent student and try to maim another one it draws attention."

"Yes, if the students hadn't been attacked, then none of this would have come to light."

Isobel felt her body tighten. The regret didn't seem so

much for the students as for all that had subsequently been uncovered.

"Probably not," she said. "I think there was a great little system going, but, obviously, the Boss lost control of his men."

"Do you think that's what happened? I saw on the news that Geo, the killer, was himself killed. Maybe that was the Boss punishing him for his stupidity."

"Do you really think so?"

Lorraine raised an eyebrow. "Of course. What else?"

"It seems more likely to me that Geo was sacrificed," Isobel said.

"Sacrificed? What on earth do you mean?" Lorraine frowned.

"I think it was a step taken to end the investigation. The murderer was found and so the investigation was over. Back to business as usual. Thank goodness it didn't work."

"Superintendent Taylor seemed confident on Saturday night that all was sorted."

"But he's arrested now. So, not such a clever boss, then. Or maybe too greedy."

Lorraine grimaced. "It appears that this was a sophisticated drug pyramid and that it has been going on for years. Really, drug dealers are like business people – supply and demand. There's a demand there and they supply it."

"Oh, I think there's a bit more to it than that. I think in this case the drug group created demand by introducing people to drugs. I also think that they targeted people and then exploited them to deal drugs. And not just drugs, they also had some people perform other functions like providing information, or influence." Her hands were white where they were gripping her glass. She let go of it and rubbed her hands together to relieve the tension in them.

Lorraine swirled her brandy. "That sounds as if they were clever enough."

Isobel met Lorraine's gaze. "Not clever if they get caught."

Lorraine kept her eyes on Isobel and sipped her brandy. "Maybe they're not all caught."

Isobel's hands tightened on her glass again. "Maybe not."

She could feel the challenge in Lorraine's words and knew her suspicions were correct. This woman was raging about what had happened. She hoped that Jack was listening and that he understood what was happening and that the picture she had sent Malcolm of the pub had made him realise what she was doing.

Isobel reached into her bag and pulled out the blister pack of tablets. "Let me return these to you. Jack never used any of them." She set the tablets on the bar.

Lorraine looked down at them a long time then up into Isobel's eyes. "When Jack said that his aunt was here to help, I imagined someone less," her mouth pursed up as if she wanted to spit, "less . . ."

Isobel raised an eyebrow.

"*Less interfering*." Lorraine's lips curled in a snarl.

"So interference is what has brought down this Boss, this drug dealer, this spider at the centre of a web?"

"Is that what you see it as? I like it, a spider at the centre of a web."

"That is how I see it but I don't see Taylor as the Spider. He doesn't have the subtlety."

"Subtlety, that's a good word." Lorraine's lips curled as if in a smile. "I think you're right – it takes subtlety to organise and run such a successful business."

Isobel felt her breath catch in her throat. She prayed that Jack could hear all of this. It wasn't a recording, it was a live call. She hoped that made a difference and that whoever was on the end of the line could testify as to what they heard.

"Everyone thinks that the Boss has been captured but I don't agree. I don't think that Taylor has the finesse to be the Boss."

"Finesse, now that's a word I like more. You're right, he doesn't have the finesse."

"And who do you think could do it?" Isobel challenged her.

"Oh, someone clever, a planner, a strategist, innovative."

"You sound as if you admire the Boss."

Lorraine smiled.

Isobel could feel tension all over her body now. Her heart raced. Her chest felt tight. Her eyes were locked on Lorraine's. This was the moment, the moment to take the risk, like stepping out of a plane with a parachute and praying that it would open. One step that you can't go back from. She felt peace settle on her. Everything had brought her to this time, this place.

She smiled back at Lorraine. "Let's cut to the chase."

Lorraine gestured for her to continue. "Let's do that."

"*You're* the Spider at the centre of the web. *You're* the

Boss. *You're* the influencer, the ruthless seducer and destroyer of young people for financial gain."

Lorraine clapped almost silently. "*Bravo!* You figured it out but no one is going to believe you and, let me tell you, Taylor won't say a word about me. He knows that he won't live long if he does. There'll be nowhere safe for him."

Isobel shook her head. "Playing the helpful landlady of the pub, helping students, when all the time you were running the whole show."

Lorraine smiled. "I know. I was their Muse. They would have got nowhere without me. And, trust me, within a few weeks I will be back in business again. I'll have to find a different method. I may have to buy another premises but I have plenty of money."

Isobel looked at Lorraine and saw the avarice and ruthlessness in her face.

"And I have plenty of influence. I'm safe."

Isobel shook her head. "Poor Patrick Magill. He never had a chance with you."

Lorraine shrugged. "I had such high hopes for him. He could have become a partner in the law firm, or even a judge. He had that potential. It was a real shame that we had to kill him."

"I thought he overdosed?"

"It's always better when a death can be ruled as an overdose rather than the mess of going through a murder enquiry."

"I can't believe you're admitting to that."

Lorraine's face contorted and she almost spat. "You have no way of proving anything. I would sue you for defamation of character and enjoy the pleasure of destroying you too."

There was a faint scraping sound from the doorway.

Lorraine stood still.

Isobel heard the inner doors open. Turning, she saw that Malcolm had stepped into the bar.

Lorraine looked at Isobel and then at Malcolm. He held up his phone.

Lorraine reached under the bar and pulled out a gun.

Malcolm put his hands up. "Lorraine, you have a gun. But you don't need to do that. There are police outside. You'll never get away with shooting us."

"*Give me your phone.* If you touch anything, if you try to send a recording, I will shoot Isobel." She trained her gun on Isobel.

"Stay where you are behind the bar, Lorraine. I'm walking towards you. *Please don't shoot.* I'll give you the phone. No tricks, I promise."

"Move slowly. Set your phone on the bar."

Malcolm inched forward. "So you're the Boss. I didn't believe Isobel when she tried to suggest it."

"Believe her. It's true. Taylor and his like, they did my bidding."

"So Taylor was your lackey?"

"He did what he was told. It was great having a man in his position. He told me about raids. Obviously, we had to sacrifice some people occasionally to keep the crime figures up but that was my choice not his."

"And Aaron McGuinness too. Was Aaron one of your acolytes?"

"Yes. He was very ambitious and thought that he could, or should, have more power – but, let me tell you, a lot of his ideas caused more trouble than they were worth. He had Taylor shoot an undercover garda. I thought that was going to cause no end of trouble but thankfully his body was never found. Now I'll have to start again but I can do that. I've told you more than I should. There may be no other option but to kill you both. I can always use a plastic bottle for a silencer. And, believe me, I have plenty of people who can dispose of your bodies."

Isobel felt her teeth clench in fear.

"Isobel, we're going to have to lie down under this," said Malcolm. "Despite all the success, we can't prove anything – we may have to take a fall now."

Isobel frowned. Malcolm was talking in a very strange way – not sounding at all like himself. Lie down under this? We may have to take a fall now?

"I'm glad that you know that," Lorraine said. "Step up and put the phone on the bar."

"I hate to have to do this but what can I do? You have to know the moment *and the moment is now*."

Malcolm set the phone on the bar. Lorraine reached for it.

A moment later Isobel was lying stunned on the floor, Malcolm twined around her, her barstool on top of her.

Lorraine shouted and a shot rang out. There was a scream and the crash of something hitting the floor.

Malcolm shifted slightly. "Are you alright, Isobel?"

Isobel felt her ears ringing. She looked towards the

door. A policeman in a bulletproof vest had a gun clasped in both hands. He moved out of his shooting stance and stepped forward. A second armed officer moved into the bar behind him. It was Inspector Williams. The two policemen moved towards the bar and the shooter ran behind it. Isobel heard him kick something.

Isobel rolled out of Malcolm's arms and he sat up slightly.

"Jesus, I'm getting too old for this. Isobel, are you OK?"

"Yes, I'm fine." She freed her legs from the barstool and, using her hands on the floor, tried to stand up. It took an effort but she straightened shakily.

Williams reached for Malcolm's right hand and helped him to his feet. Malcolm stood cradling his left arm.

"Are you OK, Malcolm?" Isobel asked him. "You've hurt your arm?"

"I'm OK. I took the force of the fall on my shoulder but no big deal."

"*Sir, we need an ambulance immediately! She's still alive!*" the police officer called.

The words slowly registered in Isobel's mind. Two more officers had entered. She moved towards the bar. One of the policemen put his hand on her chest to stop her.

"We can manage," he said.

"I know first aid. Let me help."

He glanced behind Isobel. Turning her head, Isobel saw Williams nod. The policeman let her move forward.

She moved behind the bar. She saw the gun well out of Lorraine's reach. Lorraine's breathing was noisy, her shirt dark with blood. Isobel saw a tea towel and grabbed it. Kneeling, she pressed the cloth to Lorraine's chest. Malcolm arrived beside her.

Lorraine stared at Isobel. "They heard everything?"

Isobel nodded.

Lorraine grimaced in pain.

"Hold on," Isobel said. "The ambulance is on its way."

"You want me to live?"

"I want you to stand trial."

There was a noise at the door. Two men in fluorescent ambulance coats appeared behind the bar. They took over from Isobel.

Isobel and Malcolm moved out from behind the bar. Isobel looked at her hands. There were smears of blood on them. She couldn't speak. She turned towards Malcolm. He opened his arms. As she felt his arms go around her, she started to cry.

"You're alright," he said. "We're both alright. Thank God I realised what you were doing when you sent the picture. Thank God Williams was still nearby and all the arrests earlier today meant that there were lots of officers around. Jack phoned us too. Williams tuned into the call on the group chat. I knew he could hear us. I tried to talk so he knew she had a gun. I told him what I was going to do."

Isobel dried her eyes and stepped back.

Williams came up to them and slapped Malcolm on the back.

"I knew what you were doing. You did good, mate!"

Malcolm shook his head. "No, you did. I owe you a bottle of very good whiskey. You saved our lives."

"And you saved mine, Malcolm!" said Isobel.

"Well done, Isobel!" said Williams. "Lorraine might have got away with it. She was planning to start up all over again. That would have been a bitter pill to swallow after all that we achieved."

Malcolm laughed. "Yeah, good that you figured it out, Isobel! We just have to work on your game plan a bit more, eh, champ?"

Isobel grinned and hugged him.

Two more ambulance men brought in a stretcher. They loaded Lorraine into it. Holding drips up, they carried her out of the pub to the waiting ambulance.

Isobel looked around the bar as Malcolm led her away. She would be glad to leave this corrupt and invasive case behind. One good thing was that the thought of going back to her work as a psychotherapist seemed very, very, appealing.

Chapter 49

Isobel and Malcolm went first to the hospital. They both were bruised and sore from where they had hit the floor but had no other physical injuries.

They then went to Grosvenor Road police station to give statements. When they had signed their statements, an officer brought them to Inspector Williams' office. Doran was waiting for them too.

"Well?" said Isobel.

Damien grinned. "Taylor is under arrest. He is going to be charged. Lorraine implicated him too when she was talking to you, Isobel."

"What about Aaron?" Malcolm asked.

Inspector Williams smiled. "We have Tim-Tan for Michael's murder with our two witnesses. When he heard about them, he knew he was caught. We talked to him about Gary Wells' murder and to earn some leniency he told us about Aaron. He was determined that he wasn't going down alone."

Isobel nodded. It was a relief. "And what about Professor Clarke?"

"He'll be charged but I'm sure he'll be treated with compassion," said Williams.

"And Robin?"

"He has played a significant role as a dealer but isn't implicated in any murders. He's spilling any beans he can to help his case," Damien said.

"Any news on Lorraine?" Malcolm asked.

"She's holding her own in the hospital and is likely to survive," said Williams. "Her comments to you, Isobel, were very clear as to her role and a few of us heard those. And we have her for threatening you both at gunpoint. Between now and a trial more people may come forward with what they know. All in all, a very good result. Thanks a million for your help."

He stood up and shook hands with them both.

As they left the station and walked along the Grosvenor Road, Isobel looked at her watch. It was three o'clock.

"I want to see Jack," she said, "and then I have a few people I want to talk to."

"Who?"

"Charlene, Mrs. O'Neill and Róisín Magill."

Jack was waiting in the foyer of the Park Hotel when they arrived back. When he saw Isobel he ran over and hugged her. Dave was behind him. Isobel hugged both of them, her eyes wet with tears.

"I heard what Lorraine said!" said Jack. "I heard the gunshot. I was terrified."

Isobel nodded. "Me too."

"I can't believe that Lorraine McNally was the Boss, the ringleader. I thought she was really nice."

Isobel nodded. "That was all part of her cover."

"How did you guess?" Dave asked.

"It wasn't a guess, was it, Isobel?" Malcolm said. "You never thought that either Taylor or Aaron was the Boss."

Isobel shook her head. "I had talked to Lorraine a few times and I think that unconsciously I suspected her. When Neat told us about her influence over everyone, I couldn't get it out of my head."

"I think I'm back to not liking you investigating." Dave smiled as he said it but he looked shaken. "It's too dangerous."

"I can understand that," Malcolm said. "I should have listened to your doubts and then maybe we could have come up with a plan together."

"I couldn't bear the idea that she would be able to keep doing what she was doing," said Isobel.

"I think I egged you on, Isobel, with my speech about the harm people do who don't get caught."

"Maybe, or maybe you inspired me," she replied. "But I also think that Charlene and Michael and Patrick deserved us to do the most, the very best that we could. Thank God it worked out OK."

The others nodded.

"Which reminds me, Jack, I want to go and see Charlene again and also Mrs. O'Neill."

"Let's go! Who first?"

Isobel pulled out her own phone. "Mrs. O'Neill?"

"Fine by me."

Isobel drove to Antrim with Jack and Malcolm.

Michael's brother opened the door and led them all into the sitting room. Gerard and Stella O'Neill were on the couch with their daughter.

Jack remained standing next to the brother while Isobel sat in one of the armchairs and Malcolm took the other.

Stella kept her eyes on Isobel. "What did you find out?"

"The man who killed Michael was Tim Tanner, known as Tim-Tan."

"I thought it was Geo!" Gerard said, shocked.

Isobel shook her head. "No, it was Tim-Tan. Michael and Charlene saw Geo and Tim-Tan in the alley. The two men were involved in a massive drug ring. Tim-Tan killed Michael because he saw them and he and Charlene were a danger to that drug ring. Because of Michael and Charlene, a massive drug operation has been shut down. In addition, the investigation sparked by Michael's death has led to the uncovering of corruption north and south of the border. A senior policeman and a senior garda are in custody."

"Who?" Stella asked.

"Confidentially, I can tell you that it's Superintendent Taylor and Garda Inspector McGuinness."

"*What?*" Gerard said. "The two men investigating Michael's murder?"

"Yes."

Stella shook her head. "I never trusted Taylor."

"You were right."

Malcolm said, "I realise it may not be any comfort to you but the collapse of the drug ring only happened because of what Charlene and Michael recorded and passed on. They've saved many young people."

Stella studied him and then nodded. "Thank you."

An hour later, Tony met Isobel, Malcolm and Jack as they stepped out of the hospital lift. He shook hands heartily with all three of them.

"Charlene is still very tired but she is well on her way to recovery." He smiled at Isobel. "Malcolm can tell me all about the arrests while the other two catch up with Charlene."

Jack and Isobel opened the door to Charlene's room. She was sitting up in bed with her head still bandaged. She looked pale and there were shadows under her eyes.

Jack said, "Hi, Charlene."

"Jack, Isobel, come in!"

She reached out her hands to Isobel.

Smiling, Isobel grasped her hands and sat next to the bed.

"Daddy told me about the drug ring you exposed and all of the people arrested. Of course I'm glad, but Michael is still dead."

"I know," said Isobel.

"It all seems so awful."

"It is awful, Charlene, but you did so good to send the pictures to your cloud account. If you hadn't done that Michael would still be dead and no one would have been caught. Your act in sending the photos has enabled this drug ring to be brought down, the leader of it identified and corrupt police officers exposed. I know that doesn't bring Michael back but remember loads of other lives will be saved and will benefit from these people being caught."

Charlene's eyes filled with tears. She squeezed Isobel's hands. "Did you tell Mrs. O'Neill that Michael stepped in front of me?"

"I did, a few days ago. It helped her a lot to know that. We've also been to see her today and told her about all of the arrests."

"Maybe it will be some comfort to her."

"Maybe."

"Will you come and see me tomorrow? You too, Jack. I want to hear all about your investigation."

"We'll see," said Isobel.

Tony put his head around the door.

Isobel stood up. "We'd better go."

"See you both tomorrow."

Tony opened his mouth as if to protest.

Charlene cut him off. "It's to help my recovery, Daddy."

"Oh, yes, of course."

"Dad is taking you all out to dinner to say thank you for what you did for Michael and me, aren't you, Dad?"

"Yes, I am."

"And when I'm better I'll go out for a meal with you too."

Jack grinned. "Sounds good."

Everyone came to dinner at the Europa where Tony, Joan and Nathan had organised a function room. Eoin and Alanna travelled up from Limerick, retired Inspector Jim

Daly came from Dublin. Gareth and Audrey travelled in from Holywood. Inspector Williams and Detective Damien Doran arrived, tired after a long day. Róisín Magill came and brought Henry. Jack, Rachel and Noah were already there with Dave.

Isobel managed to have a quiet word with Róisín before they sat down at the table. She told her all that Lorraine had said.

Róisín went pale.

"Remember, Róisín," she said, "that it was the statement Patrick took from Joe that meant Taylor was caught. What Patrick did made his arrest possible. He couldn't get out of the drug scene himself but he helped bring them all down in the end."

Róisín nodded. "He did, didn't he?"

Isobel nodded. "Yes, he did."

"I'm proud of him, of what he did."

Isobel squeezed her hand. "And so you should be."

Isobel, Malcolm, Jack and Dave were the last to sit down to dinner.

"Order whatever you want," said Tony. "This is on me."

It was Halloween night but thankfully at last it felt as if the monsters were vanquished and the miasma surrounding this case had cleared.

When the food arrived and everyone had a drink of some sort in front of them, Tony stood up. He raised his glass.

"To Jack who helped my daughter on the worst night of her life and who found the vital piece of footage!"

"*To Jack!*" everyone responded and sipped.

Tony continued. "And to Isobel for her investigation and Malcolm for saving her life!"

There was a bit of a cheer.

"To all of the police and gardaí here tonight who ensured that as many people as possible were arrested!"

Everyone laughed.

"I know that your work has saved many young people from exposure to drugs. Well done, all of you!" He leaned down to hug his wife. "And to our daughter Charlene who by sending those pictures managed to let us know the identity of Michael's killer and who, thank God, is making a great recovery!"

They all raised their glasses. Isobel knew it was going to be a long and very social evening. She wished that Patricia and Peter could be here too but she knew there would be other times and other cases for them.